℞OMULUS ℬUCKLE
& the
Luminiferous Aether

The Chronicles of the Pneumatic Zeppelin:
Book Three

Richard Ellis Preston, Jr.

Published by Westmarch Publishing

Cover illustration by Eamon O'Donoghue
Map illustration by Roberto Calas

For my wife,
Shelley,
with love.

PART ONE:

BLOCKADE RUNNER

I

AN UNFRIENDLY PORT

Night fell and brought the Founders with it. The small, cramped port of Vera Cruz, a refuge for air pirates, sea scoundrels and plague victims, was suddenly brought to heel under martial law.

Captain Romulus Buckle hurried through the shadows of the old brothel quarter fronting the quay, his boots thumping on icy boards. He followed close on the heels of his guide, a harsh-eyed woman with a veil across her face. She called herself Ursula but the word crossed her lips with such unfamiliarity Buckle doubted it was her real name. Ursula, or whatever her name was, further obscured her identity under a rough brown cloak and hood as did Buckle and his two crew members: Lieutenant Sabrina Serafim and Ensign Wellington 'Welly' Bratt. The ancient Atlantean automaton named Penny Dreadful, rescued from the melting pot in Spartak, accompanied them, strapped to Welly's back. The burden wasn't as tasking on the slender Welly as it first might seem — the robot was lighter than it looked.

Ursula paused at a junction where the boardwalk merged onto a main street. Buckle didn't like how dark the town was. The few surviving street lamps, their sunken candle flames fluttering in the sea drafts, cast molten pockets of illumination upon a world where everything was worn down. The buildings, boarded up and teetering, ramshackle wrecks of gray weathered wood, threatened to collapse on cobblestone streets rattled loose by decades of barrels hauled up from the pier.

A rotten fish stench assaulted Buckle's nostrils — it came from the fishmonger tables — the head-chopping blocks and gutting boards shimmered silver-green in the weak moonlight, encased in a greasy layer of fish scales and blood which decades of buckets of water thrown across the wood failed to completely wash away. The hobnails of Buckle's boots stuck to the ground — he felt the microcosmic sink of the leather into the filth — and it annoyed him.

Ursula hesitated, glancing back and forth along the street.

Buckle's spine rose up. "Move!" he hissed. All he needed now was the guide losing her nerve. They couldn't stay outside for long. The narrow avenues of Vera Cruz were under curfew. As their small boat had slipped into the harbor Buckle had pressed his night telescope to his eye and glimpsed knots of heavily armed soldiers clad in steampiper black and Founder's navy dark blue, brandishing torches in the faces of frightened passersby, clearing the streets of rabble.

A flash of gold coins on the slum side of the quay wall had bought Buckle the services of Ursula who, sleek and sober and elusive in her motions, seemed perfectly at home in the hardscrabble world of Vera Cruz.

"One moment," Ursula whispered. "We are almost there."

Buckle clenched his teeth and glanced up. A yellow-skinned Founders airship floated one thousand feet overhead, boiler pipes issuing streams of black-gray smoke, the moonlight gleaming on brass cannon muzzles poking out of her gunports. Twenty minutes earlier the airship had released a platoon of steampipers, elite Founders soldiers equipped with maneuverable steam-powered flying backpacks. Buckle and his two mates had crouched low in their boat in the middle of the harbor and he had cursed their luck, head down in the vaguely rancid bilge water, listening to the knock of the waves striking the boat with what seemed like the loudness of gongs, feeling exposed and helpless. He had yanked a crumpled tarpaulin over Penny Dreadful to hide her glowing amber eyes.

The steampipers had descended into some quarter or other, firing their guns at something in scattershot fashion. It was unlikely the Founders were looking for Buckle and his team specifically; the invasion of Vera Cruz was a logical stepping stone in the Founders clan's strategy of outward expansion, a well-placed port on the doorstep of the Pacific which up until this evening had been securely inside the Atlantean sphere of control.

Move, Ursula! Buckle thought, hedging against her back, his right hand clamped around his sword grip. He snorted in a deep breath of air and with it came the stink of mussel soup on the boil. The empty street beckoned, its cobblestones gleaming with black ice — there was a lot of sea ice but very little evidence of snow in Vera Cruz.

"Patience, dear sir, and have faith." Ursula said. "If you die, I don't get paid."

Patience. The word galled Buckle. The search for Atlantis had thus far proved an utter failure. The *Pneumatic Zeppelin* had been searching for six days and nights in their attempt to locate the great underwater city, all the time dodging Founders airships in the sea mists. Penny Dreadful's directions, despite its certainty, had proven circular and quite half-mad. The talking machine, battered and childlike and growing ever more tiresome, was as unreliable as one might have expected, but even Buckle's own abilities had failed him in the attempt to locate the submerged metropolis.

The search, the time wasted, had been a trying ordeal. With the exception of the somber sea burials of the crewpersons killed in the battle with the *Bellerophon*,

Buckle had hardly left the bridge. He had spent watch after watch at his chair with the ship's dog, Kellie, curled up at his feet, his hat plugged into the zeppelin's steam system, its vents pumping warmth down his neck. Buckle's unrelenting tensions ruined whatever ease he might have mined from such long, empty, eye-glazing hours. The weather over the Offing had been odd, unpredictable, snowy, both too warm and too foggy, and the density of the rolling fog banks had often forced the airship to halt her search because the lookouts couldn't see their hands in front of their faces, much less the surface of the ocean seventy-five feet below. Buckle dared not fly lower, for towering icebergs loomed in and out of the mists like the ice-bound peaks of great prehistoric mountains, mountains that would prove deadly in collision.

Long, sleepless hours gave way to a captain's many worries. Staring into nothingness under the bright but indistinct spheres of the sun and moon crossing above the endless cloud cover, untasked by the familiar duties of the airship, by the regular reports of the fog-blind lookouts, by the turn of the hourglass and the ring of the watch bell, gave way to one's darkest thoughts. A turn to melancholy was impossible for Buckle to avoid. His desperation at the loss of his sister, Elizabeth, and her captivity at the hands of the Founders, lived in the beatings of his heart. Seeking an alliance with the Atlanteans was a convenient excuse to chase Elizabeth and he knew it: but if Andromeda Pollux's prophesy was true, that Elizabeth was the key to winning the war, he had no other choice. Granted, Andromeda was the leader of the Alchemist clan and considered by many to be a suspect oracle — she seemed to effortlessly hypnotize Buckle on some level whenever they spoke, her dark eyes hinting at a quantity of Martian blood in her veins. But he trusted her — that was the long and short of it — and Elizabeth had to be recovered at all costs, even if it meant his death and the death of every crew member aboard the *Pneumatic Zeppelin*.

The fate of the entire Snow World was at stake.

Elizabeth was in Atlantis. Every day Romulus Buckle had grown more certain of this.

And there was Max, his Martian Chief Engineer, who nearly lost her life to a sabertooth beastie as she came to save him on the Tehachapi Mountain. She now lay recovering in the Punchbowl infirmary, far, far away, and he fretted for her pain. She had gladly risked her life in his protection. How could he ever repay such loyalty? He missed having her on the bridge, missed her terribly; he needed her there.

Valkyrie Smelt, the blonde Imperial Princess was there, acting in Max's stead, manning her engineering position nearly twenty-four hours a day. By the third night Buckle had no choice but to order Valkyrie to retire to her cabin and get some sleep. She was stricken,

Buckle knew, by the loss of her brother in the destruction of the *Cartouche*, but her cool blue eyes never betrayed her emotions. Yet she radiated sadness and Buckle felt it. She was a member of his crew and he wanted to reach out to her, to give her a chance to open up and grieve, but he felt it better not to broach the subject if she did not come to him. There was no bridge to traverse between them.

And then there was the Penny Dreadful. The old automaton had been so sure of itself in the search, so certain that it knew the location of the great but mysterious underwater city of Atlantis. Penny had crouched in the nose dome for days on end, motionless, its cold yellow eyes locked on the sea. Sometimes in the long hours it had looked far too human, too much like a forlorn and determined child, and Buckle had caught himself worrying about it on several occasions.

Penny Dreadful's faulty memory resulted in Buckle's decision to venture to Vera Cruz, an island port town known to be within the Atlantean sphere of trade and control. In Vera Cruz there would be mercenary submariners, shady customers who knew the way to Atlantis. He just had to find one of them. And match their price.

"Here they come," Ursula hissed, pressing flat against the wall as she reached back and planted her gloved hand in the center of Buckle's chest. A group of Founders soldiers, their torches burning far brighter than the scattered streetlamps, passed along the main street.

Buckle held his breath, looking down at an uneven gutter running with filthy, slush-laden water. After the footfalls of the Founders faded away he whispered, "I'd prefer to be moving."

"Just clearing the blind spots is all, Captain," Ursula replied without looking back. Buckle could see nothing of Ursula but her hood. Her voice was steady but he wanted to see her face. He wanted to see if there was fear there.

"Are you sure he'll be there?" Buckle asked.

"If he's not on a job, he lives at the Sybaris — and I know he's not on a job," Ursula said. "Let's go." She struck out across the street, the folds of her robe flowing in the sea breeze, and Buckle hurried after her.

II

THE SYBARIS

The dash across the street was quick and quiet and the stealth of it, the tapping of their leather boots on the cobbles and the flutter of their cloaks on their backs like crow's wings in shadows, made Buckle feel better. Ursula paused against a large building with boarded-up windows; Buckle tucked in beside her with Sabrina at his side and Welly next to her, Penny Dreadful peering from the harness on Welly's back. Penny's metal face was dark; it had either shut off its glowing amber eyes or sealed them somehow.

Buckle smelled the familiar tavern stench of stale beer and sailor sweat but everything on the street was closed up and dark.

"We are here," Ursula said, stopping in front of a large oak door.

"We are where?" Sabrina asked. "I don't see any tavern."

"Most of our social establishments go to ground when the authorities come, which hardly ever happens except when the Atlanteans send troopers for one reason or another, usually to collect unpaid debts," Ursula answered. She rapped on the door, sharply, six times, in an odd pattern.

A door slat slid open, striking the end of its slot with a thunk, revealing two mean eyes fringed by red-yellow firelight. "Bugger off," a muffled voice rasped.

"For the love of the bloody Martian's knickers, open the door, Grady," Ursula snapped.

"Why are ye such a bitch, Ursula?" Grady asked.

"I'm not your mother," Ursula replied. "The Founders are afoot. Open the door!"

The slat clicked shut and the door swung back, flooding the blue-back depths of the street with amber firelight. Grady, a fat fellow with sweaty jowls and a head as bald as a child's marble, eyed Buckle and his company with suspicion. "Get yer arses in here!"

Buckle turned sideways to squeeze past Grady's mass. Hit by a wall of sour-smelling heat, he blinked, for though the low-ceilinged inn was poorly lit by candles and a sputtering fireplace it was still considerably brighter than outside. It was something of a feat of crude carpentry that the warping walls were sealed up so tight that not one hint of its internal light leaked out into the street. Grady slammed the door shut and threw the bolt, cutting off whatever fresh sea air followed Buckle and his party in. Buckle's throat squeezed against the reek of gin, beer and body odor weighing down the overheated atmosphere.

Buckle stayed close to Ursula as she wove through a jumble of empty tables and chairs, the only occupied section of the tavern being the bar where a half-dozen grubby locals peered sideways at them from their stools. Ursula headed into the corner furthest from the door where a honey-colored man in a worn, black peacoat worked on a half-eaten slab of ham and a beer. The man sat at the table liked he owned it, eying them as they approached. Buckle saw the man's right hand slip under the table to his pistol belt.

Buckle glanced at Sabrina.

"I see it," Sabrina said, her hand already tucked inside her cloak, resting on the handle of her pistol.

Ursula arrived at the table and threw back her hood, showing a small head with a pale skinned, plain face framed by short-cropped black hair and obsidian earrings. "Captain Felix, I bring you customers," she said.

"They look desperate," Felix murmured through a mouthful of ham, casually replacing his right hand on the surface of the table. "I don't like it when you bring me desperate ones, Ursula."

"Your customers are always desperate, you mercenary," Ursula retorted. "Otherwise they would pay two farthings for the ferry." She turned to Buckle. "I'll claim my finder's fee now."

Buckle drew a fat leather purse from his pocket and dropped it in Ursula's hand.

Ursula stuffed the purse into her cloak. "I'm not stupid enough to count this here," she said, firing a glance at the half-turned faces at the bar, "but if you short me, I'll be back to collect the rest from your bloody corpse, you hear me?"

"Fair enough," Buckle replied pleasantly.

Ursula glanced at Felix, then hurried away, exiting through a side door.

Buckle turned to find Felix studying him with a pair of big brown eyes that were childlike in comparison to the unshaven roughness of his face. "So you pay, at least the small fees, eh?"

"And the big ones," Buckle said.

"Unless that was a purse full of slugs," Felix added as if he might laugh.

"A pleasure to meet you, Felix," Buckle said. "I am Romulus…"

Felix raised his hand abruptly, palm open, thumb folded over his fork. "No last names. There is no need for last names. Either we enter into a transaction or we do not. And your female companion can release her grip on her pistol as well—that might lighten up the proceedings."

Sabrina slowly pulled her hand out of her cloak and rested it on her hip.

"What is it you want from me?" Felix asked, lifting his beer to his mouth. The mug was fantastic, a large nacreous nautilus shell halved and fitted into a carved wooden base; it looked far too fragile and expensive to survive the tables of the Sybaris and Buckle figured it was Felix's personal cup.

"Passage to Atlantis," Buckle said.

The fabulous beer mug paused in midair, the bottom dripping condensation. "Who told you that I could get you to Atlantis?"

"The young lady who just departed with a purse full of my silver," Buckle replied. "How about we dispense with the dodging, shall we?"

"The Founders have blockaded the port," Felix said.

"We are aware," Buckle replied.

Felix took a big swig, replaced the mug on the table and winked. "If getting you to Atlantis was possible, and I ain't saying it is or that I might have any means or knowledge of the means to get there, it would cost."

"We can pay," Buckle replied.

"What's your clan?" Felix asked.

"Crankshaft," Buckle answered.

Felix nodded. "Crankers, eh? Crankers are known to have deep pockets. But, if I were able to help you, and that is a big 'if,' I'd need to see the coin."

"Of course," Buckle said again. "But not here."

"Of course not here," Felix replied, jabbing a square of ham into his mouth.

"We're not here to play games," Sabrina said.

"Ah, but life is just one big game, isn't it?" Felix said.

"Can you provide us with passage or not?" Buckle asked.

Felix turned serious. "Very well. Sit down. Let the negotiations begin."

Buckle took a seat across from Felix, with Sabrina settling in on his left. He glimpsed her face in her hood, her small, strong chin jutting forth. Welly took a seat at the empty table on their immediate right, swinging Penny Dreadful from his back and lowering her to the floor as he did so.

"What the hell is that?" Felix asked, glaring at Penny.

"Our automaton," Buckle answered.

"It looks like one of the old ones, the ones the Atlanteans made," Felix grumbled, scraping a bit of fat to the edge of his plate. "They don't like them. If we make a deal for transit I'd suggest you leave the thing behind."

Buckle shook his head at a pang of disappointment; he'd hoped that the presence of the Atlantean robot would prove an icebreaker with the Atlanteans but apparently not. "The machine stays with us."

"Dig your own grave, then," Felix grumbled. He glanced into the shadows and nodded. A woman emerged with a pistol at her side, the trigger cocked.

She was squarish and middle-aged, probably of about the same age—thirtyish—as Felix, and of Asian descent. Her demeanor was serious and unpleasant, like a person who never smiled.

"I don't negotiate with a loaded pistol at my back," Buckle said.

"We all have our hands close to our pistols," Felix answered, cutting what was left of his ham into impossibly tiny pieces, the knife blade squeaking on the ceramic platter. It was as if he wanted a reason to keep the sharp blade in his hand. "That's how business gets done in Vera Cruz. If you don't like it, you can take your leave."

"You have a submarine, yes?" Buckle asked.

In went another bite of ham. Felix chewed and swallowed. "Perhaps. But if I did I would not be happy about taking on questionable cargoes when the current environment is as unfriendly as it is."

"We have no cargo," Buckle said. "All we seek is passage to Atlantis."

"Oh, is that all?" Felix said with a false smile; several of his teeth were missing. "That takes a heap of silver on the barrelhead."

Romulus dropped his heavy leather coin purse on the table.

Felix stopped chewing. His eyes flicked to the Asian woman and back to Buckle. He started chewing again. "The Crankshafts always have money. Few things are certain in life. But the Crankshafts always have money."

"Good merchants," Buckle said.

"Good pirates," Felix countered.

"Former pirates," Buckle said.

Felix nodded, then pointed his chin at the coin purse. "What's in there?"

"Two thousand in silver," Buckle replied.

"A lot of velvet," Felix said, his brown eyes narrowing. "But it ain't enough. You may have noticed that the Founders have seized the town. Just getting you out of port will be worth every halfpenny of that two thousand, if we even survive it, that is."

Buckle tossed another leather purse onto the table. "A thousand more in gold. That includes return fare."

Felix rested his hands on the table, his grease-streaked fork and knife gleaming in the firelight. "You want me to being you back to Vera Cruz now that it is crawling with Founders?"

"No. Another location. Not far off."

Felix laid his knife and fork on the edges of his plate and nodded at the Asian woman. Buckle heard a click as she uncocked her pistol hammer. "This is Kishi," Felix said. "My partner."

Buckle turned and nodded at Kishi. She gave him a smile so big and mean it surprised him.

"We need to go and we need to go now," Buckle

said.

Felix stood up, drained his nautilus mug and stuffed it into his coat pocket. "Very well. Three tickets to the bottom of the sea it is, then."

III

THE SEAGREEN BARREL COMPANY

With the Founders patrols everywhere, the journey back to the Vera Cruz wharf was quick, a hurried, snaking rush along gray-iced alleyways so narrow they were barely wider than Buckle's shoulders. Occasionally he stepped over blanket-covered bodies, lumpy leper shadows underfoot, beggars alive or dead it was impossible to tell but in a sorry state most certainly, lying as they were on stones dense with frozen mold, garbage and corruption.

They were losing the darkness; dawn approached rapidly — the Snow World dawn — the tumultuous pink glow of the eastern sky where the overcast heavens both muted and amplified the light. The *Pneumatic Zeppelin* was out there, keeping inside the sea mists two miles to the north, stationed for the rendezvous. Buckle's brother by adoption, Ivan Gorky, was in command of the airship, assisted by the Imperial princess Valkyrie Smelt. Valkyrie was acting as chief engineering officer in the absence of Max.

Part of Buckle recoiled at the idea of a foreign clan officer on his bridge, but Valkyrie was first rate: her bravery under fire as they boarded the *Bellerophon* had won over much of the *Pneumatic Zeppelin*'s crew, her cool exterior notwithstanding.

At the southeastern end of the docks they passed through a long row of large, decrepit buildings, several of which had burned down to blackened posts a long time ago, and arrived at the reinforced door of a large, ramshackle warehouse. Felix drew a set of skeleton keys and began opening three massive padlocks. A sign creaked overhead, the dawn sea breeze rocking it on its rusty hooks: flaking gold lettering read THE SEAGREEN BARREL COMPANY and painted over that in thick strokes of red paint was the word CONDEMNED.

The padlocks clanked open and Buckle found himself descending a rickety stairwell into a large space reeking of tar, salt and rotting wood. Sunlight shot down through a broken skylight and gaps in the warping roof boards, riddling stacks of cobwebbed wooden barrels with gray shafts of light. Oily black harbor water gurgled in a forty-foot rectangular hole cut in the warehouse floor, lapping up against the teardrop-shaped conning tower of a small submarine.

Two chairs with high wooden backs and red velvet cushions, expensive and most certainly stolen, sat beside the submarine. The first chair contained an

27

old man with a liver-spotted face and stubbly white beard, his body little more than bony protrusions under his denim coveralls. In the second chair lounged a young woman in a blue and white striped sailor's blouse. They were both smoking pipes, and the curls of smoke formed lazy wreaths in the air above the chairs. They jumped to their feet when they saw Felix, their heads spinning the tobacco smoke in little tornadoes.

"Rachel! Husk! We are away!" Felix shouted. "With all speed!"

"Aye, Captain!" Rachel replied, knocking the contents of her pipe into the water before hopping onto the conning tower ladder. The old man, Husk, clamped his pipe between his teeth and began untying the submarine's mooring lines from their cleats.

"I present to you the *Dart*," Felix said without ceremony. "She's a true submarine, small and fast. She'll outrun the Founders tubs if necessary but stealth is her finest quality."

"She looks leaky to me," Sabrina said.

"And what does a sky dog know of sea boats, I ask?" Kishi growled.

Buckle appraised the iron hull plates and rivets of the steam-powered *Dart*, being most impressed by her two big copper screws surrounded with what looked to be a half dozen smaller propellers. She looked to be about fifty feet long. The crew likely totaled little more than a half dozen. "I like the cut of her," he said.

Kishi smiled at him but this smile didn't look mean.

Buckle followed Felix up the *Dart*'s conning tower ladder to the small bridge. The main hatch was open and they clambered down another ladder into the dark interior of the boat. The stink of bioluminescent boil and stale seawater hit Buckle as his boots landed on the metal deck of the control room. He stepped aside as Sabrina descended behind him, followed by Welly wedging his way down with Penny strapped to his back.

Buckle shivered at the idea of being submerged — even though the submarine was only halfway down. Dark seawater lapped at the bottoms of two large, oval window ports at the front of the cabin and Buckle felt as if he were looking out of the eyes of a great sea beast. Instruments of copper, brass and glass packed the control surfaces; Buckle recognized many of the gauges and dials — compass, chadburn, pitch pendulum, drift indicators, pressure tank indicators and on and on — the controls of a submarine were in many ways similar to those of a zeppelin.

Kishi came down the ladder, closing the hatch and winding the wheel lock shut above her.

"Vessel ready for departure, Captain," a voice rang down the chattertube.

"Lines are away," Kishi announced.

"Dampers are open and boilers are being stoked, Captain," Rachel announced from her post immediately to the port side of the helm wheel. "Minimum propulsion available in one minute."

"In one minute we take her down to ten," Felix said.

Rachel watched the red liquid in her pressure gauges rise, then turned her head to stare at Sabrina.

"See something you like?" Sabrina asked.

Stone faced, Rachel held her stare. She was pretty in the way a lioness was pretty, with a high forehead and the face that might belong to a noble. She looked to be a well-cooked mix of races, with wide-set eyes, a thick orb of densely curled reddish-brown hair and medium-brown skin. "And what trouble is this?" she asked Felix.

"Well-paying trouble," Felix replied.

"We have negotiated a passage to Atlantis," Sabrina said.

"They won't let you in with that thing," Rachel said, flicking her eyes to Penny Dreadful as it dangled from Welly's back.

"You have to forgive Rachel here," Felix said with a smile. "She only makes friends with money and wealthy widowers."

"It's a pleasure, Rachel," Buckle said with a nod.

Rachel turned back to her dials. "Engines are ready, Captain."

"Take her down," Felix ordered.

Kishi and Rachel spun hand wheels and the hissing sound of escaping air filled the cabin. The *Dart* sank into the water which surged and bubbled up and over the glass portholes until the warehouse interior lifted away and all Buckle could see in the darkness was the shadowy outlines of the warehouse pier supports.

Buckle's stomach felt queasy. It was his first time in a submarine and he liked it.

IV

THE BOTTOM OF THE SEA

To Romulus Buckle, who had never seen the underside of the ocean before, the submarine's slow glide beneath the surface of the Vera Cruz harbor was every bit a journey into another world.

He enjoyed slipping through suspended darkness and streaming bubbles, the weak light playing across the rippling surface above, throwing undulating shadows across the rocky bottom. The hulls of ships towered against the quay wall and soft-looking pier timbers as if the world had been filled with water and flipped upside-down. He felt the body of the ocean around him, the liquid density of it pressing up against the glass and metals of the submarine, making everything creak and rattle. Water leaked in at various places, little dribbling streams skittering down the edge of a panel or dripping from an overhead pipe. But Felix and Kishi took little notice of the sea's intrusions.

The *Dart* advanced slowly at a speed of three knots. Ahead of them the harbor bottom sloped deeper into the shallow depths, cut in sharper angles by dredging, and the near transparent quality of the water deepened into a pleasant green-blue. The harbor floor, amidst its carpet of propeller-clipped seaweed, was a jumble of discarded ship-jetsam and hastily-tossed cargoes — barrels full of anyone's guess — and had the appearance of an overgrown junkyard. There were no ships active on the surface — the Founders blockade had seen to that — and the water ceiling responded only to the breeze, washed by wind-ripples.

Once clear of the docks, Felix clanged the chadburn handle, signaling the engine room. "All ahead half."

"All ahead half," came the response on the chattertube.

The bridge remained quiet for several minutes, the bioluminescent green boil instruments glowing in the sea shade. The *Dart* slowly navigated her way toward the harbor entrance where the seaweed lawns of the shallows fell away into the depths of the deep blue sea.

"Lovely and quiet," Sabrina said, pulling back her hood.

"Nobody's out," Felix said, tapping his head at the temple. "None of 'em are quite addled enough in the brain pan to try to run a Founders blockade."

"Or not being paid well enough to do it," Buckle said.

"Fair enough," Felix replied. "There's a Founders submersible lurking just outside the harbor, here, so we need to be damned cautious,"

"I thought you could simply outrun him," Sabrina said.

"Aye, but I can't outrun a torpedo," Felix answered.

"Do the Founders know where Atlantis is?" Welly asked.

"Of course," Felix said. "Most of it, anyway."

"How is it that you know the location of Atlantis, Captain Felix?" Buckle asked.

Felix shook his head as he nursed the helm wheel in his big, rough hands. He took on a new aura on the bridge of the ship, looking taller: here he was the captain, ever-powerful and wise, compared to the shadowy, elusive man who haunted the back tables of the Sybaris. He and Kishi never took their eyes off of the windows or the green boil-lit instruments surrounding them. "Passed down from my father. But finding Atlantis isn't the hard part when you live underwater. The getting in, well, there's the rub. And Atlantis is far more than just one underwater city. There are seven main domes, one for each of their gens, or houses, and many of 'em don't get along. Now, let's keep an eye out for that submersible."

Buckle nodded. The news of the Founders blockade hadn't surprised him—he expected such tactics. The Atlanteans themselves were surely experiencing the particularly brutal version of diplomacy the Founders liked to practice, but such aggression should work in Buckle's favor.

The Grand Alliance sorely needed the Atlanteans as a partner, but that wasn't the main reason Buckle was there. He was lying to himself if he thought he was there for any reason other than to rescue his lost sister Elizabeth. If Elizabeth was in Atlantis he would find her. And he would bring her home. The prophecy of Lady Andromeda, her warning that Elizabeth somehow was the key to winning the war, had taken root ever more strongly inside of him with each passing day. He felt strangely attached to Lady Andromeda, as if he could hear her voice operating within him, gently and insistently, alongside the voice of his own conscience. He had now fallen victim to a gray vagueness, to a sense of insecurity at what he was doing because he wasn't certain of himself. And he knew that time would only make this condition worse. Perhaps it was for the better; his father, Admiral Balthazar, always said that certainty was the realm of fools and dead men.

"The Founders boats are big, ugly brutes—we'll see them coming long before they see us," Felix said, craning his neck to peer up. "And they're mostly surface runners, not true submarines, so odds are you'll spot them overhead if you're running at any depth at all."

"I didn't know the Founders had submarines," Sabrina said.

It first struck Buckle as odd that Sabrina would not know if the Founders had undersea machines, but on further reflection he realized it wouldn't be surprising if the secretive clan's elite avoided discussing military secrets with their own children — and Sabrina had been little more than a child when she had left the city.

"Not submarines, but submersibles," Felix replied. "They're not much more than modified ironclads. They can't stay submerged for long. Their machines don't hold a candle to the Atlantean submarines as far as elegance and efficiency goes, but there are more of them and they're big — big old piston-jammers loaded with torpedoes."

"That sounds like the Founders to me," Sabrina said softly. "Big and clumsy."

"And deadly," Kishi added.

The *Dart* cleared the harbor mouth where the sea floor tumbled down into murky dark blue depths below with the blue-green surface sparkling above. A silver mass of fish appeared like a tornado, swirling above the windows until, directly overhead, they turned black, their forms silhouetted against the surface light.

A *Dart* crewman appeared on the bridge, his boots clanking across the deck grating, shoving his way between Welly and Penny Dreadful. The *Dart* probably ran with a crew of five or six, as far as Buckle could tell. "You called, Cap'n?" the man asked; the dozens of tools lining his coverall pockets gave him the look of a machinist.

"Get in the belly pod, Marsh," Felix said. "Dawn is a perfectly bad time to try to skim bottom to Atlantis. The Guardians will be out, active as rabbits and likely to latch on."

"Aye," Marsh answered. "Dawn is sure as hell a perfectly bad time." He hurried out.

"Guardians?" Buckle asked.

Felix nodded as he eased the helm wheel back and forth in his hands, keeping his submarine close along the contours of the seabed. "Trained octopi and other nasty Martian brutes. The Atlanteans have domesticated the beasties as best they can, trained them to patrol the reaches under the city. The handlers will keep them under control, if the handlers happen to be around. Otherwise the creatures, they'll get ahold of yer boat and pull it apart. Don't worry yourself, however—my crew knows how to handle the Guardians."

"All systems are good," Kishi announced.

"Stay on the bubble," Felix said.

"Aye," Kishi replied.

"And no sign of that Founders boat," Felix said. "Hold yer breath. Nowhere to hide in this stretch."

"I was always under the impression that the Founders and the Atlanteans were trade partners and tight bedfellows in that sense," Welly said. "I am surprised by the existence of the blockade."

"They're both strange collections of bastards and there's no love lost between them," Felix replied. "But both need what the other has and they're both greedy. They have always overlooked their differences to make way for trade. It is well known that the Founders clan cannot feed itself, locked up the way they are in that corrupted city surrounded by poison, and the Atlantean fishing fleets are a friend they cannot do without."

"So why bite the hand that feeds you?" Welly asked.

"Why pay for it when you can control it yourself?" Buckle asked Welly.

Kishi nodded. "It is no secret that the Founders are uncomfortable relying on someone else for a big chunk of their food supply; now they are moving to take control of the fishing fleets."

"And then there is the matter of Lombard," Sabrina added.

Felix glanced back at Sabrina, taking full measure of her slender form with his eyes. "Aye.

Lombard."

"Who is Lombard?" Welly asked before Buckle did.

"Long ago the undersea complex of Atlantis was built by a renegade Founders scientist, a genius named Cassandra Lombard. The Founders were sore to lose her and they've always been suspicious of Atlantis."

"I heard stories about Lombard as a child," Sabrina said. "All of them bad. Sour grapes."

Felix nodded. "Yes. But the Atlanteans have always dominated the ocean trade routes and held sway over the Spice Traders, the Oriental Compact and the fishermen. The Founders never dared cross them because of that."

"It seems the situation has changed," Buckle said. The Oriental Compact—he'd heard of the mysterious people of the west, hidden beyond the ocean, more fragments of legend than real. He peered into the fluctuating currents below where schools of fish flashed and vanished. The ocean floor dropped off in steeper and steeper angles, darkening as it plunged away from the surface where the sun glowed aqua blue through sheets of ice There was barely perceptible movement in the depths, large, indecipherable shadows whispering of behemoths down below.

Buckle felt an eerie, familiar twinge. He was well aware of the alien monsters cast down upon dry land by the Martians but he knew nothing of what they had released into the water. There were many stories of sea-beasties more mighty and terrifying than sabertooth or kraken but the descriptions varied so widely it was difficult to make head nor tail out of them in the end. They made wonderful tales for landlubbers, certainly, but now that he was here, under the ocean with them, he hoped that he might not make their acquaintance.

Icebergs soon appeared, their craggy hulks blocking out the light, massive underwater cathedrals of deep blue glass, inverted, ponderous titans drifting as the ocean willed.

"I know a chasm—Neptune's Rift—well hidden, that we can use to bypass the patrols," Felix said. "We should arrive at Atlantis in about an hour. If you take the main passageway, you'll find a parlor on your right. It has a big window for you to watch the sea as you landlubbers love to do so much."

"Thank you, Felix," Buckle said. "We shall retire to the parlor, then."

"You interesting in selling that robot?" Felix asked, jerking his head towards Penny Dreadful.

"Not at this time, no," Buckle replied with an odd sense of indignity.

"Very well then," Felix replied. "I'll tell you one thing, I will, this robot shall be something of a problem in Atlantis."

"Why is that?" Sabrina asked.

"The Atlanteans don't like their old

automatons," Felix said. "They despise them, really. Don't use them anymore."

"And why do they despise them?" Buckle asked.

"Malfunctions," Felix said. "It's difficult to get a straight answer out of an Atlantean, especially when it concerns anything which they fear looks to be a failure. But I know that they were damned proud of their automatons long ago. Then all of the sudden they collected as many as they could, sending out scouts to recover the ones they'd sold or lost. In the end, the automatons were all melted down into scrap."

"Such a thought gives me the shivers," Penny said quietly, though it wasn't shivering.

"We shall retire to the observation parlor," Buckle said, gently herding Penny toward the hatchway. It annoyed him that Felix had told such a story in front of Penny, though he wasn't sure why it might bother it — it was just a machine, after all. Perhaps he was angry with himself for bringing a potentially dangerous member into his company. But how dangerous was Penny Dreadful?

"Keep an eye open for boats," Felix said over his shoulder.

"Aye, we'll do that," Buckle replied as he ducked through the rear hatchway, walking down the metal passageway that stank of oil and rust. Sabrina and Welly were close at his back with the sound of Penny's metal shoes clanking behind. Odd, Buckle mused, that he took some measure of offense when the suggestion of selling the robot was tabled; despite its appearance it still felt more like a child than a machine to him.

The observation cabin was impressive in comparison to the other utilitarian chambers of the *Dart*: a tall, circular window secured with polished bolts provided a spectacular ocean view along the port beam; two aquariums inhabited by bizarre species of red, black, yellow and orange sea creatures intensified the cabin's underwater feel; a round table made of dark, expensive wood was polished to such a sheen that the faint sea light undulated across its surface as if it were glazed with water; bookshelves lined the bulkheads, framing three old oil paintings drawn from the ruins of the old world depicting cavalry charges whose significance were lost to time.

The hefty transit payment might just buy Felix another one of those rare paintings.

Buckle knew why the *Dart* was designed with such a well-appointed parlor. Yes, she was an infamous mercenary submarine but she was also a business tool to wine and dine and impress clients. The captain's quarters and the library aboard the *Pneumatic Zeppelin* offered similar sky-windows and displays of elegance, for the airship was a machine of both war and diplomacy.

Sabrina stepped to the window, looking out at

the sea. "We must be twenty fathoms down. I don't like it, being underwater in this cockleshell."

"Why not?" Buckle asked, taking a seat at the table, running his hand across the smooth surface of the wood. "We're floating, much as we do in the air."

"You don't like being submerged overmuch, either," Sabrina said, removing her leather glove to press her finger at a water droplet on the window's metal collar.

"Well, I'd wager submarining is less dangerous that zeppelineering," Buckle said.

Sabrina peered at the droplet on her fingertip. "Aye, but a little hole in a gasbag won't sink you in the sky."

Sabrina showed the water droplet to Welly, who looked amused. Welly always responded well to Sabrina's attentions, laughing at her dry humor because he was openly smitten with her.

Sabrina sat alongside Buckle, rubbing the droplet between her fingers. "I still doubt the Atlanteans shall be willing to admit us, considering the current antagonistic climate."

"We are a diplomatic mission," Buckle answered. "The current state of affairs will help us. The Atlanteans are looking for allies even if they are unwilling to admit it. They're just as interested in self-preservation as we are."

"It would have been good to have Elizabeth with

us on this one," Sabrina muttered.

Buckle nodded. "My sister does handle people well."

"And if they have her in Atlantis, somewhere, sequestered away as your strange prophet suggests?" Sabrina asked.

"Then we shall recover her, one way or another," Buckle responded.

"I still do not understand why you think she is in Atlantis if you are certain that the Founders kidnapped her," Sabrina said. "Regardless of the jabberings of that moonchild you ran across, that old Shadrack."

"Moonchildren don't lie," Buckle replied softly.

"It doesn't mean they understand the truth," Sabrina said.

"Lady Andromeda told me Elizabeth was the key to winning the war," Buckle said, soft but pressing. "Lady Andromeda's words, sober and cold as the dawn of day. And if there is the slightest possibility that Elizabeth is in Atlantis, within my grasp, then I have no choice but to seize the opportunity."

"You do understand that Lady Andromeda is a politician and politicians—" Sabrina paused, looking behind Buckle.

Buckle turned to see a tall, thin woman bending in through the hatchway. Her skin was black and she wore the stained white smock of a cook. She only had one arm, the right sleeve of her blouse pinned up neatly against her shoulder. In her left hand she balanced a large metal tray with a teapot, cups, and neatly squared bits of food.

"Felix wants to see you served," the one-armed cook said as she placed the tea service on the table. Her voice was accented in a way Buckle didn't find familiar. He wondered if it bothered her to be constantly stooping through the low hatchways. Submariners tended to be small. "Do you want anything to eat?" she asked. "I have varieties of fish, fowl and sea vegetables."

"What is a 'sea vegetable?" Sabrina asked.

"Sea palm, kombu and agar pudding," the cook said.

"No idea what those are," Sabrina said with a toss of her head. "I'll stick with tea."

The tea tray was well supplied with cream and sugar cubes, and the liquid in the teapot smelled of a sweet spice that was new to Buckle. The tidbit plate was stacked with white crackers cradling greenish white gobs of something that looked like it might be fish eggs.

"For me, the tea shall most certainly suffice," Buckle said.

"What fish have you got?" Welly asked.

"Fish," the cook replied, prickly.

"What *kind* of fish?" Welly asked again.

"Cod," the cook said.

"I'll have some of that, then," Welly said.

"Very well," the cook sighed and took her leave, stooping low on her exit.

Buckle watched Welly pour tea for Sabrina and then himself.

Drumming her fingers on the table, Sabrina waited until the cook was long gone. "You still have not explained, dear Captain, "why you believe the words of a madman."

"Not good enough?" Buckle asked, knowing it wasn't.

"Good enough for me," Sabrina replied, blowing on her tea. "But it feels like we are chasing a ghost."

"I can't tell you how, but I know she is there," Buckle answered. "Lady Andromeda said that Elizabeth is the key to winning the war. That is why the Founders took her and that is why we must take her back."

"Lady Andromeda is an Alchemist and I for one have never trusted the Alchemists," Sabrina said, pouring one shot of cream into Buckle's tea.

"And what clan outside of Crankshaft do you trust, dear sister?" Buckle asked.

"None," Sabrina answered with a wry smile.

"I trust Lady Andromeda," Buckle said.

"She does owe you her life, saving her from the Founders prison as you did," Sabrina said, then turned to Welly with the sugar tongs ready. "And for you, Ensign?"

"Triple cream and triple sugar," Welly said. "My mother trained me to like my tea far too sweet." He smiled at his comment and then immediately bit his lip, as if perhaps he had offered too much for it to be appropriate. He wanted desperately to impress. "Many thanks, Lieutenant," he added quickly. "I thank you with my utmost gratitude."

"It wasn't an offer of marriage, Ensign," Sabrina replied. She shot Buckle an annoyed look. She hadn't wanted Welly to accompany them on the trip, though she had never voiced her displeasure. "And if the Atlanteans refuse to admit us, Romulus — what is your plan?"

Buckle blew on his tea and shook his head.

V

LADY FORTUNE BETRAYS *THE DART*

The awkward unfamiliarity of underwater transit soon melted away into a pleasant interlude. Buckle enjoyed the sensation of the submarine, the hum and vibration of its underwater steam engines — he would have liked to inspect them. Max would have loved to look at the engines as well.

Buckle's teacup rattled on its saucer. The *Dart*'s engines were running hot, the boilers bursting with steam in case a quick escape was required, but the propellers were spinning slowly. The submarine's pressure hull quivered, its metal vibrating with the energy of the engines in a fashion similar to the way the *Pneumatic Zeppelin*'s structure responded to the same forces. The *Dart*'s movement even felt familiar, the sensation of the underwater machine passing through resistance was something akin to an airship up against a sharp headwind. But there was also the omnipresent grip of liquidity, a grip tighter than the air. One might plummet to the depths, Buckle supposed, but it would be a far slower, smoother drop than if one fell out of the sky.

Finishing his tea down to the brown detritus of leaves in the bottom — the new and distinct flavor faintly similar to caramel — Buckle stood and strolled to the observation window alongside Sabrina. The muted sun was out now, high and far away above the sparkling surface, and the ocean bottom, a sandy desert populated by clumps of streaming seaweed, was alit. Everything had a blue-green tint to it except for the spots where the sunlight penetrated the ice in bright beams of aquamarine. Schools of fish, big and small and all with names unknown to Buckle, appeared, whirled and vanished in rippling typhoons of silver, black or yellow.

The *Dart* skimmed over a deep, narrow trench. Visibility was good, perhaps a half mile, but everything vanished into the wavering murk beyond that.

Sabrina looked at Buckle and smiled. The crimson ringlets of her hair looked even redder in the mix of greenish ocean illumination and the glow of the observation deck lamp. "I do believe that we shall gain entry into Atlantis," she said. "Though I don't trust Captain Felix to be there when it's time to leave."

"You think he'll skip out on us?" Buckle asked. "We paid for a two-way ticket."

"Overpaid up front."

"I wasn't in the mood to bid and barter," Buckle

whispered. "We'd wasted enough time with that little robot making us chase our own tail."

"Ah, our dear Penny Dreadful. She is so certain of herself, is she not?"

"I'm afraid its nuts and bolts have been rattled far too many times," Buckle sighed. "I have no idea what I shall do with it."

"She's an orphan like you and I," Sabrina said.

Buckle cleared his throat. The tea had a sweet aftertaste but it also gummed up the windpipe. "If it was human I would concur. But it's not."

"What do you plan to do? Jettison her into the ocean?"

"That would save everyone a great deal of trouble, I suspect."

Sabrina laughed. "You are not so heartless, Romulus. Machine or not, she has the heart of a little girl."

"Oh, I would most gladly fire that thing out of a cannon," Buckle said, but he didn't mean it.

Sabrina nodded with a grin. "Of course you would."

"I would most certainly not like to be shot out of a cannon," Penny Dreadful said mournfully in its all-too-childlike voice, its machine eyes glowing from the forward bulkhead where it stood in the shadows — the automaton seemed to like to hover in the darker corners of whatever room it was in. "I know that I was unable to locate the surface entrance to Atlantis, but I assure you I shall prove my worth to you as a traveling companion on this quest. I shall."

"Alright, then," Buckle said. He felt bad. He would never have thought the automaton would be able to hear his whispers to Sabrina. There was a lot about the Dreadful that Buckle didn't know — its capacities, motivators, flaws — and he didn't like it.

Sabrina's green eyes narrowed at the ocean. "There it is, I think."

Buckle followed Sabrina's gaze and he saw, far off in the fluctuating murk of the depths, the pale suggestion of lights, many lights, curving, undulating, the soft yellow emanations of an underwater city. "Aye," he whispered, in awe of such a thing.

Penny Dreadful stepped to the window and pressed its hands to the glass. "Home," it said in a low, metal voice that was almost a purr. "Home."

Sabrina took a deep breath and said, "Yes, well, I don't relish the idea of being stuck down here at the mercy of the fish people."

"It is a good place," Penny Dreadful said quickly, its metal fingers clicking as it planted them on its hips. "It is a wonderful city, white and full of light, the new civilization built upon the old human civilization. You shall see. You shall see."

"It does seem to exude a great deal of illumination," Welly said, arriving at the window.

"That is the greatest invention of the Atlanteans: the liquid-bound light, the luminiferous aether," Penny Dreadful said.

"The luminiferous aether?" Sabrina asked.

"You shall see," Penny Dreadful replied.

"There!" Sabrina said, in a near shout, thrusting a finger towards the fore. "A submarine. A submarine!"

Emerging from the currents, perhaps five hundred yards off the *Dart*'s port side, materialized the front of a large underwater machine. It was of bulbous construct with a large circular window framed by two small ones on each side, all flickering with the dull orange glow of seal-oil lanterns. The black hull loomed behind, oval in shape, with two horizontal fins sweeping out on each flank. Four torpedo tube hatches lurked under the nose; they were dark and Buckle figured that meant they were flooded and ready to fire. "Is it a Founders craft?" Buckle asked, but already he was certain that it was.

"We have to assume it is," Sabrina said.

Penny Dreadful clanked alongside Buckle, peering out the window. "It is," Penny Dreadful said, though Buckle did not trust its judgment anymore.

"Have they seen us?" Welly asked.

"The submarine is coming straight for us," Sabrina said. "Intercept course."

"I think Captain Felix described them as 'submersibles', Lieutenant." Welly offered.

"Shut up, Welly," Sabrina snapped.

"The question is, has Felix seen her yet?" Buckle said.

"Torpedo!" Sabrina shouted, pointing. "Coming straight down the beam!"

Buckle saw it, a small round green-brown dot spewing a long trail of rising bubbles behind, bearing down on them at considerable speed.

A warning klaxon rang through the ship. The approaching submarine rose out of view as the *Dart*, deck angling, engines throttling up to a pounding roar, dove into the blackness of the chasm below.

VI

NEPTUNE'S RIFT

A sheer wall of uneven blue rock blurred past the *Dart*'s observation window as the small submarine plunged at a steep angle.

"To hell with tea time," Buckle shouted, gripping the window frame. "Let us see to circumstances on the bridge!" Angling his center of gravity back to compensate for the *Dart*'s forward pitch, he swung his way out of the observation cabin and into the main passageway. He arrived in the control room to see the black maw of the rift looming in the windows. Felix, Rachel and Kishi manned their stations, feet planted wide, spines stiff against the backs of their jackets. Another crew member, a fair-skinned woman wearing a black beret, hunched over a brass tubed sound-collecting device with a pair of mufflers clamped against her ears.

"Both all ahead flank!" Felix ordered. "Set diving planes to maximum."

"Aye, Captain," Rachel responded. "Planes at maximum."

"What have we here?" Buckle shouted over the rumble of the engines and propellers.

"We are cursed," Felix shouted back. "I've never seen so many submarines in one place. We dodged three Founders boats before the fourth one spied us, we did. We'll shake this one off in the Rift."

"You said you could outrun them," Sabrina said, clambering in beside Buckle.

"My edge in speed shan't be much," Felix replied. "And I cannot outrun torpedoes." He turned to the woman with the beret and headgear. "Listen for those fish, Gustey."

"Be quiet, then," Gustey replied, clamping her earphones tighter.

"Is your sea craft capable of greater depths than that of the enemy?" Buckle asked.

"I'm afraid not," Kishi said. "The Founders boats can submerge deeper than we can, though nowhere as quickly. We have the advantage in rate of descent and endurance, for they cannot remain down for long."

"How long?" Buckle asked."

"Forty minutes, perhaps fifty if they want to choke," Felix said, snapping a pair of levers above his head. "Worry not, zeppelineer—we've dodged them before. Once we're under the gloom we can find a place, a nook, to nestle and hide. The big Founders boats are coal pigs. They must soon return to the surface to exchange atmosphere and vent exhausts. We can stay down for six hours, perhaps six and a half if we risk it with masks. We can't outgun him but we can outlast him. Once he surfaces we'll finish our run to Atlantis."

Water erupted from the periscope housing, streaming down into the well. Buckle stared at it with apprehension.

"Don't mind that," Kishi said with a smile.

"Six degrees down to starboard," Felix said, nudging his rudder wheel. The sheer, black face of the rift wall slipped past the windows. The sunlight was dissipating and being replaced by murky shadows. "Watch the trim."

"Torpedoes coming out of tubes!" Gustey shouted. "Two propellers coming on fast, rear port quarter."

"Hard a starboard!" Felix howled, spinning the helm wheel.

The submarine lurched to the right. Buckle grabbed hold of a map table as the deck angled.

"Can't you shoot back?" Sabrina asked. "Haven't you got stern guns, er, torpedo tubes?"

"Afraid not, girl," Felix replied, his jaw tight as he held the wheel pinned as far to the right as its swing would let him. "A blockade runner like the *Dart* is all engines and propellers in the arse. No room for stern fish."

"Two torpedoes passing to port!" Gustey

shouted.

Buckle saw two long tubes whiz past the left bridge window, rusted metal columns fifteen feet long, their sharp noses festooned with fuses, tails whirring with double propellers as they whirled past into the chasm.

"No explosions," Gustey reported.

"Good call, Gustey," Felix said. "Keep your ears open. There shall be more."

"Aye," Gustey replied.

"He's not setting timers," Kishi muttered. "Interesting."

"He wanted a lucky shot," Felix said. "It's difficult to aim on the dive."

"Can they still see us?" Buckle asked.

"He'll get a few glimmers of us at this depth and distance," Felix replied. "But it'll be enough to let him know where we are. He wants to crack us before we reach the gloom. The throat of Neptune's Rift narrows considerably at this depth and his boat needs far more maneuvering space than ours."

"Turn to port in three, two, one" — Rachel stared at an instrument which was a strange combination of illuminated chart and two hourglasses, one of which she turned upon speaking her last word — "now!"

Buckle saw the face of a cliff emerge head-on from the darkness. Felix pinned the helm wheel to the right. "Hard a starboard," Felix said calmly. "Edge of the chasm."

The towering wall of sea moss and granite slid past the *Dart* and her nose found open water once again.

"That was close," Sabrina muttered. "And awfully fast."

"Ah, plenty of buffer," Felix said. "The Rift run is timed down to inches and seconds, even adjusted for varying depths."

Again and again, Rachel shouted instructions for Felix and he whipped the helm around, repeatedly veering the *Dart* away from collisions with the sea cliffs.

There's what an abundance of propellers gets you, Buckle thought. *A brilliant rate of turn.*

Felix turned to Kishi. "Depress diving planes to fifteen degrees. Let's get under the light."

"Acknowledged." Kishi pushed the controls on the diving planes as she kept her gaze fixed on a depth meter, a glass instrument set in a wooden frame carved with angels. The needle swept toward the red section of the dial.

A crew member's voice rolled out of a chattertube hood. "Enemy still on our stern, Captain. Two hundred yards. He's turned on his lamps."

"The sore bastard is coming on fast," Felix muttered, spinning the helm wheel. "Hard a' port. Flood all tanks."

"Flooding all tanks, aye," Kishi replied.

The *Dart* heaved to the left, banking so sharply Buckle had to take hold of a rail or tumble across the deck. He caught a glimpse of the Founders boat out of the corner of the port window, the black, oblong shadow of the submersible between the dark, irregular cliffs of the Rift with the bright ocean surface shimmering above. The surface looked so very far away now. The dark bow of the submersible held two yellow lanterns encased in lensed apparatus which focused their light somewhat, like the glowing eyes of a huge squid.

A pipe at Buckle's left hand burst, spraying water.

"Six hundred feet and descending," Kishi said casually. "Approaching our depth rating."

"I know what our depth rating is," Felix grumbled.

"They're trying to crack this little tin can," Sabrina said to Buckle.

"Ah, she's good for it, and at least a hundred feet more," Felix retorted as Kishi pressed the *Dart* straight down the maw of the rift where there was nothing but darkness.

"I assume you've run her this deep before," Buckle said.

"Something like that," Felix answered. "Slippery fish — this is how we earn our money, Captain. Once we get our arses under the gloom they won't be able see us from above anymore."

"Torpedoes!" Gustey shouted, clamping her hands on her headphones. "Two props—coming straight into our baffles!"

"Damn it!" Felix snapped, turning to Kishi. "Take us down to six-seventy, now!"

"Six hundred and seventy, aye!" Kishi said as she depressed her diving planes. A new tension in her voice made Buckle uncomfortable.

"Torpedoes passing overhead," Gustey said, removing her headphones.

Buckle heard the distant drumming of torpedo propellers and shared a worried glance with Sabrina.

"They're close," Felix said softly. "Let's hope they haven't had the sense to set their timers."

Buckle's stomach rose into his mouth as he felt the *Dart* dropping fast, her metal flanks creaking against the pressure. He heard the muffled thump of an underwater explosion, followed almost instantly by the hammer force of its concussion. The *Dart* was flung to starboard and everyone and everything in her was hurled to the right.

Buckle slammed against a bulkhead, taking a blow to his right cheek as he fell. He scrambled to his feet. The sea lantern bounced in the stream of a ruptured steam pipe, fluttering as its oil either sloshed away from the wick or swamped the feeder valve.

"Seawater! I smell seawater!" Penny Dreadful cried out.

"What do you care, robot?" Felix scowled. "You can walk home!"

"We've stopped!" Rachel shouted.

Buckle realized Rachel was right. The forward momentum, the floating cut of the *Dart*, was gone. The deck no longer vibrated nor the air hummed with the rumble of the engines. She was drifting into a slight yaw to port. The hot metallic smell of overheating boilers and coal fumes assaulted Buckle's nostrils.

"Propulsion has lost power, boilers on overload," Rachel announced, pointing to a set of glass-plate gauges at her engineering station. The boiler pressure needles rattled at the red end of their measures.

"We're drifting to port," Kishi said. "Losing steerage."

"Awwwright." Felix steadied the deck with a swing of the helm wheel. "Keep your heads. We ain't food for the fishes quite yet."

"Boilers are off-line, Captain!" a voice gasped from the chattertube. "The damned hit shook 'em loose and bent the shafts with 'em. We had a fire but we put it out. We must purge pressure and shut boilers down or they'll explode!"

Buckle wanted to take command. It was his instinct to do so. The fate of himself and his officers should be in his hands. But he held himself back, though he slowly bit through his tongue in frustration. This was Felix's boat and Buckle was no submariner. It was time for the *Dart*'s captain to earn his money.

"Damn it to hell!" Felix shouted into the chattertube hood. "Do it, then. Shut 'em down before they send us out of this world and into the next."

"Torpedoes in the water!" Gustey shouted, her headgear back on.

Buckle looked up at the ceiling, at the dripping pipes, as if he could see through them, see what was coming, see the outlines of the torpedoes against the ocean sky.

"Of course," Felix muttered calmly. "Well, there's only one thing for it now. Take us down, Kishi. Vent the safety tanks. Drop us like a stone to eight hundred."

"But we are already exceeding maximum depth," Kishi said, growing more frightened. "We're already in the dysphotic. He can't see us."

"He knows where we are." Felix replied grimly. "Take us down. And on the double quick."

VII

THE GLOOM

The *Dart* fell into a gray-green darkness, her iron skeleton groaning as the ocean welcomed her descent, reaching up to crush her. Water streamed down the inside of the bulkheads. A peculiar odor arose, similar to the smell of a hot gun barrel, and Buckle wondered if the pressure hull, compressing down at a molecular level, was emitting some sort of frictional heat.

"Seven hundred and falling," Kishi said, her voice thin, tight.

"Be quiet," Felix whispered. He leaned into the chattertube. "Running silent," he ordered.

For thirty seconds there was no sound except the aching complaints of the hull, the bursting of pipes, the trickle of water. Buckle screwed his fingers around in his ears, cranking open his jaw. The descent seemed to be concentrating in his eardrums—the increasing pressure, the puttering rattle of bubbles escaping the submarine as it descended into their grave.

"Seven fifty," Kishi said, almost breathless.

"What's the exact rating on this thing?" Buckle asked, watching the darkness deepen rapidly by degrees.

"You don't want to know." Rachel replied.

"Ratings are subjective," Felix said. "Right now, vanishing into the gloom is the only chance we have."

"Gloom?" Sabrina asked.

"Six hundred and fifty-six feet and below," Felix replied, staring at lines of silver mercury rising in a bank of glass pressure tubes. "Where the sunlight fails and the true darkness of the sea begins. Where the monsters live."

"You're not helping," Sabrina grumbled.

"The Founders boat can't see us now but he must suspect that he crippled us," Felix said. "We have to get under his depth charges." He opened a small cabinet door set in the binnacle and drew forth a bottle of rum, which he uncorked with a pop and tipped up for a big swallow.

"That cork was a bit loud," Sabrina whispered.

Felix grinned. "If the blokes up there hear it, they'll understand." He offered the bottle to Buckle, who shook his head as he stared straight up. Buckle couldn't stop staring straight up.

"I'll take a swig of that," Sabrina said, and Felix handed her the bottle. Sabrina took a large gulp.

A weird, unsettling moan echoed through the ship, followed by a loud crumple of metal.

"She's a finicky boat she is," Felix whispered. "But she's tough. Her sides are dimpling, but they're not giving way."

Sabrina took another long gulp and handed the bottle back to Felix.

The bulkhead rivets started rattling. The glass plate on the compass cracked with a sudden, sharp smack.

"I've changed my mind," Buckle said. "I shall take a snort of that rotgut if the offer is still open."

Felix handed the bottle to Buckle, who tipped the bottle and swallowed one, big, syrupy-sweet slug of rum.

Outside the windows the last hints of light vanished. The ocean went black.

"The gloom," Rachel muttered.

Buckle could see no more dim glow overhead. It was if the *Dart* had dropped through a curtain and into a void, the only light now provided by the small sea lantern and the green bioluminescence of the boil-lit instrument panels.

"Eight hundred," Kishi whispered.

"Level out, stop descent," Felix ordered.

"Aye," Kishi replied.

Kishi and Rachel wound a set of hand cranks and threw a lever. The glass cover on the ship's compass shattered and fell in on the bobbing, phosphorescent needle.

Felix took a deep breath as Buckle handed him the bottle. "Well, this trip is surely eating away at my profit." He corked the bottle and tucked it back into the binnacle cupboard.

Gustey lifted her mufflers. "Enemy boat slowing to three knots, almost directly above us at five-fifty."

"Ah, he isn't in the mood to test his iron, is he?" Felix said through gritted teeth. "The coward."

"Cavitation," Gustey said as she listened hard in her earphones. "Engines reversed. He's stopped."

Everyone peered up at the dripping ceiling.

"He's a suspicious sort, he is," Felix muttered. "I'll give him that."

"What do we do now?" Welly asked.

"We wait," Felix whispered. "We can stay down much longer than he can. Once he is forced to surface we'll be clear of him."

A metal bolt fired out of the aft bulkhead and ricocheted off of the chadburn.

"Is your little submarine going to last?" Buckle asked.

"You'll know it if she doesn't," Felix said. "I see no reason for her to let me down."

Buckle's ears ached in the following silence, so intent was he upon listening. He heard the huge Founders submarine's boilers, a low, distant, constant rumble.

"Enemy boat holding position, directly above us," Gustey said.

"He knows where we are," Welly whispered.

"He heard our propeller shafts clang when they became unseated but he does not know our depth," Felix said grimly. "He's listening. Don't make a peep."

The *Dart* shuddered along her entire hull, a long shriek of tortured metal.

"Well, I'm pretty sure he heard that," Sabrina said dryly.

Felix took a seat in his captain's chair. Buckle wasn't sure, but in the sea lamp and boil-lit darkness it seemed that Felix's face had paled. Buckle coughed, his lungs irritated by the thickening atmosphere, contaminated with burnt coal smoke and agitated mold.

"He needs to flush us out before he is forced to surface," Felix said. "Ready yourselves for a rough ride."

"I hate depth charges," Rachel said.

"Depth charges?" Welly asked. "What kind of weapon is that?"

"Underwater canister bombs," Felix replied, scanning his instruments as he spoke. "Devil crackers. They are expensive—only big clans can afford them. They're unreliable: the internal fuse is set so close to the powder charge that I've heard tell of entire ships and zeppelins being obliterated after they lit their poorly sealed ordnance. But if a live one catches a submarine, well …"

"Iron coffins," Rachel whispered.

Buckle shot a glare at Rachel. The woman was no ray of sunshine, to be sure. The sourness of her personality seemed entirely at home in the gloom.

Gustey slapped her hands against her ear mufflers as she strained to hear. "Hatches opening, Captain," she said. "Metal rolling on metal."

"Here we go," Felix whispered.

Kishi slipped her pocket watch out of her coat and started counting silently, her lips moving but making no sound.

Felix placed his hands on the armrests of his chair, his fingers digging into the leather coverings. "They'll have set the timers on these bastards."

"Big objects coming down," Gustey said. "I hear hissing. Fuses in cans."

Buckle's heart started pounding. "How closely can they estimate our depth?" he asked Felix.

"They'll have a good sense of it, unfortunately," Felix replied. "They'll suspect that I can't go far beneath the gloom ceiling, and that my hull is ready to pop. They'll set the charges to blow at six seventy-five or thereabouts. No more I hope — it won't take much more than a granny's squeeze to finish us off down here."

"So we just sit here and take it, then?" Sabrina asked. She sounded pissed off.

"Felix ignored Sabrina. "Gustey — is the Founders submersible stationary or drifting?"

Gustey recalibrated her equipment and listened.

"She hasn't stopped entirely. Momentum and the current are carrying her forward from her last position, perhaps a quarter knot, by my calculations."

Felix nodded and made eye contact with Buckle, who saw Felix hatching a desperate plan, the kind of plan requiring Lady Fortune's good graces to work. Buckle grinned, feeling his bravado fueling up. Felix offered a smile back, a wild, we're-in-this-mess-together kind of grin.

Gustey discarded her listening equipment and crouched beside her chair.

Felix also crouched, clamping one hand around the helm wheel stanchion. "I would suggest that you all find something solid to grab ahold of," he said. "But stay away from the bulkheads—the force of a depth charge blow against the hull will kill you."

Taking a firm grip on the periscope housing, Buckle knelt. Sabrina and Welly tucked in beside him. Penny Dreadful huddled with them, its eyes glowing in the dark.

"I am quite frightened," Penny Dreadful said.

"As are we all, Penny," Sabrina answered, patting the automaton's metal shoulder.

Everyone looked up at the piped ceiling, cringing, waiting. Water trickled and sprayed but the wetness of clothing and skin was forgotten now.

"I hope somebody sold the Founders a nice set of duds," Welly whispered, his voice hoarse.

They listened and they waited. Time for Buckle became suspended in the wavering dark. He felt the approach of the unseen depth charges, fuses burning inside watertight barrels packed with explosives, falling upon them at great speed. A group of strange underwater creatures floated past the bridge windows, their near transparent, jelly-fleshed bodies glowing a faint purplish-red, propelling their fragile bodies by thrusting water out of dozens of tubular appendages. Buckle did not know if they were earth animals or alien transplants.

The dull thud of an underwater detonation made Buckle tense, with Welly and Sabrina clutching alongside him, but the distance of it took the bite out of his apprehension. The *Dart* rocked gently, pressed down from above.

"Too shallow," Kishi muttered. "Maybe this captain thinks we didn't have the brass."

"He'd never suspect we're this deep," Felix said.

"There are two canisters," Gustey said. "And they have probably dropped more. I'd suspect that first charge's fuse detonated prematurely."

"Always the pessimist, Gustey," Kishi said.

An elephant — at least, that was what it felt like — landed on Buckle's back and if he hadn't been holding on to the periscope he would have been driven flat to the deck. In the wallop of sound and pressure that hit him, the bridge shuddered so violently that everything blurred. Metal screamed and braces twisted. Pipes burst, spraying water and steam. Instruments cracked, firing splinters of glass and fountains of green glowing boil.

"Fire in the engine room!" a voice shouted from the chattertube.

"Damn it to hell!" Felix roared, throwing himself to the chattertube hood. "Shut down all boilers! Shut them down!"

"We've lost all internal pressure readings," Rachel shouted as loose mercury wiggled across her instrument panel. "All gauges are shot."

"Stand fast," Felix answered. "We're either dead or we're not."

"Fire extinguished," the voice on the chattertube rang out.

Felix leaned back into the hood. "Good show!"

"Brace yourselves," Gustey said, back on her headgear. "Two more coming down!"

"We've got to move, Felix," Kishi said, clicking her stopwatch, her face etched with fright. "They've got us on the hook, you hear me? We've got to move!"

"We can't move," Felix snapped. "We sit here and take it. We take it."

Gustey placed her headgear aside and crept under the map table.

"We're between the devil and the deep now," Felix muttered, eyes shining, looking up.

Buckle took a good hold of the periscope housing. It was dripping with boil and now his hand glowed with little green rivers. Thick smoke crept onto the bridge, the result of the engine room fire, and made him and everyone else cough. Take it, Felix had said. Sit down and take it. Buckle grew angry. Iron coffins indeed.

Another concussion hit them, more violent that the last. The force of its hammer blow through the deck slapped Buckle's heels so hard it felt like his foot bones had separated from their ligaments. Knocked reeling through the spray of boil and debris, he grabbed ahold of Sabrina and she grabbed hold of him, both of them toppling into a heap.

The second depth charge went off within two seconds of the first. There was nothing to do but cringe. A wooden cabinet near Buckle's head splintered with a loud crack. Boiling steam rocketed from a dozen compromised pipes, churning the bridge atmosphere into a dense, choking fog.

The sound of the depth charge echoed away and the submarine went still. But the quiet, with what it promised to bring with it again, was almost as loud as the explosions. "Blue blazes!" Buckle said as he rolled to his feet, slapping at his stinging ear. "Is everyone alright?"

"Aye," came the uneven response from Sabrina and Welly.

"I am undamaged," Penny Dreadful announced.

Buckle looked at Felix; the man's face was calm, his mouth working. At first Buckle thought Felix had gone into shock—and that was most disturbing—but then he realized the *Dart*'s captain was counting, maintaining some equation of time and distance in his head. "How many more, Gustey?" Felix asked.

I don't know, Felix," Gustey replied. "I only heard the two before I took my gear off."

Felix leapt to the forward windows, peering upwards. "Quickly, very quickly, Gustey—I need to know exactly where that submersible is. Then get those earpieces off."

"Aye, Captain!" Gustey said, retaking her station and planting the mufflers on her ears.

"Felix—" Kishi started in the dribbling silence.

"Shhhh," Felix said.

Gustey cocked her head and closed her eyes, turning a direction finder dial in front of her. "He's drifted forward, just forward of us by a league or a league and quarter," Gustey answered. "Depth still holding at five hundred."

Another depth charge detonated off to starboard. The *Dart* reeled against the punch. Buckle and the others were thrown toward the port bulkhead. A voluminous gush of seawater burst down around the periscope housing, fresh with the fish-salt stink of the sea.

Gustey screamed and threw off her headphones, gripping her ears. Blood rushed out between her fingers. She collapsed. Felix caught her before she hit the floor.

"Gustey!" Felix shouted, lowering her gently. "You, scarlet," he said, looking at Sabrina. "Hold her — keep her head off the deck!"

Sabrina scrambled forward to cradle Gustey.

"We're flooding!" Kishi coughed as she reached for a set of wooden handles. "Engaging emergency pumps."

"No!" Felix howled, lunging through the smoke to peer at the engineering station instruments beside Rachel. "Don't' waste the pressure left in the boilers. Ready to blow tanks!" He jumped to the chattertube. "Torpedo room! Flood tubes one and two and ready to fire!"

"Aye, Cap'n," came the breathless response. "One and two!"

Felix fired a grim-jawed smile at Kishi. "Shall we ride the monster, my dear?"

The fear in Kishi's face dropped away, replaced by a buccaneer's grin. "That is the most romantic thing you have ever said to me."

VIII

THE DEVIL AND THE DEEP

The *Dart*'s metal heart boomed as Felix and Rachel wound two control wheels around, releasing pressurized air into the ballast tanks. The submarine responded, jumping upward into the darkness, rising at the nose so abruptly everyone had to grab hold of the nearest bolted-down object or risk sliding away.

The wounded *Dart* heaved to port, threatening to roll over on her back. No matter. Buckle was relieved to be moving *up*.

"Trim! Trim! Maintain even keel, damn it!" Felix ordered.

Kishi, her neck reddening as she fought the stabilizer controls, made a sound like a choked-off guffaw. "Get over here and do it yourself, jackass! You keep this overinflated bitch from rolling!"

"I'm docking your pay!" Felix replied, rather ineffectually.

"I'll dock your manhood with a gutting knife!" Kishi countered.

"It's an asylum down here!" Sabrina yelled.

75

The *Dart* lurched onto a more even keel, accelerating, hurtling upward as if shot out of a cannon. A harsh vibration rattled through the boat.

"You're doing a fine job, Kishi!" Buckle shouted. "Captain Felix, what's the plan? You do have a plan, correct?"

"We're going to put a pair of torpedoes right up that Founders' arse," Felix said. "His stern observer will see us, he'll try to run—blow his tanks, even—but we'll get the angle on his tail before he can get that behemoth going."

"Doesn't he have stern tubes?" Sabrina asked.

"Won't help him," Felix replied. "Not at the speed we're going. But we can't stop our ascent. We'll only get one shot at this. If we miss we'll be stuck on the surface and he can sink us at his leisure."

"I do like being on the attack after all of this punishment, Captain," Buckle said.

"So do I," Felix answered, slapping two levers shut above his head and leaning into the chattertube hood. "Torpedo room, on my mark—ready to fire!"

"Ready to fire, aye!" came the hearty response.

The *Dart* continued to rise, faster and faster, the upward rush against gravity making Buckle feel heavy on his feet. A blast of hot, coal-smelling air hit him, expressed from one valve or another, but it did clear the smoke out of his face.

Hints of light fluttered on the windows and then

the great green-blue sunlit surface of the iceberg-laden sea exploded into view. The brightness of it hurt Buckle's dark-accustomed, smoke-irritated eyes and made him blink. But he would much prefer to die on the surface, with the light on his face, with decent air for a last breath.

Three hundred feet above them, a huge black oval silhouette blocked the sparkling surface illumination. The Founders submarine, a spiny metal leviathan fluked and bristling with hatches and glass, amber-lit window ports, arrays of tubes belching streams of black, white, gray and clear bubbles, sat motionless in the ocean sky. The *Dart* was rising so tightly under the Founders' stern Buckle began to worry they might collide with the enemy's motionless propellers.

The *Dart* continued to rocket up and up.

"If we hit our mark and sink this bastard we buy ourselves time," Felix said. "Once we breach the surface we'll vent for air and submerge to periscope depth to effect repairs. All we have to do is get one shaft back on line. We're inside the blockade area now. Atlantis isn't much more than a thousand leagues ahead."

"They've seen us," Rachel reported.

In a sudden, cyclonic explosion of air bubbles, the Founders submarine began to ascend. The captain, realizing his situation, had blown her tanks.

But the little *Dart* was much faster. Buckle watched through the mist-wreathed interior of the bridge as they rose behind the submersible's two huge bronze propellers, both mottled light green and bigger than the *Dart* itself. The blades began to turn. Buckle saw two navy blue uniformed figures moving around inside the submersible's stern observation window, located in a bulge on the keel twenty feet forward of the propellers.

"Ready to fire!" Felix shouted into the chattertube.

"We're too close!" Kishi screamed.

"No matter," Felix said. "This is our only chance."

Buckle looked up. They were now tantalizingly close to the surface of the ocean and rising at such a speed that they would surely throw themselves into the air before coming back down again. The stern of the Founder's submarine loomed squarely in front of the *Dart*, and no more than thirty feet away.

Felix leaned into the chattertube hood. "Fire! Both tubes! Fire!"

Buckle heard the buzz of propellers, the sudden wallop of compressed air, the scrape of long metal objects rattling out of metal tubes.

"Fish away!" shouted the voice on the chattertube. "Numbers one and two away!"

"We're too damned close!" Kishi screamed.

"Brace for impact!" Felix shouted.

Buckle saw the torpedoes race through the water: long, dark tubes with flashing propellers, both striking the Founders submersible just above her screws. On impact the projectiles exploded in great flashes, the detonations throwing up gigantic, cathedral-like pressure bubbles filled with fire. The two propellers wrenched apart, swinging sideways as the stern section of the Founders boat split at the seams.

The sound, the deep, horrible sound of the collapsing bulkheads was as if the ancient bed of the sea itself was ripping apart.

"Victory!" Rachel howled.

A concussive wall of roiling white bubbles rolled back into the *Dart*, cracking her bridge windows as it hurled her backwards. Buckle and everyone grabbed for handholds as the submarine tipped back almost on her tail, the deck shifting into a near vertical position under them. The force of the breakneck ascent kept Buckle pinned to the spot; he had some sense that the metal body of Penny Dreadful was under his boots, that he was standing on it.

"Pressure hull compromised!" Rachel shouted. "We're taking water in forward compartments one, two and three!"

"Bilge pumps inoperative!" Kishi shouted. "You've killed us, Felix — you soddy bastard!"

Small, tight jets of cold water shot into the

bridge through the jagged fissures in the windows and a hundred other piping cracks, filling the cabin with spray. His eyes stinging with sea salt, Buckle felt the *Dart* breach the surface and launch into the air. For that moment the forces of gravity which had so sorely pressed him in the ascent suddenly released and he was weightless — floating, flying, with the cabin suddenly filled with brilliant sunlight, all of the people and objects suspended around him in whirling, glittering arcs of spray — until the submarine, captured once again by gravity, dropped, slamming into the water with bone-crushing force.

Stunned, Buckle looked up from where he lay on the deck. He saw the shimmering light of the surface darken as sea flooded over the windows, sucking the *Dart* down. As they plummeted he shouted something — he never would remember what — at the wonderful, dappling surface light as it turned greener and blacker as they fell further and further away into the depths.

"Hold on!" Felix shouted. "We're going straight to the bottom!"

It didn't feel like a victory to Romulus Buckle.

IX

AN IRON COFFIN

Buckle clawed his way to his feet, his vision blurred, the bridge a running cascade of seawater. Boil spilled into the flow everywhere, growing brighter and brighter as it streamed in the deepening darkness. The *Dart* waffled downwards, leading with her stern.

"We're descending into the Rift!" Kishi shouted. "Abandon ship!"

"Belay that order!" Felix roared. "Hold fast!"

"We're doomed!" Kishi yelled. "We must detach the lifeboat now!"

"There isn't time!" Felix replied. "The blast threw us clear of the chasm. We'll land on the sandy bottom, easy as you please. Hold fast!"

"Damn you to hell if you're wrong," Rachel said.

Kishi slid across the deck to assist Sabrina as she held Gustey "There's no bottom here!" Kishi groaned. "We're going into the Rift, I tell you!"

"Show some faith, woman!" Felix howled.

The starboard forward window cracked again under the renewed pressure, this time in a thousand spiderwebbing, glittering white fractures. More water sprayed in from a dozen new fissures.

"Clear the bridge, damn it to hell!" Felix shouted, pointing to the rear hatch. "Clear the bridge!"

Buckle lifted Gustey's legs while Sabrina and Kishi, slipping on the tilted, wet deck, maneuvered her limp body through the hatchway.

"Come on!" Felix hissed through clenched teeth as he fought the stabilizer controls. "Back on the bubble, little lady — that's it!"

The *Dart* righted somewhat on her keel, making the going easier on the deck. The starboard window cracked again, loudly, the sound of thick glass breaking. Pin-point streaks of water turned into small torrents.

"Get out!" Felix roared. "We've got to seal the hatch!"

Buckle let go of Gustey's legs, letting them trail along the grating as Kishi and Sabrina stumbled down the flickering passageway. He leaned back into the bridge as Rachel hurried out of the green-lit waterfalls and slid past him. "Welly!"

"Coming, Captain!" came Welly's reply as he emerged from the watery tumult, lugging Penny Dreadful with him.

"You need not carry me, Ensign," Penny said.

"Leave the damn thing behind!" Felix shouted as he crowded behind Welly. "It's a damned Jonah, it is!"

"Damn your eyes, sir!" Buckle replied. "Move, Ensign! Move!"

Once they had all piled into the passageway, Felix took hold of the hatch and pressed it against the rapidly growing torrent of water. "Lend a hand!" he shouted. "We must seal this hatch now, before the water overwhelms us!"

Buckle and Welly threw their weight against the hatch. Slowly they forced it back against the monstrously dark fall of water. The *Dart* continued to level out, easing the weight of the water against the hatch, and they heaved it shut. Felix wound the locking wheel until the handle clanged against the end of its wind.

Buckle felt relief but he knew one sealed door would not save them if the *Dart* was plummeting into the rift.

A metallic boom deafened Buckle. The deck grating leapt up and slammed the wind out of him. Everyone dropped as if the strength had gone out of their legs, joining him in a heap.

The *Dart* had hit bottom.

Buckle blinked and lifted his head slightly to pull his front teeth out of the places they had sunk into his forearm. Smoke hung heavy and thick in the *Dart* passageway, the boil emergency lights casting a ghostly green illumination into the writhing haze. The roar of floods crashing into bulkheads was gone, replaced by the patter of dripping water and the rustling of the others as they struggled to rise. Buckle focused on the bright sheen of boil on his hand and sleeve; it smelled fishy.

"See?" Felix grumbled as he stood up and wound an overhead wheel. "Soft bottom. No Rift."

Buckle peered up to see Penny Dreadful standing over him, its eyes glowing under the iron lashes, the glistening metal of its skin dimly reflecting green.

"Are you alright, Captain Buckle?" Penny asked, and there sounded like genuine concern in its childish voice.

"Yes." Buckle answered, tasting blood in his mouth as he drew himself up onto one knee.

"It seems we are lucky this day, Captain," Penny said.

"Luck?" Felix snorted. "Bah! I saved our skins. I did. I should have turned and ran but I did what you paid me for. And it's taken a mighty chunk out of my profits."

A deep, metallic groan swept in and shook the *Dart*. Buckle gripped a water-dripping rail and hunched, expecting the bulkheads to collapse in upon them in one brutal, cold heave.

"That's not us," Felix said. "The Founders boat. Implosion."

Buckle found Penny Dreadful pressed at his

flank. Sabrina and Rachel assisted Gustey, who seemed to have recovered her senses enough to stand. A faint glow of aqua-colored sunlight rippled in the observation parlor hatchway. "Where do we go from here?" Buckle asked. His tongue dragged, stuck with salt.

"There's always options when one isn't dead," Felix said. "José! I want a report!" he shouted at two crew members cranking a watertight door shut at the far end of the passageway. One of them was Marsh.

"Aye, Cap," the other crewman responded, a dark brown fellow with a thick black mustache — he had to be José. "It ain't good."

"You don't say?" Felix barked. "Come with me." He ducked into the observation parlor.

Buckle followed Felix into the cabin, blinking at the ocean-filtered sunlight as it poured ever-so-softly from above. A dozen silver-white fractures laced the round porthole glass but it had not sprung a visible leak.

"Your window has a lot of cracks in it," Sabrina grumbled.

Felix smiled and tapped the glass. "Purchased special from the Friars. Four inches thick. Lady Fortune is both a witch and an angel. The blast of the explosions wounded us, yes, but it also threw us clear of the chasm."

Buckle looked out into the ocean — a great

expanse of sandy bottom, populated by large rocks and outcroppings of tall, dancing seaweed, undulated away as far as the eye could see. But what grabbed his attention was the sight of the Founders submarine, slowly sinking into the maw of the Rift, her stern spilt apart, spilling oil and debris. Another shriek of her bulkheads collapsing echoed through the depths. It was an awful thing to witness, the death of a huge sea machine.

"Look at that," Sabrina muttered at Buckle's shoulder. "Look at that."

They stood in silence until the corpse of the submersible vanished into the crevasse. Buckle again saw the soft, glimmering lights of Atlantis beyond, thousands of lights surrounding a complex of domes glinting glass, gold, green and white. Despite the peril of their own situation the group needed this pause, gasping and dripping, the strangely intimate sounds of trickling water soothing their battered nervous systems.

Rachel opened a medical cabinet and took a roll of gauze to wrap around Gustey's head and ears.

"My report is that we're sunk, Cap," José announced from the hatchway, glaring at Penny. He was a short fellow, a boilerman from the look of the sweaty flush of his skin and his soot-stained blue coveralls. His hands, streaked with coal dust and blood from a wound on his palm, were far too big for his short arms. Coughing, he sucked in lungfuls of air under his prodigious mustache as if the smoky cabin offered a vastly preferable atmosphere to what he had been breathing in the engine room.

"Casualties?" Felix asked.

"No more than a bump on the nob for Marsh," José answered.

"And damages?" Felix asked. "Give it to me straight."

"Straight is we're dead in the water, old salt," José said, glancing back at Marsh, who, rubbing a bloody spot on his head, watched them from the passageway. "Negative buoyancy and no power. Propulsion is inoperable. Port shaft is bent. Propeller packings leaking and aft bilge flooded. I purged the combustion systems to save the oxygen and kept the seawater out of the boilers. Pumps are no good."

Felix looked at Buckle. "By default I shall still get you to Atlantis, Captain. Kishi, muster the crew in the airlock and gear up. Help José prepare a sling for Gustey."

"Aye," Kishi replied, ducking out of the hatchway with José.

"Everyone into the corridor," Felix said, turning to Buckle. "We are in sight of Atlantis, at the edge of the latifundium, so we continue the rest of the way in diving suits." He tucked his chin into his chest and muttered. "I'll have to pay for the Atlanteans to send a team to recover the *Dart*. The damned greedy fishmen will stick me for it. But they probably won't risk it until the blockade is over. Damn it," he added softly.

"You have enough suits for everyone?" Buckle asked.

"Yes," Felix answered. "We use them for hunting expeditions. Wealthy sea merchants love underwater safaris. But we need to hurry. Follow me."

Felix screwed the observation hatch shut and led the group aft, down the passageway to an open deck hatch where a column of yellow-orange light shot up into the smoke-filled air. Felix swung down the ladder and Buckle followed, landing in a spacious chamber lit by three lanterns on hooks, a compartment dense with the smell of seawater and salt-saturated leather. Bulky copper diving helmets lined the bulkheads, their thick glass viewing ports glowing greenish orange in the lamplight. Leather-strapped sealskin diving suits, air tanks and scuffed weight belts hung in rows. A cylindrical iron chamber, half sunk in the deck, waited with its hatch swung open like a massive nautilus shell.

Kishi, José, Marsh and the tall black female cook worked hastily amidst the gear, preparing air tanks and opening suits.

"Captain!" Welly shouted from the top of the ladder hatch. "Automaton coming down!"

"Aye," Buckle replied, taking hold of Penny as Welly swung it down. Once again, Buckle was surprised at how light the robot was.

"I can climb ladders on my own," Penny complained.

Buckle and Welly helped Gustey down the ladder as Sabrina and Rachel lowered her from above.

"Over here, Captain," Felix said. "Tonda will get you into your diving suits." He pointed at the black cook as she pulled a diving suit open like a narwhal hide, its shoulder buckles attached to hooks so he could step into the heavy boots and have the suit drawn up around him to the neck. "There's a waterproof satchel for your pistols and put your swords in as well," Felix added. "The Atlanteans don't allow anyone but their soldiers to have firearms inside the city. They'll confiscate them. But you can keep your swords."

Buckle placed Penny on the deck and stepped into the diving suit. The weighted diving shoes were large enough to accommodate his boots and once he was in position Tonda yanked the squeaking suit up against his back and began stuffing his hands into the armholes. The suit was reasonably light, made of sealskin and doped canvas leather strappings; it smelled like every inch of it had been saturated by the sea, as if the materials, even left in a desert, would never completely dry out again. "I'll carry Penny," Buckle said to Welly, who was disappearing into another diving suit under Marsh's supervision.

"No need," Penny said. "I am designed to

function underwater."

"All Atlantean robots were made to walk on the ocean floor," Felix said. "Quite the inventor's dream, they were, to start with."

"She's not dangerous," Sabrina said, looking tentative as Rachel tugged, snapped and buckled her into a diving suit.

"The Atlanteans won't accept it," Felix answered as he screwed his feet into his diving boots. "It'll doom your negotiations before they even begin. Why risk it? I'll pay you one hundred gold coins for it. I'll keep it here and collect it once the *Dart* is salvaged."

Buckle shook his head. "Enough on that. The automaton is coming with us." Penny Dreadful was so old and banged up he wondered if its shell was still waterproof. He half-suspected its ancient seals would fail under the pressure and the cold seawater pouring into its little onboard boiler would blow it to pieces, claiming it forever in the depths. Though that, in a way, Buckle suspected, would be a sort of return home.

"Never say I didn't try to take that Jonah off your hands," Felix grumbled, now helping the one-armed Tonda secure the raft of leather fasteners running up and down Buckle's torso and legs. Each expert tug of a strap squeezed Buckle a little tighter, the hug of the leather promising safety from the sea.

"This is far too fine a mess for me." Sabrina planted her chin on her diving suit collar, her green eyes bright, nervous as she watched Kishi seal her in. "Don't you have another submarine? A little one? A lifeboat? Skiff?"

"We walk from here, Lieutenant," Buckle said with a grin. Chains rattled behind his ears as Gustey lowered a diving helmet onto his head.

"Just peachy," Sabrina replied, and she didn't look happy about it.

X

THE LATIFUNDIUM

Romulus Buckle, his head locked inside a copper diving helmet with windows of green glass, stepped out of the *Dart*'s flooded airlock and dropped into the freezing squeeze of the ocean. It wasn't much of a drop — five feet to the sandy bottom — and the uncomfortable heaviness of his suit was replaced by a pleasant sensation of buoyancy held in check by the bulk of his boots and weight belt. The oxygen tanks and helmet felt familiar, similar as they were to a zeppelineer's high altitude and poison gas equipment, though they were bulkier and more rigid in their construction. He gripped two weapons: a long-handled underwater spear and a small crossbow harpoon with a firing mechanism which combined tension and compressed air.

The Atlantis Approaches were a dangerous place, Felix had said. The Guardians, nasty creatures, operated in loose platoons under the command of vile beasties called 'gagools'. Kill the gagools first if you can, Felix had said. Kill the gagools first and your odds of survival increase exponentially. One can beg an Atlantean sentinel or herder for one's life but not a gagool.

The tan-colored bottom reflected the morning light but it all felt melancholy, surely the effect of the greenish glass of his helmet windows deflecting much of the light. He was also still in the shadow of the *Dart*'s belly. Bending as low as he could to clear the keel, he trudged out into the weak, undulating light, half-stumbling in slow motion as he learned how to move his boots over the bottom swells. It was humid inside his helmet and the faceplate trickled with condensation. The sounds of his breathing and the ping of the oxygen valves were oppressive but when he straightened up and saw the glorious green-blue-white play and sparkle of light and water on the surface he felt better.

Buckle turned, slow and awkward, to join Sabrina, Welly, and Penny Dreadful, who were collecting under the guidance of Kishi. They looked like phantoms in a netherworld, faces ghoulish in the round green portals of their helmets, the interiors lit by tubes of bioluminescent boil. It was near impossible to tell who was inside each suit except for size. Penny Dreadful, wearing no gear of any kind, moved toward him, smoothly, half-gliding across the bottom, looking like it was at home. Its golden eyes had a buggish bulge to them, enlarged by translucent lenses which had dropped from the metal skull and sealed the sockets.

The machine had transformed itself once it was in the water: a sheer metal webbing had unfolded from its hands and feet, turning them into flippers, and a shark-like dorsal fin now thrust up from a slot in its back.

It took five more minutes for the remainder of the *Dart*'s crew to descend from the airlock, with Marsh and Rachel carrying Gustey between them on a basket stretcher. The last man out was Captain Felix. Once his boots hit bottom, Felix was on the move, leaning forward as he drove his legs, his boots sending up punches of dislodged sand. He jabbed his gloved finger forward as he passed Buckle, his face looking compressed and angry inside his helmet.

Buckle swung around and hauled his boots across the sand, staying close to Felix and Kishi as they took the lead and humped toward the towering domes of Atlantis. Buckle could see all seven of the domes, one large one surrounded by six more of varying sizes, and they all pulsed with a mysterious white light.

Buckle tested the unfamiliar balance of the spear in his hand. Felix had warned them to keep moving at all times and not to get spread out, for on foot they were likely to encounter the Guardians. If there was no Atlantean sentinel present with the Guardians—and apparently there often wasn't—there would be a sharp fight to make their way through. The group numbered ten souls—not counting Penny Dreadful— and they were all well armed.

Atlantis loomed closer slowly, very slowly. Buckle leaned into his stride, throwing one heavy boot ahead after the other, plodding through the resistance of the water. He stopped and glanced back at Sabrina, Welly, and Felix's crew, a ragged line of shambling ogres, faces lost in glowing green orbs, blasting clouds of bubbles out of the tops of their skulls. Beyond the group, the wreck of the *Dart* fell away in the murk. From this distance she looked undamaged, sitting neatly on her keel on the sandy bottom. Forty yards beyond the *Dart* the great black maw of Neptune's Rift loomed and Buckle could *feel* the gaping cold of its black seam. There was no trace of the Founder's submarine. Swallowed up and gone.

A fate the *Dart* had escaped by forty yards.

But there were many more Founders boats. The underwater blockade continued in full force, the gargantuan black silhouettes of the Founders submersibles dark against the wavering columns of sunlight overhead, their propellers chopping the depths as they circled Atlantis in trails of black and gray bubbles.

If the Founders were aware of the loss of their boat they did not respond to it. If they had noticed Buckle and the divers it seemed they didn't care.

Soon the open sandy bottom gave way to a high, waving seaweed forest, its mossy floor glowing with a beautiful green bioluminescence. Felix and Kishi led the group along a narrow trail through the seaweed, a path so overgrown the plants constantly threatened to tangle harpoons and lead-soled feet.

After two hundred yards of hard slogging, the seaweed forest vanished and Buckle peered through his faceplate to see the sea floor spread wide and flat and take on the regimented, sectional appearance of farmland. Endless rows of tall, evenly-spaced plants with dark green stalks bobbed stiffly in the currents. Massive oyster beds, shrimp farms and phalanxes of lobster traps unfolded as far as the eye could see, well tended by Atlantean divers wearing tan suits and assisted by odd, centipede-like alien creatures, spotty orange-blue in color, which seemed to be weeding out dead and unwanted plants. The group reached an undersea road, its interlocking flat stones jarring to Buckle in their mathematical precision after he'd sweated his way through so much tangled flora and sand.

One diver stopped her work and stared at them as they passed.

In the distance Buckle saw the ruins of a great white and green metropolis emerging from a rise on the sea floor between them and the domes of Atlantis. He realized the drowned structures were of the ancient Roman style — the ruins of a once great city. That made no sense but Buckle didn't care. His diving helmet echoed with resounding pings as he slogged, breathing harder and harder. Felix pressed the advance and it was work to keep up with him. Buckle glanced back, turning his entire torso to do so, and saw the group following with Penny Dreadful at their head, its machinery transformed into a streamlined form cutting through the water more smoothly than the humans in their bulky suits. Buckle swung around and threw his muscles into the plod forward.

Felix suddenly halted. Buckle stopped alongside him. Felix delivered a hand signal to his crew, who quickly assembled a circular formation with Tonda hovering over Gustey on her hammock in the center. Sabrina and Welly took places alongside the *Dart*'s crew in the defensive wall.

Buckle cursed the heat in his helmet and the sweat flowing into his eyes. He cursed the dribbling condensation, low quality of his window glass, though they were as about as effective as Crankshaft gas mask ports, no worse or better. He couldn't see anything but seaweed waving in the green-blue murk. The weight of the sea now pressed down on top of him. He calmed himself through long, deep sucks of the ocean-cooled air from his tanks and felt his battle nerves kick in. The swirl of the water outside slowed down and his eyesight improved, piercing the shadows. He tightened his grip on his harpoon.

The Guardians. It had to be the Guardians. *Bring it on*, Buckle thought. *You'll get the first blow. But I shall deliver the last.*

And when the first blow came, it came in a lightning flash of silver.

XI

THE GUARDIANS

Something slashed through the middle of the group, whipping back and forth in silver whirls of knife-edged fins. There was more than one. It was some kind of fish, or eel, some kind of razorfish. Buckle spun around. He heard muffled shouts, people screaming into their helmets. Blood billowed into the water, nearly black but showing red in its thinner surges.

"Kill it!" Buckle shouted into his helmet. The razorfish darted, too quick for the wallowing swipe of his harpoon. Don't swing—jab. One of the divers crumpled forward, both gloved hands clutching at their inner thigh as blood erupted out of the diving suit in volcanic bursts.

Sabrina. It was Sabrina. Horror slapped Buckle. In the next instant he realized it wasn't her but a *Dart* crewperson—Sabrina was beside him, stabbing at the razorfish with her spear—the wounded unfortunate was José, who was about the same size.

The two razorfish, perhaps six feet long apiece, zipped in and out of the circle, lashing their bodies back and forth like whips. Someone lost their spear and it drifted to the rocky bottom.

Rachel's weapon discharged, firing a weighted net that blossomed and caught one of the razorfish, thoroughly wrapping it up, and the creature sank, thrashing the rocks in the middle of the circle, quickly shredding the ropes dragging it down. Rachel surged forward with as much speed as the water allowed, planted her boot on the razorfish and plunged a long knife into its skull. The razorfish jerked and fell limp, its tail wobbling in the current.

The second razorfish vanished. Buckle spun around, aiming his harpoon into the empty sea in front of him. The razorfish were only the opening salvo, he knew, a way to disorganize the defense, and now the brutes would come and finish them off.

The brutes came.

Looming out of the darkness, the nightmares came.

They came with light, brilliant light, shining in three tight, bouncing pairs.

Buckle blinked hard at the blinding, turquoise-edged illumination. What he could see made his guts tighten. A half-dozen razorfish slithered at the fore. Behind them heaved octopus-like beasties, pink flesh engines with lavender eyes glaring over rafts of black suckered tentacles pulling their huge bodies across the bottom.

The paired columns of light beamed down from the crowns of the octopi, pouring forth from the large eyes of the gagools. The gagools were awful creatures, manlike in form but scaled along the length of the body and equipped with skull crests that gave their heads a rabid, hippocampus-like appearance. Long gill rows, a darker blue-green color than the rest of their bodies, lined their necks. They jabbered in high-pitched shrieks, fangs bared, waving their arms above their rubbery octopus perches.

Buckle lifted his harpoon and took aim at the dark sliver of skin between the eyes of the lead gagool, but the creature saw him and ducked behind his octopus mount.

The octopi launched the first assault. Charging the circle on three sides, the cephalopods lashed with their orange-purple tentacles, the razorfish darting in beneath them in blurs of silver barbs. Buckle, Felix and Sabrina thrust their harpoons forward, forcing the razorfish aside and slashing the octopi's squirming arms that jerked back in trails of purple blood.

At the edges of his peripheral vision Buckle saw the other two Guardian octopi and their gagools swing around on each flank, aiming to overwhelm the small knot of divers by encirclement. There was nothing he could do for that. His hands were full with the lashing, lithe tentacles of the octopus in his face, a gagool peering over its neck, the light from its eyes blinding him. Buckle ducked and staggered backwards to prevent being enveloped by the tentacle mass. Felix and Sabrina retreated alongside him, but to fall back much further would collapse the circle.

Buckle aimed his crossbow into the center of the octopi looming over him, into the underside between the tentacles, and fired. The crossbow bucked as the harpoon bolt zipped through the water and buried its point in the beastie. The tentacles jerked back. The octopus released a burst of bubbles and a shriek so piercing it battered Buckle's ears inside his helmet.

The razorfish switched from harassment to full on attack. Buckle jabbed his harpoon left and right, fighting off blur after whipping blur of silver. Yellow-green blood streaked the water as his blade bit into one writhing body after another. The survivors, snapping at their dying fellows as they sank as if in disdain of their clumsiness, seemed undeterred by casualties.

A tentacle wrapped around Buckle's harpoon and tore it free of his grasp. He grabbed at the knife on his belt, unsure of exactly where it was, and found it. He drew it in front of him, the metal blade flashing in the wobbling underwater sunlight, but it seemed pitifully small.

A shadow arched overhead; a gagool, launching from its high beastie perch, kicked aside a harpoon point and landed in the center of the company's defensive ring. Kishi and Marsh turned but the monster knocked them aside as it charged, its white-hot eyes locking onto Buckle's as it barreled straight at him.

Sabrina stabbed at the gagool but the creature hurled her aside. Slashing his knife back and forth, Buckle could do little but hold his ground. The gagool sprang, grabbing Buckle's knife hand at the wrist with one massive webbed claw and taking hold of his chest plate with the other. It flung its mouth open, impossibly wide, the green tongue writhing in a cavern lined with rows of sharp triangular teeth rippling down the musculature of its throat. Buckle threw his free hand against the gagool's chest but the gagool was stronger than he was. His muscles shaking so hard the bones threatened to shatter, he barely heard his own gasps in his helmet. He was done for.

Buckle jammed his hand into the gagool's gills, attempting to rip one out, but it was no good. No good. The gagool yanked his head into its mouth, the fangs and horned tongue scraping his faceplate in cringe-inducing squeaks as it stuffed his helmet in.

The gagool was swallowing Buckle. It was swallowing his head whole, helmet and all. He could see down its throat, down the sucking funnel of teeth and blood-red muscle.

Buckle thrashed but the jaws had him locked in. The gagool stated swaying, jerking back and forth. Now the damned thing was trying to rip his head off.

All of a sudden, in a flash of white light and blue

darkness, Buckle was free. He was hurled aside, his bruised body floating down to the flagstones. The gagool had flung him away.

The gagool clawed at its right leg. Buckle saw Penny Dreadful, the little robot not higher than the gagool's waist, glowing red at the seams, bubbles streaming out of the back of its metal skull as it emitted a low, profoundly deep sort of wail. Two long-bladed daggers slashed in front of Penny; it wasn't holding them — the blades had snapped out from its forearms, the metal hands now folded back, and it drove them with great speed, again and again, deep into the thigh and hip of the gagool. Dark blood gushed out of the beastie as it frantically snatched at Penny's blades. But the automaton was too quick, cutting the monster to ribbons.

Finding his balance, Buckle swung to his feet and rushed the gagool but his dagger blade bounced off its neck. The gagool no longer noticed him. Penny Dreadful plunged both of its blades into the gagool's right knee joint and yanked them out on each side, severing the creature's lower leg.

Staggering, the enraged gagool snatched Penny and pressed both claws around its head in an attempt to crush its skull, even trying to sink its teeth into the unyielding metal. Penny continued the murderous assault, driving her knives over and over into the gagool's midriff. The water inked thick with black blood. Buckle continued his attack and his stabs found thinner armor across the small of the gagool's back, the knife snapping through the exoskeleton, followed by the easy plunge into the flesh.

The gagool crumpled forward, obscured a drifting shroud of its own blood. It took all of Buckle's strength to pry the beastie's hands off Penny. Once the automaton was free, the gagool drew its arms and legs into a fetal position, the light fading rapidly from its eyes, and sank.

The silver tornado of razorfish eased back, apparently stunned by the death of the gagool. Buckle staggered through the blood-filled water. Everyone still roughly held the circle but the octopi had snatched away their harpoons and spears and they were now slashing with daggers. The two surviving gagools remained on the backs of their mounts, hurling javelins tipped with nasty-looking barbs. The riderless octopus attacked with a particular fury and its big cold eyes looked like they were locked on Buckle.

The company was being overwhelmed, rotating, slowly squeezing into a tighter and tighter fighting formation; they were almost back-to-back, the signature of the last stand. There was no way to break out, no hope of reinforcement, and they had to either defeat the beasties or die on the bottom.

Penny was still emitting its ear-throbbing, siren-like wail as Buckle knelt to collect a fallen harpoon from a bed of seaweed. As he rose he saw one of the *Dart's* crew—it was Marsh—staggering backwards, both hands wrapped around a gagool's javelin buried deep in his stomach, bubbles and blood flooding out around the shaft. The man's face was ghastly, his mouth flung impossibly wide in a silent scream inside the glass. Buckle reached for Marsh but he dropped, his weight belt dragging him down onto the rocks.

The razorfish attacked the gap in the line, tornadoing in as they tried to wedge the opening wider. Buckle jumped in front of Tonda and Gustey, attacking the razorfish with his harpoon. Penny Dreadful was alongside him, its long, sharp knives at the ready, and he continued to be surprised at how easily the machine moved through the water and how powerful its movements were.

The two surviving gagools increased the illumination from their eyes to a blinding level, uttering long, demented shrieks. Lost in a tunnel of white light, Buckle saw the shadows of tentacles coming in from all sides, felt the surge of the barbed javelins brushing past as they cut through the water. The razorfish swirled, forming a violent, half-seen wreath of bladed, flashing silver bodies constricting around the company, threatening to cut to ribbons anything unfortunate enough to be caught in the wall of their churn.

Buckle gripped the handle of his harpoon as hard as he could and it was immediately torn out of his grasp. Drawing his dagger again, he shared a desperate glance with Sabrina on his immediate left.

She shot him a brave, encouraging smile.

Buckle smiled back.

XII

THE ROAD OF TOMBS

The Guardians closed in. The cyclone of razorfish — there seemed to be even more of them now, judging by the height of the wall — wound tighter and tighter, with the lashing tentacles of the cephalopods looming behind, and atop them the horrible blazing eyes of the gagools, the beasties terrible in aspect from atop their perches, their long black claws fully extended. It seemed to Buckle that Penny Dreadful was the only member of the group who could inflict any real damage on the gagools and he doubted it could take them all on.

A great horn sounded, a soulful, whale-song blare, low and dense and ancient, throbbing inside Buckle's helmet though he hardly noticed it, so immense was the desperate gallows-gasp of his own breathing in his ears.

Penny Dreadful's baleful siren stopped.

The razorfish vanished abruptly, the currents of their whirlpool whipping around Buckle and his company in empty whorls of disturbed sand. The octopi retreated, tentacles retracting, the two gagools snapping their heads back and forth in some kind of indignant rage, releasing high-pitched cries as the lights in their eyes quickly faded to a glowing, red-black that looked like fire embers.

Above the heads of the gagools appeared a beautiful, dolphin-like machine with an open deck, its hull colored white and gold with copper and brass elements polished to a brilliant sheen. It was an Atlantean patrol boat, the keel burning with the same bright light pulsing from the domes.

One Atlantean diver stood at the boat controls while another, gripping a long white pike, glared through the clear glass bubble of her seahorse-shaped helmet. Both divers were encased in white diving suits laced with the same brilliant light as the hull. They shut off their booming horn, leaving Buckle's ears to ring in the odd silence of his pinging oxygen tank. Through the scratched glass of his helmet window the Atlanteans looked blurred, bathed in the mysterious light.

Penny Dreadful strode forward, cresting a small rise of rocks glowing with green algae. It snapped its arm-blades back into its forearms, allowing its hands to click back into their normal positions. It raised one reset hand and waved, waved like a little girl coming home.

The Atlanteans stared at it in cold silence.

Buckle waited, shaking off his adrenalin, waiting

for his heart to stop pounding in his chest so he could swallow and ease the parchment of his throat.

Felix stepped forward in his bulky diving suit; he shoved Penny Dreadful aside and made a dramatic, awkward bow to the Atlanteans. He pointed back in the direction of the *Dart* and made some kind of signal with his hands.

The female Atlantean nodded. She disconnected an umbilical line from her suit and hopped off the boat, descending to the bottom in a vault of glowing light. Once on the sea floor she motioned for them all to follow her to Atlantis.

Felix hurried back, joining the surviving members of his crew as they secured the bodies of their two dead crewmates. The Atlantean aboard the boat made no effort to assist, wheeling around and speeding away, the sea machine's engines running bizarrely silent and clean. Sabrina helped Rachel and Tonda with Gustey's stretcher. Within moments they set off after the Atlantean woman, who was already fifty yards ahead of them, not looking back, cutting through the water far more easily than the weight belt-encumbered *Dart* divers could ever hope to manage. They trudged after her at their best speed.

Buckle pushed his aching muscles on without letting up. Penny Dreadful fell in alongside him and the automaton looked to Buckle to be both excited and worried, though he didn't know how he might read such emotions from a machine's inflexible metal face and body.

The walk to Atlantis took some time — the domes, their glass exteriors illumed by the strange yellow-white light, loomed taller and taller out of the murk — but still looked to be at least three quarters of a mile away. Buckle had lost track of how long he'd been in the diving suit. The gagool's attack had ripped away the pressure gauge apparatus on his right wrist so he had no way of knowing how much air he might have left in his tanks. But since there was nothing for it he decided he needn't worry about it.

The seaweed fields fell away as the Atlantean diver entered the sunken Roman city. The road turned into a thoroughfare, striking a straight course through the magnificent ruins fringed by fluted columns and surging schools of fish. Statues of Neptune, tridents held high, the white marble overgrown by fantastic patterns of glowing green sea algae, watched.

Buckle was familiar with the *Iliad* and the *Odyssey* — two books which had survived The Storming — and much of the Snow World's knowledge of ancient human civilizations was drawn from those pages. The sacred Victoriana was the blueprint of the new society reconstructed from the ashes of the apocalypse and the fragmented ancient histories were given an elevated importance in the education of the young, at least in the Crankshaft schools. Buckle had been taught about the Greeks and Romans but much of it was extrapolation. The difference between a Doric, Ionic and Corinthian column had somehow survived while so much else had been lost.

Buckle realized that the glorious city was a façade, an elaborate sham, a beautiful replica — up close it was easy to see most of the structures were shells, hollow and well braced. The false Roman city was beautiful and alive with sea life, silver and orange fish flitting through the loggias and porticoes like flocks of lovely birds. But it was nothing more than an elaborately constructed piece of scenery, built for the leisure and contemplation of the Atlanteans looking out their windows into the ocean. Buckle both liked and disliked the idea; the memory of the great civilizations had been reduced to an artificial background for the Atlanteans to appreciate as they sipped some form of seaweed tea.

It all seems so still and quiet down here, Buckle thought, *once one got past the gagools*.

But the war-footing of men intruded: the Founders submarines constantly rumbled just under the shimmering surface overhead, their dark outlines veering, haunting and not dissimilar to zeppelins in the sky.

The nature of the ocean bottom changed once again after the company cleared the false city. The road plunged through golden-brown and yellow-green sea fields waving back and forth as far as the eye could see, the rows dotted with groups of diver-farmers and their helpful sea creatures. Thick layers of bioluminescent algae filled the cracks between the road flagstones, giving the path a honeycombed glow.

Buckle was struck by the appearance of tomb markers and mausoleums lining the sides of the highway, ornate statues and scrolls of marble, granite, pink-orange coral or lapis lazuli, running to the very gates of Atlantis itself. The gravestones were chiseled with the words of a language Buckle recognized as Latin, surely listing the names and accomplishments of the Atlantean dead. How odd to line one's grand avenue with sarcophagi, he thought. It felt a bit macabre to a man whose clan burned their dead on funeral pyres, but there were many ways to ensure the dead might not be forgotten—at least, not forgotten too quickly.

Once the company reached the nearest dome they marched under it, into its vast shadow away from the sunlight. Buckle felt the presence of the massive, barnacle-coated underside of the dome as it passed twenty feet above him. The Atlantean diver, now seventy-five yards ahead, stopped in the middle of a circle of seven green-coated pillars, jammed the end of her pike into the sand and waited for the group to catch up with her. Once he arrived alongside the woman, Buckle realized they were standing under the surface of a glittering pool, an oval opening into a large interior chamber flooded with light.

Buckle's skin tingled. Hovering on the other side of the biggest column, one which had some kind of lift built into it, was a gagool. The creature, floating easily, its webbed feet inches above the sand, watched them with its red-ember eyes, motionless except for the constant pumping of the thick reddish-blue gills at the neck.

The Atlantean diver unclipped her weight belt and sailed upward, breaching the surface of the pool. Felix, Kishi and Rachel relieved themselves of their belts and nursed Gustey's stretcher on their ascent. Tonda followed suit. Buckle signaled for Sabrina and Welly to follow them up.

The last one on the bottom, Buckle glanced up at the surface of the dome pool, now agitated by the many swimmers treading water at its flashing surface. Activity flickered above that, people pulling the divers out of the water. He glanced at Penny Dreadful and pointed up. Penny nodded and shot upwards in a burst of bubbles.

Now alone, the last man, Buckle felt the hairs standing on the back of his neck as he turned to look at the gagool; it stared at him, its big flickering eyes as reflective as two big cauldrons full of clear water. Buckle saw his reflection, his green face inside the diving helmet, looking back at him from the two mirrors of the gagool's eyes; it looked like his soul peering back at him from the land of the dead.

That was damned unpleasant, Buckle thought.

Buckle dropped his weight belt and his body ascended, feeling light as a feather after being anchored by lead bricks to the bottom for so long, up into the shimmering white light above, plunging upwards into the sparkling white light of the unknown.

XII

THE MOON POOL

Buckle's head broke the surface into a glaring wall of light flooding through his greenish window glass. The weight of the helmet above the water was a struggle but he felt relieved, relieved to be away from the gagool. It would be good to get the helmet off, to breathe air that wasn't stale.

A pale white hand reached down from above, the fingers impossibly stiff. It was the arm of a statue, a beautiful marble woman leaning over the water. Flesh and blood human beings worked diligently alongside her, their pink and brown faces leaning over the edges of the pool as they fished the divers out of the water. Strong hands soon found Buckle, leveraging harness straps under his armpits and winching him up.

Swinging through the air until his diving boots landed on the deck, Buckle's faceplate fogged and his suit felt heavy, dangerously so, to the point where he was impatient for someone to pry him out of it even as he felt expert hands unstrapping, unscrewing and unbuckling him from the gear. The helmet locks clicked and it lifted, straight up, over his head. The gush of cool air gave him a heady rush as it swept across his damp skin and flooded his lungs with sweetness. The diving chamber smelled like fish and wet leather, along with another deep ocean smell he did not recognize. The busyness of the space assaulted his psyche, used as it was to the muffled claustrophobia of the helmet. The low ceiling pulsed with glass tubes full of a bright, white-amber liquid. He had never seen such a kind of illumination before.

The bulkheads of the oval diving chamber were packed with straightjacket-tidy rows of diving suits, air tanks, weight belts and harpoons, everything gold and cream colored and decorated with elegantly carved seahorses and ocean flora. The four Roman statues anchoring each compass point of the pool were both lovely and given utilitarian purpose, for their heads, arms and tridents sported built-in pulleys for the harnesses as they leveraged bulky divers out of the moon pool.

Buckle's diving suit was pulled away and he stepped out of the boots. His own leather boots—his entire body—felt weirdly light, even detached from gravity, and it made him a bit woozy. He scanned the crowded bay to make certain Sabrina, Welly and Penny were there—they were—then placed one hand against a bulkhead to steady himself.

For thirty seconds the only sounds were the

clank and rattle of the air tanks, the jingle of loose metal buckles and the brush of fabric and sealskin as the Atlanteans—four men and one woman—pried the last members of the *Dart*'s company out of their suits. Buckle noticed the Atlantean men and woman were lean and strong, though a little short—not one exceeded five foot and a half in height—and they smelled odd, emitting body odors not unpleasant but unfamiliar.

"Curse the depths to hell," Felix muttered.

Buckle looked to Felix, who was supporting Gustey along with Kishi. Gustey looked better, for some color had returned to her face, though she appeared to be uncertain of where she was. Rachel and Tonda stood with them, free of their suits and grim-faced. The *Dart*'s crew had been decimated by the Guardians, losing both José and Marsh in the fight. "I am truly sorry for your losses, Captain Felix," Buckle said.

"Welcome to Atlantis," Felix grumbled, his voice heavy and sad. "The price of transit is always too high."

"Please accept my condolences as well," Sabrina said. "I hope your submarine can be salvaged."

"It can and it shall," Felix said. "The *Dart* isn't finished yet. That's for damned certain."

"I shall send further compensation to you, to help pay for the damages," Buckle offered. It was a pathetic way to try to ease the loss of life but it was the best he could do.

"Much appreciated, Captain," Felix said.

"Silence!" the Atlantean diver, freed of her suit, snapped as she eyed the company from the hatchway. Her face was unpleasant, with small eyes and the jawline of a windswept ridge, her skin pearl-pale and her sand-colored hair pulled back against her head with a flat, silver barrette. She wore what looked to be a standard uniform, a tight white blouse and trousers, with rows of leather straps around the biceps and thighs. Her legs below the knees were wrapped with cream-colored puttees down to a set of gray oilskin boots. Air whiffing in and out of her nostrils, she glared at the dripping Penny Dreadful and ducked through the hatchway.

The five Atlantean helpers stepped back and looked uneasy. No one spoke. Buckle waited for Felix to take the lead; the mercenary was the one who knew the Atlanteans, after all. Bubbles gurgled in the moon pool and a gentle rush of fan-driven air whistled faintly from cantilevered vents overhead.

Buckle looked at Sabrina, who shrugged.

"I hope we didn't get this wet for nothing," Sabrina whispered.

"They don't like unannounced visitors," Kishi said.

"And we killed one of their gagools," Welly

added.

"The Atlanteans know me well and they are a hospitable clan," Felix said, louder and somewhat angry. "But your insistence on bringing that thing" — he pointed at Penny Dreadful — "has endangered us all!"

"The only reason we survived the Guardian attack was because of this little automaton," Sabrina countered.

"Silence!" the Atlantean diver roared, returning through the hatchway.

A group of Atlanteans followed the diver into the chamber, led by a woman with the straight-backed bearing and rich perfumed breeze of nobility. Her skin was dark brown and her face, with big blue eyes, high forehead, and a great punch of black curly hair held up in gold lace chains, carried the aspect of a lioness. She wore a full-length stola, a draped wrap of white wool edged with thin purple stripes at the sleeve and shoulders, held in at the waist by a white belt studded with brilliantly colored seashells. Her jewelry was prodigious, in the form of gold and emerald earrings, bracelets and rings, and at her throat hung a cameo carved out of deepening layers of precious blue stone.

More concerning to Buckle were the four men and women flanking the lioness, soldiers wearing bronze breastplates and Roman-patterned helmets over white tunics and knee-length skirts, with seahorse-engraved greaves on their shins and laced sandals on their feet. All four brandished well-polished tridents in their white gloved hands. Each of them also had a smooth, oblong device lined with valves built into the throat guard of their breastplates; Buckle assumed they were some kind of underwater breathing apparatus.

One of the female soldiers, an older woman with four golden seahorses sewn into both sides of her high white collar, held a pistol in her free hand. It may have been the tension that exaggerated Buckle's vision but to him the muzzle of the firearm looked extraordinarily big, like a scattergun.

As soon as the tall noblewoman's eyes found Penny Dreadful her demeanor shifted from annoyance to anger. "How dare you, Felix?" she said. "How dare you bring this mechanical abomination back into our city!"

"My passenger insisted, Lady Cressida," Felix responded quickly, with a quick bow. "And since he is a clan ambassador in a time of great uncertainty I felt compelled to bring him in."

"And how many gold coins did it take to compel you, Captain Felix?" Lady Cressida replied. "You know our laws. Your mercenary judgment has failed you once again." She turned to Buckle and Sabrina. "None of you look anything like an ambassador."

"I am acting for my father," Buckle said. "Admiral Balthazar Crankshaft of the Crankshaft clan."

"Turn the machine over to us immediately,"

Lady Cressida ordered.

"Lady Cressida," Buckle answered, "I am here to negotiate an alliance with the leaders of your city."

Cressida's eyes whipped to Buckle and back to Penny Dreadful. "Turn the abomination over to us so that it may be destroyed immediately. Then we can talk."

Buckle glanced at the dripping Penny, then back at Cressida. "This automaton is my property. I shall not turn it over."

"You have no choice," Lady Cressida said evenly, menacing in the way of the calm before a storm.

"You have no right to take it," Buckle replied. He heard Sabrina open the watertight oilskin satchel behind him and felt the press of a sword handle into the palm of his right hand.

"I have every right, for we built it," Lady Cressida replied and stepped back. "Appropriate the machine," she ordered.

The four soldiers stepped forward, their trident points gleaming in the light. The older woman advanced with her pistol ready, the wide muzzle looming like a sabertooth cave.

Buckle jerked his sword around in front of him, whipping the blade out of the scabbard in the same motion. He heard a swift snap of leather, cloth and steel as Sabrina and Welly followed suit, their two blades joining his in front of the tridents.

The four guards paused. Sword blades and tridents wavered under the bright lights.

"Bad idea, Captain Buckle," Felix muttered, hedging away, shaking his head. "Bad idea."

"Crankshaft!" Lady Cressida roared. "You have no idea what that thing is. Do you really wish to die here in a vain defense of this infernal machine?"

Buckle gritted his teeth. He wasn't going to give up Penny Dreadful. It would be a lousy place to die, however. He felt he should respond, but no words came.

No one moved, the steel blades hanging in the balance.

"Well, this has all gotten off on a rather bad foot," Sabrina grumbled.

XIV

A MARTIAN CONSTITUTION

Water. Nothing but darkness and the need for water. Max awoke, aware of returning from the longest slumber she had ever taken in her life, clawing at a bedside table for the cup she was certain would be there. The Martian half of her brain, that miserable never-stopping calculator and repository of endless details and bad memories, knew she'd been unconscious off and on for the better part of a week and, though she had yet to open her eyes, knew it was evening. She lay on her right side, away from the wounds the sabertooth beastie had inflicted upon her, not wishing to recall the dreams she'd been having, instead concentrating on the steady pump of the iron lung at the back of the room where her comatose brother, Tyro, lay entombed. Other sounds intruded: the soft murmurs of Dr. Edison Lee talking in the orderly room, the distant, joyous cries of children playing outside, hurtling through the wide spaces of the citadel parade grounds, the same spaces where as a child she had stood by and watched the others play.

Grogginess lingered, muddling Max's return to full consciousness. She denied herself a sense of frustration. She sensed the morphine fading in her bloodstream. Dr. Lee, knowing full well her dislike of sedatives, had kept her drugged in order to force her to sleep.

Anxiety struck Max and she knew why. Romulus Buckle was gone away. The *Pneumatic Zeppelin* was gone away. A message had arrived from Spartak, how long ago she wasn't sure — perhaps four days — which Nurse Florence Herzog had read to her; Romulus had joined the Russians in their defense against a Founders invasion force and won a great victory over Muscovy.

She was not with them. With him.

Max sucked in a long breath of air, its pinch of antiseptic and ammonia helping wake her more fully. She realized she was up against a wall of pillows, stacked to prevent her from rolling onto her heavily bandaged back.

She relaxed. She would wait to open her eyes and call for water. Taking inventory of her body, she measured the pain in her neck and back where the sabertooth mauled her. Martians, even half-Martians, healed at a much faster rate than humans. No burning or fever, no signs of infection. A rocking of the shoulders proved the flesh sufficiently scabbed shut even if it hurt her to move.

The sabertooth beastie lunged in the darkness behind her eyelids.

Max jerked her eyes open, blinking in the sunset-colored light of a kerosene lantern on the table beside her bed. She watched the dancing lantern flame with its whirling scarves, imparting a lovely glow to the strips of salted blue cloth inside the glass bowl. Her eyes stung with their normal irritation. Damned dry earth air — although she had no idea what the more humid atmosphere of her father's unnamed planet would feel like.

She saw her leather flying helmet with its aqueous humor-filled goggles lying next to the lantern. Rolling forward, she inched up onto her elbow and collected the eyewear. Ignoring the agonies accompanying the movement, she eased herself into a sitting position. It was less uncomfortable than she had expected. She paused with her head down peering at the goggles as they sat in the folds of the gray woolen blanket in her lap, her long black hair flowing around her vision like the walls of a cave. She allowed the ligaments in her lower back and behind her knees a luxurious stretch against their invalid-bed tightness.

She liked being alone. She liked the illusion of being hidden from the world. She and Tyro were alone in the infirmary. Her constant roommate of the last two weeks, other than a child who spent one night under observation with a terrible cough, wasn't there — a rough-edged *Pneumatic Zeppelin* boilerman named Cornelius Valentine who had lost his right leg below the knee to the kraken over Tehachapi and somehow survived the trip home.

Max parted her hair with her right hand so she could see Valentine's bunk. He wasn't dead because his bunk was a mess, a spill of blankets, and the nurses would have immediately replaced the sheets if his corpse had been carted away. His absence was a relief. He snored when he slept and sulked or shot bitter expletives at the nurses when he was awake. The man never wanted his wound dressed and when the prosthetic inventor came to take measurements he shouted the poor fellow out of the room, bellowing that his temporary wooden peg would be sufficient to serve what worthless scrap of life he had remaining.

Valentine did not want to be healed. He wanted nothing but to escape the infirmary, collect his severance pay with its hefty wounding bonus and drink himself to death with it.

In the despair of uselessness, Valentine and Max were one. She, too, desperately wanted to escape her recuperative imprisonment. The Snow World had fallen into war and it was inexcusable for her to be away from her station aboard the *Pneumatic Zeppelin*. At one point Dr. Lee mentioned that Max's post had been temporarily filled by a foreign engineer, an Imperial clan princess, and Max could not stand the idea of her airship being cared for by such a woman. Yes, the *Pneumatic Zeppelin* had been built by the Imperials and the Crankshafts had stolen the air machine from them but it was Max's airship now. And she needed to be on her.

And Max needed to be alongside Romulus Buckle. She could deny herself any outward show of affection toward him but she could not deny herself his companionship. And if he was to die in battle then she must die with him.

Max swung her legs over the side of the bed, planting her bare feet on the freezing floorboards, enjoying the little shock running up her legs. She heard the soft padding of shoes, someone walking into the room from the nurse's station behind her.

"Back into bed, Max," came the warm, familiar voice of Dr. Lee. "You Martians heal quickly, but not that quickly. You're not ready to take on the world again. Not quite yet."

"Is there word from the *Pneumatic Zeppelin*?" Max asked.

"No. No word. Not since the report of the battle over Muscovy." Dr. Lee halted, looking at Valentine's bed. "Ah, and where is Mr. Valentine?"

"They should have returned days ago," Max muttered.

"Where is Mr. Valentine?"

"I don't know where that foul-mouthed

boilerman is," Max grumbled. "Is that not your department, Doctor?" She stood up and almost fainted. Her helmet and goggles dropped from her lap, a vertigo-inducing tumble of leather, metal and flashing glass, falling with a thump on the floor.

"Lieutenant!" Dr. Lee shouted, taking hold of her as she grabbed the cast iron headboard to stall the spin of the room. "Lie down, Lieutenant," he ordered as he tried to guide her back onto her bed. "Nurse!" he yelled.

Stiffening at the doctor's touch, Max shook her head and locked her hands on the rail. She felt as if she had been still for a hundred years. She'd be damned if she was going to lie in that bed for another second. "I am sufficiently recovered," she said. "I am more than ready to return to my duties, Dr. Lee. And I would advise you to keep your morphine syringe very far away from my bloodstream."

Dr. Lee released his hold on Max's forearms. "Be sensible, Lieutenant," he said gently, reaching down and collecting her helmet from the floor. "At least sit down. And put these on before your eyes dehydrate."

"I shall sit," Max said, tucking her bottom on the mattress—it did feel better than standing—and fitted the helmet over her head, cinching the leather until the lens pockets pressed securely around her eyes. She switched open the aqueous humor reservoir, flooding the lenses with the cool, clear fluid, an environment her eyes much preferred.

"Yes, Doctor?" Nurse Flora Herzog asked, scurrying in.

"Where has our other patient disappeared to?"

Flora glanced at Valentine's empty bunk and screwed up her face. "Oh, my. He was here at lunch. He wouldn't eat his pudding. Complained to no end and wouldn't eat it." She hurried to the infirmary closet. "His clothes are gone." She walked back to the nurse's station. Max heard her open and shut the lavatory door.

Dr. Lee sighed and crossed his arms. "What is it with you zeppelineers? Why don't you have the sense to stay put when you're hurt? Do I have to tie you all down?"

"He went where he needed to go," Max said. But Valentine's disappearance made her anxious. As the *Pneumatic Zeppelin*'s first mate she was responsible for the wellbeing of her crew. And Valentine, yet to be discharged, was still her responsibility.

Flora returned to the doorway with a helpless sigh.

"He isn't ready to be upright," Dr. Lee replied. "He isn't part Martian like you, Lieutenant. His body isn't recovering from the amputation with the speed or efficiency of the constitution you have, which sews you up back up again like a mad seamstress. His wounds need to be disinfected and dressed. If he wants to kill himself he's doing a bang up job of it."

Valentine did want to kill himself.

"It is my duty to recover Mr. Valentine," Max said. The old boilerman saw his looming discharge from the air service as a trip to the guillotine. He would receive a decent pension as a crippled zeppelineer, a good pension, but money was not the problem for the old salts—idleness was. Rough and tumble sorts who had made the airships their lives, often coming aboard as cadets or apprentices at the age of fourteen, often fell apart when suddenly banished, broken and dismayed, to the ground. The veterans did not know how to live in towns and, with no experience regimenting or regulating their own lives, they became melancholy and drank until they turned yellow and died.

Dr. Lee shook his head. "No, it is not. Valentine is under my care and I'll see to it. He'll be easy to find. I'm sure he's already soused in one of the Friendly Society taverns. I'll send a citadel officer to collect him. Your responsibility is to get back into your sickbed."

Sickbed. The sound of the word turned Max's stomach. She was sure she knew where Valentine was; he would be sucking beer in the taverns of the Roustabouts, the Friendly Society supporting the men and women of the sky engineering corps. Friendly Societies were tightly knit, lower-class collectives created to pool money to assist members in hard times and find homes for a small but endless stream of orphans. They were also rawboned drinking clubs where alcoholism was the norm and brawls tended to cap off each evening's festivities. Each Friendly Society was based in one or more taverns, depending on the size of their membership rosters. The Roustabouts laid down their rum shillings at The Blonde Bastard and The Ophir. The older salts preferred The Ophir. "I am well able to get about," Max pressed.

A bemused smile lifted Dr. Lee's face though it was betrayed by the concern in his brown eyes. "Ah, but I do not concur. And since I am the one who went to medical school my assessment wins."

Max glared at her feet. Below the cuffs of her warm gray woolen infirmary trousers she saw her glaring white feet, her feet the same color as the white painted floorboards except for the tips of the black stripes reaching nearly to her toes. They looked alien even to her.

"Into bed, please," Dr. Lee urged. "Let me assist you. Please don't make me post a guard."

"I do not appreciate being sedated with morphine, Dr. Lee."

"It was necessary," Dr. Lee replied. "You were having nightmares, Lieutenant. Violent thrashings in the night. You were tearing your stiches open and bleeding. Reopening a partially healed wound, especially one as messy as yours, is almost guaranteed to invite infection, whether one has Martian wonder blood or not. My choices were to sedate you or strap you down. And those still are my choices."

"I acquiesce to your authority, under protest," Max said sharply, though she had no intention of remaining inside the infirmary once the coast was clear. Crimson flickered in Max's goggles; seething undercurrents of anger. Where were her clothes? When Flora had opened the infirmary closet it was empty. There was a small wardrobe in the nurse's office; surely her clothes were in there. "I want to be informed of my father's condition."

"Balthazar is well," Dr. Lee said. "It is as if all of this activity has improved his health. Ah, he thrives on difficult circumstances, I suppose." Lee helped ease Max down onto her right side, adjusting the pillow as she winced. "Don't worry. I'll send a man after Mr. Valentine right away."

"Thank you, Doctor Lee," Max said. "And may I trouble you for a glass of water?"

"Of course. You must be parched. You must drink as much as you can."

Dr. Lee strode out of the room. As she listened to the clink of a brass jug on glass and the gurgle of water in the nurse's office, Max devised her escape plan.

XV

THE OPHIR

Martian cheeks became frostbitten easily. Even with a heavy green scarf wrapped round her face, the Snow World air had never felt colder on Max's skin as she hurried through the darkness. Dr. Lee and Flora had kept a close watch on her until the long shadows of the purple evening, but a well-timed emergency — some unfortunate ground crewman's arm had been crushed by a crate on the loading docks — sent them out to the airfield in the ambulance.

Max had jumped out of bed and pieced together a harlequin's set of clothes to put on over her heavy infirmary tunic — a cream-colored woolen sweater with a tea stain on the front, a mothballed green sentinel's scarf and an old pair of men's blue trousers, all lifted from the wardrobe in the nurse's station. Max also took a spare pair of oversized boots and her toes floated in the soft, velvety interiors. Max's own uniform wasn't there — the ripped and blood-soaked clothes would have been discarded and her flying boots, weapons, and personal belongings probably transferred to her bedchamber in the citadel.

Taking a large gray cloak—surely one of Dr. Lee's due its expensive weave and silver buttons—Max had slipped out of the infirmary and made her way outside to the front gate. The cloak's voluminous hood obscured her identity completely and she, wrapped up in her fur and wool togs like everyone else on this particularly frigid evening, strolled out of the citadel gates unnoticed.

Max now strode along the rambling streets of the Devil's Punchbowl. Her back hurt, every inch of every cut aching, but she was more worried about her baggy-fitting, oddball-colored clothes attracting attention. All black was so much better. One could sink into the shadows in all black. She rejected her instinctive desire to hunch her back against the pains assailing it; she walked deliberately with her characteristic smoothness, her boots making no sound upon the cobblestones, passing ghostlike under the low-burning street lamps. She felt as if no one could see her, even if she brushed their shoulder in passing. Now that she was free of the sickbed she dared her wounds to slow her down, and somewhere inside of her that challenge was exhilarating.

Max had also borrowed a pair of dog fur-lined gloves from the infirmary wardrobe; her striped hands needed to remain hidden along with the rest of her. It was dangerous for Martians to walk alone in the hardscrabble alleys of the west-end Punchbowl. The Crankshaft citizens distrusted Martians even though they knew their beloved Admiral Balthazar had adopted a half-Martian daughter. Most had never seen her. Max had always remained sheltered in the citadel as a matter of choice and as an adult she had spent her life aboard airships and not in the town. She never walked to the market to buy a greenhouse apple nor donned her best gown to attend a performance in Playhouse Alley. But the most unpredictable threat lay in the many foreigners who were always present in the Punchbowl taverns: traders and air merchantmen who loved the grog and the rough-and-tumble, men and women who easily lost their minds to bloodlust and the whims of the mob. And they hated Martians.

Despite the chill and Max's discomfort, it was a lovely evening and excellent to be outside. The still atmosphere hung crisp and snowflakes drifted down from the moonlit clouds, their silver edges catching the yellow gleam of the street lamps. Max's breath misted inside her hood and flowed with her as she walked. She had to pick up her stride as she crossed the market square. Her stamina was on a shorter rope than she had expected. She forced her legs to pick up the pace but she paid a price for it. She felt her strength reserves, already near empty, draining away.

Ahead of her, beyond the western edge of the square, she could already hear music, singing and shouting wafting from the streets of the Friendly Quarter. At least it wasn't much further to Cornelius Valentine. The one-legged old salt, hobbling in to join the company of his Roustabouts at The Ophir, would have been encouraged to drown his sorrows. Free rotgut was irresistible to a man like Valentine who had probably bloodied his freshly amputated leg as he stumped down the cobblestones to get it. Yes, free grog. His comrade engineers would happily lay out their hard-earned shillings — those who had shillings — until he was under the table. His friends would continue to do so night after night, thinking they were easing his misery, but in reality easing his way to a befuddled, yellow-skinned, early death.

Max coughed, a dry rattling hack. She hadn't slaked her terrible thirst. While devising her devious escape from the infirmary she had forgotten to sip from the big cup Dr. Lee had brought her. She had not looked for anything to drink on her way out of the citadel. She thought about sucking on a handful of snow but that would only make her thirstier, and she was almost to the threshold of The Ophir as it was. She decided she would order a drink in the tavern but then she realized she didn't have any money.

Elusively hooded in a fancy, obviously stolen cloak, penniless, and hacking as if consumptive, she would fit right in with the Friendly Society.

Turning the corner and heading onto a seedy

side street, Max merged into a loose, milling crowd of people, arguing and smoking as they lingered outside the Friendly Society taverns and inns. Two men in rigger leathers raged at each other, poking fingers into chests. Brawls were frequent here. Balthazar had assigned a unit of the Punchbowl constabulary to patrol the Friendly Quarter — the officers with their dark blue piths were officially named "The Tavern Watch," but on the streets they were better known as "the Truncheons" due to the liberal use of their nightsticks on inebriated zeppelineers. The Truncheons were notoriously corrupt. Max did not see one of their light blue uniforms anywhere among the crowd.

Max disturbed hazes of listless tobacco smoke as she slipped through the crowds. The reek of the pipe irritated her unprotected eyes but it was far preferable to the other smells endemic to the place, notably rotting garbage and urine. She was in the midst of the worst elements of her own and foreign merchant aircrews, the villainy who inhabited the night, faces half lit by street lamps: Crankshaft marines jingling their purses, looking for vials of poppy tears, Spartak firemen looking to fight, Gallowglass skinners looking to steal, and local prostitutes, wrapped in their signature dirty red shawls, looking to earn. The frantic beat of the these desperate souls battered Max's psyche, her Martian physiology absorbing the hum of physical anxiety generated by human beings when they packed together looking for stimulations both life affirming and destructive. War was coming and it made the urges worse. Deliver the best you can. Go out with the biggest bang you can.

Ducking as deeply inside her hood as she could, Max maneuvered her oversized boots through a group of zeppelineers collected on the front stoop of The Ophir, her nose assaulted by the hot stink of rum rolling off their breaths. They didn't give her a lopsided glance. Cloaked, anonymous people were a fixture in the Friendly Quarter: fugitives, crazies, and the snake-voiced sellers of Morgause weed, laudanum, poppy tears, peyote and the risky, powerful Martian hallucinogen called cassiderium, commonly known as "delirium" because it slowly destroyed the addict's brain.

Wide open, the doors of The Ophir sent a flood of lantern light into the street, casting the idlers in silhouettes and shivering the icy cobblestones with a coat of pumpkin orange. Max plunged into the light, squeezing between two burly women with the intricate hand tattoos of the Pale Traders. Whatever awful odors existed in the street were no match for the sour miasma of body sweat, stale beer, and ancient vomit The Ophir offered; Max would have sunk her head deeper into her hood if she could have, so repulsive was the smell at first contact.

Max worked her slender form through walls of

bodies of every imaginable size and shape, sidling around scattered tables and chairs as her boots skidded on spilled beer and bits of food. Again she worried about the expensive quality of Dr. Lee's cloak with its fine Vaquero wool—but wealthy citizens often sent finely dressed servants on discreet missions into the Quarter. Regardless, she had to remain hidden or there would be trouble; most of The Ophir's patrons tonight were foreigners—the outbreak of war had brought on a frenzy of trading from the northeastern clans who feared what the future might hold for any stockpiled goods they already had on hand. The local Crankshaft societies tended to meet at more sociable hours.

Max sensed a faint coming on. She slowed to a stop, placing her hand on the back of a patron's chair to steady herself, cautious that her gloved fingers not brush his back. Her eyes itched terribly. The vile, damned smoke. Her aqueous humor goggles sat in her pocket but there was no way she could use them here without drawing attention to her black-violet eyes. She focused her vision on the fire roaring in The Ophir's massive stone fireplace where stuffed deer heads, antlers broken or ripped away, stared back at her from above the mantle. Her queasy lightheadedness lessened and she felt better for a moment— until she saw the stuffed head of a sabertooth beastie leering at her from the rafters.

Max shuddered, her vision telescoping down the

tunnel of her hood, unable to tear her gaze away from the dead glass eyes of the sabertooth. Coward. Squeezing her grip on the back of the chair, it took great effort to turn away from the monster. She caught a whiff of antiseptic — her heart accelerated and cleared her mind, her senses sharpening up to a point where they actually hurt. Only one person would trail a sanitized smell among the scab-riddled carcasses packed into the tavern.

Strength returned to Max, flowing, cascading, for she was now on the hunt. It was easy to follow the bright ammonia scent through the unwashed throng — she could almost see it — and before she knew it she had arrived at the bar alongside Cornelius Valentine.

XVI

THE FRIENDLY SOCIETY

Max took a seat on the stool alongside Cornelius Valentine.

"What'll it be?" the barmaid asked, leaning towards her.

Max kept her head down, sending the woman off with a wave of her black gloved hand.

"You come in, you buy something, damned —" the barmaid said through gritted teeth. "Sell your cursed apothecaries outside!" She slapped the counter and moved away, responding to the call of another, paying, customer.

Max peered sideways through her hair and around her hood at Valentine. Slumped forward, he had his hands around a half-empty tankard of ale sitting in a pool of beer and half-sunk penny farthings. Short white and brown hairs bristled on his head and surrounded his red ears. His jaw hung slack, his eyes unfocused, and he stank of blood and antiseptic. He was dead drunk or very close to it.

"Valentine," Max whispered.

Valentine did not respond. Perhaps he had passed out with his eyes open.

"Valentine!" Max shouted into his ear. There was no reason to whisper in the noisy tavern. And she wanted to leave.

Valentine jerked and turned his head towards Max. "What do you want, woman?" he asked, slurring the words. "If you came to rob me, I have spent all of me paltry coins. If ye came to offer the bordello, I have spent all of me paltry coins."

"It is time to go," Max said.

Valentine narrowed his brutish eyebrows as he tried to focus his eyes on her. "I am not your eunuch, woman." He grumbled.

Max opened her hood, just a fraction, enough for only Valentine to see her face within.

Valentine's eyes shot wide. He shook his head. "Go away, Lieutenant," he whispered.

"No," Max answered. "Come with me."

Valentine slapped his hand on the counter. Max felt droplets hit her chin. "You are not my officer anymore, you hear me?"

"You are still a crewman of the *Pneumatic Zeppelin* and under my command," Max said.

"I quit," Valentine moaned. "I quit before you drummed me out. No zeppelin can use a one-legged boilerman. Now leave me be and let me die in peace."

"Have you signed your discharge?" Max asked.

"No."

"Then you are still my crew," Max insisted. "Leave with me."

"Ha!" Valentine laughed bitterly. "I am out. Do you think that if I leave my mark on the discharge, which I cannot read as it is, makes any difference to the way things are? I am out. You go, Lieutenant!"

Max lifted her hand to try to calm the rising volume of Valentine's speech. A handful of patrons glanced their way, glassy-eyed, probably hoping to witness a fight. The Ophir was no place for a Martian, yes, but it was also no place for officers. "Follow me out, crewman. Now."

"Leave me be," Valentine hissed. "And stay out of my head. I cannot abide you knocking about in my head!"

Max blinked. The man remembered when she had entered one of his dreams where he had recognized her as an intruder and awakened. The act had been unintentional, a weird function of her Martian side. "My intrusion into your dream state was unexpected and unfortunate and for that I apologize," she said. It was unforgettable however, the dream's misty scene — laden with the telltale elements of old memory, fuzzy at the edges, layered with emotion and grafted with elements and textures filtered through the always busily re-inventing subconscious mind — of a woman waving farewell to him as his airship lifted away from an airfield. Max leaned in closer, the edge of her hood touching Valentine's cheek. "I am not leaving until you come with me."

"You are breathing on me."

Max leaned back. "I am not leaving unless you leave with me."

Valentine hunched his shoulders and stared straight forward. Max coughed, parched, her throat like sandpaper, crackling with an itch that made her choke and her eyes water. "May I trouble you for a sip of your beer?"

Valentine stiffened. "If you promise to leave," he grumbled, sliding the half-full beer mug across the counter, spilling a portion of it in one looping slosh.

"Thank you," Max whispered. She took the mug in both hands, lifted it inside her hood cave and swallowed all that was left of the bittersweet beer. Rum was her preference though she tended to eschew alcohol, but in that moment nothing had ever tasted better and it soothed her throat. Slightly dizzy, she placed the empty mug on the counter and slid it back to Valentine.

"Leave … me … be," Valentine snarled, pushing the mug away with one finger and sinking his head between his shoulders.

"Enough of this. I order you to come with me." Max said.

"Leave … me … be," Valentine repeated

through gritted teeth, head lower, his voice shaking.

"Get out of that chair and come with me, Mr. Valentine, or I shall have you clapped in irons for insubordination."

"Leave ... me ... be!" With the last word, Valentine lashed out, swinging his right arm on the backhand.

Max had not expected her crewman to strike her. His forearm, big and muscled from a lifetime of shoveling coal, struck her across the base of her throat and knocked her off the stool. The tavern whirled and she landed on her back on the beer-splattered floor. The stitches running up and down her torso felt like they blew apart and she released a sharp cry of pain.

Perhaps she had pushed Valentine a little too hard.

Max rolled over onto her hands and knees and leveraged herself up onto her feet. The squeak of her boots on the wet floorboards was too loud. The tavern had fallen silent. She froze, lantern light piercing through the rivers of her black hair hanging over her face, hurting her eyes. Her hood had fallen back, the weight of the wool soft against the back of her neck, the humid heat of the tavern tickling her ears.

"Martian!" someone shouted. "A damned Martian!"

Chair legs scraped across the uneven floor as seated patrons jumped to their feet. A low, angry howl rose from the assembled crowd.

"It surely is!" a woman shouted, drunk and belligerent, her clipped accent unique to the Black Diamond clan. "Hidden among us like a snake, she is!"

Ignoring the brutal throbbing in her back, Max stood as tall and straight as she possibly could. She threw her hair back and faced the sea of slack-jaw, snarling faces. Valentine sat on the floor, the swing of his blow having also carried him off his stool. He looked stunned and hurt, gripping the joint where his peg leg attached to his knee, the shortened trouser leg now stained with fresh blood.

"Vile zebe!" a Gallowglass zeppelineer, a big, burly lout with a blond beard, yelled, drawing a knife from his belt. "Here selling delirium poison!"

Max backed up a step. She both saw and sensed the predator-like encroachment of The Ophir's rough crowd as they left their drinks on the tables and slowly, pack-like, crept up to encircle her. Max did not recognize one face among them. If the *Pneumatic Zeppelin* had been in harbor there might have been a few of her own crew there and, regardless of their personal feelings, duty would have brought them running to her defense.

Max's hand instinctively slid to the spot on her hip where her saber handle would have been but even as she grasped for it she knew it wasn't there. She should have borrowed a sword on her way out of the citadel. Martians were strong but, unarmed and hurt, she would not be able to hold so many with her bare hands. She snatched an iron candlestick holder off of a table, the paraffin candles tumbling across the floor in rolling flickers. The holder made for a worthy club but it would do her little good once the crowd pinned her down.

The blond-bearded Gallowglass brute, his drink-bright eyes gleaming with the prospect of easy violence, led the advance upon Max. "I take first crack, you blackhearts!"

The mob surged in, tightening the circle. Max saw the gleam of brass knuckles and knives. The beer aftertaste in her mouth turned sour and she wanted to spit, though that was something she would never do, etiquette-wise. Her eyes itched terribly, needing moisture; rapid blinking eased the discomfort but it also blurred her vision.

Blood-weak and half-blind. *Perfect*, Max thought.

Someone stepped in front of her with the clomp of wood thumping on wood, placing his barrel-chested form between Max and the Gallowglass man. "Stand down," Valentine shouted. "There shall be no violence here."

"You have been hypnotized to stand with this freak, brother," the Gallowglass man raged, though he looked surprised. "Brain-addled by a zebe. We shall teach her a lesson! Do not interfere with your own revenge!"

"Nay, brother," Valentine replied. "She is Max of the Crankshafts, the adopted half-breed daughter of Admiral Balthazar. You hear me? Lay not one hand upon her, charlatans, for if you harm a child of Balthazar's it shall be most unlikely that you escape the Punchbowl with yer lives. Stand down!"

"Balthazar is not here," the Gallowglass trader replied, aghast. "And you, brother, you stand with this monster? You, a sky dog? A Roustabout? One of us? One of us whose leg must be paid for?"

"She is my officer," Valentine growled, rocking between his good leg and peg leg in his drunkenness. "I do tend to dislike her, you see, but she is my Lieutenant and I am bound by oath to defend my shipmates to the death. Such is the oath of all zeppelineers and I wager that all of you have taken it. So if you pick a fight with her you pick a fight with me, brother."

The forward lean of the mob shifted back in a tiny, near imperceptible way. Max felt it. She was rescued.

The bearded Gallowglass man grimaced, glancing back at the group. He threw his arm out, pointing at Max over Valentine's shoulder. "You are most lucky, you stinking zebe bitch, that your filthy hide is owned by the leader of the Crankshafts and that one of our own has stood up for you in this public house. Because if it were not this way I'd already have your striped hide tacked up on that wall."

"Time to go, Mr. Valentine," Max said.

Valentine held up a penny, glaring at her with half-open eyes. "But I got enough for one more beer — "

Max snatched Valentine by the collar and, at the cost of more pain in her back, yanked him around table after table and knot after knot of leering faces until she squeezed him out the door.

The cold of the night air focused Max's mind. She dropped the candlestick without being aware of it and the loud clang of its iron on the cobblestones startled her. Faces turned in the dark street, peering at her in the weak lantern light. Max threw her hood back over her head. Valentine tore free of her grasp to stumble up against the side of the tavern, bend over and vomit.

It seemed to take forever as Max waited for Valentine to finish puking. The people in the street had turned back to their own nefarious deals, however — the sight of a Martian, a cassiderium dealer, perhaps — did little to rattle them.

"You owe me a shilling's worth of beer, damn you," Valentine spit, gasped and vomited again.

"I shall reimburse you," Max replied. She felt as if she had slipped into the surreal where the flickering snowfall and ice-rimed cobblestones gleamed weightless under the illumination of the street lamps.

Everything pulsed red-yellow, red-yellow with the throb of her barely healed wounds. Most painful was the knowledge that Valentine had saved her from a beating, saved her perhaps even from death, and she was unhappy owing anything to a man like him.

XVII

AN ODD COUPLE

The journey through the Devil's Punchbowl was slow but much easier for Max. With her hood on and Valentine at her side, drunk and argumentative, hobbling along on his peg, they fit right in with the town's nocturnal crowd. She was a cloaked apothecary of dark drugs, he the addled and addicted customer, out for a stroll. The cold air, sweet after the sickly warm miasma of The Ophir, braced the body. Above the yellow haloes of the streetlights the clouds glowed with a peculiar sheen of moonlight, a rippling silver and blue ceiling the people called 'Pearlie's blanket.'

Valentine's wooden leg slipped across the cobblestones and he nearly fell. "Blast the frog-eared ghost of the frog-headed bastard who fathered me!" he roared.

"The airship corps shall provide you with a mechanical leg," Max said. "Traversing cobblestones shall be no hindrance then, and less cause for babblement."

Valentine spit, wiping his mouth his sleeve. "I

don't want nor need no clockwork device attached to my person. The peg suits me just fine, it does."

"Suit yourself," Max said.

"How about we just don't talk at all, Lieutenant?" Valentine grumbled. "That would suit me."

It would have suited Max as well. Valentine's breath stank of bile. "You need to sleep. Go home."

"You damn well dragged me outta my home," Valentine grumbled.

"I meant where you sleep, Mr. Valentine."

Valentine sighed. "I always slept on my flying machine."

"You have no home, no place to sleep beyond the *Pneumatic Zeppelin*?"

"I always slept on my assigned airship from the day I was brought on at sixteen, with the exception of a few inns here and there on leave. I started with the *Albert*, then the *Bromhead* and now the *Pneumatic Zeppelin*."

Valentine's lack of a ground home did not surprise Max. The crew who came into the zeppelin service young and poor often need no other residence, especially if they remained unmarried. "I'll find you a bunk in the citadel, then."

Valentine guffawed. "What, Lieutenant, do you plan to bed me? You are far too young and pretty to fancy a rough old coot like me, even with your nasty skin."

Max halted, not out of any affront taken from Valentine's words—the man could spew insults all night long and not bother her—but the street had taken a steep rise and her strength, falling away, threatened to fail her again; she feared another step might result in her knees collapsing.

Valentine cleared his throat and she felt him looking at her hood. "Begging your pardon, Lieutenant. My mouth runs ahead of my brain more often than not."

"The open sewer of your mouth is of no concern to me, crewman," Max whispered. Every intake of breath hurt her back. Something hot trickled down the left side of her ribcage.

"Yes, well, I did save yer striped hide this evening, did I not?" Valentine replied, heartiness returned, born to deliver unintentional insults. "I suppose that might buy me a little room for my indiscretions."

"I am making exceptions because you are hurt and drunk, Mr. Valentine," Max said. "But continue after such a fashion and it will buy you the brig in the morning."

"Aye, Lieutenant," Valentine responded softly, almost with a tone of remorse, as if melancholy had suddenly overwhelmed him. "I do expect a punishment."

"A punishment?" Max asked, still, fighting dizziness.

"For striking a senior officer. I am still on the ship's roll. I expect punishment."

"I recall no such transgression," Max said. "And let us leave it at that."

"I do regret hitting you, Lieutenant."

"No such thing happened. Do not speak of it again."

The earth tilted. Max would have toppled over had not Valentine caught her in his big, dirty hands.

"Hold fast, Lieutenant," Valentine said gently, his arms around her. "Are you injured?"

"I just need to sit, to sit down," Max whispered; her voice sounded weak and it angered her.

"Here," Valentine replied, guiding her to a seat on the stones of a low wall.

Max removed her gloves and pressed her hands against her aching eyes. She had gone too long without the goggles, the irritation exacerbated by the stinking smoke of The Ophir. "Thank you, crewman."

"Aye," Valentine answered softly. "Is it your wounds, Lieutenant? The surgeon, he told me about how you saved Captain Buckle, about how the sabertooths ripped you up at Tehachapi."

"No," Max answered. A burst of frustration brought her new energy and she stood up.

Valentine chuckled to himself and nodded. The

boilerman was odd. But then, again, most pure humans struck Max as odd much of the time. "Where are we going, Lieutenant, if you don't mind me asking?" He sounded less drunk than before. "This isn't the way to the citadel."

Max took a deep breath and felt more blood meander down her back, which she ignored by resuming her walk, briskly this time. "Our destination is the public jetty. If we are going to get back to the *Pneumatic Zeppelin* we'll need a fast ship to get us to her."

"Shouldn't they be on their way back to us already?" Valentine asked. He looked pale in the pools of lamplight and the intervening shadows, his peg clicking on the cobblestones as he drew himself alongside her.

"Unknown," Max said. She had no idea how she knew it but she was certain Buckle was not heading home. "Our airship needs us."

"Your airship needs you, Lieutenant," Valentine said. "I am no good for her now."

"You shall remain a part of my crew. I shall see to it."

"And how shall you do that?" The shred of hope in Valentine's voice made putting up with him easier.

"Captain Buckle has accommodations for a personal steward, a station he has resisted filling. I shall draft you into that service." This was the solution Max had devised on her way to The Ophir, the way to keep Cornelius Valentine on the *Pneumatic Zeppelin*. Buckle would fight the idea, deeming the job unnecessary because he ate what the crew ate, but she knew how to outmaneuver him on such matters. The Captain's steward was one of the few idler positions which would allow a disabled airman to remain with his airship.

"Captain's steward?" Valentine spluttered. "Me? I can't boil a rat in a bucket. I would poison the captain with my cooking skills, I would."

Max wanted to smile. "You can fry an egg on a boiler, can you not?"

"That's not going to make a captain happy."

"It is a start. You shall learn. And our captain shall endure that difficult journey with you. Do we have an agreement?"

"I ... don't the Captain pick his own steward?"

"He has not done so and now I have done it for him. As second officer I am responsible for recruiting."

They walked for a quarter mile in silence, Valentine considering. Max smelled fabric stiffening dope and the parsley-infused aroma of Gallowglass lamb stew; they were approaching the jetty.

"Maggots in the biscuits," Valentine muttered. "I accept the position. But why do this for me?"

"Since Lady Fortune has both damaged us and cast us together I recommend we do all we can to make the best of it. And let's just say I owe you one, Mr. Valentine."

Valentine cleared his throat and belched with it. "Since you have salvaged me from certain beggary in the gutter I suppose I have no choice but to accept, and with gratitude. But I still do not enjoy your company overmuch, Lieutenant."

"The feeling is mutual, I assure you."

XVIII

A FAST SHIP

The high wooden structure of the public jetty was located on the southwestern outskirts of the Devil's Punchbowl stronghold. Six small, sleek airships floated at the docking towers, overpowered corsairs and cutters with masters ducking the scrutiny of their cargoes required at the main airfield, running errands known only to them and the customers they served. Normally the jetty's long stretch of boardwalk was well-lit by lamps but now, in near blackout conditions, only a few night lanterns glowed here and there, joined by the faint glow of buglights inside the gondola windows of the airships.

Max stopped at the broad staircase leading up to the jetty boardwalk. "Can you make the stairs?" she asked Valentine.

"Bah! Don't worry about me, Lieutenant. This old salt has a new lease on life, he does," Valentine replied. "Burning captain's eggs."

"A simple 'yes' would have sufficed," Max replied, starting up the steps.

"Aye, but then the breath is wasted. It ain't got no color to it. You see what I mean, Lieutenant?"

"You are loquacious. I'll give you that."

"I don't know what that means but I'll take it as a compliment," Valentine said, his peg leg thumping on the wooden stairs as he kept pace with Max. She was operating at a reduced speed; it galled her but she dared not push her body any harder.

The public jetty provided an expansive view overlooking the stronghold, maze-like in appearance because its fortifications and streets weaved around hundreds of rock outcroppings. The lanes were lit up here and there by a lantern-carrying citizen and the factory quarter glowed red and orange with the illumination of the forges, burning coal overtime to produce war materiel, and the color gave its streets and alleys a hellish aspect. The black silhouette of the citadel loomed over the town and, beyond its towers, the high black rectangles of the airship hangars hunched like sleeping giants at the base of the mountains.

The ellipsoidal shadows of docked Crankshaft war zeppelins hung massive and silent at the airfield. The entire fleet had been recalled and most of them were there, minus those on patrol.

Max and Valentine moved through the anchor ropes, supply carts and unmarked crates crowding the jetty. The stretch was unattended except for a female air constable who sat cross-legged on a bench, whittling at a stick and looking drowsy. She gave them a long but disinterested glance as they passed.

"Which one of these little bilge rats strikes your fancy, Lieutenant?" Valentine asked.

"The black," Max replied, pointing to a sleek corsair with a black envelope and an impressive array of six irregular propellers.

"The *Shenandoah*," Valentine said. "I've heard of her. She's fast. Her captain is Prisco, a Gallowglass by birth and a real piece of work, so they say."

"Who are 'they'?" Max asked, terribly thirsty once again.

"They are the ones who know," Valentine replied.

Max and Valentine arrived at the corsair's gangway, a simple, sturdy ramp of unfinished boards stamped with the name *Shenandoah*. They paused, waiting under the creak and groan of the corsair's mooring ropes straining against the light breeze.

"Who comes a calling?" A man's voice rang out from the airship. He emerged from the gondola cabin, holding a buglight that lit the side of his long face and accentuated the shadows of his heavy-lidded eyes.

"Two travelers seeking passage to Spartak," Max said.

"Spartak, eh? There's a war on. Come back and make suicidal requests at a decent hour."

"I am Balthazar Crankshaft's daughter and I must be away at dawn," Max said. "We settle a transaction now or your competitors get my pretty penny."

"One of Balthazar's daughters, eh?" The lantern man coughed. "If you were one of Balthazar's daughters you'd have your own airship, wouldn't ye?"

"Do you want my gold or not?" Max replied.

"Hold your horses," the lantern man sighed and disappeared into the gondola.

"Gallowglasses," Valentine muttered. "Gallowglasses, Lieutenant? Give your money to someone else."

"I would appreciate it if you would remain silent, Mr. Valentine," Max said.

"That goes very much against me nature, Lieutenant," Valentine whispered.

"Nonetheless," Max replied.

They waited for several minutes, listening to the familiar whispers of the wind as they pressed the flanks of the docked airships. The mouthwatering smell of the Gallowglass stew, rich with beef, onions and potatoes, was thick on the air and had to be flowing from the *Shenandoah*'s galley. A dog barked somewhere in the town, an echoing, lonely sound. Max heard the regular scratch of the air constable's whittling knife on the stick, a sound that bit through the air even though she was out of earshot. Max began to wonder if the

Shenandoah's night watchman had simply gone back to bed.

Boots thumped across the corsair's deck as two men appeared at the top of the gangway. The first was the lantern man, a small, thin fellow, and the other was a much rounder man, bigger and taller, with unkempt brown hair and a huge fur coat thrown over his underclothes.

"What do you want?" the unkempt man asked, looking annoyed.

"Are you the captain of this air vessel?" Max asked.

"Aye. I am Captain Prisco, Ibsen Prisco, and this is the *Shenandoah*. And who might you be and what do you want? I don't take kindly to desperate souls waking me up at ungodly hours unless they have a lot of money."

"I'm sure your man told you who I am," Max responded. "And I am certain that you do most of your work at ungodly hours. I want to charter the *Shenandoah* for a voyage to Spartak. Two passengers departing at dawn. That is, if she is fast enough to get us there by noon of the following day."

"Oh, she's fast enough," Captain Prisco said, sniffing and peering at her through the weak, undulating glow of the lantern man's buglight. "But it shall cost you. And as for who you are, well, people who appear in the night are rarely who they say they are anyway. But I don't give a damn as long as your coins are in my pocket."

Max didn't have a penny farthing on her. She threw back her hood. Prisco and the lantern man reacted with shock, followed by looks of disdain.

"You be a Martian, eh? Here among us?" Captain Prisco said. "My word."

"Half-Martian, Captain Prisco. As I said, I am Max, the adopted daughter of Admiral Balthazar. I did not lug the treasure chest you're going to ask for up here with me now but I assure you I can pay my way."

"The half-breed Martian daughter of Balthazar's?" Prisco muttered. "I've heard of you and aye, surely you have the coin. You Crankshafts are genius merchants. I know you keep your coffers loaded with treasure, far more than any of the other clans might imagine."

"No zebes," the lantern man hissed into Prisco's ear, but the captain waved him off.

"To Spartak at dawn, is it?" Captain Prisco asked.

"And perhaps beyond that," Max replied.

"Ah. A destination far and the dangerous journey open-ended," Prisco said, his eyes glowing with greed. "Expensive."

"Name your price. I have no time to quibble."

"Five hundred," Prisco said matter-of-factly.

"Five hundred gold?" Valentine spluttered.

"Five hundred silvers would be excessive for a ride in this ballast balloon!"

Max slapped her gloved hand over Valentine's mouth. He glared at her, too drunk and startled to move. Not the most gracious muzzling, but Max was worn out and her eyes ached. "Done," Max replied to Prisco. "We shall be here at dawn with the money. Bunker now if you must but be ready to go."

"Oh, we shall be ready," Prisco said.

Max removed her hand from Valentine's face — he looked like he was about to explode, so badly did he wish to speak, but he held his tongue. "Lady Fortune save you if you are not," Max said to Prisco, throwing her hood over her head and turning on her heel.

"Lousy zebes," the lantern man grumbled behind her.

Max strode away with Valentine thumping along behind her, moving past the constable to descend the staircase. Her exhausted, half-healed state would make the walk back to the citadel an arduous one but it was the beginning of her return to Romulus Buckle and the *Pneumatic Zeppelin*, and that was fuel enough to drive her anywhere she needed to go.

"Five hundred?" Valentine grumbled behind her. "Gold? Five hundred?"

Max halted halfway down the stairs, Valentine almost blundering into her. Steadying herself by planting her hand on the wide, heavy rail, she closed her eyes. Her back hurt like the sabertooth had just slashed it open again; more streams of hot blood trickled down her cold skin and soaked into her shirt at the base of her spine. "Did you smell that Gallowglass stew?" she asked.

Aye, how could I not?" Valentine replied. He rubbed his bewhiskered chin and the sound of his fingers on the stubble was loud and abrasive. "Reminded me how hungry I was."

"Get the recipe. The captain likes Gallowglass stew."

"Aye, Lieutenant."

XIX

THE MIRROR

Max stared at her face, her long, well-shaped face staring back at her from the mirror. She hated her face with its violet-black eyes — betrayers of emotion — and the black stripes tapering across her cheeks and forehead, stark against the white skin. A thin, light pink scar stood out in a small arc over her right eyebrow, the result of Romulus Buckle knocking her into a door jamb when they were children. Her reflection held motionless except for the flickering movement of the lantern's candle flame in her pupils, trapped butterflies of fire.

Setting her hairbrush aside, Max pulled on her leather flying helmet, drawing her goggles down onto her face and pressing the lens casings squarely against her cheekbones. She switched open the helmet's reservoir valves, submerging her eyes in soft, soothing, aqueous humor.

Her eyes looked bigger now, magnified slightly as they were by the liquid.

Such alien eyes.

She turned away from the Martian in the mirror.

Max crossed her arms and stared at the wall. Two hours before dawn and she was fully dressed. She couldn't sleep. It wasn't due to Valentine's snores rolling down the hallway from the guest bedchamber. It wasn't due to a fear of being found after her infirmary breakout—she had sent word of her imminent departure to Balthazar via the butler and she knew her father would not stop her. It wasn't due to the pain of her aggravated wounds. An anxious, nervous energy had driven her out of bed so many times she had let it win. It was surprising that, since the visit by the Gravedigger, she'd somehow buried her near-obsession with the immortality equation, lost the desire to think about it at all. Yet her brain churned, working furiously on other things like measuring her first-blush appraisal of Captain Prisco and the *Shenandoah* over and over.

The thin pink-white scar.

She wondered where Romulus Buckle and the *Pneumatic Zeppelin* were, worried about him and how difficult it might be to locate them in the Spartak Territory. She felt her heart accelerate of its own accord. She wanted him. She wanted Romulus Buckle so badly her body threatened to quiver. Damn the weaknesses of the Martian race. Max's father had warned her of this uncontrollable biological compulsion even when she was a child. Martians selected a mate through a blind, physiological urge which left the brain at the mercy of the yearnings of the flesh. And, once the heart locked on, the mating choice would stick for life. In full-blooded Martians the linking was almost always mutual and thankfully so, for rejection was catastrophe. Max's Martian half, she was now certain, had transfixed itself upon Romulus Buckle. But he was human; his body did not recognize the alien chemical shower of her unspoken affection. He couldn't *feel* it.

But Max could say nothing. She could not expose herself in such a way. At least her human half gave her that modicum of control. Being his lieutenant, his second mate, his comrade-in-arms, provided her with the line she would never cross. If Buckle never turned to her, if he never offered her the kind of love she so desperately needed, she would go to her grave in loyal silence, unrequited, quietly angry with herself for the pathetic vulnerabilities of her bright red Martian blood.

And the kiss, the kiss, delivered as she lay at death's door in the Tehachapi mountain cave; it haunted her. She could explain it away: shock delirium, morphine-doped groping—and Romulus would never mention it, suspecting she would not remember and be embarrassed if it was revealed. But she remembered. It was a memory more alive than any other inside of her; the warmth of his mouth on her freezing lips, the tightness of his initial surprise followed by an open-lipped, willing response—a response which was an act of pity and accommodation—an allowance to a dying friend. But his intimate kindness had sealed her doom, for it stoked her smoldering Martian chemistry into an inferno. She had entered him, ever so slightly, with her quivering tongue, and the effect would have been the same had she been able to pour her entire body into his.

Max crossed her arms tighter and turned to stare at another wall—anything but the damned mirror. Romulus was such a cad. Beautiful, warm and intelligent, but still a cad. He was a poor choice for her, she told herself.

And yet she had chosen. Or, more accurately, her Martian heart had chosen for her.

Max stood up and started pacing. Get the blood flowing. Shut the sleep-deprived confusions out of the head. She lifted her duffle bag from the bed but it was already well packed, heavy with extra outdoor clothes and boots plus a spare pistol and three sets of instrument calibration tools in wooden boxes. The hospital had transferred her sword and personal belongings to her room but there hadn't been enough left of her shredded uniform to salvage the clothing. Her boots had been waiting for her, freshly polished, but she could still smell her own blood on them.

The clothing borrowed from Dr. Lee and the infirmary lay neatly folded on the chair. She would have a servant return them.

A small metal chest emblazoned with the Crankshaft treasury seal sat beside the duffel bag, sinking into the mattress, loaded with gold coins for Prisco.

There was nothing to do.

She couldn't stand it.

Was it possible that Valentine was snoring even louder? How could she hear him so distinctly with both her heavy oak door and his being shut?

She took in a deep breath and looked around her bedchamber. It wasn't like her to seek distraction and she didn't know how to occupy her idle self. She hadn't grown up in this room. She moved in here after Balthazar and the family had relocated to the Devil's Punchbowl the year before, after the destruction of the stronghold at Tehachapi. The attack had been the Founders' doing, of course, posing as Imperials, and the bombs had killed many Crankshaft citizens and crippled the air fleet.

The family had lost Calypso, Balthazar's wife and Max's adopted mother, and her death had hurt Max so deeply she had no idea how to deal with it. So she buried the agonies over and over until they sank away into the oldest layers of sediment inside where they no longer tortured her. The others, her human brothers and sisters, wept openly and bled out their grief, but she did not. Sometimes she had caught them looking at her over Calypso's funeral pyre, a familial indignity in their eyes at how she, alien-blooded or not, could be so tearless and cold.

The way Martians handled tragedy, their external stoicism, "the stillness," her father had called it, did not blunt emotion—it threw feelings into higher relief, in fact—but it accelerated recovery. But Max was a half-breed. Instead of burning her pains away the hybrid mechanism boiled them—and they threatened to explode when the crucible cracked.

If she could let the Martian half of her swallow the human side whole, in there would be a sanctuary from the all the hurts of the world. But she also sensed on a much deeper level such an achievement would be a trap. For Martians felt everything even more intensely than humans—they were just better adapted creatures when it came to submerging their emotional responses.

And Max had cried. She had done it alone and when such things were done alone one could, over time, almost convince oneself they had never happened at all, the brain being the poor, gullible witness it was. She hadn't wept in her cabin aboard the *Pneumatic Zeppelin*; the ventilated ceilings offered little privacy and the wooden chamber partitions were light and thin. But she had found a place to cry herself almost into a faint, bawling for nearly half an hour—the amidships observation pod, built into the roof and well insulated with a lockable entry hatch, was a place where she would sometimes retire to enjoy isolation.

That was where she hid and wept. And when it was over she had felt humiliated.

And there was also Elizabeth. As Buckle's natural sister she had always shown Max and her brother Tyro more warmth and affection than anyone else in the family with the exception of Balthazar and Calypso. Elizabeth was the most capable person Max had ever met. She was both sweet and powerful, blessed with an intellect and intuition she wielded with nuance and skill. They never spoke much but Elizabeth always seemed to sense when Max was sad, even as little girls, and she would hold her hand on the playground or at the dinner table. Tyro adored her, and, if she allowed herself the truth, so did Max. Elizabeth certainly had her flaws but they mattered little, even made her more likeable. Max would have suffered many more beatings in the schoolyard had Elizabeth not been there.

When everyone thought Elizabeth had died along with Calypso in the Tehachapi raid, it was truly as if Max had lost a sister. The rumors that Elizabeth had not been killed but rather captured by the Founders infuriated Max. She would gladly risk her life in order to save Elizabeth.

But first she wanted to kiss Romulus Buckle one more time.

Max realized she was gazing at herself in the mirror. She nearly kicked it, wanting to destroy the alien thing in a shimmering, satisfying fall of broken glass. But she restrained herself. It seemed her entire life boiled down to an act of restraining herself.

Max kicked the side of the bed, its legs skidding across the wooden floorboards until the frame clunked against the wall. The next thump of wood made Max think a bed slat had fallen. Then she realized it was a soft knocking on the door. "Who is it?" she asked.

"Flora Herzog," came the voice from outside.

"I do not require medical attention."

"Your father's orders. He told me either you allow me to dress your wounds or you shall be escorted back to the infirmary."

No more infirmary. No more of Dr. Lee's morphine needle. Max opened the door.

Flora stepped in, smiling, carrying a tray heaped with bandage rolls, gauze, brown antiseptic bottles, an iodine vial and a tin of Fassbinders' Penicillin Paste. "How are you feeling, Lieutenant?" she asked.

"Well," Max replied, not wanting to be touched. "Far too well to require such endless attentions."

Flora set her tray on the desk. "I heard a loud noise. Is everything all right?"

"Yes. How could you hear anything over that snoring?"

Flora offered a sad little smile. "All boilermen snore because the coal dust ruins their windpipes." She glanced at the dark fireplace. "Why haven't you lit up your hearth? It's cold in here."

"I was about to leave and didn't think it necessary," Max said.

"Very well—take off your shirt, please," Flora asked as she unscrewed the antiseptic paste can.

"You won't need the antiseptic," Max said. "The wounds have closed."

"I shall be the judge of what you need, Lieutenant," Flora replied. "Shirt off."

Max unbuttoned her blouse and removed it, folding it neatly over the footboard of her bed, which rested at a slight angle to the wall since she booted it.

"What is that?" Flora asked.

Max glanced down at the heavy wool infirmary tunic she had wrapped tightly around her upper body and knotted beneath her left armpit. Her purpose had been to maintain a good pressure on her wounds and allow them to reclose as well as sop up any bleeding. "A makeshift bandage," she said. "I am certain it has been effective."

Sighing, Flora set the Fassbinders' tin on the table, untying the knot and tossing the bloodstained tunic on the chair beside the table. The blood looked brown and dry—the pressure had worked, Max thought with a small sense of satisfaction.

"Please turn around," Flora said. "I need to look at you in the lantern light."

Max turned her back to the nurse—but now she

175

was facing the mirror again—and she tightened her hands into fists.

"You're shivering," Flora announced with worry. "We should really get the fire on in here."

"I like the cold," Max said.

"Lieutenant," Flora started.

"Get on with it, please."

"Very well," Flora said with disapproval, leaning in to inspect Max's back. "You've been bleeding quite a bit."

"But the wounds are closed now, correct?"

"You've been bleeding."

The gurgle of a small bottle was followed by the stink of iodine and it stung Max's sensitive nostrils. Flora began working up and down Max's back and shoulder with a cloth, dissolving the scabs as gently as she could. The cold and pain braced Max and made her feel stronger.

"Much of the lengths of your wounds are closed but not all of them," Flora said. "In many places you've popped your stitches the blood is barely congealed. We must do our best to prevent the gashes from reopening."

"It is but a small concern," Max heard herself say, staring into the mirror again, looking without pleasure upon her stark white and black striped nakedness from the waist up. She rarely took time to look at her body. She did not want to be that body.

"Until the infection sets in."

"Then sew me up, please."

Flora sighed again. Max heard the rattle of needles in a box and the rasp of surgical thread unspooling. "I mixed a nerve-deadening agent into your iodine wash so this should only sting a little." She began stitching the wounds.

"It is fine," Max replied, wincing now and again when the needle bit too deep but keeping her body still. She looked at the bookshelf where her leather-bound tomes rested under a fine layer of dust, untouched since they had been unpacked and placed there. It looked nothing like her cubby aboard the *Pneumatic Zeppelin* where the every gap was jammed full of dog-eared scrolls, schematics, and blueprints. Nothing gathered dust there.

In the shadow between the desk and the bed lay Tyro's steamer trunk. Max had stowed his personal belongings inside it, neatly folded and wrapped, after his terrible injuries in the Imperial Raid. Tyro had been lost to her in a coma since then, his damaged body locked in the infirmary iron lung.

"There," Flora said, unscrewing the lid of the Fassbinders' tin and smearing penicillin paste across Max's back. The paste had a pleasant odor of mint and felt greasy and warm on her chilled skin. "I closed you up as best I could, but you have to take it easy, you hear me?"

"Yes," Max answered, though she had no intention of taking it easy.

Flora applied new bandages and tape and finished with a satisfied, "There." She assisted Max with her sweater and coat before collecting her tools on the tray.

"Thank you," Max said. Her fingers were so white, her hands so white, with the black stripes curving out of her coat sleeves to end in elegant swirls on the backs of her hands. She still felt naked. She reached for her black leather gloves and pulled them on.

"You are welcome, Max," Flora replied. "And best of luck, wherever it is you are going." When Max opened the door she felt a presence in the hallway.

"Did my daughter allow you to do your work, Mrs. Herzog?" Balthazar's voice boomed from the corridor. "She can prove to be rather trying."

"Yes, Admiral," Flora replied.

"Come in, father," Max said.

XX

A FATHER'S DAUGHTER

Balthazar Crankshaft stepped into Max's bedchamber, his gray greatcoat radiating the icy bite of outdoor air. Most likely he had just walked across the citadel parade grounds. His airship mascot, the grumpy bulldog Agamemnon, a mottled brown and white ball of muscle, trotted in on Balthazar's heels and jumped on the bed. "I am pleased that you did not give Flora a difficult time," he said, smiling through his heavy but well-groomed beard. The beard seemed a little whiter than Max remembered but he looked as powerful and robust as ever.

"I was a model patient."

"Which would make me suspect that you are up to something if I didn't already know what you were up to," Balthazar said quietly, his familiar bulk filling the room as it always did. "And there is little I can do to stop you from leaving beyond slapping you in irons."

"I must return to my airship."

"I know."

179

"My wounds have healed sufficiently for me to return to my duties," Max said.

"And you are taking Cornelius Valentine with you? The boilerman who lost his leg to the kraken? What good would the poor fellow be to you in the field? His condition is far more fragile than it looks and he is not a young man, Max."

Max nodded. "He will drink himself to death otherwise. Romulus needs a steward."

"Ah, steward, very good," Balthazar replied. He knew the traps of the Friendly Society taverns, good as their intentions might be. Many of the cooks and staff in the citadel were maimed former zeppelineers. "He is your crewman to post as you see fit, of course."

"Any news of Ryder among the Tinskins?" Max asked.

"Yes. We received a message from him via messenger pigeon two days ago. The Tinskin Council is assembling near their entire war fleet to join the Grand Alliance, though the decision to do so was apparently far from unanimous. They plan to take a rather circuitous route to us from the east in order to avoid any spying eyes."

"That is good," Max said.

"Yes, very good," Balthazar said. "Our chances against the Founders increase tenfold if the Tinskin fleet is with us." He took a deep breath. "Once all of the allied clan fleets are assembled, well, it will be a sight to see. Your mother would have gotten a kick out of it."

Max nodded, focusing her eyes on her father, who was always sad when he spoke of Calypso. "Things are on schedule then?"

"Yes. With ambassadors come spies but I believe every clan understands their own survival depends upon our victory."

"I don't trust the Tinskins."

"I don't trust any of them." Balthazar answered, and winked to hide his worry. "You should be asleep."

"So should you."

"Aye. But sleep does not come easy under the weight of the world."

"It does not."

"Might you stay a little longer?" Balthazar asked. "I could have the cooks put together a wonderful mutton stew for us."

"When I return," Max said.

"Of course. Now, as soon as you find Romulus, as soon as you reach him, tell him that he must return home immediately, at best speed. The Alliance needs the guns of the *Pneumatic Zeppelin*."

"I shall tell him," Max said.

"Make certain he obeys my command."

"Romulus keeps his own council at times."

Balthazar shook his head. "Not this time. None of his headstrong contrariness. Not this time. Have Ambassador Washington take him to task if he tries to go his own way."

"Aye, father. I take it that you have not received a message from Romulus since the news of the victory at Muscovy."

"No."

"Then Muscovy is where I shall start looking for him," Max said.

"What is your plan?" Balthazar asked. "I cannot spare you a Crankshaft airship but I can procure passage on a merchant vessel for you."

"I have commissioned a ship. Thank you."

"A good ship?" Balthazar asked. "A fast ship?"

"The *Shenandoah*, docked at the southeast jetty."

"Captain Ibsen Prisco's vessel, eh?" Balthazar said, rubbing his beard. "He is a mercenary from the Pale."

"And perhaps has a bad reputation?" Max asked.

Balthazar grinned. "A shady character, yes. But a mercenary would go out of business if he wasn't reliable. His airship is faster than the devil, overpowered with all those turbines and screws. Just watch yourself around him. He'll become unpredictable if he believes he is being double-crossed. Make sure he knows you are my daughter."

"He does," Max said, buckling on her sword belt. "I can read him effectively."

"Captain Prisco does not do anything on the

cheap, however."

"He most does certainly not."

"Do you need funds?"

Max pointed to the small chest on her bed. "I already raided the treasury."

"My children rob me blind," Balthazar said with a grin.

"All children rob their parents blind."

"Aye. It is worth it to get Romulus back here. We'll need every air machine we can get when the time comes to match the Founders in the sky."

"I shall bring Romulus and the *Pneumatic Zeppelin* home, I promise you, father," Max said.

Balthazar smiled at her, one of his profoundly disarming smiles, and took a deep breath. "It is difficult for a father when his children have become soldiers, when he cannot protect them, when it is no longer possible to think of you as the little creatures I once knew."

Max gazed at Balthazar. In a world which had offered her little more than suspicion and cruelty since she was a child, he and Calypso had clutched her and Tyro close to their breasts, offering love and protection to the cool, unresponsive half-aliens. But she and Tyro had absorbed it utterly, desperately, and were now eternally bound to their family. Max had rarely shown affection to Balthazar, though she had always been the good daughter, respectful and loyal. But she loved him with every ounce of her subterranean, all-consuming Martian intensity. She felt the pain radiating from him now, the uncertainty and apprehension, the worries of an old, powerful, dying bear.

Max lifted her goggles and smiled at Balthazar.

He smiled back, surprised. "Ah, that smile, so rarely bestowed," he whispered. "As precious as fairy dust to me."

Max kissed Balthazar on the bare stretch of skin of his cheek above the whiskers of his beard. She wrapped her long arms around him, pressed her chin to his shoulder. She hadn't hugged him for years. He felt broad and strong and it was like hugging a barrel. She smelled the tobacco smoke on his skin and uniform and she felt like a little girl again. She remembered him carrying her in his arms after the bullies attacked her in the schoolyard and later, when the frightened parents, hats in hand and bringing three-penny cakes, dragged their brats to Balthazar's door, how the children, heads low, eyes simmering, offered awkward, forced apologies.

Max felt Balthazar's big heart beating through the cloth against her chest, and it was here, only here, that she felt absolutely safe. He had chosen her. He had chosen to be her father. She held the embrace for a long moment, the rough wool of his collar against her neck, and suddenly her back didn't hurt any more.

"I love you, child," Balthazar whispered.

She held him tighter. She wanted to say that she loved him, but he already knew.

PART TWO:

ATLANTIS

XXI

LIQUID LIGHT

The brilliant illumination of Atlantis threatened to blind Romulus Buckle even after his eyes had adjusted to it, so accustomed was he to the overcast grays and muttering oil lanterns of the cloud-bound surface world. Transparent glass tubes channeled light across every ceiling of the underwater city, carrying streams of yellow-white liquid, both bright and soft, and if one stared straight into it one could make out a barely perceptible pulsing at its center. Atlantis dazzled with light and warmth as if everything flowed from its own secret sun.

The Roman-styled passageways, wide and fitted with faux columns over plush crimson and green carpets, verged on garish: freshwater fountains gurgled at the main intersections, marble splashers with sculptures of old gods and green-crusted bronze fish on gears wheeling back and forth across the basins.

Beautiful seascape paintings lined the white walls and sometimes incorporated existing utilitarian fixtures and instruments of copper and brass, making them appear like submarines or fantastic undersea wheels. Buckle had yet to see one surface scene in any of the art, as if the Atlanteans had no need to remember the world above the water at all.

An Atlantean harpoon prodded Buckle's back as he walked. There were two Atlantean soldiers behind him and two more in front, led by Cressida. Sabrina and Welly strode at his flanks and in front of them was Penny Dreadful, clanking as she moved, for her arms and legs were bound with heavy iron manacles. That had been the deal with Cressida. The automaton had to be chained if Buckle wanted an audience with the First Consul. Buckle had reluctantly agreed. Furthermore, Buckle and his crew were ordered to surrender their sealskin bag containing their firearms. Felix and his crew, well known to the Atlanteans, had been whisked away; Buckle didn't know where they'd been taken.

Cressida glanced back at them, her regal chin up, her gaze high and suspicious, lingering on Penny. Buckle smelled Cressida's perfume — the sweet scent of cinnamon — and it mixed well with the pleasant aroma of ambergris incense which burned in tiny braziers near each fountain. So far, Atlantis had proven to be a thing of beauty and it structure underfoot offered a solid, land-like feel — unlike that of a submarine — built to last.

They arrived at a large glass bubble with doors that looked like some kind of pneumatic elevator. Cressida ushered everyone in with a wave of her hand. The doors slid shut with a sound of sucking atmosphere and sealed them in the chamber. The sea surrounded them on three sides, deep and green outside the glass.

One of the Atlantean guards pulled an ornate metal lever with a copper squid as a handle.

With the roar of rushing air and the rumble of metal sliding along oiled rails, the elevator shot upward. Bending at the knees, Buckle watched the sea through a blur of metal girders, glimpsing the looming glass mountains of four smaller sister domes, all glowing with their secret amber light.

"Better than being tossed into the sea," Sabrina said.

"Aye," Buckle replied. The spacious vault of the underwater landscape dizzied the head after being inside a diving helmet and constricted passageways for so long. The sprawling ruins of the artificial Roman city stood in the near distance, visually magnificent, thought-provoking and haunting. The blue-green forever of the ocean was calm, undulating with white-blue flickering at the surface and darkening near the bottom where schools of fish rose and dove like flocks of birds over the vast seaweed fields waving in the currents.

But what caught Buckle's attention were the shadows moving at various depths in the distance: Founders submersibles, dozens of them, massive machines, their rows of dark yellow windows glowing faintly like the eyes of monsters, circling Atlantis, circling again and again.

The view vanished abruptly as the elevator zipped inside a shaft and slowed to a halt. The doors hissed open and Cressida stepped out. The Atlantean guards ushered the group into a grand foyer where seven large, curving staircases made of polished, pink-white rock swung off in seven directions like the tentacles of a massive, well-balanced octopus, its suckers springing upwards in the form of columns. A long, vaulted ceiling, its ribs designed to look like the huge white plates of a leviathan's spine, terminated at the far end over a great marble statue of Neptune, its eyes filled with Atlantean liquid light that cut two columns through the faintly smoky air, the haze provided by braziers hanging on the walls, burning sticks of ambergris.

"Come with me," Cressida said.

"What is the source of the illumination in this, this fluid?" Buckle asked. "Other than boil, which is far weaker, I have never seen anything like it."

"It is the luminiferous aether," Cressida replied without glancing back, the quick bite of her words announcing that there would be no more information forthcoming.

"I'd like to take a jar of this liquid back to the ship," Welly said. "Ivan would love to see this."

"Cressida, wait!" a female voice rang out.

Buckle stopped with the others as they turned to see a woman, flanked by an Atlantean soldier with a purple robe, hurrying down one of the staircases. The woman was slender and shorter than the others, but the confidence in her bearing gave no doubt that she was accustomed to commanding a room. Her thick black hair was up, intricately braided, and her skin was a lovely shade of olive. She wore a white stola edged with patterns of purple and pulled in at the waist by a gold and purple sash. Gold rings adorned her hands between the first and second joints of the fingers and a single gold bracelet was looped around her right wrist, carved in the shape of sea snake.

"Lady Julia," Cressida replied and bowed. The guards lowered their heads.

Buckle attempted a quick bow but Lady Julia was coming at him so fast he more or less bungled it. "Lady Julia, I am Captain Romulus Buckle."

"I have been informed of what it is you Crankshafts want from us, Captain," Lady Julia replied, now directly in front of him, slightly out of breath. "Save your speeches for the First Consul."

"As you wish, of course," Buckle replied. Lady Julia's abruptness belied a tight nervousness, a sense of duress.

"I was ordered to bring them to the Senate floor," Cressida said.

"Change of plans," Lady Julia replied and glared at Penny Dreadful. "This thing. Where did you get it and why did you bring it here?"

"Is she not a creation of yours?" Buckle asked.

"Yes, she is," Julia answered in a measured way, as if to be careful about not saying too much on the subject. "She is from a very old time. We were certain that every one of this model had been destroyed."

"Why were they destroyed? Sabrina asked.

"Because they are failed abominations," Lady Julia replied.

Buckle glanced at Penny Dreadful. The little robot stood still in its heavy chains, its eyes glowing, apparently taking no offense, not responding at all. Sabrina stepped closer to it and placed one hand on its shoulder, protectively, as if the machine were some kind of real child.

"I haven't seen anything to make me think—" Buckle began.

"Because you don't see them coming," Lady Julia said. "It must be dismantled or it shall cause you never ending misery."

"It saved my life in the battle with your Guardians," Buckle said flatly.

"Oh, yes," Lady Julia said, colder than before.

"You killed one of my alpha gagools, a fabulous, loyal creature. Your appearance has been an unexpected disaster, an unwanted disruption."

"Oh, stop posturing!" Sabrina groaned.

Lady Julia snapped her eyes to Sabrina, then back to Buckle. "And you are already in bed with the Founders, I see."

"By what means, if I may ask, do you ascertain that?" Buckle asked, though he knew what she was getting at.

Lady Julia huffed. "Don't play me for a fool, Captain. You have a scarlet in your company."

"Just because my hair is red does not mean I am Founders," Sabrina said through gritted teeth.

"Oh, it is much more than that," Lady Julia said. "You have a Founder's face."

Sabrina took a step forward. "What does that mean?"

Buckle needed to change the subject before Sabrina said something that would get them in serious trouble. "It is urgent that we meet with your First Consul."

"The First Consul has agreed to see you over lunch in the triclinium," Lady Julia said. "You are fortunate that I spoke up on your behalf, for his first reaction was to have the automaton melted down and the three of you jettisoned into the sea."

XXII

THE TRICLINIUM

Lady Julia, Cressida, and the soldiers led Buckle and Sabrina along a maze of corridors into the private interior quarters of the Atlantean elite, or at least Buckle assumed so, counting how many purple-robed guards they passed along the way. Buckle tried his best to shake off worrying about Welly and Penny Dreadful, who had been separated from them. There was no way on earth the hated automaton was going to be brought into the presence of the First Consul — both Lady Julia and Cressida had been adamant about that — and Buckle had been compelled to leave Penny behind with Welly as its protector. Although from what he had seen of Penny's ability to fight, it was more likely it would be protecting Welly if it came down to it. The boy and the robot would be placed in comfortable quarters and in complete safety, Cressida had promised, and Buckle had no choice but to trust her. But if they were truly in danger it was because he had brought them here.

Buckle and Sabrina, passing two more hulking guards in purple robes, were ushered into a spacious dining chamber with a green carpet and one wall entirely of glass, its frames supported by white statues of Roman gods cast in poses akin to Atlas, appearing as if they supported the weight of the shimmering sea above and beyond the windows. A rectangular table with wide benches on three sides occupied the middle of the space, sumptuously set with serving plates of white ceramic loaded with foods both colorful and bizarre. Five servants in white togas stood at the ready, lined up in front of the window-wall with towels folded over their forearms.

Two men awaited them in the room and the first, an average-sized fellow wearing a plain toga similar to Lady Julia's stola except his purple trim was laced with gold thread — had his nose in the air. Though the man's short, balding physicality was unimpressive he overcame it through the way he held himself, the power of his presence, the serious angle of his eyes, leaving no doubt that it was he and only he who carried the weight of the world on his shoulders as the Atlantean First Consul. Buckle sensed a tightness in the man, a thread so taut it hummed under his regal straightness: under the calm façade he was harried, anxious, cornered.

At the First Consul's side stood another man, taller and broader with the wide shoulders and narrow waist of an athlete, a magnificent body type which would have been more pronounced had he not been wearing a splendid set of Roman armor; a gold breastplate covered his chest, two frogs on the shoulders bearing the knots of a large red robe, and he held his cheek-plated helmet in the crook of his left arm, the tall crimson brush as high as his chin. His face was pale-skinned with deep crow's feet at the corners of his eyes and he radiated more worry and less pomposity than the First Consul.

"May I introduce Octavian, First Consul of Atlantis and *pater familias* of the Aventine House," Lady Julia said.

"First Consul," Buckle said as he made a deft bow. "It is an honor."

"And this is Marius, our Master Equitum," Lady Julia added.

Buckle nodded to Marius and returned his attention to Octavian. "First Consul, I am Captain Romulus Buckle of the Crankshaft clan. I—"

"If you are a captain then where is your air machine?" Octavian asked.

"It is close by," Buckle replied.

Marius strode forward, drew his sword in a flash, whipping it up so the blade kissed Buckle's throat.

"Bastards!" Sabrina whispered. Her hand was on her sword handle but she too held herself motionless, for the tips of the Atlantean guard's harpoons pressed at her back.

Buckle held still, trying to look bemused as he listened to the low hum of the aether tubes overhead. "A little overdramatic, wouldn't you say, First Consul, considering we are your guests."

"Guests?" Octavian smiled. "You came uninvited, if my memory serves."

"Tell us why you are here," Marius asked, his voice as cold as the glimmering steel under Buckle's chin.

"As envoys of —" Buckle started.

"A lie!" Marius blurted. "You are no envoys. Where is your Ambassador?"

"My Master Equitum is a very good judge of character," Octavian said. "I'd like you to clear things up before we sit down to eat. Tell us why you Crankshafts, the very son of Balthazar himself, running a Founders blockade no less, appear to us so suddenly and with a Founders scarlet and a banned automaton in tow."

"I'm no Founder," Sabrina snarled.

"You were not spoken to, scarlet," Marius snapped.

Buckle locked his gaze on Marius. "I do not negotiate at the point of a sword."

"All negotiations take place at the point of a sword, one way or another," Marius replied.

"I'll concede that point," Buckle said. "I'd even nod if I didn't risk cutting my own jugular in the process. I can tell you that my original intent was to come here to find my sister, Elizabeth Crankshaft. The Founders abducted her and the evidence led me here."

"We are not harboring this sister of yours," Octavian said. "There are no Crankshafts here."

"Aye, well," Buckle replied. "Upon discovering that you were under blockade by the Founders I decided it was a good time to request that you join my father's Grand Alliance, all in the name of mutual self-preservation."

"Ah, yes. Balthazar's great secret eastern alliance. That sounds a little more believable, hmmmm?" Octavian said. "What do you think, Marius?"

Marius lowered his blade from Buckle's throat.

The First Consul nodded to the guards, who eased back on their weapons. "Now that we have cleared that up, allow me to formally welcome you to the Aventine house, the greatest house in all of Atlantis. Shall we eat? I am famished." He clapped his hands together and the servants scurried out two side doors on the left which offered steamy glimpses of a busy kitchen.

"I would like to say—"

Yes, yes, Captain," Octavian blurted dismissively. "Please sit. I prefer to handle negotiations over good food—a full stomach keeps the mind settled, don't you think?"

Buckle didn't move. "With all due respect First Consul, if I may—"

"You may not," Octavian snapped. "Your unexpected arrival has come at a time most inopportune, Captain, and I am going leagues out of my way to accommodate you. Now, sit down." Octavian swung his arm across the table in dramatic fashion; Buckle noticed Octavian's forearm was sculpted with dense, ropy muscle, quite unexpected for a politician of the elite class.

"As you wish, of course," Buckle replied, and took a seat at the table, Sabrina tucking in beside him.

Octavian smiled, his irritation vanishing as he took his seat. "Ah, much better," he enthused. Marius took up a station at Octavian's back, joined by Lady Julia and Cressida. "I hope you brought your appetite with you, Captain," Octavian said, rubbing his hands, "along with your political maneuverings."

A female wine-pourer carrying a large jug entered, deftly delivering peach-colored wine into golden goblets, of which there were seven. The five servants returned and served three white plates, the first to Octavian and then to Buckle and Sabrina.

Buckle realized the contents of his plate were moving. It was a pile of small octopus tentacles, freshly cut from their owners, still sucking and twining in a pool of thin black sauce.

"Fresh salted octopi tentacles in anemone

sauce," Octavian said with a grin, lifting his fork. "Knocks the palate wide open."

"Are you expecting more guests?" Buckle said, motioning toward the four unattended goblets before he used his fork to prevent a squirming appetizer from wandering off his plate and into his lap.

If Octavian heard Buckle's question he did not acknowledge it. "One cannot help but be civil when holding a glass of fine Sargassum wine. Marius, have some wine."

"I am on duty, First Consul," Marius replied.

"You are always on duty!" Marius growled. "Sit down, Marius, and take the damned edge off!"

Marius gritted his teeth and took a seat on the bench to Octavian's right, landing with a crunch of squeaking leather and clanking armor.

"Ah, you prefer the sweet mulsum, do you not, my dear general," Octavian said. "Philo! Chilled mulsum for the Master Equitum!"

"Of course, First Consul," an older servant said, snapping bolt upright and nodding to the wine-pourer, who hurried out of the room.

Sabrina lifted her fork—a tentacle wrapped tightly about the tines—and gave Buckle a disgusted look. Through the windows behind her, Buckle saw a Founders submarine churning past in the distant depths of the sea, its yellow portholes and tubular mass just visible. "First Consul, if I may—"

"Ah!" Octavian replied, raising his hand as Philo placed a goblet on the table in front of Marius. "Wine is served first."

The wine-pourer returned with a glass bottle and began pouring pale yellow liquid into Marius' cup.

"I want it so full it can't hold another drop!" Octavian said.

The wine-pourer carefully loaded the goblet with so much wine that surface tension was the only thing preventing it from overflowing. Buckle noticed the wine, lit up as it was under the luminiferous aether, appeared to have hundreds of tiny sparkling creatures swimming on the surface.

"Philo!" Octavian ordered. "It would appear that our guests are unaccustomed to food from the sea. Bring the next course now. They will certainly be more comfortable eating mammals."

"Yes, First Consul, Philo replied, and hurried into the kitchen with one servant in tow.

"If it is undercooked again I'll send the chef to the Latifundium fringe for the rest of her miserable life!" Octavian shouted after Philo. "Tell her that!" He glared at Marius, who, calm and stoic, seemed quite accustomed to being glared at. "Don't sip at it like a sick old woman, Marius," Octavian grumbled. "Show me the seven."

Marius threw back his head, his throat working as he drained the goblet. When finished he banged the empty cup on the table.

"Ha!" Octavian laughed, much amused before he glared at Buckle and Sabrina. "You two! Follow suit." He tilted his goblet to his mouth, gulping loudly.

Buckle turned to look at Sabrina but she, head back and cup upended, was already more than halfway through her wine.

Suppressing a grumble, Buckle swallowed his drink as fast as he could, suspecting that the First Consul was a man who measured others by how effortlessly they could imbibe alcohol. The wine wasn't bad at all, the flavor light and full of fruit. Traces of mandarin spice traveled in a thousand sweet flickers across Buckle's tongue in way that felt physical but he did not want to think about what might be swimming in the wine. When he emptied the goblet he saw seven pearls set in the bottom.

Octavian slapped his empty goblet on the table. Sabrina slapped her empty goblet on the table.

Buckle slapped his empty goblet on the table and cleared his throat. "First Consul, it is important to talk. Our shared situation is perilous. You are under blockade and we —"

Philo returned with two large silver serving trays which he laid on the table.

"Please," said Octavian, "help yourselves to some edible dormouse. You'll eat nothing tastier in your life, I assure you, and they are land-bred. An ancient Roman delicacy, you see."

Buckle peered at the small, skinless rodents roasted on skewers. With the heads and legs still attached, they looked like nicely cooked squirrels, the skin crispy and brown over the meat underneath, dripping with greasy juices. The creature's long, pock-marked tail was also well done, wrapped around the skewer. It smelled good, like peppered and salted venison. Sabrina ripped the tentacle off of her fork, stabbed an edible dormouse and laid it on her plate.

"Sir, about our shared situation," Buckle said.

"Our shared situation?" Octavian repeated as if the words stabbed him, watching the wine-pourer as she refilled the goblets, the jug gurgling with each pour. "Our situation is not shared, Captain. Do not dare presume our situation is shared. You have no idea of what Atlantis is capable of or what our condition is."

"Fair enough," Buckle replied. The wine generated a pleasant warmth in his nostrils.

Sabrina leaned in close to Buckle's ear. "I don't know what an edible dormouse is," she whispered, "but this is a rat." She shoved her knife under the rodent and slid it to the opposite side of her plate, leaving a juicy streak as she tucked it up against her pile of still-quivering tentacles.

Octavian looked at Buckle as if he had just popped into the room. "Tell me once again who you are exactly, Crankshaft?"

"I am Romulus Buckle, captain of the *Pneumatic Zeppelin* and son of Admiral Balthazar, leader of the Crankshaft clan."

"And remind me of what you want and why you risk so much to come here," Octavian asked.

"The Founders threaten us all, First Consul," Buckle said, deciding not to bring up his search for Elizabeth again. "The Crankshafts and many other clans have formed a grand armada in the spirit of mutual defense and I come here today to ask you to join our alliance." Not exactly the specific truth of the matter but there was no doubt that the Grand Alliance would benefit greatly from having the Atlanteans on their side. "And I see that you are already under duress."

"Atlantis is not under duress," Lady Julia blurted. Her voice was even and steady and cold but she was lying. Buckle noticed a close resemblance between her face and that of Octavian's; small forehead, wide-set eyes, square chin. "We hold our own."

"Of course," Buckle said gently. The Atlanteans were in trouble. And he wasn't sure, but he got the feeling that the unannounced arrival of his Crankshaft contingent had made things worse.

"So you hire a mercenary to run the blockade, kill one of our finest gagools and bring that vile, murderous, demented robot in here with you, eh?"

Octavian said.

"I am truly sorry about the loss of one of your Guardians," Buckle replied with sincerity. "It was an act of self-defense. As for the automaton, we had no knowledge of the machine's history."

"If the Crankshafts wish to negotiate they should do so properly and send an official ambassador," Lady Julia said.

"Julia, that is enough," Octavian said, but not without affection.

Lady Julia lowered her head. "My apologies, father."

"My daughter is high spirited and sometimes forgets her station, but she raises a good point," Octavian said. "Where is your ambassador? All I see is low-ranking intruders bumbling in unannounced, on foot, and in the company of mercenaries."

"Our ambassador was dispatched to Spartak along the way, First Consul," Buckle said.

Octavian sighed. "No matter. There you have it. Atlantis does not takes sides nor join confederations of any sort. You may have your war, Captain Buckle, but keep us out of it."

Buckle noticed both Octavian and Marius casting furtive glances toward the opposite doorway. They were expecting someone — whomever the four extra goblets were for — and they were nervous about it.

"From the looks of things outside you are

already neck deep in it," Sabrina said.

Octavian turned his gaze directly on Sabrina. "And how do you, a red-haired Founders woman, count yourself among the Crankshafts?" he asked.

"My blood is that of the Founders, aye," Sabrina answered, barely covering her exasperation. "But my heart is Crankshaft."

"The snake becomes a hawk?" Marius said. "I don't think so."

Buckle didn't like the Atlanteans pushing at Sabrina. How were they so sure she was a Founders child? Redheads were rare, yes, but they certainly existed in bloodlines outside of the city. "It would be great folly to throw your lot in with the Founders," Buckle said.

Marius threw his shoulders back, the result of his spine stiffening.

Octavian's eyes flashed. "Atlantis throws its lot in with no one."

"It appears to me the Founders are attempting to coerce —"

"Coerce?" Lady Julia bristled.

"Atlantis throws its lot in with no one," Octavian repeated.

"You throw your lot in with no one, First Consul?" a deep voice boomed from the doorway. "Yet here you sit, breaking bread with a Crankshaft."

Buckle jumped to his feet as two people stepped

into the opposite archway. The first, the speaker, was a mountain of a man with black and silver hair and a white scar running diagonally across his heavy face. The blow that caused the injury had sunk deep but the weight of his brows, the depth of his small eyes, and the huge bridge of his nose must have saved him from blindness, even death. He wore a black suit with a notched red collar and a red cape, black-lined, pinned at the shoulders.

But Buckle barely saw the man. Beside him, a slender, familiar form stood, wearing the black uniform and silver lace of the steampipers. She had bright red hair and beautiful Asian-influenced face, her nose smattered with freckles.

If Buckle hadn't known that Sabrina was beside him in that moment he would have sworn that he was looking at her now. "What the?" he gasped.

"She is Odessa, my twin sister," Sabrina whispered.

XXIII

THE VICAR

Octavian glared at the big man in the archway. "I shall host whomever I wish in my own house, Vicar. And how dare you be late!"

Marius stood from his seat, never taking his eyes off the Vicar.

The Vicar strode in with a smile and Odessa matched his every step. "Now, now, Octavian," the Vicar said. "This is no way to treat one's honored guests."

"You are not 'guests'," Lady Julia hissed low, but Buckle heard it.

Though he could not take his eyes off Odessa, Buckle did not like what he was hearing. Octavian and the Founders man, this Vicar, knew each other. The Founders had gotten there before them. Octavian might have already cut a deal with the Founders.

Odessa looked straight ahead, her gaze never wavering from Octavian. She cut a fine figure, buttoned up tight inside the stiff collar and silver buttons of her steampiper uniform with her crimson hair pulled tightly into a bun at the back of her head. In the angle of her jaw, the curve of her nose, she was in every way identical to Sabrina. Buckle realized Odessa was the steampiper he had fought aboard the *Pneumatic Zeppelin* during Balthazar's rescue. She was the woman who had jumped from the bowsprit in order to avoid capture. She was the woman who had been shot in the abdomen by Katzenjammer Smelt.

"Sit down, Vicar," Octavian said unpleasantly. "And you as well, Marius."

The Vicar stopped at the table, taking possession of the stage in a way that Buckle didn't like, so he stood up as well. "If you shan't provide the introductions, Octavian, I shall," the Vicar said, looking at Buckle and Sabrina.

"You shall address our leader as the First Consul," Cressida said.

"I am called the Vicar," the Vicar said without acknowledging Cressida, "Founders clan envoy and Gentleman of the Tar. With me is First Lieutenant Odessa Fawkes—though you seem to have picked one of her up for yourselves along the way." He narrowed his small brown eyes to Sabrina. "Yes, Sabrina, the lost sister. We have been looking for you."

Sabrina and Odessa stared at each other, neither betraying any emotion at all.

The Vicar—the name struck Buckle. The representative of the Founders at the Palisades conference where Balthazar had been kidnapped was said to be called the Vicar. The names. The Vicar. Odessa Fawkes. Fawkes. The leader of the Founders clan was Isambard Fawkes. Odessa was Sabrina's sister so that would make Sabrina a Fawkes as well. "Captain Romulus Buckle of the Crankshafts," Buckle said.

"Of course you are," the Vicar replied to Buckle with the look of the cat who had caught the edible dormouse. "And you have with you the lost daughter of Isambard Fawkes. Impressive. Hello, Sabrina."

Sabrina remained silent, bristling.

"What?" the Vicar grinned. "Do you not remember me, my dear? All those hours you spent riding on my shoulders, bouncing on my knee?"

"I left that life behind long ago," Sabrina said slowly.

The Vicar's face turned cold. "Shunning Fawkes royalty to become one of Balthazar's adopted pirate brats. What a shame."

"Watch your mouth," Buckle said.

The Vicar smiled with a sickly version of being pleasant. "Forgive me if I misspeak, Captain."

"Sit down!" Octavian bellowed, pulling Marius into his seat. "Damn you all—I will not have it! Sit down!"

"Oh, Octavian," The Vicar sighed. "You and your obsession with food. As you wish. Though I must say I am dearly famished." He took a seat on the bench opposite Buckle and Sabrina. Odessa sat beside him.

Buckle sat down and looked into his plate for a moment, at the naked, well-cooked dormouse and the still-jerking octopus tentacles, one of which had slithered onto the table and now, with its last ebb of life, curled around the base of his goblet. He watched the Vicar take a big bite out of a dormouse and, jaws working, swig from his goblet and make an approving nod to Octavian. The Atlanteans glared back at him.

Oh, how much Buckle missed having Elizabeth alongside him! She would be able to read the people and the circumstances so much better than he. It did feel like the maneuverings before a battle and he was familiar with that, but these were people and not warships and the layers of deception and intrigue were nigh impenetrable to his intuition, stonewalling him. The Vicar had strutted in like he owned the place. The Atlanteans, Octavian, Lady Julia, and the others stood defiant but they also cringed with fury and humiliation. Negotiations between them had been ongoing, perhaps for a considerable length of time. The Vicar had them by the short hairs. Somehow, he had them. The Atlanteans may not have surrendered to the Founders demands quite yet but they were afraid and it was coming. Elizabeth would have handled this properly — but Buckle was on his own. He had to get Octavian and Julia alone, quickly, in order to circumvent whatever devil's pact the Founders were about to force upon

Atlantis.

If the Founders hadn't forced it upon them already.

"It is very kind of you, Captain Buckle," the Vicar announced through his mouthful of dormouse, "to drop in and congratulate the Founders and Atlantean clans upon the completion of our brand new mutual protection agreement and trade alliance."

There it is, Buckle thought without responding. The devil's pact. More than one, even.

"We have agreed upon nothing," Octavian said flatly.

"Please," the Vicar replied in a kind but vaguely exasperated fashion, as a parent might gently chide a child, "delaying the inevitable does no one any good, Octavian. Especially you."

If there still existed a crack between Octavian and the Vicar, Buckle had to try to jump right into it. "It appears that we have arrived in time to throw our hat into the ring, to represent the interests of a great many other clans."

The Vicar smiled as he chewed. "You do not belong here, so very far away from your own sphere of influence, Captain. Why in the world would you think to stick your nose into the business of us here in the west?"

"Because we are at war," Buckle said.

"My dear Crankshaft captain, there is no war

here," the Vicar said. "We are all in neutral territory. There is no reason why we cannot be civil with one another." His practiced, perfect gentlemanliness could not entirely hide the wolf lurking beneath the skin.

"Why have you blockaded Atlantis?" Buckle asked.

"The blockade is only temporary, of course," the Vicar said. "Negotiating tactics, you see, to assure the safety of Founders shipping both above and below the waves until our mutual protection agreement can be put into effect."

"And that's why you're here," Buckle said.

The Vicar grinned. "Of course. "Which brings us to the question of why are you here."

"For purposes quite similar to yours, it appears," Buckle replied.

"Really?" the Vicar shot back, and Buckle sensed the threat under his words. "Yet you are so very far from home, Captain."

"Enough!" Octavian shouted, stabbing angrily at an octopus tentacle with his fork, the tines clinking loudly on his plate. "You act as if Atlantis is a carcass you can fight over. Well, we are not. We belong to the sea and want nothing to do with you surface clans."

"The entire Snow World is at war," Buckle said. "It affects us all."

Octavian snorted. "Not Atlantis. Not *under* the sea. As for you, Vicar, there are and shall be no agreements. You attempt to apply your typically overaggressive diplomacy when you know that my clan responds poorly to threats of force. Enjoy your meal and after that you may take your requests and go."

Buckle liked that, liked Octavian bucking the Vicar, but he didn't know how much of it was some kind of face-saving show.

The room fell silent, the atmosphere heavy under the glare the Vicar now foisted upon the First Consul. "Go?" the Vicar asked as if he were uttering a curse. "Why, my dear Octavian, you suddenly sing a very different tune now that the Crankshafts have arrived. A very dangerous tune."

"Dangerous for you," Marius said quietly, straight at the Vicar.

The Vicar looked at Buckle, then to Octavian. "If you send me away now. If you refuse to join our mutual protection agreement and send me home empty-handed, then you shall leave the Founders Parliament with no choice but to act in its own defense. If you are not a friend in this time of conflict then you are an enemy. If you refuse us we shall unleash our sharks and Atlantis shall not survive our wrath. Think well upon what you say next, Octavian, for the fate of your clan hangs in the balance."

"You shall address him as the First Consul," Cressida blurted, her voice shaking.

The First Consul swallowed hard, a jerky, nervous working of his throat, and Buckle knew the man was afraid.

The Atlanteans were already beaten. Buckle had arrived too late. He wouldn't get a chance to win them over. The Atlanteans were going to fold, to submit under the Founders' pressure, and Buckle and the Crankshafts and all that his clan knew could well be doomed.

Octavian snapped his head around. "Where is the goddamned food!"

XXIV

THE ORPHANMAKER IS A FINE DISH

The kitchen doors burst open with Philo in the lead, followed by four servants hauling a huge silver tray. The tray was leveraged onto the table and Buckle raised an eyebrow as he scrutinized its offering; a gigantic fish-beast, sturgeon-like except for the eyeless, tubular head, perhaps six feet long from the tip of its bulbous nose to the end of its shovel-shaped tail. The fish looked like it had been boiled but now it was cold and the scent of it was bitter with vinegar with salt. Scales nestled along the body in tight rows, each one a slightly different shade of silvery gray with shimmering rainbows in its reflection. The mouth, a long barracuda-dinosaur trap with overlapping rows of teeth, was propped open and stuffed with purple-green sea fruit that looked like the cross between an apple and a cabbage.

Octavian stood up, looking newly confident, as if his bombast was refueled by the arrival of the elaborate dish. "The orphanmaker—some call it a jawfish—is a rare delicacy here in Atlantis. The flesh is delightful but poisonous unless cooked and served properly and I have had one prepared just for you on this occasion, my distinguished guests. The animal is warm-blooded, an alien transplant, courtesy of the Martians, and it does quite well for itself in our oceans."

"It is a most beautiful creature," the Vicar said. Buckle couldn't tell if the man was being sarcastic or not.

Octavian laughed. "A beautiful creature, eh? Don't let her looks deceive you, ladies and gentlemen, this beastie is a killer." He tapped a silver serving spoon on the serrated teeth and they made a musical sound, something like a child's xylophone. "Hollow. You can hear them coming sometimes, if they gnash these hollow teeth. But they still manage to kill our sea farmers with unfortunate regularity—we lose perhaps four dozen citizens to these beasties every year, far more than we lose to sharks, picked off in the seagrass fields—the creature scissors them in half in one bite, usually. That is why we call it the orphanmaker."

"They eat you so you eat them," the Vicar said with a grin and gulped his wine.

Octavian nodded. "Yes. Such is the way of the underwater world. Eat or be eaten. Destroy or be destroyed. There is no such thing as prisoners."

Buckle looked at Sabrina, who stared uncertainly

at the beastie. Crankshafts were an inland clan; they lived on meat and greenhouse vegetables. Fish could be traded for and it wasn't unusual to find common seafood of one sort or another popping up in one of the Punchbowl market stalls, but exotic undersea creatures were unusual and people rarely developed a taste for them.

"It's moving," Sabrina whispered.

Buckle peered at the orphanmaker. Its flanks rippled back and forth, faintly, the flesh beneath shivering the rainbow prisms on the scales. Something was moving around inside the orphanmaker, indeed.

"Food should be dead when you eat it," Buckle muttered.

"Aye," Sabrina whispered, stabbing a crawling tentacle appetizer with her fork.

"I rather like it," the Vicar said. "It is a food with possibilities."

Two more servants entered, carrying small red clay jugs which they uncapped and set at equidistant points along the table. Buckle caught a whiff of the contents of his jug—a horrible reek of rotten fish—and gagged.

"Ah, the garum sauce is here!" Octavian announced, taking a deep, appreciative sniff from one of the jugs. He clapped his hands and accepted a large bladed knife from Philo. "I suggest that you slather your meal with it—it sweetens it up."

The chamber went silent as Octavian plunged the knife into the side of the orphanmaker. The intrusion increased the swarming activity of whatever was moving around inside of it. The wet, rasping slither of the knife sawing through the orphanmaker's thick scales made Buckle oddly queasy and he took a big swallow of wine.

The pink flesh of the orphanmaker split open under Octavian's knife and the dark red gash was immediately filled with what looked like a hundred shaking red worms. Tubular red bodies spilled forth, legs scrambling, antennae jerking, claws slicing. The orphanmaker was stuffed with lobsters.

Philo moved quickly around the table, placing a small but heavy pewter mallet beside each plate. Marius stepped away from the table at this point but Octavian did not seem to care.

"Never, never shall you ever eat something as fine as these lobsters," Octavian enthused. "You see, once the orphanmaker is cooked we stuff it with live lobsters, who gorge themselves on the flesh all night long. The lobsters are immune to the poison, you see, the acids in their bodies absorb it and render it benign. But the orphanmaker's chemistry cooks the lobsters alive — it cooks the meat without killing them. Isn't that astounding? Then you can eat the lobster, you see, which, after stuffing itself all night with orphanmaker, marinates its own flesh and takes on the same exquisite taste as the beastie. Break one open and feast—I dare say you shall never taste anything quite like it, or more enjoyable."

"I appreciate the expense of serving such delicacies," the Vicar said, looking at the lobsters as if he had already tired of them. "But now that the show is over I would suggest we return to the matter at hand, Octavian."

"Ah, but the show is far from over, my dear Vicar," Octavian said, grabbing his mallet and bringing it down upon an advancing lobster with a loud, shell-busting crack. "The show is far from over."

XXV

TITUS AND BELARIUS

The table surface crawled with dozens of red lobsters with rough armor jackets, snapping claws and scrabbling legs, though the creatures were in poor condition from their alien juice cooking, staggering and blind. Philo and servants dashed about, collecting the lobsters, expertly binding their claws and legs with quick twists of green seaweed shoots and delivering them, one after another, into jerking piles on everyone's plates.

"Eat, my guests, eat!" Octavian enthused, ripping a large claw off his lobster and cracking it open to expose the light pink meat inside.

"I'd like an assurance from you," the Vicar said, his demeanor noticeably darker than it had been the moment before, "that the Atlanteans have made a commitment to their pact with the Founders clan."

Buckle looked at Odessa; she hadn't touched any of her food but rather kept her cool green eyes on Sabrina, who stared right back.

"All possibilities are still on the table," Octavian

said, full of his own momentum, high in the catbird seat. "So many possibilities and potential outcomes."

"That was not what you told me before," the Vicar replied, his voice shifting low and quiet, menacing.

Buckle heard a number of boots approaching, leather soles padding softly across carpet from the opposite archway, and fought the urge to jump to his feet. An Atlantean officer marched into the room, a tall man with a rectangular face dressed in high-ranking Roman armor similar to that of Marius except his robe and helmet brush were purple instead of red. Behind the tall officer walked two older men, both wearing white togas with purple trim, both looking indignant and frightened. Two purple-robed soldiers loomed at their backs.

"Ah! Now the guests are all here, finally," Octavian announced. "And the scene can be set."

"Apologies, First Consul," the tall officer said. "The senators would not come willingly. They had to be arrested."

"That is most unfortunate, Horatus," Octavian replied. "Senators should be loyal, don't you think?"

"What is the meaning of this, Octavian?" the older of the two senators, a man with a shock of white hair and a pugilist's nose, roared with a powerful voice made for the pulpit. "This is an outrage!" Buckle saw his eyes widen when he noticed the Vicar.

Octavian tossed aside his lobster claw and clapped his hands together. "Captain Buckle, may I introduce to all of you the leader of the official opposition in the senate, my good enemy Titus Septillus, and his boot-lapping lackey Belarius."

"Does loyalty to one's own ideals warrant such name-calling, First Consul?" Belarius asked pleasantly. He was a well-built man with a handsome face and he held himself with far more grace than Titus.

"I ask again, Octavian. What is the meaning of this?" Titus repeated.

"You always wish to be included in important matters of state, my dear Titus," Octavian said. He was relishing the moment, Buckle realized. "And so here we are. This is the Vicar, envoy of the Founders. But wait, I do believe that you and the Vicar have met before, have you not?"

"I haven't had the pleasure, no," Titus replied smoothly.

"I've never seen this senator before," the Vicar said. "Be careful with what games you choose to play, Octavian."

"Games?" Octavian said. "I am too old for games. Ah, I am mistaken then. Wouldn't be the first time." He laughed. It was a smug, dark, self-satisfied sound. "Everyone please sit and indulge in the orphanmaker. More food is coming, far too much of it. The vomitorium is down the hall should any of you feel the need to overindulge."

Philo pulled out an empty bench but Titus and Belarius did not move, staring at it with trepidation. "With all due respect, First Consul," Titus said. "I want to know why we have been brought here."

Octavian swung his mallet down atop another lobster, resulting in another crack of carapace, a splatter of blue-black liquid and the sickly wet smack of crushed flesh. "Sit down, Senator. I have invited you, Titus, not for your brilliant etiquette and table manners, but because we have a problem."

"Surely any problem the First Consul may have should be brought to the floor of the Senate and not here, in his private chamber filled with Praetorian knives." Titus replied.

"At least my Praetorian's blades are clean," Octavian said, "and not stained with the blood of men's backs like those of the filthy Capitolines. But then, you are well familiar with the Capitoline house, are you not, Titus?"

"I shall not stand here and be insulted," Titus answered evenly.

"Then sit," Octavian replied.

"If you plan to accuse me of something, I would prefer you do it now," Titus said.

"Why doesn't anyone wish to sit down and eat today?" Octavian blurted with exasperation. "Very well, Titus, though I was hoping you might have an opportunity to enjoy the orphanmaker first." Octavian nodded to Marius.

Marius pulled a piece of folded parchment from his pocket and approached Titus, shoving the paper into his hand. Titus stared at the paper like it was his own death warrant.

"I believe that belongs to you, Titus," Octavian announced, chewing, working on his lobster.

"I do not know what this is," Titus said.

"Read it," Octavian pressed. "Read it out loud."

Titus didn't move.

"If Titus is unwilling to read it I can elaborate," Octavian announced. "It is a secret transmission, intercepted by my faithful Guardians who managed to catch and kill the messenger porpoise in transit last night. The recipient was to be a notable Atlantean, a member of the Capitoline House, a criminal I know well: one Lavinia Pompey, who has since her birth, along with her wretched family, been plotting to overthrow our Aventine House and usurp the power of Atlantis for herself. The sender, well, the letter marks the signature and signet wax of our very own Titus Septillus." Octavian pointed at Titus, whose face reddened with fury. "Do you deny that this letter is yours? Do you deny that this be your own handwriting and your own senatorial seal?"

"This is criminal," Titus hissed.

"Would you like to read the letter out loud, my

dear Titus?" Octavian asked. "Or would you prefer Marius do you the honor?"

Titus yanked the parchment open, reading: "Lavinia Pompey, let it be known among the House of Capitoline that the time has arrived for us to act. Soon the Founders shall take the Aventine dome by whatever means necessary. We shall do our utmost to assist them in this action and we shall reap the rewards predetermined. Titus."

"Do you deny that you are the author of this message, Senator?" Octavian asked, dropping the scooped-out claw of his lobster on the table with a splattering thump.

"I have the right to defend myself from this false accusation," Titus roared, but he was trembling. "I have the right to defend myself on the floor of the senate and in front of my peers!"

"Defend yourself, hah!" Octavian snapped. "This is indisputable evidence of a conspiracy hatched between yourself, the Capitolines, and the Founders."

Buckle glanced at the Vicar, who did not look the least bit perturbed by the goings-on.

"This paper is not mine," Titus replied. "The message is not mine. You prove your own unworthiness, Octavian, in the attempt to disgrace me in such an obvious manner. I am loyal to the office of the First Consul. I am loyal to Atlantis."

"As am I," Belarius added.

"And this is not your seal, Titus?" Octavian asked, pointing to the wax mark on the parchment.

Titus shook his head. "No, it is not. It's a forgery."

Octavian glared at Titus. "Bring the next course!" Octavian shouted.

XXVI

THE KETTLECRAB IS A TERRIBLE DISH

Philo and three other servants took hold of the dining table and hauled it away with one practiced heave. Marius retrieved his helmet from the table as they passed. The remains of the eviscerated orphanfish and its surrounding stacks of lobsters vanished through the wide kitchen doorway, the creaking of the doors the only sound in the room afterwards. Buckle glanced at the Vicar and Odessa — it was odd to no longer have the broad table between them, now replaced by open space.

The Vicar stood from his bench, Odessa immediately standing with him. "Perhaps we Founders should take our leave. I have no desire to witness petty internal squabbles."

"Sit down!" Octavian shouted.

The Vicar and Sabrina remained standing.

"Sit down," Octavian repeated, this time with less volume but more poison.

"I do not take orders from you, First Consul,"

the Vicar replied.

"You shall obey me as you sup at my table and find yourself implicated in a conspiracy against me and my house," Octavian growled. "This is far from over, negotiator."

The Vicar seemed to grow larger, more ominous. "I assure you, First Consul, that the Founders need not connive in shadows with pipsqueaks in order to make House Aventine do our bidding." He motioned toward the windows. "Have you not seen our mighty submersible fleet? If we wish we would crack your domes open like rotten eggs and be done with it."

"If you think I would believe one word spilling from your silver-tongued mouth you sorely underestimate my intelligence, Vicar," Octavian said.

Odessa grabbed the hilt of her sword but a wave of the Vicar's big hand stilled her. "If you wish to make these negotiations unpleasant, Octavian," the Vicar said with measured cool, "things will go badly only for you."

Marius leaned into Octavian's ear but Buckle heard his whispers; "Be careful, First Consul, of whom you openly impugn," Marius said.

Octavian, his jaw working, glared at the Vicar.

The kitchen doors banged open as Philo and the three servants, all wearing ornate silver face masks and black rubber gloves pulled up to the elbows, carried another big table—this one with a fine white tablecloth—into the room. As the table was inserted into the midst of the benches Buckle saw it was empty except for a large black cauldron, boiling hot from the fire, resting on an ornate copper trivet, its contents hidden under a heavy cast iron lid.

Buckle placed his hands on the table and he suddenly felt an odd, almost buzzing sensation. His fingertips tingled and the hair on his arms stood on end.

Titus gasped.

"The kettlecrab," Belarius whispered, his voice shaking. "The kettlecrab."

"Yes, the kettlecrab," Octavian announced. "The traitor's favorite dish."

"This, this is assassination," Titus mumbled, as if he could not believe what was happening. "The Assembly shall not stand for this, this infamy and coercion."

Octavian nodded to Marius, who lifted the lid of the cauldron. Inside, a blood-red soup bubbled and steamed. Buckle saw things swirling within it— slithering, snake-like things. A head popped up from the greasy liquid—a cobra-like, dark blue-green head with slit red eyes atop four antennae shoots and a circular, sucking mouth festooned with hundreds of tiny white teeth.

Sabrina gasped.

Octavian laughed. "One should fear the

kettlecrab, my dear. Actually they are delicious to eat but they have to be dead. They're a crossbreed of electric eel and an alien snake-crab called a pontu. They're boiled but boiling does not hurt them, you see—the boiling is to get them agitated and mean—one must lop their head off in order to kill them, much as one must do with traitors. I have heard of a number of Atlanteans who, drunk at parties, forgot to decapitate a beastie before forking it from the bowl and, sadly, lost an eye or tongue when the creature was lifted to the face for eating."

"Quite the entertaining meal," the Vicar said coldly.

Octavian turned to Titus. "I give you one more opportunity, Senator, to confess your crimes against Atlantis and my ruling house. Do so and I can promise you that your family shall be spared after your death."

"Death?" Belarius shot back. "It is you who has betrayed us. This is an outrage!"

"Save your words, Belarius," Titus said. "The First Consul has baited us into his trap. He has already decided our fate."

"Confess!" Octavian roared.

Titus raised his chin. "You cannot do this. I am a senator! You sent your Praetorians to arrest us over our lunches, threaten our spouses and frighten our children. You are no republican. I call you Rex. I call you tyrant."

Octavian nodded to Horatus, who wrenched Titus' hands behind his back, tying them with a long strip of leather he had at the ready.

"Confess, and do it quickly, Titus," Octavian said.

"I am innocent of all charges," Titus replied, his eyes darting around. "You cannot condemn me without trial. I can only be sentenced to death through a verdict of the senate."

"Confess," Octavian continued. "It won't take the kettlecrab long to realize you're on the menu."

"Damn you to hell, King Octavian," Titus spit back.

Octavian nodded to Horatus again. Horatus shoved Titus to the edge of the table and forced his head down until his face was within a few inches of the swirling orange-red soup in the cauldron.

"I am innocent!" Titus howled.

"Innocent?" Octavian laughed. "An innocent senator? You would be the very first, then."

"Stop this, First Consul!" Belarius shouted, lunging forward. "You know the senate shall not stand for it!"

The Praetorian yanked Belarius back, belting him in the midriff with the butt of his sword handle. Belarius crumpled to his knees, retching.

"Titus!" Octavian exulted. "I await a confession!"

Buckle rose to his feet, backing up from the table. Sabrina was at his side. They both had their hands on their swords.

Titus, blinking against the hot steam, howled as he fought to shake free of Horatus' grasp. His struggles only caused him to dunk his face in the soup. The orange liquid roiled as the creatures under the surface grew more and more agitated. Titus froze, his nose dripping.

"You only have a few seconds, Titus," Octavian announced.

Titus strained, his neck muscles almost bursting out of his skin. "Go to Hades!"

Blue flashes erupted inside the cauldron, some of them striking Titus in a way that made both him and Horatus jerk. A green-black head slashed up out of the soup, followed by a long exoskeleton lined with hundreds of small, webbed fin-legs in the manner of a centipede. It bit and vanished. Blood poured from a ragged hole in Titus' left cheek. Titus screamed.

"Missed the eyes," Marius growled. "Lucky."

The blood gushing into the soup sent the kettlecrabs into a frenzy of coiling black spines whirling in the orange whirlpool.

"Better you talk quickly, dear Titus," Octavian said. "They have tasted blood now."

"Vicar! Help me!" Titus howled.

The Vicar raised his hands. "I do not know you,

sir."

"Tell them to release me or die!" Titus shrieked, though his words were slobbered by the hole in his cheek. "Tell Octavian the Founders are coming to crack Atlantis open unless they submit! Tell them House Capitoline is with us! Now! Damn you, now!"

The Vicar tossed an easy smile at Octavian. "Your man has lost his mind from terror, First Consul."

"Let him up," Octavian ordered.

Horatus, maintaining his grip on the back of Titus' neck, slowly lifted the man into an upright position. Titus gasped, his white hair sticking up in all directions, eyes half-rolling in his head, black burn marks on his forehead, ripped red muscles and bloody teeth visible through the gaping hole in his cheek.

"The senate will not stand for this!" Belarius growled, having recovered from his blow and returned to his feet

Marius shoved Belarius against the wall "Speak again and you may also kiss the kettle." Belarius swallowed and looked at the floor.

"The senate will accept what I must do to defend it!" Octavian said. "Do you, Vicar, still claim the confession of the traitor Titus to be a lie? He has implicated you in every word."

"Lies," the Vicar replied. "Every word. Every syllable."

"Mercy," Titus mumbled. "Mercy."

"There is no mercy for traitors in Atlantis," Octavian snarled, nodding to Horatus. "And you are a traitor, Titus. You are a traitor to your house, to me, to the senate, to all that your life has stood for."

Horatus took one step back from Titus, holding him at arm's length as he drew his short sword and, in one fluid, powerful motion, drove the blade into Titus' back with enough force to make the tip of the blade erupt out of his chest.

Belarius gasped and covered his eyes, but no one else moved.

Titus looked down upon the bloody steel protruding from his torso. "Damn you, Octavian," he gurgled.

"Let him swim in the soup," Octavian commanded Horatus. "And I shall feed the broth to his children before I slit their stomachs and take it back."

Horatus slammed Titus' face on the table, stepped back and chopped the Senator's head off with his sword.

Blood sprayed across the fine white tablecloth in front of the Vicar. "Well, that ruined my appetite," he sighed.

As the quivering body of Titus slid to the floor, Horatus dropped his severed head into the kettle. The alien-eels went wild, sending up dozens of blue electric arcs as they swirled, rotating the head like some ghastly planet in the midst of a turbulent orange galaxy. It only took a few seconds before the kettlecrabs wrapped the head, slithering and wriggling as they gorged themselves, plunging into the eye sockets, mouth and ears and out again.

Octavian turned to Belarius and placed his hands on his hips. "And now what must I do with you, lackey?"

The Praetorians released Belarius and he raised his chin, defiant. "I shall not beg you for mercy."

"Let it be known that Octavian and the Aventine House do not suffer conspirators gladly," Octavian said. "You shall not die this day, Belarius, for you shall be my winged raven, my whispering snake. Though we have arrested some of your cabal I am certain there are many more of your fellow rats in the senate, rats who conspire with the usurper Capitolines, rats who have sent secret messages to the Founders. Run to them now. Tell them of what you witnessed here. Tell them that in this time of war they must prove themselves either friends or enemies upon the floor of the senate. Tell them the First Consul has eyes and ears among them. I know of their every collusion, every transgression. Tell them they have one chance to save themselves and the lives of their spouses and children, and that is to recant, to confess and throw themselves upon my mercy. If they do, I shall spare them. If they do not, then the senate floor will run with their blood and the kettlecrabs shall be busy. Now, go!"

Belarius held his ground though his obvious wish was to run. A loose lobster dragged itself across the floor, skittering in what looked like death throes. Something inside of it burst and it collapsed, its claws clicking as a blue-black pool widened underneath it on the carpet.

"I will tell them," Belarius said. He turned and strode out of the room, his sandals clicking away down the corridor.

Octavian spun to the Vicar. "And you, you and your submersible may take your leave as well, Vicar."

The Vicar looked Octavian up and down as a butcher might inspect a slab of meat. "Very well. May I inform Isambard Hawkes that the great clan of Atlantis has elected to join our pact of mutual protection?"

Octavian appeared as if he was about to scream but controlled the urge, though his voice rattled with anger. "I have the evidence of your conspiracy, Titus. I have taken it apart piece by piece." He pointed at the head of Titus rolling in the soup cauldron, now more white skull than anything else. "You have been unmasked by the confession from the very lips of Titus Septillus himself."

"A man will say anything while he is being tortured," the Vicar said evenly.

"Tomorrow the conspirators shall be purged from the senate in a river of blood," Octavian answered. "You underestimate me, fogsucker. I hold power here by knowing more than men think I know. And I know far more about your machinations than you could imagine I might."

"I would be careful if I were you, First Consul," the Vicar responded.

"A thousand earth-eels might swarm an oyster, Ambassador, but never crack it, never win the pearl and find their ruin in the attempt," Octavian said before flinging his arm out and pointing to the archway where the Vicar and Odessa had entered. "Now, get back on your boat and go tell Isambard Fawkes that his assault upon Atlantis from within has failed, and to attack us from without is suicide."

"I thought we'd already come to an understanding but, very well," the Vicar suddenly grinned. "Thank you for a lovely meal. And I shall say this: you Atlanteans are most surely not lacking in dinner entertainments. And to you, dear Sabrina, it is wonderful to see you again. Are you certain that you do not wish to come home with us?"

Sabrina said nothing.

"Very well, then," the Vicar nodded to Sabrina and exited with Odessa at his side, never looking back.

XXVII

CONFINED TO QUARTERS

"How did it go, Captain?" Welly asked, waiting at the hatchway as Buckle and Sabrina, escorted by two grim-faced Atlantean guards, entered the undersea quarters which Lady Julia had assigned to them.

"A little bloodier than I expected," Buckle replied, surprised at the luxurious comportments of the chamber as he entered, unclipping his sword sheath from his belt. If this was a prison it was also an undeniably beautiful cabin: luminiferous aether tubes glowed warmly upon furniture and grand fixtures fashioned like sea creatures out of copper and brass. A circular window portal dominated the far wall, the convex glass providing a breathtaking view of the ocean. The false Roman ruins haunted the distant sea bed, lit by the last effects of evening light and passed over occasionally by the yellow-portaled silhouettes of the big Founders boats patrolling the perimeter.

Penny Dreadful stood at the window, turning its gaze from the sea to look at Buckle. Its look was contemplative, in appearance at least, for an

241

automaton. And it still wore the manacles.

"Did the Atlanteans join us?" Welly asked, looking confused.

"No," Buckle said.

"They're too busy killing each other," Sabrina said. "Atlantis is rife with internal unrest and conspiracy, it appears, and that will make them easy prey for the Founders. Lambs to the slaughter, I say."

Welly nodded though he obviously did not quite understand. "Did you eat? They have yet to deliver any food at all here and I am famished."

"From the way they seem to adore their food I'm sure something is forthcoming." Buckle said.

"A word of advice, Welly," Sabrina said. "Avoid the soup."

"You are speaking in riddles, Lieutenant," Welly replied.

"Starvation is certainly preferable to consuming the highlights of the Atlantean menu," Sabrina continued, grinning.

"It's that bad?" Welly asked.

"Not if you like your food still moving," Sabrina sighed.

"Is that what you mean by things were 'bloody'? Welly asked.

"A hoard of brutal buggers," Sabrina said. "They're no better than the Founders. I'd be loath to ally us to them."

"They would be dangerous friends, aye," Buckle added. He was glad to have Welly and Penny back in his field of vision—he had become profoundly concerned for their wellbeing once he had seen Atlantean diplomacy in action.

"The Atlanteans have provided a second chamber for Lieutenant Serafim, just across the hall," Welly said.

Buckle shook his head. "They mentioned that." He didn't like the idea of his command being separated in the night, not with conspirators loose in Atlantis. "I think we should all sleep in here tonight."

"I agree," Sabrina said.

"They did bring us tea," Welly said, offering the elaborate teapot. "Anyone for a cup? Captain? Chief Navigator?"

"I'll gladly take one as long as there isn't a skull floating in it," Sabrina said, taking a seat at the table and crossing her legs.

"A skull?" Welly asked as he poured the tea.

"Don't ask," Sabrina replied.

"Captain?" Welly inquired again, the teapot spout poised over a second cup.

"Certainly, and thanks," Buckle said.

Welly poured the tea and handed it to Buckle.

"You sit, Welly," Buckle said.

"But there are only two chairs, sir," Welly replied.

"I am in the mood for standing," Buckle said. "Take advantage."

"Yes, sir." Welly took a seat beside Sabrina as he poured himself the third cup. "Thank you, sir."

Buckle nursed the strange Atlantean tea which, after a lip-stinging first sip, he strongly suspected was brewed from seaweed.

"So we are staying the night, Captain?" Welly asked. "Does that mean the Atlanteans are still considering our offer?"

Buckle stirred his tea. "No. They gave us our walking papers, I'm afraid. We are confined here only as long as it takes them to salvage and repair the *Dart*. After that we shall be sent on our way."

Welly nodded. They fell into a comfortable silence, looking out into the ancient depths. It seemed a shame to speak and break such a pleasant interlude, especially after all the awfulness they had been through in the morning. Buckle smelled ambergris, the lingering effect of a cold incense burner on the table.

"May I say, Lieutenant," Welly offered tentatively, though in a fashion which hinted he could not stop himself from speaking. "That you do look particularly lovely in the aetherlight." Welly lifted his teacup to his mouth and it lingered there, as if he was trying to hide as much of himself behind it as he possibly could.

Sabrina shot Welly a glare that would have

made a centaur shiver.

Buckle felt like laughing but held his tongue. The enamored Welly always confounded Sabrina despite her superior rank — and absolute rejection — and he still managed, undeterred, to ball-up the occasional compliment.

"The Ensign does make a point," Buckle said. "You do look lovely."

"The next man to compliment me, I'll spill his intestines on this table," Sabrina grumbled.

"Reading from the Atlantean book of etiquette, are we?" Buckle mused.

"How about a little bit of silence?" Sabrina asked. "I could use some of that, especially from the junior officer at the table."

"Grand idea," Buckle said. He strolled to the window and stood alongside Penny Dreadful. Penny's eyes glowed with a softness Buckle always noticed before it shut down at nighttime. In the quiet, Buckle heard the tiny rumble of the steam engine inside its torso. It was an incredible feat of engineering, even measured by its brain alone. Buckle wondered what malfunctions had caused the Atlanteans to destroy their own automatons and if it had anything to do with the robot's considerable killing ability, a talent he had witnessed in full display in the battle against the Guardians.

Buckle had to admit — he did worry about the

robot. But Penny had acted to save his life when they fought the gagool. It would appear that his death was not an item on its mechanical agenda. Damn it — the little robot was the least of his worries. Instead of rushing home after the Muscovy sky battle and joining his clan at the outbreak of war he had spent the better part of a week searching for Atlantis. Now he had left the *Pneumatic Zeppelin* hovering in the sea fogs northeast of Vera Cruz while thrusting himself and two of his officers into the safekeeping of the mysterious and apparently bloodthirsty Atlanteans in the midst of a Founders blockade.

Yet his search for Elizabeth was everything. She was alone. He was her only chance and here, somehow, deep in the ocean he knew she was close. All of his life he had known when she was close. The old moonchild named Shadrack had been right when he said that Elizabeth would be in Atlantis. So was the First Consul lying about her presence here? But why would they do that? It was unsettling, to say the least, to find the Founders already in the wings and applying pressure. The Vicar was bad company.

And now there was Odessa.

Buckle trusted Sabrina Serafim. Dark pasts were common in the Snow World and she had hers and she was the one who had to deal with it. The appearance of Odessa had visibly shaken her but she had said not a word about it.

Buckle gazed up at the surface of the sea. Somewhere out there the *Pneumatic Zeppelin* lurked, waiting for the passage of night and the arrival of the morning sea mists to steam to the first rendezvous point. If Buckle and his officers never made it home, Ivan and Valkyrie would become the new commanders of the *Pneumatic Zeppelin*, at least until Max returned. Promotion in the Snow World was often of the quick variety, through senior ranks killed in action or disappearing on missions, never to return.

There were many of those zeppelineers, the disappeared.

Buckle knew that he wasn't going to get any sleep that night. He figured the others wouldn't get much either.

"If I may speak now," Welly said, "I would very much like to know what happened in your meeting with the Atlanteans."

"Oh, bother," Sabrina replied. "It's a fine mess, Welly. It seems there are many conspiracies afoot, and, well, and the Founders have envoys here — they beat us to it, I think — oh, and a senator's head was severed and consumed by eel-beasties in a kettle."

Welly's eyes widened.

"Kettlecrab?" Penny asked softly.

"Yes," Buckle said.

"Most unpleasant," Penny said. "What was the name of the senator?"

"Titus," Buckle said. "Titus Septillus, if memory serves."

"Septillus," Penny repeated. "The family Septillus was a grand and powerful gens when I was last here."

"Gens?" Buckle asked.

"A chain of families connected by daughters, referred to as a 'house'," Penny Dreadful replied. "All the patrician families in Aventine Atlantis are descended from the head of the first family, that being the rogue Founders inventress, Cassandra Lombard. Such matters of bloodline and lineage are all important to the Atlanteans."

Buckle felt as if he could sense sadness emanating from Penny, but that would be impossible for a machine. "Penny, tell me about Atlantis if you don't mind," he asked.

"I shall try, though it seems many things have changed since I was last here," Penny replied. "When I knew this place it was a tight alliance of seven separate houses in seven separate domes. This one, the Aventinus dome, appears to still be the main seat of government for the coalition, containing the primary senate and the dwelling of the First Consul, who is always Aventine. The Palantine and Capitolium are also large and powerful houses while the remaining four, Caelius, Esquilinus, Quirnalis and Viminalis are much smaller and possess lesser degrees of influence, though the Esquiline submarine force was once unmatched."

Buckle nodded. "From what I saw, it seems the First Consul is facing a rebellion from the Capitolines who may have allied themselves secretly to the Founders, but it is difficult to tell how realistic Octavian is being about everything."

"There is no doubt in my mind," Sabrina added, "that the First Consul is beset by paranoid delusions, or is at least being debased by them."

"The Atlantis I once knew was the realm of great statesmen and citizen merchants, of rigorous debates and open votes on the senate floor," Penny Dreadful whispered, gazing out of the sea.

"Well," Buckle replied, "it appears that things have changed."

XXVII

FAR FROM HOME

Romulus Buckle found himself once again at the sea window, watching the twilit ocean creep from the last shades of purple-blue into darkness. Everything shifted in form, changed in color. Bubbles streamed up from below, rattling as they leapfrogged up the surface of the window glass. Twice Buckle had heard the distant churn of propellers from the patrolling Founders submarines, now obscured by the depths and their descending shadows.

The guest quarters were quiet and dark, the aether lights reduced to a bare glimmer for nighttime. Welly lay sound asleep on the divan. Penny Dreadful stood near him, eyes glimmering gold, her boiler metals pinging occasionally as they cooled, shutting down for the night.

At least they had been properly fed. The Atlanteans had brought food earlier in the evening, something that looked, smelled, and tasted like peppered lamb. Buckle, Sabrina and Welly had eaten ravenously without worrying about what the meat might actually be.

Sabrina arrived alongside Buckle and looked out at the ocean with him.

"We are far from home," Sabrina whispered.

"And in a viper's nest," Buckle replied.

"What troubles you so sorely, Romulus?" Sabrina asked.

"I could ask you the same thing."

"I asked first."

Buckle smiled. "Many things."

Sabrina crossed her arms. "I am impressed that you have been able to contain yourself from inquiring about my sister."

Buckle nodded. "Your old family is your business, just as it is with every one of Balthazar's orphans."

"It is lovely to be trusted so implicitly," Sabrina said.

"I can stand beside you in no other way, sister," Buckle replied. He gazed at Sabrina. Ready for bed, her hair was down though not brushed, hanging in a cascade of half-curled crimson locks. Buckle rarely saw Sabrina's hair loose and he was surprised at how long it was, nearly halfway down her back. He had never seen anyone with hair as vibrantly red as Sabrina's except for her mysterious sister.

"Ask a question if you'd like," Sabrina said. "About Odessa."

"How long has it been since you saw her?"

"Twelve years, in all," Sabrina said, "or very near to it."

"She is a Fawkes?"

"Yes."

"And you are a Fawkes," Buckle said. A Fawkes. Somewhere in a corner of his being that knowledge rattled him.

"We are nieces of Isambard Fawkes, the children of his older brother. But blood means everything and nothing to Isambard. He murdered our mother and father and perhaps many of our relatives—I don't know much of what happened and who died, really — in the great purge. I was carried out of the city by a family servant, a tutor who had once been a soldier, a man named Marter, but my sister did not escape. She has done well since, apparently, judging from the lace on her sleeve."

"I saw her, once," Buckle said. "She was among the steampipers who attacked us over the city of the Founders when we rescued Balthazar."

Sabrina nodded. "She was always more capable than I—at least, in my memories of her. She was more serious." She smiled a little, forcing a light rush of air out of her nose in the way a vaguely self-amused person did.

"You were raised inside the city, then," Buckle asked.

"Until the night of the purge, yes. I left when I was seven years old."

"And you left via the route we used to enter the city when we rescued Balthazar."

"Yes," Sabrina replied. "Marter had gas masks. I don't remember it well at all."

"If I may ask, where did you and Marter go after your escape?"

"Up the north coast," Sabrina said. "Refugio. Marter was killed when the Founders eventually hunted us down. I became a vagabond after Marter's death, at least until Balthazar adopted me and gave me a new home and a new family." She turned to Buckle and looked at him, her green eyes reflecting the glint of aether light on the window. "You are my family, now, Romulus. The Crankshafts are my family, my clan, to the death. You need not worry."

"I'm not worried," Buckle said quickly. "I'm not."

Sabrina returned her gaze to the window and took a sip of her tea. "Vile stuff," she muttered. "This would be an idyllic view, restful, if not for the sharks."

"I fear the Founders are applying far more pressure than the Atlanteans would care to admit," Buckle said. "And if the Atlanteans are forced to fall into line with the Founders they will control the eastern sea and all of the trade which comes with it."

"The Atlanteans are arrogant, far too proud, and

they have descended into internecine viciousness," Sabrina said slowly. "They long have had many trade deals with the Founders, and even as a child I saw many precious items which came from them: sea grass, fish delicacies, pearls. But we were always aware of their arrogance. And it was a sticking point for the Founders that they would never give up their secret of the luminiferous aether."

"Does it provide power as well as light?"

"It is electricity, Romulus," Sabrina answered, blowing on her tea. "Somehow the liquid allows the Atlanteans to generate and harness electricity, at least under the sea."

"Electricity," Buckle repeated softly.   That magical word. Electricity. "It would go badly for us if the Atlanteans ally themselves with the Founders."

"I had always believed that Atlantis was one of the few clans strong enough to resist Founders aggression," Sabrina said. "But now they are frightened, on their heels. Whatever the Vicar is coercing them with I think it is working."

"I agree," Buckle said. "Octavian could have dispatched the senator in a far less brutal and public way if hadn't wanted to make a show for the Vicar. It was the act of a desperate man, a man brandishing a sword in front of a firing squad. We have offered the First Consul his salvation in the form of the Grand Alliance. There is little more we can do."

"The Atlanteans must come to us. They must reach out to us."

Buckle suddenly felt a bit lightheaded. He stared into the ocean to straighten out his senses. It was an odd feeling and he had experienced it several times within the last half hour or so. Perhaps the depths were affecting him. But it was more than mere dizziness. It was as if he were ever so slightly slipping out of one state of consciousness and into another, or almost falling asleep where he stood before snapping back into full consciousness.

Sabrina asked: "How is your neck? Where the kraken sucker ripped you?"

"Stings, then itches, then stings," Romulus said. "The bandage chafes between the sorry flesh and my collar.

"Do you wish for me to look at it? I can change the bandage."

"It is fine for now, thank you."

"You don't want infection."

"It's fine for now."

"Sometimes you are exasperating, Romulus," Sabrina sighed.

"That I am," Buckle replied.

Buckle heard the rustle of Sabrina's shirt as she turned to look at Welly. "That boy sure can sleep," she said.

"Yes, he can."

"I'm certain you brought him along simply to enjoy him torturing me with his poorly expressed affections," Sabrina said. "I cannot thank you enough for all of those awkward moments."

"You're welcome," Buckle said with a smile.

Sabrina took a deep breath and exhaled. "I think that I would like to speak with my sister."

Buckle nodded. There it was. "Difficult under the circumstances," he said. "But even if it can be arranged you shouldn't expect too much."

"I would anticipate nothing pleasant," Sabrina replied. "It could only prove painful in every imaginable way. But perhaps I could open an avenue of negotiation." She paused. "Well, that is a ridiculous lie. I want to see what Odessa has become. That is the long and short of it."

"We'll frame the request as a negotiation tactic anyway," Buckle said. "The Vicar is game enough to let her bite, I think. But the Atlanteans have to agree to it and that might prove the tricky part."

Sabrina laughed. "I trust the Atlanteans less than I trust her."

Buckle placed his hand on Sabrina's shoulder and she gave him a wistful smile. He felt immensely protective of her in that moment, the way he felt about Elizabeth. "I'll send a request through the officer of the watch," Buckle said. "Now go and get some sleep. I have a feeling things are going to be crazy in the morning."

"You should sleep as well," Sabrina replied. "You take the bed."

"No, I'm fine with the chair. Look at the cushions. It's sumptuously appointed." As he spoke, Buckle became aware of a light thumping sound on his left, emanating from the bulkhead.

"Do you hear that?" Sabrina asked, turning her head to listen.

Buckle peered at the bulkhead. "Yes, I do. Someone tapping from the other side."

"It is a secret passageway," Penny chimed in lightly.

"What?" Buckle asked. "How do you know that?"

"I am well versed with the blueprints of the seven domes of Atlantis," Penny replied.

The sound of scraping metal — a wheel or latch being rotated — rumbled from the bulkhead.

Sabrina jumped to the bed and grabbed her sword, half-drawing the blade from its sheath.

"I don't think it's assassins," Buckle said.

"Why not?" Sabrina asked.

"Because they came a' knocking," Buckle replied. He stepped to the divan where Welly slept. "Welly!"

Welly remained sound asleep. Buckle kicked the divan. Welly twisted upright into a sitting position, blinking. "What? Sir?"

"We have visitors," Buckle whispered, pointing at the chamber wall.

"Welly peered at the bulkhead. "I don't see anything. This place is so confusing."

"Just get your sword, Ensign," Sabrina ordered as she hedged forward toward the sound of the turning metal wheels.

"Sabrina, stand back," Buckle said. His heart hammered in his chest for now with his senses heightened, he felt he might be in the presence of Elizabeth.

XXIX

A FATHER'S DAUGHTER

A low burst of compressed air hissed from the edges of the hatch, its outline well camouflaged among the ornate decorations on the bulkhead. Buckle took a step forward as the hatch swung open with a burst of light and Lady Julia emerged, looking harried and stern. Behind her Buckle saw a narrow, utilitarian passageway lined with pipes and lit by one thin aether tube.

"Lady Julia," Buckle said, "You could have used the front door."

"My apologies, but no," Lady Julia replied. "No one can see me coming to you. The enemy eyes and ears inside Atlantis are many."

"Our strongholds have also become hotbeds of assassins and saboteurs," Buckle said.

"What do you want?" Sabrina asked, lowering her sword but keeping the bare steel at the ready.

"I have come to you to explain our condition," Lady Julia said. "The Founders arrived a full day before you did, blockading our city and threatening our latifundium fields with destruction if we did not accept their ambassadors."

"Have you joined with them?" Buckle asked.

"No," Lady Julia replied. "But now the Founders have demanded that Atlantis capitulate to their demands. If we refuse, they will attack and attempt to destroy us."

"I thought your storied defenses were such that the Founders would fail," Sabrina said.

"Yes," Lady Julia replied. "But our latifundium fields and surface ports are vulnerable. The Founders have already invaded many of our sister islands."

"We barely escaped them when they took Vera Cruz," Buckle said.

"Where is your father?" Sabrina asked.

"He and the Praetorian Guard have their hands full right now, arresting conspirators and garnering support so we can dominate the Senate floor in the morning," Julia said. "Our internal split is dangerous, especially if the powerful Capitolines have secretly joined the Founders."

"What of the other Atlantis houses?" Sabrina asked.

Julia shook her head. "We have called upon our closest gens, the Esquilines, to dispatch their submarine fleet to our assistance. But it appears that the Founders have them under siege as well."

"How long do you have to answer the Founders'

ultimatum?" Buckle asked.

Lady Julia looked at Penny as she spoke. "We have until dawn to respond."

"What is the ultimatum?" Buckle asked.

"We surrender control of all sea trade to the Founders exclusively. We are also required to place our soldiers and sea fleet under Founders command, and we must turn over the secret of the luminiferous aether."

"That is one rotten deal," Sabrina said.

"It is," Lady Julia said. "And though we have ordered them away, the Vicar's submersible is still docked with the city. They claim they're having some kind of mechanical malfunction and cannot disengage but we believe that there is a high-ranking member of their parliament aboard ready to receive our surrender in the morning."

"What do you need from us, Lady Julia?" Buckle asked.

"I come to you in this way," Julia said, "inside secret tubes and under shadows, to let you know that I have persuaded my father and our gens to join the Grand Alliance. I cannot speak for the other houses of the now collapsing Atlantean confederation but we Aventines shall prove a most capable and loyal partner to you in this war against the Founders."

"Agreed," Buckle said, offering his hand to Julia, who shook it. He didn't like the idea of taking sides in an Atlantean civil war but at this point he could not refuse the Aventines. "My zeppelin is not far off. If I can get to it we shall collect some airships from Spartak and be able to come to your aid within two days."

"Spartak?" Lady Julia groaned. "They shall not come. They hate us and we hate them."

"They must be willing to abide by the spirit of the alliance," Buckle said. "One must not refuse to support the other."

"Ah, to be friends with Spartak?" Lady Julia mused. "That will take some getting used to. But I am afraid there is no way we can sneak you out of Atlantis at the moment — the Founders have us hemmed in. But as I said, we can defend ourselves from anything the Founders might throw at us underwater. We can do them much harm, I assure you. What the First Consul and the Aventine gens need to do now is secure senatorial commitment to the Grand Alliance and reconfirm our position as the lead gens of all seven domes of Atlantis."

"And what of your own rebels?" Buckle asked.

"We shall deal with the Capitolines and any other traitors on our own," Lady Julia replied. "Once you make your way back to your own clan you may assure Admiral Balthazar that Atlantis can hold its own as far as the sea goes. We shall both choke off the Founder's vital sea trade lanes and sink her shipping at catastrophic rates. And when this is all over we shall ask for much of the spoils in return for our participation."

"That is something you must work out with the Alliance," Buckle said.

Lady Julia nodded. "I shall leave you now. I have ordered our guards to protect you as they would protect the First Consul himself. You shall be safe here tonight." She looked at Penny Dreadful and her face hardened. "That automaton should be destroyed."

"It belongs to me and I shall see to its future," Buckle said pleasantly.

"As you desire," Lady Julia answered. "But you have been warned as many times as you shall be warned."

Sabrina sheathed her sword. "Lady Julia, I have a request to make of you."

"And what is that, scarlet?" Lady Julia asked.

"My long lost sister, my twin, is a member of the Vicar's party," Sabrina said. "I would like to ask for you to arrange an audience with my sister on my behalf."

Lady Julia raised an eyebrow. "Ah, yes, the identical steampiper officer. What good will it do us to have you speak with her?"

"Someone needs to be talking." Sabrina replied.

Lady Julia narrowed her eyes at Sabrina. "The time for talking has passed."

"She's my sister," Sabrina said.

Lady Julia turned and put her hand on the hatch handle. "It is against my better judgment but I shall forward your request to the Founders submersible," Julia said. "Good night."

"Good night, Lady Julia," Sabrina said. "And thank you."

"Good night," Buckle said.

"Good night, Lady Julia," Penny Dreadful echoed.

Lady Julia halted and stared at Penny. "I strongly urge you reconsider our request to turn the automaton over to us for termination."

"What is it with you Atlanteans and your little machines?" Buckle asked, exasperated. "This one has proven nothing but loyal to us, though we have not had it for long."

"Not 'it,' but 'she'," Julia said.

"What?" Buckle replied.

"Order the machine to turn itself off, Captain." Julia said, turning back from the hatchway.

"Why?" Buckle asked.

"I don't want to," Penny whined.

"Do it," Julia repeated to Buckle, more forcefully this time. "And I shall explain to you what that thing actually is."

XXX

THE LIVING MACHINE

Buckle turned to Penny Dreadful. "Penny, go to sleep."

"I don't wish to," it replied.

"You're already halfway there—please shut down for the night," Buckle said sharply. "That is an order."

"As you wish, Captain," Penny answered in a sullen, disappointed fashion. It folded its metal fingers in front of its waist as its interior gently clicked and rattled. Steam oozed from vents in the back of its torso and thighs and its glowing eyes ebbed weaker and weaker until they went black.

"It's shut down," Buckle said.

Julia leaned close to Buckle and whispered as if she did not trust that Penny was actually deactivated. "I beg you, Captain Buckle, destroy this thing while you still have a chance."

"Is the automaton really so dangerous?" Buckle asked. "This one has proven quite helpful to us, in the short time we have had it in tow."

"The machine is a catastrophe waiting to

happen," Julia said gravely. "You must know that it is a child, a real child, or at least it once was."

"I knew it," Sabrina muttered.

"There is a human child inside that machine?" Buckle asked. "How is that possible?"

"Yes," Julia replied. "Or, more accurately, the last remains of a child. One hundred and seventy-four years ago there was a terrible sickness, a plague, which struck one of our colonies, Pontus, the furthest, deepest outpost under the western sea. Every child fell mortally ill and the parents, dying themselves, were desperate to save their children. They turned to their genius inventor, the brilliant but unstable Tarquinus Lombard, descendant of the great inventor and founder of Atlantis, who possessed the brilliance of his mother but also the mental instabilities and torments of his father's line. Since the plague destroyed the body but not the brain, Tarquinus devised a machine, an automaton, to replace the bodies of the children almost in their entirety with metal, but in a fashion which preserved both the brain and the soul."

"So Penny Dreadful is a machine with a child's brain," Sabrina said.

"Yes," Lady Julia said. "Though there is also some heart and lung tissue in the torso. Tarquinus made his living machines capable of surviving underwater and defending themselves, for the colony was facing extinction and the adults would be gone.

Most of the children did not survive the procedure; the two dozen who did were the only ones left after the plague finally wiped out the colony six months later. The Pontus dome was first quarantined, then permanently sealed. No one on the outside knew about the children until twenty-two years later, when a security expedition re-entered the Pontus on a mission to raze it. There was no trace left of the plague so we brought them home and took them in, for they were our children."

"Half human, half machine," Buckle muttered.

"More machine than human — a living machine," Julia continued. "The Pontus children were adopted into new Atlantean families but their brain development seemed to be partially arrested, somehow locked into the age in which they had been introduced to the machine. They also displayed an unnatural longevity, so one over one hundred years later all but one were still operating, passed down through Atlantean families from one generation to another. Until, all at once, fifty years ago, almost all of them broke down. The automatons" — she glanced at Penny and lowered her voice even more — "committed murders, mass killings. They tore their relatives to pieces, their families, bloodlines they had known for a century. The senate ordered immediate termination. Most of the automatons submitted willingly but a few ran, escaping into the sea and up onto the surface. It took years for our soldiers to hunt them down."

"I have seen the Penny Dreadful in action against your Guardians," Buckle said. "Your Tarquinus provided the children with lethal attributes."

"Tarquinus knew the children would have to fend for themselves," Julia said. "In the end, all of the Pontus children were destroyed except for two who were never found. And Penny—that is her name, though I don't know where the 'Dreadful' came from, fitting as it is—is one of them. She was a nine-year-old at the time of her salvation, one of the innocents, one of the Pontus children."

"And she came back here willingly, after all of that?" Buckle asked.

"It proves that she is unstable," Julia said. "Who knows where she has been for the last fifty years? Her violent deterioration is inevitable. She must be destroyed."

"She has done nothing to warrant her own termination," Buckle said.

"Neither had the others," Julia said softly. "Until the day came when they murdered everyone who loved and cared for them … and many others. Even Tarquinus knew what he might have done: he recognized the potential for evil in his new, dark science of the living machine. He burned all records of his experiments before he died of plague."

Buckle cast a worried glance down the

passageway. There was something human inside the dangerously equipped metal automaton, the ancient, perhaps on-the-verge-of-madness mind of a child. But he could not kill or abandon her now. Even if there would be a terrible price to pay. He knew that much. "But, in the end, she is still a human child," he said softly.

"You are mistaken, Captain," Lady Julia replied quickly. "As long as she remains here, the manacles stay on. As for our current circumstances, try to get some sleep—the Senate shall convene in emergency session one hour before dawn. We want to bring you to the speaker's podium as my father makes the announcement that we shall reject the Founders' aggressions and ally ourselves with you. We need to ratify the decision and turn our full attention to the defense of Atlantis, for I am certain the Founders shall prove true to their word once their ultimatum is rejected and we shall be attacked."

"I will stand with you on the Senate floor, of course," Buckle said.

"Very good," Lady Julia answered, swinging back into the hatchway. "Good night."

"May I ask something of you?" Buckle said.

Lady Julia paused, looking at him.

"I have a sister. She and I are very close, very ... connected. I have been looking for her and I feel her presence here, faintly, in a way that I cannot explain.

Her name is Elizabeth."

"I have no answer for you," Lady Julia replied. "I can swear to you that there are no Crankshaft citizens other than your company inside the Aventine dome at this time, and I have never heard of your Elizabeth."

Buckle nodded. "It is a strange thing then, what I feel in this place."

"I hope you find your sister," Lady Julia said. "Now, good night."

"Good night," Buckle said.

Lady Julia ducked out of the hatch, pulling it shut behind her with loud clicks of engaging locks and rotating gears.

XXXI

ODESSA

The chamber was plain for an Atlantean one, windowless, with copper pipes lining one wall, hatchways on opposite sides and a large table in the middle carved with leaping dolphins and winding eels. To Sabrina it felt like an interrogation room, though the diffused illumination from the luminiferous aether tubes overhead took the edge off everything. The Praetorians had brought her here without a word and now she waited.

For Odessa.

Sabrina wasn't nervous. At least, she told herself she wasn't nervous. She had no idea what to expect from her twin sister, wasn't even sure why she'd asked to see her. They'd been immensely close long ago. Perhaps Sabrina needed to see if any of their old bond still remained or if Odessa would now prove to be nothing but a stranger to her entirely.

Beside the table sat two chairs with plain wooden seats. Sabrina took one step toward a chair but stopped herself. She didn't want to be sitting down when Odessa first came into the room. Sabrina slowly slid her foot back, the leather sole brushing across the metal floor.

Odessa. Her sister. Sabrina fought her old memories, always tried to avoid dwelling in the happy days before the purge, for that meant dwelling with ghosts. But it was impossible not to fall back into them now. She and her sister were not ghosts.

Or were they?

If one vanished from one life and re-emerged into another, did that not make one some kind of ghost?

Ghosts. As much as one wished to leave them behind they always followed — not like hauntings, necessarily, but more like one's own shadow, always there but rarely noticed, popping into view at odd moments, arriving with a sound, a smell, the way someone folded their hands, or drifting into the otherworld before sleep. Odessa had been a ghost for Sabrina. One of her most potent memories of her sister was a day with their mother, Chelsea, the first day Isambard had taken the girls outside of the Crystal Palace, or at least one of the first times she could remember being outside.

***

Sabrina and Odessa had been at least seven years of

age, riding their ponies at the grand equestrian center inside the city. She remembered her pony named Wren. The girls rode every day under the strict supervision of their instructor, Peter Darling, with either their mother or nanny in attendance. The equestrian center was a large dirt arena with a grandstand where the Founders cavalry would parade for Isambard and the elite families. Lines of thick black smoke, issuing from the factory quarter's chimneys, streamed endlessly over the high ceiling of dirty glass and wrought iron, resulting in faint stripes of shadow and weak sunlight across the equestrian center floor.

Sabrina remembered looking up as she rode, the warm body of Wren under her and the depthless, glowing mass of clouds far overhead making her feel like she was floating. She would often forget to keep her little pony on line, which rather miffed old Darling.

Sabrina had loved the equestrian center with its horses and ponies and the smells of dung, wood chips and greenhouse-grown hay, complemented by the salty air blown in from the ventilation tunnels by the huge underground fans. The smells made it a lovely place to breathe in comparison to the more stuffy corners of the palace where things tended to take on the odor of decomposing vegetation and canary droppings.

It was a particularly bright afternoon—the clouds seemed thinner than normal—and Chelsea had taken the girls to their practice session with Darling.

Isambard, their older cousin, had arrived, his face pink with an enthusiasm that clashed with his long, brilliant red hair. Sabrina always remembered how happy Isambard looked that day; he did have a dark streak in him which often made him melancholy and spiteful, but today he had a new machine and he was ecstatic. The engineers had unveiled an armored train, one which Isambard's father had ordered built upon the day of his birth but only now, twenty years later, had all of the train's cars rolled out of the worksheds complete.

"Come with me, cousins!" Isambard said, clapping his hands. "I have something to show you!" Five people accompanied Isambard, all dressed in cloaks with breathing masks strapped on their shoulders, ready to go outside. The first was Isambard's engineering tutor, Rodrigo, a tall, gangly man who always looked serious but could sing everyone under the floor at dinner parties when asked to perform. The second was Shuba, a young Martian male who was Isambard's best friend and who often acted as a representative of Lotus: an older Martian female whom people rarely saw, sequestered as she was in her private chambers in the southeast corner of the palace. Lotus had the distinction of being the most trusted counselor of Isambard's father. Sabrina had seen her only once, and the tall alien woman had frightened her, both with her big violet-black eyes and the set of winged alien armor she wore which looked like it was permanently attached to her body.

The third member of Isambard's party was Greyfell, one of the military leaders of the Founders, a once-handsome man who kept himself quite fit and had a white beard and the saddest blue eyes that Sabrina had ever seen. Greyfell was unmarried, which was rare for a Founders man of his age, and the story went that he'd lost the love of his life in his youth and his heart had never recovered sufficiently to accept another. Sabrina couldn't remember a time when she had not felt sorry for Greyfell.

The other two men were steampiper corporals, big strapping fellows in black uniforms and silver cuirasses and loyal to the death despite never being able to rise above the rank of senior sergeant. Such bodyguards were necessary for elites who wished to travel outside the gilded glass confines of the Crystal Palace. It wasn't spoken of, but citizens unhappy with their station in life might sometimes express their displeasure with rocks and knives, despite risking a trip to the gallows for such traitorous behavior. No one seemed to be able to explain sufficiently to Sabrina why some citizens should act in such a way. Had not the Fawkes provided the citizens of the city with a home safe from the mustard gas? Had not the Fawkes built the city for their protection, the factories for their work, the greenhouses for their food and the hospitals for their woes? Such dangers confused and angered Sabrina.

Although Sabrina and Odessa shared many things they did not possess equal affections for Isambard. Sabrina was sufficiently relaxed with her cousin, for despite his sometimes mean teasing he cared for her, but there was always something between them—a sour note of indefinable condition which prevented them from being close friends. Odessa, on the other hand, adored Isambard and he adored her back. Sabrina never saw Isambard smile more than when he was playing with Odessa or when she hugged him or brought him a secretively plucked daisy from the palace gardens.

"The girls are not yet finished with their lesson, Isambard," Chelsea said pleasantly.

"Please indulge me, Aunt Chelsea." Isambard grinned. "I have waited all of my life for this train and today I have shown it to everyone except you three!" He motioned toward the steampipers, who carried cloaks and masks for Chelsea and the girls. "I have brought your outdoor gear."

"Very well," Chelsea said, laughing. "It is a momentous day."

Odessa urged her pony over to the rail where Isambard stood, dismounted in one easy motion and hugged him about the lower waist. Isambard smiled and blew a kiss to Sabrina as she trotted her pony over.

"Ah, my favorite girls!" Isambard enthused. "I am happiest being able to show my train to you."

Sabrina cinched her black cloak around her shoulders and pulled on her elaborate breathing mask. Masks were worn by the elite during extended stays outside the Crystal Palace, for they were designed to filter out the coal and tar smoke which hung thick in the city's air. They provided some protection from hurled rocks as well. Each mask was stylized in a sort of masquerade ball fashion, with Sabrina being a little owl, Odessa a wolf pup, and their mother the face of a doe. The steampipers donned their standard-issue helmets while Isambard put on his large mask, a grotesque metal hybrid of a lion and a raven. Sabrina always thought it was odd that Isambard did not wear a mask similar to that of his father, the traditional Fawkes phoenix with three large metal feathers thrust up at the top and a long, wickedly curving beak. But Isambard tended to go his own way; some even whispered that his own way was the way Lotus wanted him to go.

The filtering masks served two functions: to purify the air of the noble person breathing through it and to separate the royals from the masses in the street. Sabrina agreed with keeping one's distance from the unwashed mob because, though the palace servants were lovely and clean, the general citizenry suffered from scabrous maladies and lived in various unhealthy and filthy conditions. The citizens coughed a lot and many succumbed to black lung disease from years working underground in the pits.

Odessa grabbed Sabrina's hand, clutching it as they approached the equestrian center door. They'd rarely been taken outside, never to the railway yard, and now it was happening so fast, so easily. The steampipers swung the doors open and Isambard stepped in between Sabrina and Odessa, taking their hands in his. Sabrina had not minded, for she was always impressed with Isambard; he referred to Sabrina as the "older" sister—she'd arrived from the womb first, beating Odessa's appearance by seven minutes—and Sabrina had always liked that. Mother and Greyfell followed close behind, Greyfell wearing the mask of a sullen bear which was barely more somber-looking than his own hang-dog appearance.

As she stepped outside Sabrina was immediately struck by the bottomless, upside-down heave of the sky, the high, ribbed-cloud ceiling of it, causing a headiness one did not feel while looking up through the palace glass. The still air chilled her cheeks and she shivered, though from cold or exhilaration she couldn't tell. She'd always wanted to be outside and see the city. She'd always wanted to see the city from above. You can't see anything from the air because of the sea fog, everyone said, but she wanted to see it anyway. Sabrina and Odessa's father was a Commander of Zeppelins and he'd informed his daughters that each of them would earn an air officer commission and make a career out of the service unless they preferred politics. Sabrina had wanted to be a zeppelineer; it had been her heart's desire from the first time she could consider such things, and it was agony to have to wait until she was twelve to enter the airship cadet program.

But therein lay the sticky problem.

The Founders never flew. Their zeppelins sat docked and mouldering in permanent reserve, hidden in huge hangars in the northwest quarter of the city. Air officers spent their careers maintaining the grounded airships while only a lucky few were assigned to the extremely rare scouting mission. Sabrina and Odessa, as the daughters of a high-ranking Fawkes family, might get a shot at one of the operational missions, but probably just one. And the dreadnaughts, the mighty near-mythical dreadnaughts which Sabrina had heard of but had never seen, remained always hidden in the darkest hangar, their earthbound crews sworn to silence. Sabrina's father always said that the dreadnaughts were more effective against the enemy as ghosts than real warships that could be seen.

Sabrina despaired over the prospect of a zeppelin career on the ground, but she also knew that she wanted nothing to do with politics. She always assumed that, when the time came, her father might provide her with other options.

Everything sounded different outside. The air took noises and carried them away and brought other sounds back with it. The click of Sabrina's boot soles on the cold-brittled flagstones was new. The cold and space invigorated her and she wanted to run but there wasn't far to go. The guards standing at the railway yard gate greeted them with salutes and they passed into a different realm of oily gravel, long metal tracks and dozens of looming locomotives and armored trains.

"Here she is!" Isambard said as he led the girls to the huge gold-copper locomotive. "I present to you, the locomotive *Isambard*! Isn't she a beauty?"

Sabrina gasped, for the machine was beautiful: its metal skin curved into a thousand polished, gleaming lines. Its large, teardrop-shaped windows bulged like gecko eyes over the engineer's turret and the sleek boiler stacks angled backwards so the noxious mustard could not force its way into the combustion system. It was a mountain of a machine, perhaps seventeen feet high, and it looked like a mythical whale to Sabrina, captured and recast in bronzed metal.

"Brilliant," Sabrina breathed, and heard her mother and the others murmur their approval.

"Can we go for a ride?" Odessa asked. "Please, please, please?"

Isambard laughed. "Not quite yet, little bird," he

said, patting the top of her wolf pup mask. "Her airtight seals have still to be approved. She must pass her trials out in the noxious mustard. But once that is done, yes, you may go for a ride. With your mother's approval of course."

Sabrina looked up at Chelsea, who looked disappointingly skeptical. "We shall see," she said.

"Oh, they must!" Isambard laughed.

Sabrina and Odessa never did get to take their ride on the *Isambard*.

***

Sabrina jumped as the opposite hatch clicked and swung open, pushed by the white and gold gauntleted hand of an Atlantean soldier. Odessa stepped in, wearing her black steampiper uniform and its black cloak with red lining, her face the mirror image of Sabrina's, her hair the same saturation of crimson, her features bearing the same Asiatic influence— but there was also a harshness in the green eyes and a gauntness in the line of the cheekbones which were absent from Sabrina's visage.

Odessa paused, locking her gaze on Sabrina as the hatch closed behind her. She crossed her arms, her black-gloved fingers sinking deep into the folds of her uniform cloth above the elbows. She was nervous also.

"Hello, sister," Sabrina said.

"Hello, sister," Odessa repeated coldly.

Odessa's voice was strong, with a hoarse quality that Sabrina remembered. "You look well," Sabrina said.

Odessa nodded. "As do you." She motioned for Sabrina to sit at the table, sweeping her cloak aside as she seated herself.

Sabrina sat down. It was strange, unsettling, to suddenly be so close to Odessa, and she could not tell if there was any connection left between them or not. If there was, it was at first blush entirely imperceptible.

"You wished to speak with me," Odessa said. "I am here."

"Had you never wanted for us to see each other again?" Sabrina asked.

"I had thought you to be dead for the longest time," Odessa said slowly.

"In some ways I was."

Odessa folded her hands on the table in a slow, deliberate movement. "Not long ago, perhaps a year, I was informed that you had survived the purge and now lived among the Crankshafts. At least you could have picked a proper clan to live with and not trader-pirates."

"At least they don't murder each other."

Odessa stiffened. "Was it you—were you the traitor who led the Crankshafts and Alchemists into the city that day, the day Balthazar was taken from the prison?"

"Yes, I did."

Odessa's mouth tightened. "You are my blood, my sister. I do not think I need to speak with you anymore."

"What has become of you, sister? Sabrina asked. "Isambard murdered our parents, everyone we knew."

"That is not true."

"Yes, it is."

"Who told you that — Marter?"

"Yes," Sabrina answered.

"You should not believe the things Marter said," Odessa replied. "Look at what his association has brought you to. A life of hiding? Leading enemy forces against your own clan? Many good citizens, comrades of mine, were killed during your incursion. Since when did you become my enemy, sister?"

"If Isambard has not stolen every last bit of who you are, Odessa," Sabrina said, unable to contain an anxious current from rising in her voice, "you must listen to me. You must believe what is the truth!"

Odessa looked angry for an instant and recovered with a dark, pond-still calm. "Why am I here? Not to comfort the enemy. Ah, yes. The Vicar thought it would be appropriate that I invite you back into the family."

"The Vicar? What about you?"

Odessa did not blink. "Isambard approved of

the request. He too, wants you back. You are one of us. You are the blood of Fawkes. Come home and you shall be forgiven."

"I left the family of Fawkes with its rivers of blood. I no longer wish to be a part of it."

Bristling, Odessa leaned forward. Sabrina felt her sister's anger and frustration and she knew that the connection between them, deeply submerged, was still strong. "You have no idea what happened," Odessa whispered, "why it was necessary for Isambard to order the purge. Many of the people you remember were not as innocent as you might think."

"Including mother and father?"

"Including mother and father," Odessa said slowly, leaning back.

"What kind of monster—" Sabrina stopped herself. She was shaking on the inside. She had to choose her words carefully. Isambard had raised Odessa. "I may no longer wish to be a part of Isambard's family but no matter how long we are apart we shall always be a part of each other."

Odessa's eyes had now gone cold, their sleek green mirrors betraying nothing, no vulnerability or emotion, but Sabrina could feel the tightness of her muscles vibrating the chamber air. "I am Fawkes. You are Fawkes. You are a part of Isambard's family whether you think you wish to be or not."

"I reject all of it but you," Sabrina whispered.

She almost said something else, words rushing from her mouth unbidden, but she stopped herself. The memories upon seeing Odessa, some long repressed, flooded back to her, reawakened echoes, vague childhood memories of sunlight in the atrium and birds in the Crystal Palace, of her father's bouncing knee and statues of the three Founders, of gurgling fountains and red-headed relatives and the lurking, rarely seen shadows of the tall, black-violet-eyed Martians standing in the shadows wearing hoods over their strange black and white faces, whispering into the ears of the powerful.

Sabrina grabbed Odessa's arm and squeezed. The move shocked Sabrina — as if a part of her she did not understand was now taking action. "Sister," she whispered.

Odessa ripped her arm out of Sabrina's grasp and stood abruptly, her chair legs screeching across the metal floor. "There is no family here, as you have said. If you are here to negotiate with the Founders, know this: Isambard will accept nothing less than the unconditional surrender of the rebellious Grand Alliance. Is this what you offer?"

Sabrina's stomach hurt. The woman sitting across from her looked exactly like her, shared memories with her, but perhaps they were not sisters anymore. "Odessa, please be reasonable," Sabrina said. "You have the ear of Isambard and I have the ear of

Balthazar. Perhaps the two of us can help stop this war."

"I do not know what you have become, sister," Odessa replied coldly. "But you disappoint me. I am Odessa Fawkes, blood of the Fawkes, adopted daughter of Isambard Fawkes, and I do not negotiate with the enemy." Odessa spun on her heel and swung the hatch open, vanishing through it without a glance behind her.

Sabrina placed her hands palms down on the table, unsure as to whether she was upset or not, unsure as to whether there had ever been another person in the room with her or if she had been speaking with a ghost.

XXXII

THE PONTUS CHILDREN

"I am a child but I am also very old," Penny Dreadful said.

Buckle nodded. He sat on the edge of his chaise lounge as Penny Dreadful stood in front of him, her eyes glowing, her arm manacles rattling on any occasion she might move. She whispered with a metallic whir and she seemed not averse to answering his questions about her past ... but he could not shake the sense that she was an unreliable narrator of her own history.

They were alone, at least, alone in the sense that Welly was fast asleep again. Buckle had not removed his clothing, not even his sword belt, since Lady Julia's visit. He didn't trust the Atlanteans with their secret passageways. "How did you survive after all of the adults died in the Pontus?" he asked Penny. "You were just children."

"It was terrible, of course, for all of us little ones," Penny said. "Uncle Lombard did his best to save as many of us as he could but so many died during the transfer of brain to machine. I was distraught when my parents died of the plague, but it was so long ago I can speak of it with little emotional distress now. There are good memories of my first family and the families I lived with after."

"But how did the twenty of you children survive alone for decades?"

"We played a great deal in the beginning," Penny said.

"That isn't surviving, Penny," Buckle said. But he had to be more careful now. This was a child, a very old child, but a child nonetheless.

"It was surviving for us, you see, Captain. Once we had recovered from our bereavements and disposed of the decomposing bodies in the ejectae tubes we needed joy. But the urge to play left us, perhaps within a year. One of our machines, Teresa, malfunctioned after thirteen months. Just dropped dead. That frightened us. We had a ceremony for her and buried her in the sea. After that we put ourselves on very low settings and waited. For decades, we just waited. Our biological elements are maintained through a mixture of water, carbon, and minerals drawn from steam humidity and byproducts of fuel incineration, so food was not a problem. With the exception of combustibles and oil, my system is largely self-sustaining."

"But the organic elements of yours, how could they be immortal?"

"They are not immoral. They do decay, though slowly, I suppose. Uncle Lombard constructed a system whereby our human parts are refreshed with a mix of carbon and electric currents. I have lived through many families, Captain. In my first adoption, cousins of my mother, I was treated as a child, and over time, as one family more distant in relation took me after another, I was handled in different ways: as a baby, a servant, a pet, and even some kind of coat rack providing amusement at parties."

"What happened when they came to terminate you?" Buckle asked. "How did you escape?"

Penny paused as if considering her answer carefully. "At the end I lived with a nice family and they had a little boy. His name was Hallas and I was something of a nanny to him. We were related. He was a descendant of my original family. He was six years old when we heard of the other living machines malfunctioning in such horrible ways, killing people. Fourteen of us, fourteen of the nineteen metal children, fell apart within three months of each other, as if we had all been intentionally set with the same biological expiry mechanism."

She turned her head and looked at the viewing window. Buckle heard a sigh, a very human sigh, pass from her metal lips. The neck rotated and she looked at him again. "I was once comforted by the presence of water. But no more. There were leaks in the Pontus dome, small ones that gradually grew larger and larger over the decades we were locked inside. We could not repair the cracks. We did not know how. I remember, I remember shutting myself down just so I would not have to listen to that sound, that sound of the water trickling down the inside of the dome, every day increasing ever so slightly. Tarquinus Lombard had not informed us that our metal bodies were equipped to survive submersion. We assumed that if the dome failed we would drown. It was awful, shutting down to wait to drown."

"I am sorry that you had to go through that," Buckle said. "Losing your family. Everything."

"I appreciate your concern," Penny said, her eyes glowing a touch brighter, the hum of her engine rising a chord higher. "I am sound, Captain. I am not about to malfunction. I shall warn you if ever I sense my mind, my control, slipping away."

"I trust that you shall, Penny Dreadful."

Penny's glow pulsed as if she was well reassured. "Hallas, the little boy—when the senate ordered all living machines be taken to the foundries for immediate destruction—that little boy made me promise to him that I would run, that I would escape, that I would live. I promised him. I hugged him and slipped away. I climbed into the ventilation shafts and exited through an exhaust tube. I walked on the ocean floor for, well, for what seemed like a lifetime. I did not know where I was, nor where I was heading. I eventually hit a place where the sea floor rose up and kept rising until it broke the surface of the sea. I had arrived at the coast. I remained in hiding after that."

"What of the other living machine who escaped?"

"I know not who the other survivor was though I suspect it was a boy named Cassius," Penny replied thoughtfully. "He was always the smartest of us, and our leader, in a way."

Penny sighed and sniffed, signaling she was done telling whatever part of her story she was willing to tell.

"Thank you for telling me this," Buckle said. "One day I do very much wish to hear you tell of your adventures afterwards."

"There were no adventures afterwards, Captain. Just running. Just hiding. Just having nowhere to belong. I cannot say as I blame Atlantis for wanting to destroy us, if the stories of the horrors committed by my companions so long ago are true."

Buckle looked at Penny's metal face. He still had a difficult time believing there was a human child behind it. Surely there was very little human residue left. And where had she been for the last fifty-odd years? "If you were under an execution order, why did you come back to Atlantis with us?" he asked.

Penny lifted her hand to her face and rubbed her

cheek, absentmindedly, in the fashion a human might do. But what kind of itch might copper skin have? Buckle wondered if the familiar movements were part of the machine's attempt to appear humanlike or if they were the moldering scraps of a human brain telling the fingers to wander the way they once did when they were flesh and blood. He heard the cogs gently turning inside Penny's metal skull, supporting the old remnants of her human brain. She smelled like hot metal because her insides were hot metal. "Because you gave me a home. Because you needed me, Captain."

Buckle nodded. She was loyal, though she had not proven much help in finding the underwater city. More of an enthusiastic disher of red herrings, to be accurate. An enthusiastic disher of red herrings who, rather than being perturbed when her suggestions failed, readily offered another with promises of certain success, even though those instructions led them nowhere as well. He was certain her shamblings were well intentioned but he also worried they might be a sign of her impending mental collapse. He felt sorry for the child. He wondered, for a fleeting instant, if she now considered him her father, but that seemed an idea too weird to entertain. "You could have told me what awaited you here."

"It does not matter," Penny replied. "I wanted to see Atlantis again. Now you should get some sleep, Captain. I shall stand watch."

"Yes," Buckle said; though he knew that he would be unable to sleep, he needed to try. He was tired, emotionally drained, and lying down would at least provide some measure of rest, even if his brain refused to stop spinning. He stood, stretched and walked to the chamber basin where he splashed cold water on his face.

"I hope Sabrina returns soon," Penny said. "I worry about her being alone in the presence of the Founders."

"As do I," Buckle answered as he dried his skin with a towel. He considered pouring himself a glass of rum from a bottle the Atlanteans had provided but he was too tired to do the work required to uncork it. He sat on the chaise lounge where he would try to fall asleep and fail, considered and rejected the idea of taking a shot at the rum bottle again, and rubbed his face with his hands. Already he had to fight the urge to jump up and pace. He was jealous of Welly, always ready to slumber, snoring softly on his lounge.

The Atlanteans were going to fold. Buckle was certain of it. For all of their blustering and promises they were going to cut some kind of deal with the Founders.

But there was nothing Buckle could do for it now. He forced himself to lay back and rest his head on the pillow. The chaise lounge was soft. He crossed his legs, adjusted his scabbard so it rested neatly alongside his hip, folded his hands behind his head and looked up at the dark lines of the luminiferous tubes on the ceiling.

In his peripheral vision Buckle caught the glimmer of Penny's two yellow eyes. She had moved into the area of the secret hatch, her manacle chains swinging lightly in the shadows. He scratched his chin through his beard, which seemed to be getting thicker. Was Penny as dangerous as the Atlanteans had warned? He wanted to comfort her, but what was she? The last of the plague children, the Pontus children, a will-o-the-wisp essence of a child in the armored body of a machine, an unknown, a frantically designed hybrid in a state of advanced mental deterioration.

And now she watched over him as he slept.

What was Buckle to do? Shut her off? She had stood with them against the Guardians, fought to protect the group. He wasn't going to do anything about it now. He felt better having her there.

The main door opened, spilling light from the passageway as Sabrina entered. An Atlantean guard shut the hatch behind her, cutting off the illumination. Sabrina paused, most likely allowing her eyes to adjust to the dark chamber.

"Good evening, Lieutenant," Penny said.

"Good evening, Penny," Sabrina whispered.

"How did it go?" Buckle asked, sitting up.

"The Founders offered nothing but ultimatums,"

Sabrina replied. "My sister offered nothing at all. That is the long and short of it. Nothing more."

"Unfortunate," Buckle replied. He wasn't surprised but still he felt disappointed.

"Welly is asleep, I see," Sabrina said. Buckle could sense her smile as she spoke. She walked to the washroom door and engaged a small, round glass orb, frosted on the interior, which lit up with a faint, soft aether glow designed to not interfere with sleep. Sabrina entered the washroom and shut the door.

Sabrina didn't want to talk about her time with her sister, Buckle knew. Understandable. Buckle hoped to have the opportunity to meet with the Founders himself, but it looked like that wasn't going to happen. He thought of the Founders zeppelin officer, the man he had saved from the *Bellerophon*, lying in the *Pneumatic Zeppelin*'s infirmary. Buckle had very much hoped to have a conversation with him but, according to surgeon Fogg, the man would die of his wounds without ever regaining consciousness. Pity. It was all such a pity.

Buckle looked out the viewing portal into the dark ocean. Now and again the Founders submarines slipped past in the murk—they looked like they were closer than they had been before. Buckle laid back and took a deep breath. The air was salty and sweet, freshly pumped down from the surface, tempered by the musky scent of the ever-present ambergris incense. He considered closing the viewing portal but decided to leave it open.

Buckle thrust his head against the pillow, trying to invite sleep. He ended up gazing at Penny and wondering if those golden mechanical eyes were the last thing the unfortunate Atlanteans saw before their own beloved automatons tore them to pieces in the night.

XXXIII

REFUGIO

Sabrina stood in a dark room lit only by one lantern. Shafts of sunlight filtered through gaps in the rickety wooden plank ceiling, the same gaps that poured water when it rained. The space was full of crates, some opened, some nailed shut, the dirt floor littered with bits of packing hay. Outside in the filthy street the shopkeepers haggled with customers, donkeys brayed, and children shrieked with laughter. Sabrina heard Sato, the neighboring cobbler, arguing with his wife, their voices barking through the paper-thin walls. The smell of the peppered fish-head soup boiling in the pots of the Kaminski's leaked in from the other side — the Kaminskis always had their big meal at noon and it was always fish-head soup and black bread.

There was so little privacy in the slums of Refugio.

Sabrina clenched her teeth and blocked it all out, blocked out everything but the target in front of her, a crude bull's-eye she'd painted on a wooden pillar. In her hand she weighed her knife, the leather-bound surface of its handle, the balance of its blade. She stepped forward and whipped her arm at the target, releasing the knife in a spinning whirl. The knife struck the target center and stuck there.

Sabrina walked to the post and yanked the knife free. Two swords, bonecutters far too expensive for a poor spice seller and his twelve-year-old daughter to possess even as pretenders, hung on the wall, one of them two inches shorter than the other.

"Sabrina," Vadim said, poking his head around the doorway leading to the shop. "The Master needs your help." Vadim was nineteen years of age but cursed with the appearance and thin build of a fifteen-year-old boy; he was the fifth son of the Refugio harbormaster and his apprenticeship under Marter was part of a black market trading agreement. It was obvious, however, that Vadim preferred the get-rich-quick schemes of the street hawkers to the slow plod of a semi-honest living. Easygoing on the surface, Vadim never seemed to mind when Marter couldn't pay him on time but he also had a greedy streak—Sabrina knew that he coveted both the shop and her, though he would never admit such jealousy. He also had a damaged right arm, one which he always kept sleeved, and he did his fine work and handwriting with his left hand. His normally placid face was tight this afternoon, his eyes bright and darting; he was nervous and Sabrina didn't like it. He was up to something.

Sabrina nodded, sheathing the knife into a belt hidden under her tunic. She checked herself in a mirror, tucking her black-dyed hair under her bowler hat before she stepped into the shop.

Marter, a tall, thin man with a balding head, smiled at Sabrina. In front of Marter stood a portly gentlemen of Asian descent who wanted to look wealthy—his silk cravat and amber-topped walking stick aimed to make that impression—but the elite didn't shop in the Refugio slums. The Asian man was most likely a userer or a high-end criminal.

"Dear, please bring me the new shipment of saffron," Marter asked.

"I want the pure Oriental spice," the Asian man grumbled, shoving aside a set of display samplers. "No salt-cut garbage cooked up by the Russians. But if you don't have saffron I'll take turmeric."

"Pure oriental saffron is expensive," Marter said gently.

The portly man huffed. "Does it look like money is a concern for me? I have a forgotten wedding anniversary and an angry wife on my hands. Show me the good stuff."

Marter smiled at Sabrina. "Get the Yokuni, then."

"Yes, father," Sabrina replied, ducking into the back room. Marter was not her real father but rather a sort of step-father. He'd been the family tutor at the

Crystal Palace and he'd carried Sabrina out of the city on the night of Isambard's purge. After six months of constant running they'd ended up settling in the trader port of Refugio, a backwater town serving the hinterlands of the Spartak Territory. Refugio had a strange Asiatic-Russian feel to it, in its culture and its people, and it was a rough place.

Marter and Sabrina had lived in Refugio for three years. It offered a life of hard work and always looking over one's shoulder. Marter paid half-pennies to the local street urchins, with their eyes and ears always attuned to the narrow, crowded lanes which passed for streets in the slums, to be on the lookout for any authority figures. Refugio had very little by way of local government beyond the organized gangs which controlled specific zones and ran extortion rackets for merchant *protection.*

Danger never caused Marter to pause. He'd been a soldier — an officer of the Interior Ministry — before he turned his attention to tutoring, though few traces of his military career were noticeable outside of the erectness of his bearing. In the years since the purge he'd taught Sabrina the arts of self-defense and killing with firearms, swords, daggers, rocks and her bare hands. In her soldier's education Marter never relented, whether the classroom was a barn in the forests of the Palisades or the dingy back room of their Refugio spice shop. Marter's lessons were serious business and

Sabrina bore plenty of little scars on her forearms and fingers to prove it.

Marter was ever the protector, ever the provider, and he became well invested in the Refugio underworld though it was a side of his operation he worked hard to conceal from Sabrina. If days passed without customers and they got hungrier and hungrier, she could sense a growing rage in him even though he tried to hide it. In the difficult times Marter would put on his cloak and vanish, sometimes for one night, sometimes for a few days, but every time he returned he had money or food or both.

Where the treasures came from, Sabrina never asked, and Marter never told her.

Sabrina located a small crate and carried it out to the counter. Marter opened the lid to reveal a dozen glass vials filled with orange saffron and sealed with black wax, nestled amidst packing wraps. Sabrina remembered eating food spiced with the metallic hay-tasting saffron off of ceramic plates when she had been a small child inside Founders City. Now she ate gruel and questionable meats out of a wooden bowl.

"How many vials do you wish to purchase?" Marter had asked. They'd paid a small fortune—the last stack of coins in the reserve tin can they kept hidden under the floorboards—on the black market for the case of saffron, surely lifted by sea pirates out of the hold of some unfortunate Oriental Compact trader. It would be nice to turn a profit and have some money, perhaps even to buy a chicken for dinner.

The Asian man lifted a vial to the light and grimaced at the orange powder. "This is one dozen?" he grunted.

"One dozen," Marter replied. "Twenty-two apiece or two hundred for the set."

The Asian man had plunked the vial on the counter. "If this was purple crocus, even red, I would find the price acceptable. But surely you can't expect much for this weak chaff. I'll pay half that."

"The price is the price, good sir," Marter said pleasantly. "And it is a very good price for orange."

"One hundred or I walk out of here," the customer said.

"Fare thee well, then," Marter replied.

The Asian man glared at Marter and then at Sabrina and then back to Marter. "This is unfair, for I have given you too much information," he huffed. "I slipped up in announcing my anniversary."

"Would you like these wrapped?" Marter asked.

"What would that cost me?" the Asian man sighed, digging in his pocket for his purse. "No."

"Vadim, watch the street," Marter said.

"Yes," Vadim said, hurrying to the shop entranceway. It was always good to keep an eye out when coins exchanged hands, for the shysters, the rampmen, and the pistol-toting thieves always seemed to be able to sniff out money on the table, and they hit hard. Marter was careful but he also kept two loaded pistols under the counter.

The Asian man counted out his money — Founders coins, which were the best currency — and handed them to Marter.

"Thank you for your patronage, kind sir," Marter said.

"Harrumph," the Asian man replied and hurried out into the busy lane, lugging his little crate.

Marter turned to Sabrina and smiled. "Here, little one, this is good for us. We can keep improving our stock."

"May I go to the sweet shop?" Sabrina asked.

Marter laughed, pressing a silver coin into Sabrina's hand. "Yes. One shilling for the sweet shop."

"Thank you, father!" Sabrina said. Marter insisted that they call each other father and daughter ever since they had left Founders City. In Refugio they were known as Leonid and Sabrina Serafim. Sabrina was a fairly common name, especially in the north, so Marter had seen no harm in her keeping it, but the surname of Fawkes was never to be breathed again.

"Master Serafim!" the voice of a young boy cracked, high and sharp, from the doorway. The hair stood up on the back of Sabrina's neck. "Master Serafim!" The boy was Gaspar, a street urchin whose clothes were dirty and tattered but he was well fed because he was an excellent pickpocket.

"Gaspar—what is it?" Marter asked.

"Men are coming this way," Gaspar said. "Black cloaks and pistols."

"How do you know they are for us?" Marter asked.

"Vadim met them at the intersection," Gaspar answered, turning to peer into the street. "He's leading them here."

"Vadim," Sabrina snarled under her breath. She should have known better. She should have known.

"Get out of here!" Marter shouted to Gaspar, then spun to Sabrina. "Get in the tunnel."

"Not without you," Sabrina replied, her fright making her words snap.

Marter snatched her by the shoulders. It was the first time she'd ever seen him angry, the first time he'd ever gripped her roughly. "Go!"

Sabrina obeyed. She scurried into the back room, shoving aside a wicker table and a rug to expose a trapdoor.

"Good afternoon, dear sirs," Marter said loudly in the shop. "What can I find for you today?"

Sabrina hauled the heavy trapdoor open and paused. She crawled to a gap in the wall where, with the right side of her face pressed against the rough wood, she could see through into the shop. Marter's back was to her; his right hand resting on one of the pistols hidden under the counter.

Five people stood in the shop, their dark forms blocking out the noise and light from the street. Vadim was with them, off to one side, looking scared. The leading man in a dark leather hat and overcoat grinned, a gap-toothed smile through his scattershot black beard, his blazing blue eyes standing out from his dirty face; he was a mercenary from the looks of the irregular knives and pistols jammed in his bandoliers. The mercenary stepped aside to allow a tall, strawberry-haired woman and two equally tall blond-haired men to advance in front of him, soldierly in their bearing, wearing black airman clothes and black cloaks, all gripping pistols.

"This would be your man, I believe?" the mercenary announced to the strawberry-blond woman.

"Yes, it's him," she answered without taking her eyes off Marter. "You've earned your reward, Mr. Hackett."

"Ah, Lieutenant Tunney," Marter said, a tense strain in his voice. "What brings you to my little shop? Spartak is awfully far afield for a Founders interior agent and her steampipers."

"My rank is captain now, Marter, you filthy yellowjacket," Tunney answered. "Where is the girl?"

"Long dead, I'm afraid," Marter said. "Carbuncle plague. Very sad."

Tunney's eyes narrowed. "Put your right hand

on the countertop, Marter." Tunney and her two steampipers raised their pistols. A firing squad.

Hackett laughed.

Sabrina gasped. Marter's head shifted slightly, a barely perceptible jerk back towards her. He'd heard her. They had heard her.

"Dead, eh?" Tunney roared.

"Run!" Marter shouted, whipping his pistol up.

The three Founders' pistols fired as one.

Hot blood hit Sabrina's cheek and she jerked back, her legs knocking the trapdoor shut with a resounding thud. There was no time to pull it up again. Already she'd spun to her feet and was on the run, bolting out of the box-crowded storeroom and through the tiny kitchen into the sleeping quarters. Her few personal possessions rested in a metal box under her bed — but there was no time to get it.

In the rear corridor Sabrina snatched a kerosene lamp from its hook and hurled it back into the kitchen. The glass shattered, the spraying fuel bursting into flames. She hurled herself at the back door, slamming into it and staggering backwards. The lock. The damned door was always locked.

Sabrina threw the bolt and kicked the door open, charging into the cold blue light of the narrow alleyway. She croaked for breath — the blow against the door seemed to have collapsed her lungs — but breathing was less important than escaping now. She raced along the gap between the tar-paper shacks and wooden buildings, a space hardly wider than the breadth of her shoulders. Her lungs opened up just as she thought she might faint, her chest expanding in one painful heave. She charged ahead, head low, her boots splashing in the filthy, steaming, slushy black sewage streaming down a central channel, floating with dead rats and other, less-sanitary things. She could smell nothing but urine.

She heard the splashes of boots coming after her.

Dogs barked on Sabrina's left, their fangs snapping in a two-inch gap between the ground and the bottom of a corrugated tin wall. Her breath fired white bolts in front of her face and she knew she was stupid because the Founders would have stationed someone at the other end of the alley. She was stupid not to have flung herself into the escape tunnel, the tunnel Marter and Vadim had secretly dug to emerge behind a garbage pile on the other side of the Kaminski's hovel thirty feet away.

Vadim. He had betrayed them. And there would be a Founders' man waiting for her at the other end of that tunnel.

The bang of a Founders' pistol thundered behind Sabrina, the wallop of it funneling down the alley. The lead ball zipped past her ear with a rattling buzz and dinged off something metal where the alley exited into the street twenty feet ahead.

"Don't kill her!" Tunney shouted somewhere behind, a thousand echoes behind. "Fawkes wants her alive!"

Sabrina burst out into the busy street, sliding and slipping, and cut to the right, dodging the currents of pedestrians as she'd done for years as a child. She knew how to lose pursuers, how to use the crooked streets to her advantage as child pickpockets do. Don't look back. Never look back. She heard the shouts of the steampipers behind her, the dismayed grunts and cries of people as they were knocked aside.

Sabrina slid under a wagon, the rippled ice bruising the skin of her right thigh before she hopped to her feet and sprinted down another alley. Now that she could breathe freely she wanted to sob, to scream her heart out of her body, to throw herself down and die. But she had to run. She had to live. Because so many had to pay for what they had done, and now there were three more.

Tunney, Hackett, and Vadim.

Sabrina clambered up the bricks of a collapsed wall and dashed along the shantytown rooftops, her feet banging on the wooden planks and scrap metal. Dodging the loose coverings and tarpaulins, she accelerated and made the six-foot leap to the drainpipe of the old church and pulled herself up hand over hand. On the high church roof she scrabbled across the ice-slickened, crumbling clay tiles until she made it to the bell tower and squeezed through a hole in the belfry.

The tall, wooden square compartment which housed the old bell was just big enough for Sabrina to stretch out and this she did, lying still, waiting for her lungs and heart to ease back from nearly bursting. The belfry hole was her own private discovery. She'd hidden here before, the coin purses of angry merchants clutched to her stomach, laughing silently. The belfry had been closed up long ago and though the old rusty nails still held the original boards in place, the wood had grayed and shrunk and warped. It was all white and gray. The bird and bat guano was white and gray and the outside light filled the space with a hundred gray-white columns.

Sabrina heard Tunney shouting in the square below, frustration ringing in her voice as it bounced off the stone walls. Sabrina envisioned Tunney striding through the churchyard with its bare concrete pedestals, their bronze statues long gone and melted down, their inscriptions dissolving away.

"Where is she?" Tunney howled. "You promised us the girl, Hackett!"

"You had your girl!" Hackett roared. "I'm not responsible for you bungling a capture!"

"This way!" It was Vadim's voice, frightened and high, girlish, but it was Vadim's voice. "I know where the urchins hide!"

Sabrina lay still, breathing through her mouth now. She was glad Vadim didn't know about the bell tower. Actually, Vadim didn't know about a lot of things. The Founders had chosen a poor snitch.

Sabrina remained in the bell tower for two days. She was cold, wearing only her ratty woolen sweater, but she didn't allow herself to suffer. She thought of Marter, all warm memories, and she occasionally had to remind herself that he was dead. She wasn't going to cry. She wanted no food, no water, no sleep, only a whip with which to lash the world. By the morning of the third day she started to hallucinate. The peaked roof of the tower expanded and contracted and the universe expanded and contracted with it. At times she floated in white-gray nothingness or drifted through wooden-ribbed space. She gave herself up to the comforting oblivion for a while, becoming nothing more than the whistle of the wind through the cracks, the glimmer of the ice on the edges of the cantilevered vents, the swirling peel of white paint lifted up from a board the color of an old man's beard.

At noon on the third day in the bell tower Sabrina drew her dagger from her belt and laid it over her heart.

XXXIV

SEMAPHORE BRIDGE

At midnight on the third day in the bell tower Sabrina climbed down from the church roof and walked to the Semaphore Bridge.

Vadim—a snake-oil-salesman to the core—always wanted to make the big score, to get rich quick, and he was most comfortable with a little gang of dangerous pretenders who always gathered under the Semaphore Bridge.

Gliding across the snowy walkways, Sabrina reached the concrete side of the Semaphore riverbed, now nothing more than a big snowy concrete ditch with a bottom of yellow ice. Fires, their wooden fuel purloined from abandoned houses, burned under the bridge as they always did, warming the hands of the homeless beggars. The light of the flames gave the iron bridge and the snowbound ravine a weird, fluttering aspect, like a wavering orange tunnel leading into eternity.

Sabrina skidded down the embankment and found herself walking past knots of sleeping people huddled under mountains of blankets or packed inside ramshackle shacks, their fires burning, dozens of them, along both sides of the ravine. Directly under the bridge, the choicest spot because it was sheltered, burned the largest fire. Around it three young men and one young woman sat on old dining room chairs, sipping from ceramic mugs. Drawing her knife and holding it behind her back, Sabrina strode directly toward them.

The first to notice Sabrina was Leper, the shortest of the group, a mean streets pretender with a real home like Vadim, and he jumped to his feet.

"What the?" Leper groaned. "Vadim — look."

The others stood up from their chairs. Vadim looked frightened, already backing up. The other two were Semyon and Birdie, shady-eyed customers, true street thugs, slick and dangerous.

"Hello, Sabrina," Semyon said with a sleepy grin. "People have been looking for you."

Sabrina smelled chocolate. They were drinking hot chocolate. One of them had recently come into a nice pile of money, then. "I want Vadim."

Semyon laughed. "Why? He isn't good-looking like me."

"You three should leave," Sabrina said, still advancing.

Semyon's smile vanished. "What's behind your back, girl?" He tossed his mug aside, sloshing dark liquid across the dirty snow. "Vadim is one of us, girl. We don't abandon each other."

"He betrayed me," Sabrina said, never taking her eyes off of Vadim, who cowered behind the others.

"And he got paid," Leper said. He threw down his mug and Birdie did the same.

"There is a fine bounty out on your head," Semyon said, reaching inside his coat for a knife or pistol as he stepped in front of the others. "I'll take you in, after I make you my girlfriend for a little while, first."

If outnumbered you must run, Marter's voice echoed in Sabrina's head. If you choose not to run then you must act first, before the enemy thinks you're willing to act. Take advantage of them before they can organize to take advantage of their numbers.

Sabrina kept walking straight at Vadim, Leper, Birdie, and Semyon, almost right into their fire in the midst of them.

Hit them, Marter would say. When suddenly and unexpectedly hit, even when they see you coming at the last moment, most human beings will freeze. It may be only a fraction of a second, but the brain needs time to understand, to sort out information before reacting with something more than instinct.

Sabrina planted her foot, hurling her knife at Semyon's throat. The blade flashed once in rotation, so short was the distance between them. Semyon staggered, clutching at the knife buried in his throat. He dropped his newly drawn dagger and fell backwards. He landed hard, convulsing in the snow, his blood spurting, glittering in the air.

"You bitch!" Leper shouted but his voice squeaked with fear. He clumsily yanked a pistol out from inside his big overcoat.

Sabrina rolled, grabbing Semyon's dagger out of the snow. She sensed the blade was ill-weighted but she had no intention of throwing this one. Springing up in front of Leper, she knocked aside his gun hand and thrust Semyon's dagger deep into his stomach. Leper shuddered, his eyes wide and dark and peering into hers. She wrenched the blade around inside of him. He jerked and gurgled, mouth splayed wide open, and fell to the side. Sabrina lifted the pistol out of his hand as he dropped.

Birdie turned and ran.

Vadim was already running.

Sabrina cocked the pistol. A thundering roar rose in her head, deafening her, making the world shake beneath her boots. Chunks of snow dropped in reams from the trestles above. She realized a train was passing overhead, the locomotive pounding over the bridge. In the shadows dozens of faces looked at her, dirty faces poking out of blanket piles and holes in the tarpaper shacks. These people would do nothing. All they wanted was to ransack the bodies once Sabrina left.

And they were welcome to it. Sabrina was already on the run, scrambling up the embankment, her boots kicking apart the crumbling footprints Vadim had made just seconds before. Birdie was out of sight but Sabrina didn't care. Birdie could go. Sabrina leapt through the snow like a gazelle. Ahead of her, Vadim stumbled and shambled, gasping and weeping, slowing himself down as he clawed with his good hand at whatever weapon he'd stored inside his coat.

Vadim cut down an alley but Sabrina was already on him, catching up to him so fast it surprised her. She stopped, raised the pistol and fired. The gunpowder flash lit up the high brick walls, the discharge ringing sharply. Through the burst of black smoke Sabrina saw Vadim hurled forward, his arms and legs flinging out as he landed on his stomach and sent up a wave of displaced snow.

Sabrina tossed the pistol aside and approached Vadim, stepping over the red streak he had left behind as he skidded across the ice. The wall masonry dripped with blood. The ball had blown Vadim out from the inside, from back to front. Vadim gasped, face down, the hurl and ebb of his last agonized breaths puffing the snow back and forth around his cheeks.

Bits of things lay scattered in the snow; irregular chunks of pink and white and pale yellow—Sabrina realized they were cookies, wrapped in wax paper, blasted out of Vadim's coat pocket. They had been a sweet reward for betrayal, like the chocolate, bought with Marter's blood money.

Sabrina knelt alongside Vadim and yanked at his blood-soaked coat until she found his coin purse, fat and heavy, and jammed it into her own pocket. She was going to need money now. Vadim's form went rigid as Sabrina stood up. She heard his death rattle, saw his muscles lose so much tension the body almost dissolved into the snow.

Sabrina stood still in the silence, the blast of the gun and the thunder of the train echoing in her ears, her heart racing in her chest. The moon, a bright haze within the clouds, cast a silver-blue light upon the world and looked alien after the warm orange fires of the ravine. Snowflakes drifted down thick and soft and unaffected. Tomorrow the footprints would be gone, the pools of blood frozen, the bodies no one cared about buried under the white.

One down, Sabrina thought. One down and an army to go.

Sabrina froze.

Someone was behind her.

Sabrina spun around. A figure stood in the night shadows, heavily cloaked, so indistinguishable through the snowfall it seemed there might not actually be someone there.

But she was there.

It was Elizabeth.

***

Sabrina woke from her dream with a start. Staring at the dark luminiferous aether tubes on the ceiling, it took her a moment to remember where she was; her quarters in the undersea city of Atlantis. It was quiet. The dark sea gurgled outside the viewing window. Air hummed gently out of an overhead vent. She rose from the bed into a sitting position. Welly and Buckle were both asleep, Welly on the divan and Buckle flopped in a plush chair with his boots on. She was truly surprised that Buckle had managed to get some shut-eye.

"Are you well, Sabrina?" Penny Dreadful asked, a breathy metallic whisper.

Sabrina saw Penny standing in the area of the secret passageway, her amber eyes glowing in the dark.

"Yes, I'm fine," Sabrina whispered. "Be quiet now, so as not to wake the others." Sabrina swung off the bed and moved into the bathroom. She shut the door and, plunging both hands into the silver basin, splashed cold water her face. She breathed through her nose, feeling droplets of water trickle down her neck and soak into her shirt collar. She looked at herself in the mirror: the person staring back at her seemed a stranger, more like Odessa than her own face.

The old nightmares of her last day with Marter

and the killing of Vadim were as vivid as they always were. Except, this time, Elizabeth's appearance at the end was new, horrifyingly new.

I'll be damned, Sabrina thought. She wiped her face and neck with a towel and exited the washroom, returning to sit on her bed. Penny still watched her but she didn't make eye contact, choosing to gaze out the sea window instead. Sabrina felt groggy, detached, as if she was unable to pull her head out of the dream world she'd just left. The ocean pulsed outside the glass, pulsed with a pressure as old and dark as the beginning of the world, and she felt it, felt it reaching for her, felt its weight on the surface of her eyeballs. She stared into the sea until her head hurt and bits of stars flickered inside her eyes.

Sabrina shut her eyelids. A vision struck her from the darkness: the window glass shattered and the freezing sea burst in. She saw her dead body suspended, floating in a galaxy of flickering luminiferous aether and glowing, purple-bellied jellyfish. After the initial dismay it gave her an odd sense of relief.

XXXV

ELIZABETH IN CHAINS

Buckle was on his feet before his eyes opened, before he was awake, pawing for his scabbard before it fell out of his lap and hit the dark floor and he was moving as he found it, moving, moving blindly toward the secret passageway. Elizabeth was with him in his dream. She was with him even now. And she'd shown him the way to find her. He reached the bulkhead where the secret hatch was located and began twisting and wrenching at every ornament he could wrap his hands around.

"What?" Sabrina asked, sitting up in her bed. "Romulus?"

"Get this damned hatch open!" Buckle ordered. Every nerve tingled, muddying the function of his half-awake brain. "She's through here!"

"Captain?" Welly asked, rising groggily from the divan.

"Get this open!" Buckle shouted. He stepped back and kicked the bulkhead as if some expression of his frustration might knock the door open.

"I know how to open the hatch," Penny

Dreadful announced, clanking across the deck to the bulkhead.

"Quickly now, quickly!" Buckle pressed, hedging behind Penny as she began manipulating the wall decorations. She tapped her metal fingers along a semi-circular string of metal dolphins, depressing a number of them.

Sabrina jumped out of bed. "What happened?"

"I had a dream," Buckle said. Shivering, he cinched his sword belt tight around his waist. He couldn't shake the eerie sight of Elizabeth kneeling beside his chair in the darkness, the curve of her cheek lit by the aether night lamp, her hand on his forearm, its pressure so odd, incomplete, as if the fingers were more water than flesh. For an instant he feared what visited him had been her ghost — that Elizabeth was dead — but he knew she was alive. And now he was terrified of losing her again. *I shall show you where I am*, Elizabeth had whispered, the breathy issue of her voice sounded both close and distant, both intimate and as if forced toward him from far away. *You must hurry.*

"She came to me in my dream as well," Sabrina said. "Are you fully awake, Romulus?"

"But it wasn't a dream," Buckle replied. "It was Elizabeth. She spoke to me. She showed me where she is. She showed me the way. She's here, Sabrina! She's here. We must go now, this instant," Buckle said, turning to Penny. "Hurry up, damn you!"

"But how do you know where she is?" Sabrina asked, scrambling for her boots and sword belt. Welly was up now, blinking.

"Because she took me there," Buckle replied.

Penny spun a dial. Buckle heard a low hiss of compressed air as the hatch swung open into the aether-lit tunnel Lady Julia had used — the same tunnel Elizabeth had led him into in the dream. "Stay here!" Buckle ordered as he lunged through the hatchway, taking off at a run.

"Damn it, Romulus!" Sabrina shouted after him. "Wait! We'll come with you! Wait!"

Buckle couldn't wait. Elizabeth was in agony and alone and she'd shown him where she was. He raced along the long, narrow, curving passageway lit by a single tube of luminiferous aether overhead and similar to the carpenter's walk on the *Pneumatic Zeppelin*. Every pipe and bulkhead, every inch of grating, every detail matched exactly what he had seen in his dream. It was difficult for his barely awakened brain to keep the residue of the vivid dreamscape from merging into the frantic movement and impression of the now.

Elizabeth was there, running ahead of him in the passageway or, at least, her dream-memory led the way. She looked back at him, frightened, and it was a shock to witness her condition: eyes sunken and dark, cheekbones gaunt, her brown hair hanging in thick curls clotted with blood. More blood streaked her face and neck, staining her white blouse red and brown at the neck and shoulders. Buckle accelerated after her even though he was already dizzy, as if he were splitting the seams of time and space, as if the passageway was rotating around its own axis.

"Romulus!" Sabrina screamed from behind, far away in the maze. But he couldn't stop or turn to respond.

Elizabeth's boots left the metal grating and she lifted into the air, a fluttering white swan, wounded and bloody, attempting to take off in a long metal cage. Her image faded away but Buckle didn't need it—he could make the trip through the labyrinth on his own. Elizabeth had already shown him the way.

The passageway veered and branched into a myriad of tunnels, the metal veins of the underwater city, pulsing with the lifeblood of luminiferous aether. Buckle plunged down a circular stairwell in a tight spin to the right. Three levels down he reached the hatchway Elizabeth had led him to in the dream. He spun the crank and the hatch flung open with a swish of air, popping his eardrums and meeting him with the stink of wet wood, old seawater and machine oil.

Buckle jumped into a wide, brightly lit, utilitarian passageway with a grimy metal grating for a floor. Stacks of barrels and crates lined the bulkheads, all in the same configurations he had seen in his dream.

Buckle turned hard right, heading straight for a huge airlock hatch which was shut tight. This was where the dream of Elizabeth had ended. Elizabeth was in there. Whatever was behind the hatch, Elizabeth was inside of it.

"Halt!" a surprised voice bellowed behind Buckle. He glanced over his shoulder to see the far end of the passageway crowded with armed Atlantean soldiers, their white and gold armor bright under the aether tubes, their pearl-colored swords and tridents clenched in their hands. An officer, a high-ranker from the looks of his scarlet helmet comb and the large scattershot pistol in his hand, shouted: "You there! Halt!"

Buckle charged the docking bay hatch, having no idea how he might breach the towering disc. He heard the loud click of steel bolts, the squeal of a rotating wheel and felt a heave of pressurized air. Creaking, the hatch swung outward toward him.

"What the — stop!" the Atlantean officer howled.

Buckle drew his sword and plunged into the bright, rapidly widening gap in the hatchway. He was instantly face-to-face with a Founders seaman straining to push the hatch open; he was a short young man with a shaven head, wearing a dark blue uniform, and he had a striking look on his face and in his shining eyes — a look of confusion, a kind of unbelieving horror of a man who could not control himself.

Knocking the seaman aside, Buckle raced into the airlock tube, its walls pressure-ribbed like the interior of a throat, and headed for the maw of a submarine hatch at the opposite end, a dark cavern lit by the green bioluminescent glow of boil.

Elizabeth was in there. She was close.

"Close the hatch!" Someone bellowed from the interior of the submarine, a voice with a strange, high-end vibrato that did not sound entirely human. "We are betrayed! Close the hatch!"

Buckle drew his sword as he ran, holding the blade at the ready in front of him. Once he entered into the dark hatchway he would be at a disadvantage; running in from the well-lit docking tunnel into the interior darkness would put the defenders with their dark-accustomed eyes at the advantage. But as he lunged through the hatchway he realized the submarine chamber just beyond the boil-lit passageway was spacious and high and full of illumination, pulsing with blue and yellow light. He smelled lubricant oil and blood.

And there she was. Elizabeth burst into the passageway, running to him, stumbling, her regal face bloody and gaunt, her white shift stained with blood just as she had appeared to him in his dream. She threw out her arms to him, reaching for him, reaching for her salvation. "Romulus!" she gasped.

It was Elizabeth. Not a memory. Not a dream.

Not a mysterious vapor. She was only a few feet ahead of him, in the flesh. "Elizabeth!" Buckle cried. "I'm here! I am here!"

Two Founders seamen burst out of the hatchway around Elizabeth, older men, experienced salts, one sandy haired and the other black haired, both shorter than Buckle but burly in the arms and shoulders. Their look of surprise shifted to fury as they grabbed hold of Elizabeth and dragged her back. "Intruder!" One of the seamen shouted.

"Romulus!" Elizabeth screamed.

"No!" Buckle roared, hurling his body headlong, saber whirling. He burst into a large, high chamber pulsing with yellow-blue light, the high bulkheads a riot of twisting metal pipes as if it were the nest of some huge machine-beast. The two seamen released Elizabeth and grabbed for the knives sheathed at their waists.

Buckle slashed left and right. Stripes of red splattered the deck as both Founders seamen dropped. Buckle grabbed Elizabeth by the arm as she reached for him. Her eyes. He had not forgotten the immense depth of her eyes. In them he saw hope and despair, warning and need. Elizabeth was fighting for her mind. In the next instant he felt his connection to her being blocked, overwhelmed. Elizabeth fought it. She fought it. Blood burst out of her right nostril and poured down her lip.

"Run!" Elizabeth cried, and though he was

closer to her she sounded weaker. "It's all wrong, Romulus. It's a trap! Run!"

"I'll get you out of here!" Buckle shouted.

A shadow swept behind Elizabeth, a looming figure silhouetted by the lights in the submarine chamber, a tall, winged creature glimmering with metal. It moved like a spider but it was humanoid. Buckle glimpsed goggles, their interiors glimmering with liquid, but the face was obscured by a metal helmet, a weird helmet crowned with hoops of metal holding metal spheres orbiting it like the satellites of a solar system; the figure's long arm, draped in black cloth with metal-gauntleted fingers, wrapped around Elizabeth, pulling her away.

"No!" Elizabeth screamed.

The thing dragged Elizabeth back, dragged her back into the darkness.

"No!" Buckle howled, his sword over his head. "Elizabeth!"

A Martian, a tall, skinny creature wearing a gray uniform glorious with its rows of buttons and gold lace, his long black hair framing a zebra-striped face and goggle apparatus over his large black eyes, jumped in front of Buckle.

"Stand aside, zebe!" Buckle roared.

The Martian, drawing his rapier in a motion so quick it was no more than a blur, knocked Buckle's blade aside in a rip of blue sparks. Buckle lunged, barely avoiding a skewering on the Martian's quick blade. Buckle slashed, attempting to plow through the alien, but he found himself in trouble, barely deflecting swipes of steel so quick he was in immediate fear for his own life. But Buckle pressed, unwilling to sacrifice his forward momentum.

The Martian backed up a step though he seemed unimpressed by the ferocity of Buckle's attack; his Martian eyes, the treacherous, bottomless, black eyes of the full-blooded alien so much more intense than those of Max, whose half-human genetics had softened their malevolent aura to a great extent, looked somewhat amused after a deadly fashion, in the triumphant way a cat observes a mouse it has caught.

Sailors brandishing cutlasses and pikes raced in, fanning out around the Martian's flanks. Buckle was suddenly outnumbered and surrounded. He would not retreat, he would not give up one inch. He would rescue Elizabeth or perish in the attempt. He knocked a sailor's cutlass aside, chopping him nearly in half on the backhand slash. The sailor dropped away and was replaced by two more attackers, one of them wearing steampiper black and silver.

Buckle found himself fending off six weapons at once.

A commotion rose behind Buckle, a clattering of armor and shouts. The Atlantean guards had followed him in. More bodies poured into the chamber, small, blue-coated submariners and tall, light-haired steampipers, their boots ringing on the grating.

"Master Shuba! Get back!" the steampiper officer shouted at the Martian.

"Do not kill him!" Shuba bellowed. "Take him alive!"

About to be overwhelmed, Buckle slashed left and right, knocking swords and slicing hands, but the attackers wedged inside his guard, crashing into him, swamped him in fist-blows and grasping hands. The world spun upside down as Buckle fell. He knew a truncheon had struck his head but it seemed far more probable the submarine was rolling over than he would be toppling backwards.

Buckle wanted to scream Elizabeth's name but his mouth would make no sound. He landed on his back and everything fell into slow motion. Sound collapsed into the background, a trickle under the piercing ring in his ears. Above him the knives and truncheons of the Founders extended to confront the gold and white tridents of the Atlantean guards like two portcullises closing towards one another.

"Leave him be!" Sabrina shouted, her voice echoing, shouted from the top of a distant peak, "Leave him be or your lives are forfeit, fogsuckers!"

XXXVI

UNDER ARREST

"Because you are under arrest, that is why," a woman's voice trickled into the black void, whispered through the throbbing pain as Buckle returned to consciousness.

"Captain Buckle has done nothing but attempt to defend one of our own," a female voice shot back. Sabrina.

"By brawling in the airlocks?" The voice belonged to Lady Julia and she was angry. "Doing what? Carrying out his own private little war? Our guards assisted in his defense, against orders, more out of instinct than self-preservation. Has your captain gone mad, charging the Founders in such a way? May I remind you that Aventine Atlantis is not at war with the Founders, at least not officially."

Buckle remembered the dark figure snatching Elizabeth away and shivered, something primitive inside of him frightened by the height of its metal-shod wings in the darkness. Buckle remembered the Martian officer, the one named Shuba. *Do not kill him*, Shuba had ordered. Why would they not try to kill him?

"And how did you know how to open the secret door?" Lady Julia asked.

"I picked the lock," Sabrina replied.

"If you are not a Founders why do you lie like one?" Lady Julia shot back. "It was the automaton. The little machine knows too much and that makes it doubly dangerous."

"What is to be done with us then?" Welly. That voice came out of Welly. Buckle felt he should open his eyes but it seemed like far too much effort at the moment. And in the blackness he could see Elizabeth, bloody and beaten. He feared that if he opened his eyes he would lose her altogether, for he could no longer feel her presence. She wasn't there with him anymore. Despair washed through him. He had failed to rescue her. There was no reason to open his eyes.

Lady Julia sighed. "Considering how difficult and unpredictable you have already proven to be as an ally, I am uncertain as to how to proceed. A real Crankshaft ambassador might have been helpful. Now Founders sailors have been killed. This spilling of blood has yet to be answered by the Vicar. He has sealed up his submersible but it still remains at dock. Yet there is nothing for it. We shall forcibly detach his submersible if he remains unbidden much longer."

Detach. If the Founders submersible left it would take Elizabeth with it. Elizabeth. Buckle stirred himself out of his malaise, forcing his eyes open. He found

Penny Dreadful leaning over him.

"The Captain is awake," Penny said.

Welly leaned in from nearby, his eel-leather seat squeaking under his weight, "Take it easy, Sir."

Blinking, Buckle realized he was lying on a couch in the middle of a spacious, round chamber with soaring, ink-black walls. White marble columns and purple banners lined the room, reaching up to the lip of a white dome where a brilliant fresco of Neptune and Mars, Neptune under the sea and Mars above it, presided over the space. The carpet and cushions were of crimson velvet and the tables and chairs were either black or white. A white marble fountain dominated the center of the chamber, topped by a life-sized statue of a woman with a shock of curly hair — it had to be Cassandra Lombard — while fifty hippocampi leapt about her, clear water jetting from their mouths to gurgle in the basin. A great gateway, guarded by a statue of Neptune and two flesh-and-blood Praetorian guards, opened into a long corridor. A similar gateway, this one overseen by Mars and two more guards, mirrored it from the opposite wall. Two normal-sized hatchways were built into the other two walls opposing each other and while neither one was ornate their frames were brightly painted — one blue, the other green.

Lady Julia stood near the fountain with Sabrina and Welly in front of her.

"Are you alright, Captain?" Sabrina asked.

"All square," Buckle croaked, sitting up.

"You are quite fortunate that my soldiers fished you out of that Founders boat, Captain Buckle," Lady Julia said. "Or you would be dead now."

"They weren't trying to kill me, it seemed," Buckle said, planting his face in his hands and rubbing his temples.

"A hostage, then," Lady Julia said.

"Elizabeth," Buckle said. "The Founders have my sister, Elizabeth, in their submersible."

"Your sister?" Lady Julia huffed, not hiding her incredulity.

"Elizabeth?" Sabrina asked. "How can you be so certain?"

"Because I saw her," Buckle answered.

"Romulus," Sabrina said softly. "I came in right behind you. I didn't see her."

"Nor I, Captain," Welly added.

"She was taken away," Buckle said. He looked up at the others. "She came to me in a dream — I don't know how — and she showed me exactly how to reach the docking bay and find her. She is in poor condition. We must get to her. We must."

Sabrina turned to Lady Julia. "If this is true then you must not detach the Vicar's boat. You must keep him secured in place until this mess is settled. One of Admiral Balthazar's daughters is being held aboard that Founders war machine against her will."

"That makes no sense," Lady Julia grumbled. "What need have they of your sister here?"

"I don't know," Buckle said, standing unsteadily, waving off Welly's attempt to help him. "As your ally I ask your assistance in her recovery."

"I have empathy for your situation, Captain," Lady Julia replied. "But you shall make no demands of me."

Fury surged in Buckle but he recognized it as despair disguised as rage. Elizabeth was so close. Why were the Founders holding her? Had Elizabeth been used as bait? Had the Vicar and his Martians brought her close and allowed her to beseech her own rescue — through some alien-powered mind amplification, surely — in order to lure him in? But, why? What did they need from a Crankshaft airship captain? No. Nothing added up. The Founders boat had arrived hours before Buckle and his contingent did and they would have had no knowledge of his coming nor would have any sane person predicted it. No, Elizabeth was here for a different reason. "Very well, Lady Julia. If you could update me on the situation."

Lady Julia took a deep breath. "The Founders tightened the blockade at dawn. One of our submarines has gone missing and two Guardian patrols have not returned from their pickets."

"Julia!" Octavian roared from the Neptune

archway. "That is enough."

Buckle spun to face Octavian and Cressida as they strode into the room. Marius and Horatus walked behind them wearing gold breastplates and helmets, hands tight on the handles of the swords sheathed at their belts — nervous men.

"The Crankshafts are now our allies, as we all agreed, father," Lady Julia said. "I do not believe obscuring our condition is the best way to have them help us."

Octavian shook his head. "We Aventines keep our own council on military matters. You know this."

Buckle noticed a small, fat man strolling in the protected gap between the politicians and the soldiers; he was the shape of a billiard ball and his equally round head was rounded out by a spherical coif of tightly curled brown hair. His white toga swept under a golden sash at his midriff and then hung to his knees like loose drapes, imparting to him the appearance of a small table with an oversized tablecloth; he seemed to float rather than walk even though you could see his sandaled feet scuttling along underneath.

"It is best to keep one's mind to one's self," the round man growled. "There are traitors among us." He held one hand out in front of him in a deliberate, theatrical fashion, his small fingers adorned with gold rings. Foppish. Arrogant. Buckle already disliked him intensely. Nero, the *Pneumatic Zeppelin*'s ballast officer and overbearing performance artist, would love him.

Lady Julia turned to Buckle. "May I introduce you to Cicero, the Keeper of the Aether."

Buckle made a small bow. "Captain Romulus Buckle of the Crankshafts."

"Charmed, I'm sure," Cicero said. But he didn't mean it.

Buckle didn't care. His head swam, reaching for the underpinnings of a desperate plan, a plan to tackle the Founders submersible and rescue Elizabeth.

"Are you alright, Romulus?" Sabrina whispered. She had moved alongside him, her mouth close to his ear. "How is your head?"

"I'm fine," Buckle replied.

"I would like to state for the record I do not approve of foreign clan members being introduced into Atlantean affairs," Cicero announced to no one and everyone.

"It tasks me but we need the Crankshafts with us," Lady Julia said.

"Do not allow outsiders to know what we need, Lady Julia," Cicero snapped.

Octavian turned his attention to Buckle. "We are heading into an emergency session of the Senate. Once they ratify my motion for Atlantis to join the Grand Alliance your clan must openly assist us in our resistance against the Founders."

"We have to get out of here first," Buckle said.

"There are escape routes the Founders are unaware of," Octavian said. "Your mercenary submarine has been salvaged and should be repaired before nightfall. Captain Felix shall get you to your airship if his crew isn't too drunk to drive her. Cressida, have someone make sure that the crew of the *Dart* has no more access to stupefying drink."

"Yes, First Consul," Cressida replied.

Cicero tapped his fingers together. "Of what use to us is this alliance? I don't believe any of your member clans possess submarines, do they, Captain?"

"We shall secure the sky," Buckle said.

"Oh, Captain, please," Cicero snarked. "Secure the sky? Your balloons are useless to us down here if this confrontation falls to blows."

"The Grand Alliance shall soon apply immense pressure upon the Founders from the north, east and south," Buckle said. "They'll be forced to turn their weapons toward us."

"Soon?" Cicero asked. "How soon is soon, Captain? Because we are about to be attacked. Are there any Crankshaft airships on their way to us now? No. Of course not. Useless."

"It is no matter," Marius boomed in his deep, commanding voice. "Our defenses shall hold. The seven domes are impenetrable."

"Nothing is impenetrable, Master Equitum," Cicero said. "Except your daughter's chastity. But then again, perhaps not."

Marius reddened. He looked like he was ready to chop Cicero's head off.

"You are a royal jackass, Cicero," Horatus said.

"Enough!" Octavian said. "I hope you are a decent orator, Captain Buckle. Upon my signal you shall enter the Senate chamber and come to stand at my side. You shall present the Grand Alliance's offer of alliance to Senate."

"For the fools to debate it?" Cicero huffed. "Pah! Just do it. Do what must be done. The Senate is a rubber stamp as it is."

"Things must be done correctly, Cicero," Octavian said. "Especially in times of great duress. Otherwise the entire system breaks down. Remain here, all of you, and I shall send for you. Cicero shall present you on the floor, for as the Keeper of the Aether he carries great import with the Senate."

"Of course they listen to me," Cicero said. "I am the best mind in Atlantis, after all."

Octavian led Marius, Horatus and Julia towards the Neptune gate. He pointed at Penny Dreadful as he walked past her. "And keep this living machine out of sight. No one out there wants to see her. How has that thing not been destroyed?"

Octavian and his entourage disappeared into the passageway. Buckle closed his eyes. Every inch of him ached. He kept seeing Elizabeth in his mind's eye, her face and shirt ragged with blood. He kept seeing the winged creature, no more than a nightmare shade in the dark chamber, looming up behind her. He opened his eyes.

"That automaton must be scrapped," Cicero huffed. "You fools have no idea what your toy is capable of."

"We are handling her," Sabrina replied.

"Oh, and I suppose you think you're its mother, don't you?" Cicero said. "Of course you do."

"She is a lovely little thing," Sabrina said.

"Until she slices your abdomen open and makes a bow out of your intestines," Cicero laughed. "That'll be the abrupt end of your little 'mothering' adventure. A sky tramp like you isn't cut out for mothering as it is."

"Just hold it right there, Keeper," Welly snapped.

"It's alright, Welly," Sabrina said. "I'm sure your mother is quite proud of your manners, Keeper."

"My mother gave me the blood of the Lombard line," Cicero replied. "I surpassed the intelligence of my parents at the age of five. That's what she is proud of, not the ignorant game of 'manners'."

Sabrina gave Cicero a big, lovely smile. "Why don't you take your manners and shove them up your—"

"Lieutenant!" Buckle ordered, crossing his arms.

"Yes, sir?" Sabrina said.

"A proper move, Captain," Cicero said. "No one, not even I, wishes to see your pretty officer humiliated."

"How about we all stay quiet for a moment?" Buckle asked. He folded his hands behind his back, trying to stretch his arms in a way that might relax the immense tension in his shoulders, but he failed. What he really wanted to do was to draw his sword and wiggle the tip against Cicero's throat until the man pissed himself, but he kept that urge under control.

XXXVII

THE KEEPER OF THE AETHER

Cicero released a long, bored sigh and eased his portly form onto a large divan. "This shall be a little while. It takes at least twenty minutes for Marius to introduce Octavian, though he might make an exception and abbreviate his list of imaginary accomplishments and titles this one time, considering the dire and impending nature of our circumstances." Cicero clasped his hands together and his gold rings clinked. Each ring was set with precious stones and the largest, a large golden dolphin, looked too big for his short, pudgy finger. Cicero studied each of the Crankshafts with unkind eyes, like a butterfly collector peering into his killing jar. "Might I ask how a Founders scarlet finds herself among the old Crankshaft pirates?"

"I am not Founders," Sabrina said.

"Your blood is," Cicero said mildly. He cocked his head. "That crimson-haired trait seems not to exist anywhere else in such powerful expression but among the Founders, which is interesting in itself, really, genetically speaking. Inbreeding creates some brilliant results as well as the undesirable ones, wouldn't you agree?"

Sabrina looked at Buckle and grinned.

"A person is more than the clan they were born to," Buckle said.

"Aye," Welly whispered from the background.

Cicero glanced at Welly. "Ah, the pipsqueak apprentice squeaks? And so eloquently and vociferously."

"I know what those words mean," Welly said.

"Of course you do," Cicero replied as if he hardly cared. "As well as a pimply midshipman adolescent schooled in the northern backwoods might know anything."

"I am a man of action, not an eater of cake," Welly replied, but Cicero wasn't listening to him anymore. "And my rank is Ensign."

"Insulting my crew will get you prickly results," Buckle said.

Cicero tapped his temple and looked Buckle. "I see through people and into their deficiencies; it is as if I can scan them microscopically and identify defects in their evolutionary strands. This perceptiveness is both a blessing and a curse. Don't make me turn my microscope on you, Captain."

"How about you turn it on yourself, fish man?" Sabrina asked.

"I'm afraid you'd find far too many odd bugs on

my strands to make sense of it," Buckle said.

"Fear not, Captain," Sabrina said. The Keeper's insight seems restricted to little more than hair color and insignia pips."

"Ah, yes, I have restrained myself because you are guests of the First Consul, but don't get me wrong, Fawkes-girl!" Cicero laughed, a high-pitched trill both happy and mocking. "I would be thrilled to possess a few bits of your genetics, the ones which would supply me with your head of rich crimson hair. Ah, the partners I might bed with tresses such as that!" He stopped and peered into the falling water in the fountain. "Matters of love and war. Diplomacy is so childishly buggered and transparent. Boring." He paused, slipping his right forefinger back and forth under the stream flowing from one of the hippocampi, for a moment apparently mesmerized by the gurgling interruptions.

"You do understand that Atlantis cannot stand alone against the Founders," Buckle said.

Cicero continued flicking his finger through the water. "Incorrect. The Founders do not possess sufficient underwater forces to crack Atlantis, as the Master Equitum has already mentioned. The constant circling of the Founders submarines does, I must admit, unsettle me. But then it takes little to unsettle a sensitive stomach like mine."

"You must choose a side," Sabrina pressed. "We

RICHARD ELLIS PRESTON, JR.

all must choose sides."

"Or we shall all fall under the sword of the Founders and, if we survive that, be forced into a lifetime of slavery and servitude?" Cicero interjected. "Choice? Ha! Do not speak to me again of choice! We are all prisoners of the original *Cycopede* we are, our very lives locked into this circus veneer of culture, these Victorian-era aping stereotypes the four original founders used to reconstruct human society from the wreckage that was left after The Storming."

"There were three original Founders," Welly said.

"There were four," Cicero muttered under his breath.

The legend of the mysterious fourth Founder, Buckle knew. But he had never heard of a *Cycopede*. Was that the same thing as the famed *Encyclopaedia Utopia* which each clan historian possessed, the hauntingly incomplete history of the human world before The Storming?

Cicero leaned back from the fountain, wiping his fingers on the sleeve of his toga. "The reconstruction, the great new society built on a vague memory of the Victorian era, worked, it did, at least, it worked well enough, despite the silliness of much of it. Geeks, I tell you, geeks. Self-aggrandizing anti-social shut-ins playing God. Who better equipped to reconstruct the human experience, eh?" He laughed. "No going back now. And to be honest I do very much like living in the traitor Cassandra Lombard's underwater amusement park, in this re-engineered, re-imagined Greco-Roman mishmash. And with togas there is no binding underwear."

"What the hell is a *geek*?" Buckle asked.

"The very people who made this, what we are, what this is!" Cicero waved about the room. "Do you know why this atrium is black? Of course you don't. The ancient Romans once lived in one-room houses and the walls were always blackened by smoke from the fire. It is amazing what useless tidbits of information survive an apocalypse, eh? 'Atrium' is derived from the Latin word for black, which was something like 'ater." In later Roman villas the atrium became the area where guests were received, as we do here for the Senate. You see, our reconstruction of ancient society is as accurate as we could make it with the shreds of true history left to us, and knowing such details gives us great pride. As for the all the rest, well, we mimic the form and wing it, just like the Founders did."

Buckle stared at Cicero. Whether the Keeper of the Aether was truly brilliant or no more than a witty pretender he could not yet tell; the man's mind seemed to flip back and forth barely under control. Buckle knew something of the histories of the original Founders and of the clans, of how the Founders rebuilt the ruins of human society to emulate a pre-apocalypse historic era — the steam-powered age of a great empire called Victorian England. He knew how the Founders designed their expanding colonies to emulate other Victorian era model nations, which had resulted in the clan-distinctiveness of the Imperials, Gallowglasses, Spartak, the Tinskins and so on — they were based on mysterious nations of the past with enigmatic, romantic names like Germany, Ireland, Russia and Spain. This was all grammar school lesson material. But what was the Cycopede? And what were geeks?

Cicero clasped his hands on his belly. "That the original Founders would rebuild human society by reconstructing the base, dirty Victorian era never ceases to astound me. They were given a carte blanche by history. Think of it! An opportunity to remake the world! An opportunity to create a steam-driven utopia! To re-educate humanity to despise violence. And what do they do, those incompetents? They opt for the pretty clothes and the empire-mad European imperialist culture of the 19th century. Damn those fools. Those geeks, arrogant, myopic, ivory tower board gamers. Damn them."

Buckle didn't understand much of what Cicero had expressed in his final sentence. "Tell me, what are the geeks?" he asked.

Cicero yawned. "What I would be, I suppose, had I been living three hundred years ago."

"Are you suggesting that the world we live in is

nothing more than a sham?" Sabrina asked.

"No, not entirely," Cicero said. "Human beings are real and our lives are real. Culturally, the whole hastily constructed mess has evolved into its own functioning form, I suppose. We are what we are and the cities we have built, the songs we sing, and the children we have spawned, but our culture is not an organic growth. It's rather an imperfect reconstruction grafted imperfectly onto a pre-determined framework, like living plants potted on the spokes of a blacksmith's wheel by people who were neither smithies nor gardeners."

"You have difficulty speaking clearly, don't you," Sabrina said.

"Too clearly for you to understand, apparently," Cicero shot back.

"Is such not the way to rebuild something?" Welly asked. "To use the best parts of what remains?"

"Ah, the midshipman voices another opinion," Cicero sighed.

"Ensign," Welly said.

"That depends upon the quality of the remaining parts," Cicero said. "We are the phoenix rising from the ashes, eh, as the Founders believe? Humankind reborn from its finest hour? Hardly. Our Victorian rebirth is a return to the horrors of the age of industrialization, of war-worship, social inequality, and the slavery of colonization. One step forward equals two steps back."

Buckle eyed Cicero but said nothing. He hoped that the First Consul did not put too much stock in Cicero's view of the world. But, then again, the First Consul was also fond of decapitating senators and tossing their heads into cauldrons of soup. "Is that what you think of the Snow World, Keeper?" Buckle asked, pulling his pocket watch from his jacket and clicking the stem winder. "Quite the disparaging viewpoint."

Cicero waggled his finger at Buckle. "You believe that we are the phoenix, Captain, and in many ways we are. But our phoenix is imperfect. That is to be expected, of course, because we are imperfect descendants of apes or something quite like it. But what divides us is the result of pure stupidity. The Republics and Parliaments, monkey houses that they are, must stand. They must not fall to the tyrants as the Founders' parliament did long ago. Atlantis is a Republic—currently in a poor condition I admit, but a Republic nonetheless. We are the bastion of the yearnings for the greater good. You and your army of buccaneers must see to it that we do not fall or your lives of shadow-bartering and excess shall become very dark indeed."

"That same darkness threatens us all equally," Buckle said.

"Yes," Cicero answered. "And I do not wish for

things to change. I like my life the way it is." He flicked his eyes to Penny Dreadful. "Can you send that monstrosity out of the room? I don't like it watching me."

"No," Buckle said pleasantly. He said it to gall Cicero but he also didn't want Penny unprotected too far from the group. If they got the chance he was certain the Atlanteans would incinerate her and apologize without meaning it later.

Cicero sniffed. "As you wish. But when the last shred of her brain matter fails inside that metal skull case, when the last strands of what she is unravels and her machine is suddenly at the mercy of the raving mad beast of what is left in the decayed cerebral cortex, I will find some satisfaction in that she will most certainly draw and quarter you first."

"You are colorful, I shall give you that," Buckle said with a grin.

Cicero's eyes flashed mean but in the next instant he fired up a big smile. "I am the Keeper of the Aether," he said, pointing at the glowing tubes overhead. "I am electric and I am eclectic."

The green-bordered hatch to the right of the Neptune gate swung open, revealing a narrow but ornate passageway lined with green velvet carpet. Cressida emerged and waved. "Come with me, Keeper and Captain Buckle of the Crankshafts," she said. "The First Consul is ready for you."

Buckle started for the hatch. Cicero cut in front of him with surprising agility for someone so round, though he was relatively young as well, perhaps in his late twenties. "I shall lead," Cicero said, following Cressida as she turned back into the corridor. "Captain, you shall remain silent until the First Consul invites you to take the floor. The rest of you remain here — and that monstrosity stays out of sight!"

"Keep an eye out," Buckle said to Sabrina.

"Hurry up," Sabrina sighed. "I'm growing tired of being underwater."

"Be careful, Captain," Penny Dreadful said, her eyes brightening as she spoke.

"I'll be fine," Buckle replied.

"Yes, be careful, Captain," Cicero chimed in, narrowing his eyes at Penny before he swung into the green hatchway. "Be very, very careful."

XXXVIII

THE ROSTRUM

Buckle emerged from the small hatchway into the huge Atlantean senate chamber, a seven-story-high amphitheater. Its soaring glass walls undulated with the early morning light as it flowed through the turquoise currents of the sea. High above, the surface of the ocean glittered pink and white. A long silver cable soared down from the apex of the ceiling dome to swing a gigantic copper pendulum mere inches above the grand mosaic on the Senate floor. The chamber was bright, for along with the sunlight, huge tubes of luminiferous aether ran up the walls to illuminate fantastical glass sculptures installed into the dome ceiling, a breathtaking array of coral outcroppings, fish, seahorses, leaping pods of dolphins, mermaids, Roman Gods and octopi, all part of a masterpiece of glass and light.

Two Praetorian guardsmen eyed Buckle as Cressida led him and Cicero up the rear stairway of the main podium, an ornate platform decorated with Doric pillars and purple curtains. At the top Buckle saw

Octavian and Julia whispering together with Marius and Horatus close at hand. Julia motioned for Buckle and Cicero to stand beside her.

From the podium Buckle had a full view of the amphitheater: fronted by porticoes and balustrades, the long rows of polished wooden pews rose steep and high against the glass walls. Thin aether tubes laced every handrail and pew, making the red curtains and banners glow and throwing hundreds of small marble statues into high relief. Men and women in purple-laced togas packed the seats, their hundreds of murmuring voices haunting the space like a purring of a great beast.

"I have advised the Senate of the proposed alliance." Octavian said. "Make a good case, Captain." Buckle noticed that Octavian looked agitated, working his fingers against each other in a nervous, uncoordinated fashion.

"Cicero, introduce the Captain on the rostrum," Lady Julia said. She leaned close to Buckle as he passed her. "They will be contentious, but it is only for show. The First Consul has already garnered the votes necessary to approve our entry into your Grand Alliance. It would be good to impress the gallery, however."

"Do not mess this up," Cicero hissed as he led Buckle onto the low stage at the front and center of the platform. Cicero threw his arms wide. "Good members of the Aventine Senate," he boomed. "I, Cicero, the Keeper of the Aether, present to you the worthy representative of the Crankshaft clan, Captain Romulus Buckle, son of Admiral Balthazar Crankshaft. He now has permission to address the Senate."

Buckle stepped to the front of the rostrum as Cicero moved aside. The chamber gallery fell dead silent, a sea of unkind faces. Floating in the void beyond the glass walls Buckle glimpsed the small white and gold Atlantean submarines, their ports bright with the glow of luminiferous aether, patrolling the depths of the bright blue sea. He also noticed that the rostrum platform was sitting atop two large, irregular cones of metal, both pointing out toward the senate floor. The metal plates were rusted and dinged but Buckle realized they were the noses of old submarines, both adorned with the half-faded symbol of a fire-breathing sea serpent. Old enemies who succumbed to the might of Atlantis, Buckle assumed.

Buckle cleared his throat. "Senators, I come from the northeast, from the Crankshaft clan, and I act as an ambassador for Admiral Balthazar Crankshaft and all of my people. I also represent the Grand Alliance, a coalition of clans who at this very moment are assembling a Grand Armada to meet the Founders invasion, an invasion which also poses a threat to you at this very moment."

"They do not threaten us!" someone shouted

from the gallery.

"Let them try!" another voice echoed, supported by hundreds of cheers.

"Not one clan can stand alone against the Founders," Buckle said. "Not one."

A female senator stood. "How do you know that Atlantis is alone? You know nothing of our situation. You know nothing of who we have relations with or not."

"Please," Lady Julia yelled above the cacophony. "All of you. Let him speak."

"Foreigners do not belong on the senate rostrum!" someone shouted, though Buckle could not make out which face it was.

Much of the room assented with cheers.

"Let him speak! I command you!" Lady Julia shouted, and the chamber fell silent.

Buckle pressed his tongue into the inside of his bottom lip, took a deep breath and bellowed. "Shout me down, if so you choose, proud senators of Atlantis. But beware your pride. And if you choose to hear me, hear me well! There is no disgrace in a collective defense! Join us in the Grand Alliance! Together we can end the tyranny of the Founders, the blockades and coercions, once and for all!"

A long silence followed Buckle's words. Oh, if only Elizabeth, with her immense charisma and eloquence, her exacting logic and instinct for which strings of the human heart to pluck, could be on the rostrum instead of he! Whether the deal was sealed or not she would have won over many hearts in the same space of time. Buckle experienced a brief but vivid sensation that Elizabeth was there in the chamber, standing near him.

"We are quite familiar with the Founders and their strong-arm tactics," another male senator yelled, a man with a hoarse, failing voice. "Atlantis shall remain neutral as she always has and we shall bring anyone who tries to force our hand to ruin."

More cheers.

"Just what 'alliance' do you speak for, Captain?" a woman asked. "What is this great confederacy of clans you speak of?"

Buckle looked at the woman. Though the Grand Alliance had attempted to keep its nature secret the spies had immediately found them out. Even the Vicar knew of the Alliance. There was no more need to try to hide its existence or who was a part of it. "We have assembled a sky fleet capable of defeating what the Founders can muster in the air and on the ground. It includes the Crankshafts, Imperials, Gallowglasses, Alchemists, Brineboilers, Spartak and the Tinskins, with more to come."

"You have the Tinskins with you?" the female senator said, her face softer, looking somewhat impressed.

"Yes," Buckle replied, though in that moment he felt a pang of worry for the safety of his brother, Ryder, perhaps still among them.

"And for their resistance the Brineboilers are overrun," a male senator shouted. "And Spartak has a city burning and the remainder hard pressed."

"I fought alongside the Russians at Muscovy," Buckle said. "Spartak has plenty of airships and cannon, and stands resolute. The Founders now face our armada in the east, Spartak in the north and the Tinskins to the south, and with Atlantis pressing their backs from the western sea, the Founders shall find themselves fighting at every point of the compass. We must strike now, before the Founders can apply their maximum strength to each of us in turn, and, in all honesty, we need Atlantis. Do not fight for me. Do not fight for Spartak. Fight to defend all you hold dear. Fight to keep your children from slavery. Think upon that and join us!"

"Enough," Cicero hissed from where he stood on the right edge of the podium.

"It is an honor to speak before the Atlantean Senate," Buckle said. "I am most grateful to be heard. Thank you."

Buckle stepped off the rostrum, feeling the solemn eyes of the two hundred watching him, hearing their rumbling murmurs rise as they weighed his words, as they weighed their own fates.

"You have been heard!" Octavian bellowed, almost colliding with Buckle in his hurry to take the rostrum and address the gallery. "As First Consul, you all understand that I, in times of great import, must make decisions for the clan. The fate of Atlantis now hangs in the balance. Do you hear me? We are strong, yes, but we can no longer afford this dithering around. We must control our own destiny. I have chosen for all of us. I have chosen to join with the Founders."

Buckle looked at Octavian, stunned. He saw Julia stare at her father, her mouth gaping.

A roar rose in the senate, a roar of angry, dissenting voices.

"There has been no debate!" someone raged.

"There has been no approval from the senate!" another voice howled.

"We have the votes to approve!" a woman shouted.

"I have done what must be done!" Octavian roared. "There is no choice! I have allied Atlantis with the strongest clan who, despite their once mighty armaments, need us. We have been offered an agreement which advantages our position as the most powerful gens in Atlantis and I have accepted the deal!"

The roar from the senate chamber grew louder. Cries of *betrayal!*, *tyrant!*, and *traitor!* rang out.

"There is no secret agreement, father!" Julia

spun to Buckle. "Captain, I assure you—there have been no clandestine negotiations with the Founders."

"Then what the hell is he talking about?" Buckle asked.

"I don't know … I don't know!" Julia replied.

Buckle felt the thudding concussion of an underwater explosion—it wasn't close but the entire dome shook. The two hundred senators jumped to their feet as one.

A great bell, sequestered in a balcony high above the Senate gallery, began to ring, loud and deep, its peal echoing back and forth between the walls of glass.

Horatus, one hand pressed to his scabbard, purple cloak flowing, dashed to a communications station on the left of the speaker's platform where dozens of pneumatic tubes, aether-lit gauges and chattertubes were affixed. He threw out his arm and pointed high up into the sea windows. "We are under attack! We are under attack!"

PART THREE:

UNDER SEIGE

XXXIX

THE UNDOING OF THE FIRST CONSUL

Two hundred Atlantean Senators turned, togas and stolas rustling, to look up into the sea. Four massive, cylindrical shadows approached, descending in the gloom over the approaches.

Dozens of voices rang out from the voice tubes at Horatus' communications station.

"The fleet has been dispatched, First Consul," Horatus shouted.

"No!" Octavian screamed. "Recall the fleet! We must not resist!"

"We must not resist?" Marius gasped. "What kind of devil's pact have you cut, Octavian? They are attacking us!"

"Submit, my friends, my fellows!" Octavian bellowed. "We must submit!" He strode to the forefront of the rostrum, arms thrown wide open. "Fear not, good senators of Atlantis! All we do is bend one knee in a show of good faith!"

"Traitor!" a senator screamed.

"We stand with the First Consul!" another senator countered.

Marius spun to Horatus. "Do not recall the fleet!"

"Never," Horatus replied.

Do not defy me, my Generals!" Octavian said. "Your stupidity shall kill us all!"

Julia rushed alongside Octavian, clutching him by the arm. "We cannot surrender, father. What have you done?"

"I am saving your life, child," Octavian replied, taking Julia's hand in a nervous thrashing of fingers, "I am saving all of our lives. I am aligning us with the sharks of the seas, not the carrion birds of the surface."

Buckle recognized a strange shining in Octavian's eyes, a wild, shocked unwillingness, and he realized it was the same look he'd seen in the eyes of the Founders sailor who had opened the submersible hatch for him. It was the look of a man who had lost control. No—it was the look of a man who'd had his control taken from him.

"As Master Equitum I shall never surrender Atlantis to the enemy," Marius announced.

"Then you shall die where you stand, old friend," Octavian snarled. "Praetorians! Execute the Magister Equitum! Cut the dog down where he stands!"

The purple-clad Praetorian guards, swords in

sheaths, did not move. They looked to Horatus, who shook his head.

"No!" Octavian roared. "Do not defy me, Horatus!" He whirled back to the senate gallery. "Soldiers and citizens, the die is cast. I have done what it is I must, citizens. Do not mire your thinking in Plebian ideals of honor! I have negotiated what is best for our Aventine house. The Grand Alliance? Bah! No surface fleet can help us now. We are alone! Do we wish to be conquered by the Founders and displaced by the nefarious Capitolines? Do we wish to be made the servants of the Capitoline traitors? I say not. As partners of the Founders we escape the war, we remain the dominant house of Atlantis and our trade coffers shall be enriched beyond our wildest dreams. I have saved us all!"

"This is folly, father," Lady Julia said, trying to haul Octavian down from the rostrum. "You are unwell. Let Marius take command!"

"We stand with the First Consul," Belarius shouted, hurrying down from the senate rows, tall and beautiful with an imposing manner and deep voice, a man well accommodated to lead other men. Close to three dozen male and female senators, after a moment of uncertainty, came scurrying after him.

"Protect the Keeper!" Horatus shouted. Two Praetorians grabbed Cicero and hauled him back toward the rear of the stage.

"Thank you, Belarius!" Octavian rejoiced as the rogue senators crowded the podium around him. "You shall be amply rewarded for your loyalty!"

The remaining senators hammered their fists on pews and benches, raising a thunder of disapproval. Amidst the howling, Buckle realized Elizabeth was there. He scanned the faces in the gallery but there was no sign of her. How could she possibly be there?

"Surrender!" Octavian screamed, shoving Lady Julia aside. "Horatus! Order your Praetorians to lay down their arms!"

"Stand your ground, Horatus," Marius ordered.

"With all due respect, First Consul, the Praetorians shall not lay down their arms," Horatus replied.

"We shall stand our ground against the conspiracy," a senator roared from the gallery. "We shall stand our ground!"

"As First Consul I order the Praetorians to join me!" Octavian shrieked. "The Founders have been assured of our compliance. If you do not stand down, if we do not provide the secret of the aether, Atlantis shall be destroyed!"

"Father," Lady Julia stammered, "we shall never give up the secret of the aether."

"Have you not heard the First Consul, Horatus?" Belarius shouted, a man flush with a sense of momentum, of advantage. "Surrender!"

"You have betrayed us, Octavian!" Marius roared, drawing his gladius. "You have betrayed Atlantis!"

"Death to Octavian!" a senator in the gallery screamed.

A chant rose in the senate chamber, growing rapidly in volume. "Death to Octavian. Death to Octavian!"

Belarius and his thirty rogue senators backed into a defensive circle, cringing as if pressed down by the weight of the hundred and seventy voices hurled against them.

"Defend the First Consul!" Belarius shouted. "In Octavian lies our only salvation!" Belarius and the rogue senators drew swords from beneath their robes.

"Swords!" a burly senator with a head of thick black curls shouted from a front bench. "Belarius and his snakes came into the senate chamber armed. The conspirators have defiled the senate! They must die!"

"Slay the conspirators!" a female senator screamed.

The crowd of senators, set off by the appearance of the swords, transformed into a howling mob. They tore at their benches, ripping up heavy planks before streaming down upon Octavian in a tide of club-wielding rage.

"No!" Lady Julia screamed. "No!"

"We must surrender," Octavian urged, arms

open, imploring, "We must! It is the only way to save Atlantis. Marius! Defend me! Call in the Centurions! Marius!"

"I shall save Atlantis!" Marius announced, striding towards Octavian with his sword pressed at his side. Belarius moved to confront him; Marius knocked Belarius' sword away and laid him out with an armor-fisted punch.

"No, Marius!" Lady Julia wailed, jumping in front of the Master Equitum.

Marius shoved Lady Julia aside with a sweep of his arm and lunged at Octavian, his powerful sword thrust driving the blade clean through the First Consul, entering at the stomach and bursting out through the spine.

"I am undone!" Octavian shrieked, blood gushing from his mouth.

"No!" Julia screamed.

Marius kicked the dead Octavian off his sword. "Horatus," he shouted. "Now!"

"Praetorians!" Horatus ordered. "Destroy Belarius and his traitorous senators." The twenty purple-cloaked Praetorians charged forward, spears leveled, but they were not needed. The senate mob, bench planks raised, had already surrounded Belarius and his small knot of conspirators.

"Do you think we are the only ones?" Belarius raged, rising from the rostrum floor, blood dribbling from his mouth. "You have made your choice, all of you — and you have chosen wrongly. The Master Equitum has misled you! I now claim the office of First Consul. Swear your oath of loyalty to me now, Praetorians, and I shall make you all rich! The doors of Atlantis have been thrown wide open. It is done. Defy me and you all shall pay for the murder you have done!"

"Traitor! Dog of the Capitolines!" the senator with the black curly hair cried, and he slammed his bench plank across Belarius' head with a dull whack. Belarius dropped.

"Do not kill Senator Belarius, you hear me!?" Marius shouted. "Destroy the others, but leave Belarius to stand trial!"

Dodging swinging bench planks, the black-haired senator and a female senator dragged the senseless Belarius aside until two Praetorians took hold of him, pulling him clear of the massacre unfolding around them. The other conspirators disappeared, losing their swords, crumpling under the flood of infuriated senators whaling on them with their boards, continuing to smash them long after their legs stopped kicking. The white togas took on brilliant streaks and spatters of red. Rivers of blood coursed down from the rostrum and flowed between the thousands of tile chips on the gallery's mosaic floor.

Buckle saw Lady Julia kneeling in the midst of

367

the skirmish, cradling her dead father's head in her arms. Cressida, her face flowing with tears, crouched beside Lady Julia. "Father, oh father—what have you done?" Julia wailed. "These were not his words! This was not his heart!"

"Enough!" Marius roared, and the mob froze in place, gasping, their faces, togas and clubs dripping with blood.

Buckle heard a shuffling, a wet dragging, and a pathetic whimpering. He saw the last senate conspirator, an old man with flowing gray hair and a stately face now busted and bloody, dragging his broken body across the rostrum, sobbing. Horatus stepped over the man and finished him with a downward stab of his sword.

Then there was nothing but silence.

Buckle smelled the blood, the rich, sickly sweet coppery scent of it. He could even taste it.

"With the First Consul dead," Marius announced, "I, the Master Equitum, assume temporary command as dictator. Does anyone here object?"

No one raised a voice against Marius.

"Lead us to victory, Marius!" the black-haired senator shouted. "Save our city!"

The senate raised a great cheer.

"It is done then," Marius announced.

Horatus pointed up into the sea. "Be on guard, citizens, for the battle of Atlantis has only just begun."

XL

THE DOME IS BREACHED

Marius rushed back to the communications station, his sword dripping red on the marble, pausing to decipher dozens of frantic, distant voices streaming from the chattertubes. "Outer pickets are engaged and hard pressed," Marius shouted. "Dome shields have been activated. The Admiral has ordered the fleet to attack."

Once again, the senators turned to look out into the ocean. Seven sleek Atlantean submarines, pearly white and golden-copper and aglow with luminiferous aether, sliced effortlessly through the green water like the dolphins they resembled. They charged the oncoming Founders submersibles, massive bulky shadows emerging from the near distance, issuing volcanic bubble trails of gurgling oil and black smoke.

"Our flagship, the *Tiber*!" a senator cried, pointing. "She leads the fleet against the enemy!"

Buckle peered at the largest Atlantean submarine—large by Atlantean standards—as it led the seven-boat attack with three fellows spread out on each flank.

"Dome torpedo batteries are manned and ready!" Marius called out.

Lady Julia stood up from the body of her father, her hands and dress stained with blood, her eyes glassy, her hair falling from its pins. "Save the city, Marius. But at least show the decency to wipe my father's blood from your sword."

"Forgive me, Lady Julia," Marius replied, clearing his blade with a fold of his cloak. "It was a duty which broke my heart."

Lady Julia seemed to nod or perhaps she just lowered her head. Cressida pressed against her side and clutched her arm.

"Horatus," Marius said. "See to it that Guardian patrols are dispatched to defeat seabed incursions."

"Yes, Dictator," Horatus replied, stepping to the communications station alongside Marius.

"All forces are in position," Marius said. "Despite their treacheries we shall defeat the Founders soundly and then we shall turn our wrath upon them!"

The four Founders submersibles, dwarfing the Atlantean boats with their immensity, came on. Buckle saw black rectangles snap open in their huge bows — torpedo tube hatches. He felt a terrible tingle run up his spine as two more monstrous Founders submersibles appeared in the baffles of the four leaders, both just as big if not bigger than the ones ahead. Six of them now.

The senators gasped as one.

The seven Atlantean submarines fired their torpedoes, a pair apiece, the slender copper fish flashing as their propellers kicked up swirling bursts of bubbles. The Founders submersibles, lumbering behemoths, made no attempt to turn or avoid, and this was of little surprise to Buckle. Two of the Founders machines were struck, exploding in bursts of burning air; huge bubbles expanded and contracted and hurtled upwards toward the surface. The haunting thunder of the implosions and the shriek of collapsing bulkheads rattled the windows of the great Senate dome.

A cheer rose up from the gallery.

"There is some good old Atlantean backbone for you!" Cicero enthused from behind Buckle. "Served up on a silver platter!"

The surviving four Founders submersibles came on, propellers churning, plowing past their disemboweled fellows as they sank, their great black hulls spilling bubbles of fire.

The bows of the surviving Founders boats burst with multiple surges of flashing bubbles. Every submersible fired its full complement of fish, as far as Buckle could tell, in the neighborhood of four apiece. Twenty-four long, ugly, coppery-green colored torpedoes, seams glowing red, propellers chopping, hurtled at the Atlantean boats, fired near point-blank, coming in a wall like grapeshot fired out of a scattergun.

The Atlantean submarines dove and wheeled to port and starboard.

"They're too close!" a senator screamed.

The *Tiber* and another submarine, struck on the flank as they turned to avoid, exploded in massive, grotesque underwater spheres of detonating gunpowder and collapsed back in upon what was left of the wrecks themselves.

The force of the blasts rattled the great glass dome again.

The *Tiber* and her unlucky companion sank, plummeting metal carcasses, their beautiful luminiferous aether lights flickering as they died.

"The torpedoes!" Buckle shouted. A dozen unexploded Founders metal fish were heading straight at the senate dome.

The senators cringed as they saw the torpedoes approach, shuffling back, appearing as if they might break and run.

"The dome shall hold!" Marius shouted. "Our electrified aether shield will detonate the fuses short of the glass! The dome shall hold!"

The torpedoes sliced the water, their ugly, fuse-crowned, green-copper heads becoming more and more distinct until they raced up to the dome.

"This is your doing, Marius!" shouted Belarius, his chin streaming with blood, struggling in the grasp of the Praetorians who held him. "You and your pride!"

Buckle held his breath.

The dome windows lit up as if hit by lightning, shivering with splitting blue forks of electricity that made Buckle's skin prickle. As each torpedo arrived within ten feet of the glass a myriad of rising electrical arcs slashed out to greet it, concentrating their energy upon the point of contact and shattering the device. Three of the torpedoes detonated. Buckle lifted his arm to shield his eyes from the stunning blasts of light and fire. The flash and wallop of the explosions shook the floor. Luminiferous aether tubes split, spilling bright liquid high from the dome ceiling. The shuddering window glass, the sheets rocking and grinding in their iron frames, cracked in places; tiny jets of water sprayed through some spiderwebbed fissures but the great dome held.

Buckle lowered his arm, staring in awe. Every torpedo had been destroyed before it struck the glass directly. Never before had he seen such a thing. He felt the senators expel a collective sigh of relief.

"Atlantis!" someone cheered.

But still the battle raged. Buckle watched the Founders boats continue their charge, the Atlantean vessels wheeling about them.

"All north-facing batteries returning fire!" Horatus shouted.

Buckle almost lost his balance as the platform

rolled and shook under his feet, the dome rocking with a series of deep, echoing booms.

"What has happened?" Marius asked.

"Our sea batteries—the torpedoes have exploded in their tubes!" Horatus yelled. "The launchers have been destroyed! Breaches—we have multiple breaches on the battery decks!"

"Sabotage!" Marius snarled.

The senate chamber voices rose into a howl of "Traitors! Spies! Betrayed!"

"Marius!" Horatus shouted from his station, his face pale. "The main docking bays have been opened—all of them!"

"Close the bays!" Marius ordered.

"We cannot," Horatus replied. "The engineers have been locked out of the control stations on every deck."

Again the senators howled, "Traitors! Saboteurs!"

Marius, shocked, could do no more than stare at Horatus.

"You forced our hand, you fools!" Belarius shouted, still trying to wrench his arms free of the Praetorians who held him. "Many stand with the Founders, not just a handful in the Senate. And now we have opened the gates of Atlantis and they cannot be shut again in time. Surrender, Marius! Order the fleet to stand down or every one of you shall die."

Marius marched up to Belarius. "How could you betray your own house, your own gens?"

"Always side with the strongest man, Marius," Belarius replied. "My followers already have. It is not too late. Submit. Yes, it stings in the beginning but the future holds wealth and glory for us all."

"Mother of Mars!" Horatus yelled. "We have enemy soldiers inside the Number Three dome!"

"Enemy troops?" Marius gasped. "Impossible! What happened to the pickets? Where are the Guardians?"

"I don't know!" Horatus answered. "General Sulla and his Centurions are assembling the Guard on the Via Aventinus causeway. We shall hold them there."

Cicero, looking as pale as his white toga, clambered onto the bloodstained rostrum. "I fear the enemy has access to every dome. All is lost!"

"Surrender, Master Equitum," Belarius bellowed.

"Horatus," Marius shouted. "Order Sulla and his men to retreat beyond the watertight hatches. If they are about to be overrun tell them to seal the hatches and flood the dome."

"Did you not think we would be prepared?" Belarius laughed. "The Aventine house is doomed. Surrender, Master Equitum. You are a good man and we shall show you mercy."

With a roar, Marius spun around and ran his sword straight into Belarius. The Praetorians held the dying Belarius up so Marius could look him in the eyes. "Die like a dog, traitor," Marius hissed. "Atlantis shall never surrender."

Belarius opened his mouth but died before he could speak. Marius yanked his sword free and the Praetorians dropped Belarius' body on the floor.

"Clear the senate!" Marius ordered. "Get to your escape pods if you can!"

The senators dropped their planks and hurried toward the exits, though there was no panic. Buckle turned to run, to leap down from the platform and race back into the Black Atrium to collect Sabrina, Welly and Penny Dreadful. He had to get his people out of Atlantis. But how to escape? Where was Captain Felix? Their only chance was the *Dart*.

"Wait, Captain," Marius said, taking hold of Buckle by the shoulder and hauling Cicero along beside him. "We shall see to it that you get out of here."

"I cannot be taken," Cicero mumbled, opening a compartment on the golden dolphin ring on his finger. "I cannot be taken. I shall not be drowned."

"No, Cicero," snapped Marius. "Not yet."

With trembling fingers, Cicero snapped the ring shut.

"Horatus," Marius yelled. "Escort the Keeper to the First Consul's private launch. And take Captain

Buckle with you."

"Yes, sir," Horatus replied, rushing up with two Praetorians at his side.

Marius turned to Buckle. "Captain, return to your clan and tell them Atlantis is with them. We are with them."

"I shall," Buckle said.

"The Founders!" Lady Julia screamed, flinging out her arm to point at the dome wall. "The submersible!"

Buckle spun to see the lead Founder's submarine, its towering bow advancing through the water, accelerating as it charged the towering glass wall.

"Oh, Neptune save us," a senator screamed. The senators surged, now a chaotic, panicked mob heading for the doors.

"Go," Marius shouted at Buckle, shoving Cicero towards Horatus. "Get out of here!"

"With me!" Horatus announced as his two Praetorians grabbed Cicero by the scruff of the neck and, lifting his feet off the floor, raced down the stairs to the hatchway at the rear of the speaker's platform. Buckle ran alongside. As he reached the hatchway he heard a collective scream, hundreds of male and female voices erupting in terror — and he looked back.

The Founders submersible loomed larger and larger in the glass four stories up, too fast, coming on too straight. The crazy bastard was about to ram the dome.

The Founders didn't make officers like that, Buckle thought.

The submersible slammed into the dome, its bow punching through the glass like a gigantic harpoon of copper-green metal and iron, sending a titanic waterfall of seawater and glittering glass plummeting down to the gallery floor. The pendulum cable snapped and the huge bob crashed down on the grand mosaic.

A violent burp of pressure nearly burst Buckle's eardrums, making him stagger. As he stumbled through the hatchway he sensed more than saw the entire side of the dome collapse, sending a mountainous wall of churning dark blue water — and it the midst of it the falling submersible — thundering down upon the rostrum where Lady Julia and Cressida knelt and hugged each other over Octavian's dead body.

XLI

THE BATTLE OF THE BLACK ATRIUM

Buckle dove through the doorway, bounced off a Praetorian hedging against the hatch and crashed into Cicero, knocking both of them sprawling.

"Now!" Horatus shouted.

The Praetorians slammed the hatch shut. Horatus whirled the locking wheel.

The corridor shook with a deafening boom so immense Buckle was shocked the structure didn't collapse around them. The hatch sprung leaks but its seals held.

The Praetorians hauled Buckle and Cicero to their feet.

"Get going, damn you," Horatus gasped. The Praetorians took hold of Cicero and raced down the passageway.

Buckle turned to follow but Horatus hauled him back. "Captain," Horatus said, "the Keeper must not fall into enemy hands. The secret of the aether must be preserved at all costs. If the enemy overwhelms us we must make certain the Keeper does not survive to have his secrets extracted. Do you understand me?"

"Yes," Buckle replied.

"Good," Horatus answered, and set off running. Buckle followed at a sprint, breathing in air rich with the salty stink of seawater and wet ambergris. He emerged in the Black Atrium where Sabrina, Welly, Penny, and four Praetorian guards waited, swords drawn, looking confused. Buckle found himself splashing through ankle-deep seawater as he crossed the room—he saw a low torrent pouring in from the opposite blue hatchway, pooling shallow but flowing fast, turning the red carpet to a dark, ugly shade of purple.

Twelve red-cloaked Atlantean soldiers led by a man with a sideways crimson brush on his helmet charged in through the Mars gate. Buckle noticed the Mars gate—and the Neptune gate opposite—were closing, slowly, as big metal hatches slid into position to seal the passageways.

"Horatus—what has happened?" the officer with the crimson brush on his helmet asked.

"The senate chamber is lost, Centurion Numa—breached by a Founders submarine," Horatus said quickly. "We have reports of Founders soldiers entering the domes."

"Impossible!" one of the soldiers snapped, more out of rage than disbelief.

"All watertight doors are closing," Numa said. "We'll cut them off and drown them, we will, General."

The dome shuddered again, making Buckle's stomach clench. The aether tubes vibrated and the fountain spouts splattered droplets into the shallow water on the floor. Buckle heard the sound of torrents of water roaring though the interior of the dome, coming somewhere from above. Buckle picked up Penny Dreadful without breaking stride and she clung to him like a human child.

"Is it as bad as it looks?" Sabrina asked.

"Worse," Buckle said.

"We must get the Keeper to the First Consul's escape pod," Horatus told Numa. "The Founders must not take him."

"Ah, but we already have him!" A voice boomed from the Neptune gate.

Buckle spun around to see the Vicar entering through the half-shut watertight door, arms thrown open, a rapier in one hand and a pistol in the other. He wore a wide leather belt stuffed with pistols of which there must have been at least ten. A company of cutlass-armed, blue-coated Founders seamen poured in around him.

"Atlanteans!" Numa shouted. "Form up!" The dozen solders, drawing their swords, formed a line in front of the arriving Founders. "Go, Horatus! Go!" Numa barked.

"I am afraid the Keeper has nowhere to go," the Vicar said as his seamen formed a line in front of him, teeth gritted, poised and ready to pounce. "Surrender or die."

"Atlanteans do not surrender," Numa replied.

Horatus grabbed Cicero, lifting the portly Keeper off his feet as he raced to the blue hatchway where seawater now gushed calf-deep across the threshold. Buckle, Sabrina, Welly, and the six Praetorians raced after Horatus. Buckle heard splashing coming down the throat of the blue passageway. Odessa leapt out, clad in her silver steampiper breastplate, sword in hand, leading a half dozen tall, blond-haired steampipers.

"Fight your way through!" Horatus shouted, shoving Cicero behind him as he drew his sword. "Cut them down and do it quickly!"

Releasing Penny, Buckle swept his saber free of its sheath in one smooth motion of swishing steel, as did his crewmates and the Praetorians.

"She's mine!" Sabrina said, loud and clear, lunging to the fore. "Leave my sister to me!"

Buckle heard a crash of steel as the Founders sailors rushed the Centurion's company behind them. Glancing back, he saw more blue-clad seamen streaming in through the steadily decreasing gap in the closing Neptune gate. Numa and his Atlantean guards were now outnumbered. Buckle cursed inwardly —

their best chance would have been to fight in the doorways, to restrict the enemy to the corridors where their greater numbers could not be brought to bear, but it was too late for that.

Sabrina and Odessa collided first, swords clashing, as Buckle, Welly, Horatus, and the Praetorians spread out to meet the steampipers. Buckle slashed his blade from side to side, deflecting the well-delivered thrusts of the steampiper swords. The steampiper charge stalled. Horatus and his Praetorians were proving their worth. But, behind them, amidst shouts, rings of metal and agonized screams, Buckle sensed Centurion Numa and his soldiers were backing up, desperately trying to avoid being surrounded.

The watertight metal doors thudded shut in the gateways of Neptune and Mars.

Buckle knew they only had a few seconds to cut their way through the steampipers if they wanted to get out of Atlantis alive. He feinted right and slashed left, cutting the sword arm of the steampiper in front of him, following up with a backhand swipe across the throat. The steampiper fell back in a spray of blood.

Wheeling to his right, Buckle blindsided a female steampiper engaged with a Praetorian, wrenching her sword arm up and plunging his blade into her armpit, driving it deep into the thick muscles and bones of her upper chest. The Praetorian thrust his gladius under her breastplate and into her lower abdomen, finishing her off. Buckle struggled to free his blade as the woman fell, for it was angled tight against her bones and the armhole of the breastplate.

"Kill the Keeper!" Numa shouted. "Kill the Keeper!"

Pulling his bloody sword free, Buckle turned to see the Centurion and six of his soldiers — the ones not down and dying — laying about them with their swords as the Founders sailors flooded around their flanks.

Cicero, having had lost all color from his ruddy face, hunched against the fountain as a female Praetorian gripped him by the collar. "I am prepared!" Cicero shouted. Buckle saw him pluck a glass ampule out of his gold dolphin ring and jam it into his mouth.

Buckle felt calm as the Founders sailors rushed him; he was calculating, fueled by a sizzling but coiled anger. His little group had almost fought their way out. They had almost made it. But Odessa and the steampipers still blocked the escape route. "To hell with this!" He bellowed. He charged in front of Cicero, cutting down the first Founders seaman he met, sending the man tumbling into the water, his cutlass spinning away.

"To hell with them, yes!" the Praetorian who had been holding Cicero shouted, stepping alongside Buckle with her blade at the ready. "Watch your back and have at them!"

"Kill the Keeper!" Numa shouted again,

clubbing a Founders seaman with his fist. "Kill him, damn you!" The chest of Numa's breastplate exploded in a burst of blood, flesh and black smoke and he toppled face-down in the water. The Vicar stepped over Numa's body, tossing aside a smoking pistol and drawing another from his belt.

"Take the Keeper alive!" The Vicar howled. "He'll have a poison ampule in his mouth. Cut his tongue out before he finds the brass to swallow it!"

Whipping his blade back and forth, Buckle found himself besieged on the left and right as the Founders swarmed in on both sides, the cohesion of the lines collapsing in the thrashing chaos of combat. Welly was on his left, wielding his saber with excellent control, keeping two opponents at bay. Buckle was infuriated with himself. Even as he slashed and parried, the stench of saltwater in his nostrils and the fire of combat in his veins, his brain hammered like a difference engine gone mad. He had put his crewmembers in this situation, into dire straits, in his obsessive pursuit of Elizabeth. He could not allow them to be captured. "Offer no quarter and ask for none!" he shouted. "To the death!"

Buckle glimpsed Penny Dreadful, looking small as she stood against a bulkhead, unnoticed at the fringe of the battle. Head down and quivering, she glowed red at the seams, firing bolts of steam from vents in her ribcage and neck. She was attempting to pull her manacles apart.

Buckle wanted to help Penny — they desperately needed her fighting skills — but he had no idea which Praetorian had the keys. Retreating as more and more Founders cutlasses hacked at him, he backed up against Cicero. The surviving Atlantean guards and Praetorians, bleeding and hard-pressed, had formed a circle around the Keeper. The doomed circle. The last stand. This was it. *Damn it*, Buckle thought as he deflected a sailor's pike swung at his head. If they were to die he would make certain Marius' last request was honored. Cicero was behind him. If he couldn't save Cicero — and if the man had lost his nerve and couldn't bite down on his poison ampule properly — Buckle would have to kill him. And it was going to have to happen now.

Buckle made a series of aggressive sword thrusts, forcing the Founders sailors in front of him to hedge back. With his opponents on their heels he had a moment, the only chance he was going to get, to spin around and execute Cicero. He lowered his sword as he turned, anticipating a merciful kill, an instant kill, a thrust up under the Keeper's sternum to sever the vital organs in his upper abdomen. Then, in turn, the Founders would skewer Buckle through the back, multiple blades, rewarding him with his own instant death.

I have failed you, Elizabeth. Forgive me.

Cicero, still in the clutches of the Praetorian, saw Buckle come at him with his leveled sword and did not raise his hands to defend himself. There was fear in Cicero's face but also acceptance.

A coppery blur whipped through the space between Buckle and Cicero like a springing metal jaguar. The force and speed of it was enough to stall Buckle's hand. It was Penny Dreadful on the launch, snapped manacle chains trailing from her wrists, shining nests of blades jutting from her forearms. The automaton landed in the water and as Buckle spun around he saw her slam a knife into the knee of an onrushing female sailor. The woman screamed and dropped to her knees in front of Penny who, yanking her knife loose, chopped the woman's head clean off with a double armed scissoring of her two longest blades.

Penny was on the attack again before the female sailor's head hit the water, ricocheting into the Founders like a whirling dervish, her body a dodging blur, her arms delivering a hundred devastating snake strikes at once. Blood filled the air in fountains — splatters and fine, pinkish sprays. Screaming and shouting, the leading sailors — the ones still standing — hacked wildly, panicked at the sight of the golden eyed, half-submerged hellion savagely chopping at their thighs and knees, and clawed back into the crowd of their fellows behind them.

Welly moved to follow Penny but Buckle grabbed him by the collar. "No, Welly," Buckle shouted. "She can hold them."

Penny Dreadful took down nearly a dozen screaming sailors who fell, shins and thighs split wide open. She ignored the cutlass and pike blows raining down upon her. Anyone lucky enough to land a strike was rewarded with an ineffective bang of metal against unforgiving metal.

"For once one of the little monsters is on our side," Horatus shouted, yanking Cicero by the collar so roughly Buckle feared the poor Keeper might bite down on his death ampule by accident. "It'll hold them long enough for us to break out. We must clear the hatchway now!"

"Aye!" Buckle yelled, noticing the seawater was almost up to his knees as he turned to join Welly in the attack on the last few steampipers holding the blue hatchway.

But where was Sabrina?

XLII

BLOOD IS NOT THICKER THAN TIME

Sabrina may have moved to engage Odessa first but her sister was the one determined to finish it. They had exchanged only a few blows before the surge of the charge shoved them apart. A minute later, out of the corner of her eye, Sabrina saw Odessa chop down a Praetorian and come straight at her, blade straight up, a perpendicular, shining slash in the aether light, coming at her blind side in the way a sabertooth beastie cuts its victim out of a herd.

Sabrina already had her hands full battling another steampiper, a tall woman with a wicked thrust and immense power in her arms. Sabrina took a quick step back, rotating her body so she was facing both the steampiper and her onrushing sister. Sabrina had no doubt that Odessa intended to kill her. But still, as the soldiers whirled around them in a maelstrom of blades, armor, blood, and water, she hesitated slightly, a fraction of a second, in the presence of her only sister. Sabrina's hesitation nearly cost her life.

Odessa's first swing, aimed to cut Sabrina's throat, was perfect.

Sabrina parried Odessa's blade at the last instant and Sabrina held it locked against hers, locking them together in the moment, their faces mere inches apart. Odessa's hot breath seemed to scald Sabrina's cheek. Her green eyes offered no pity, no empathy, no quarter.

Where are you, sister? Sabrina thought. *Where is my Odessa?*

If Odessa had to die, if Sabrina had to kill her sister, then it was something she was ready to do.

Sabrina jumped back to avoid being skewered from the right by the female steampiper whose sword thrust missed her stomach by an inch. Sabrina knocked the woman's blade away but stumbled, unable to adjust her footing in the sucking water now up to her knees.

"Capture the Keeper!" Odessa shouted at the woman. "This one is mine."

The steampiper nodded and swung away. Sabrina lunged at Odessa with the thrust and parry, the low cut and high, exploiting every line of attack — but Odessa matched her every move. Again and again Sabrina lunged for the kill but Odessa countered her each time, often nearly slicing her on the return. They were now, even as they were then, evenly matched.

A memory darted through Sabrina's mind, fighting over a doll.

A Praetorian backed up against Sabrina's left, barely holding off a swarm of Founders. Their company was about to be overwhelmed. She felt the battle turning, the squeezing of the middle as Welly, Buckle, and the Atlanteans grouped tighter and tighter behind her. If they could not cut their way through to the blue corridor now they would be surrounded and annihilated.

Sabrina also realized that the little automaton, Penny Dreadful, was loose and in the thick of it but she doubted even the fast blades of the living machine could save them if they could not win the blue passageway.

Advancing, Sabrina rained such a reckless flurry of blows upon her sister that Odessa, parrying, retreated a few steps to the black wall. Odessa's pommel struck the bulkhead as she swung her sword, knocking her rhythm off-kilter and unsettling her guard.

Sabrina saw her chance and she stepped into it. But before her muscles drove her saber home she was hammered from the right, the brutal slam of a bigger body plowing into her smaller one, the clunk of skull upon skull, a blur of blue uniform and brass buttons. The world jumped and heaved over. Sabrina fell sideways into the churning water, the icy cold biting at her pounding heart—but it also slapped her mind clear. A Founders seaman loomed over her, his axe coming down, halfway through the descending arc that would end her existence at the end of its swing.

Sabrina's reaction was instinct, muscles firing, remembering ten thousand training repetitions, and it saved her life. Though she was halfway submerged she swept her sword up and parried his blow, though just barely, the axe blade glancing off of her saber, missing her nose by barely an inch and plunging into the water.

"Fool!" Odessa shouted.

The sailor had thrown too much of his momentum into what must have looked like an easy killing blow. Now he was off-balance and bent over Sabrina, the brass buttons on his coat pressing down on her head. She threw her left hand around his neck, forcing him to support her weight and toppling him over on top of her. With her right hand she released her sword, drew her dagger and drove the blade up into his stomach. The sailor grunted as he fell on top of her, plunging them both under the freezing water. Holding her breath, Sabrina rolled the man to her left as she wrenched the blade around inside the bulk of him. He convulsed and kicked, thrashing up foam and screaming a gargled, ghostly howl into the water.

Sabrina was already out from under the man's weight, her head breaking the surface as she scrambled to get back on her feet, gasping as she felt around for her sword which now lay somewhere on the bottom of the churning water.

Sabrina saw a flash of movement on her left. A burst of red hair. The silver of a whirling blade.

Sabrina raised her knife, deflecting a finger-stinging blow which would have decapitated her had it not been interrupted. Odessa swung again. Sabrina dove to her left, avoiding the slash by completely exposing herself to the next. She plunged her hands under the floating body of the Founder's seaman she had just gutted. She found her sword and raised it from the water in time to deflect Odessa's swing at her head.

Agony shot through the fingers on Sabrina's left hand. She had picked her sword up by the blade, her hand wrapped around the steel just above the guard and not on the grip beneath it. The force of Odessa's blow had sunk the cutting edge into the joints of her fingers. Thin rivers of blood poured down her wrist, racing fast and bright across the water-drenched skin.

Sabrina ignored the pain. The sword, no matter how she held it and no matter the cost, had saved her life; it had bought her time. She was on her feet now, tossing the saber from her bloody left hand into her right and her knife from right to left in the same motion.

Without pause, Odessa came on. Sabrina tried to back up, to buy herself a fraction of time and space but her effort nearly sent her backwards into the water again. Her right foot had been locked down. The Founders sailor, half-submerged, his mouth blubbering foam, curses and blood, had grabbed her ankle and would not let go.

Sabrina tried to kick loose of the man's grip but failed. Now she was off-balance and pinned. In a moment she would be dead. Odessa, raining down blow after furious blow, had her.

"Lieutenant!" Welly shouted, rushing Odessa from the right. Odessa, quick as a cat, knocked Welly's saber thrust aside and punched him squarely across the jaw with her free hand. Welly crashed against the bulkhead and tumbled into the water.

Welly's charge bought Sabrina an instant — and it was enough.

Sabrina lunged, stomping on the Founders sailor's face as she broke free of his failing clutch, and brought her sword down upon Odessa with all of the strength she had, chopping clean through Odessa's sword arm just above the wrist.

Odessa's hand, still clenching the sword, dropped into the water. Odessa screamed, springing backwards, her arm spraying blood. Sabrina kicked Odessa in the chest, slamming her against the bulkhead as she drew back her sword to drive the point through Odessa's throat.

Sliding to her knees as she clutched her wound, Odessa looked at up Sabrina, her green eyes flooded with agony. In those unveiled, brightly drawn depths Sabrina saw her sister looking up at her from the past.

Sabrina halted her attack. She would not deliver the killing the blow. She would not.

Sabrina remembered her own arm, small and thin, when she was six years old; an angry Odessa had raked Sabrina's forearm with her fingernails, leaving four long, thin, bloody lines that barely hurt but offered great dramatic pretext for wailing in the presence of their mother.

And now she had chopped Odessa's hand away.

Welly, rose up from the water beside Odessa, lifting his sword.

"No, Welly!" Sabrina shouted, grabbing Welly's arm. "Mercy!"

Welly lowered his sword.

Sabrina saw the way to the blue hatchway was clear. Horatus and three surviving Praetorians had dispatched the last of Odessa's steampipers. Already the female Praetorian was hauling Cicero into the passageway.

Sabrina sheathed her knife, grabbing Welly by the collar and pulling him through the red and black water. She saw Buckle, Penny Dreadful, and the few remaining Atlantean guards backing up, keeping the Vicar and the Founders in front of them as best they could. "We are leaving!" she shouted at Buckle.

No!" howled the Vicar, advancing with sword and pistol. "Do not let them escape or your backs will bleed for it!" The blue-coated mass of sailors behind him lunged forward, threatening to overrun what was left of the Atlantean defense.

Penny Dreadful jumped forward to meet the Vicar, her streamlined body slicing through the water, arms whirling, blades flashing.

"Damned machines!" the Vicar bellowed without breaking stride. He pointed his pistol at Penny Dreadful's chest, point blank, and fired.

The concussion of the weapon blast in the enclosed space bludgeoned Sabrina's ears. The belch of black smoke from the muzzle seemed to lift Penny Dreadful, blowing her small metal form out of the water and hurling it between Buckle and an Atlantean soldier; she crashed into a black-curtained bulkhead and tumbled into the water.

"Penny!" Sabrina screamed, rushing toward the bubbling whirlpool where the automaton had disappeared.

"Go!" one of the three remaining Atlantean soldiers ordered. "Go! We shall hold them! Go!"

Buckle had already run to Penny and lifted her out of the water. A dense black powder burn covered Penny's chest. Her eyes had gone black but, much to Sabrina's relief, they fluttered to life again, as bright and golden as ever.

"Stop them, damn you!" the Vicar boomed. "Sabrina!" He strode at her through the surging water, yanking another pistol from his belt. "Come to me, child," he urged. "Come to me and I shall return to you to your family. I am your beloved uncle!"

Sabrina snatched her dagger from her belt with her bloody fingers. In one smooth motion, a motion practiced a thousand times in the back room of Marter's shop in Refugio, she hurled the knife at the Vicar's head. The blade flashed in the aether light as it spun. The Vicar uttered the first hissing fricative of a curse before the dagger buried itself between his eyes. He fell backwards with a great splash.

The Founders paused, their swords and pikes wavering. Both of their officers were down.

"Do not let the Keeper escape!" Odessa shrieked, hauling herself up from the water, gripping the bloody stump of her left arm, her face so white she looked like a fire-haired ghost, her light brown freckles looking like black specks of rot. "Capture him and Isambard shall make you rich!"

"Make it quick!" Horatus bellowed as he stood at the blue hatchway. Two Praetorians and Cicero had already vanished into the passageway and Buckle was on his way in, carrying Penny.

Sabrina pulled Welly into the hatchway and with her last glimpse back she saw Odessa glaring after her with the ominous coldness of a gallows tree.

XLIII

HOW LONG CAN BUCKLE HOLD HIS BREATH?

The last man to lunge through the blue hatchway was a Praetorian, helmet missing, his arms running with blood, though whether it was his blood or someone else's Buckle could not tell. The last Atlantean in the Black Atrium, a red-cloaked soldier, turned his back to them and shouted "Seal the hatch!"

Horatus and the female Praetorian were already pressing the oval hatch shut, having the advantage of the waist-high water current flowing with them.

Outside, the Atlantean soldier screamed in agony and the sound was abruptly cut off. A Founder's pike thrust through the gap between the hatch and the jamb, the razor-sharp blade screeching against the bulkhead. Buckle grabbed the pike just below the blade and hauled it back. Horatus chopped the wooden shaft clean through with a downward cut of his sword.

Buckle joined the others as they forced the hatch shut, snapping the wooden pike shaft in the process. Horatus grabbed the door locking wheel, winding it around and around. The seawater, now dammed, began to rise at an alarming rate.

"There shouldn't be water coming in here," Horatus said. "A seal must have failed." He snapped a locking lever into place and the hatch sealed with a hiss of air and a clank of bolts.

"Are you well, Captain?" Penny asked. She looked up at Buckle from where she stood between Cicero and Sabrina, her emotionless, golden copper eyes glowing, her body submerged up to the shoulders in the swirling water. Her blood-smeared blades retracted into their arm sheaths with a slippery click.

"I am well, Penny." Buckle said.

"I am most relieved," Penny sighed.

"Let's go," Horatus ordered, wading down the corridor. "Hurry! If the emergency hatches seal before we can escape we shall drown!"

The two Praetorians grabbed Cicero and carried him after Horatus.

"You heard the man," Buckle said to Sabrina and Welly. "Let's move."

"Our best chance is the maintenance shafts," Horatus shouted back. "We cannot risk running into the Founders in the main corridors. And there is a way to get to the First Consul's emergency pod from here."

They splashed along the long passageway, the dark water surging above their waists and the luminiferous aether tubes glowing brightly overhead.

Buckle kept moving, driving his muscles through the resistance of the water, but the increasing depth slowed him down and made his legs advance in slow motion. By the time they had traversed one hundred yards down the passageway Penny had entirely submerged though he could see the dim glow of her eyes just below the surface.

"How much farther?" Buckle asked.

Horatus stopped. "Too far." He looked to the two Praetorians. "The passage has been flooded either through breach or defensive stratagem. Give them your breathers!"

Without hesitation the Praetorians unsnapped the sleek, cylindrical breathing devices from the fronts of their breastplates and handed them out. Cicero received one while Sabrina was given the other.

Horatus dropped his helmet in the water and pressed his breather into Buckle's hands. "Bite down on this and don't release and you'll be able to breathe," he said, flipping a mouthpiece out of the breather.

"What about my Ensign?" Buckle asked, looking at Welly, who, looked battered and doomed.

"We can't leave a man behind!" Sabrina snapped.

"It is unfortunate," Horatus replied. "But the senior officers must survive to protect the Keeper."

"What about you and your men?" Buckle asked, feeling his boots lift off the floor, now treading water.

"We are trained to hold our breaths for a very long time, Captain," Horatus said, inhaling and exhaling deeply. "What must be done is done. The Keeper is the only life here that matters. When we reach the end of this passageway we shall descend through a hatchway to a lower deck and then up again. Stay close." Horatus turned, and he was swimming now, his head visible in the claustrophobic two-foot gap between the water and the passageway ceiling where the aether tubes pulsed, radiating warmth.

Buckle kicked and swam, shoving Sabrina's hand aside as she tried to offer her breather to Welly, who was pushing it away.

"Never!" Welly said.

"Take mine," Buckle ordered, thrusting his breather into Welly's hand. "Take mine, Wellington!"

"Sir," Welly began.

"That's an order, damn it!" Buckle snapped.

Welly reluctantly took the breather and pressed it to his mouth.

"Romulus," Sabrina began.

"Enough!" Buckle replied. He couldn't see Penny but he was sure she was standing just below him. "Don't fall behind! Swim!"

Sabrina and Welly ducked their heads and set off after the others. Buckle sucked in a long draught of air and plunged under the surface. The water swallowed him in icy darkness, snapping shut over the top of his head. The passageway, now a weird underwater world illuminated yellow-green by the aether tubes, seemed to go on forever. He saw the indistinct forms of Horatus, Cicero, and the two Praetorians swimming away, propelling their bodies with long, expert strokes, Cicero's breather ejecting bursts of bubbles. The gloves and boots of the soldiers had sprouted webbing which further added to their speed. Cicero undulated his rotund body like a porpoise—freed of his weight by the water he was stunningly agile, like a walrus.

Penny Dreadful, striding on the deck directly beneath Buckle, moved with him. Buckle's mother had taught him to swim in the mountain lakes where he had been raised. But now, in the strong currents with his boots as heavy as lead, he felt like he was moving impossibly slow despite the energy expended by his strokes.

Buckle concentrated on swimming. Already his lungs requested another breath of air. He figured that first urge would pass, that he would overcome it and travel a good distance before the need attacked him again.

Within twenty seconds the group reached an open hatchway in the deck. Horatus, Cicero, and the Praetorians dove down into it, followed by Sabrina and Welly. Buckle swam for his life. He reached the hatchway and pulled himself down the ladder to the

403

lower deck, hearing Penny's metal shoes clank down the ladder behind him. He planted his feet on the rail and pushed off after Sabrina and Welly, propelling himself down another long passageway.

Still, Buckle was falling further and further behind. The others became more shadow-like and distant in the disturbed currents and wobbling aether light. His chest began to ache and burn. He had no experience in holding his breath. Was water leaking in through his lips? He clamped his mouth tight. The strokes of his arms, the kicks of his legs, now consumed the last wisps of oxygen in his lungs. He saw air bubbles crowd the ceiling, tantalizing as they gathered in sparkling bunches around the aether tubes, but he knew it was impossible to try to breathe them in.

Keep swimming. You can breathe later. It's not far.

And yet he slowed even more. The water grew heavier, thicker. He was spending more energy to stop himself from sinking than he was swimming.

A set of metal fingers clamped around Buckle's left hand. Suddenly he was surging through the water at great speed. Penny Dreadful was towing him. She ran along the deck, her metal shoes clunking with deep, weird echoes on the grating.

Buckle's stomach muscles jerked. His lungs burned as if a torch had been jammed inside them. His vision tunneled. In his last moments of failing consciousness he had the distinct impression of being flushed through a tube of yellow-green iron on the bottom of the ocean. The gagools caught him as he emerged, tearing out his insides, prying his mouth open with their fangs so they could vomit a great, agonizing blast of saltwater into his lungs and the black edges of nothingness would bleed in until the light was gone.

Keep swimming, he berated himself. Instead, he thrashed. His left hand struck a bulkhead and he veered to starboard. He was disoriented now, upside-down or sideways. The pressure of movement stopped and he was drifting. Penny's grip on his hand was gone. His mouth flung open of its own accord, an ancient, undeniable urge, his body mechanically attempting to save itself by breathing no matter the consequences suspected by the higher mind. He managed to slam his mouth shut again.

But now his throat was full of salt.

There had been one time before when he had nearly drowned, high in the wintery Tehachapi mountains, wading into a deep bend of a creek to rescue a fledgling duck. But that time the water had been freezing, numbing him to pain, slowly pulling him down, until his father had jumped in and saved him.

He was floating and it was pleasant. The water felt warmer, the aether light soft, and he was glad that

Sabrina and Welly would find a way home. But what of Elizabeth? Rage seized him. *Elizabeth*. How could he depart while Elizabeth was in chains? He was the only one she had. The only savior.

Buckle willed his arms to move, to swim again, but they refused. Blackness surged in upon him in its final rush, cold, and heavy. He took the breath. His mouth opened. But he could not — his lips were shut — a metal shield clamped over them, tight and sharp and no amount of frantic twisting could shake it loose.

Buckle flung his eyes open and saw Penny's face immediately in front of his, her amber irises in their copper orbits looking into his bursting eyes. He looked into her and saw the little girl looking back at him, a little girl who had hold of him and wasn't going to let go.

Buckle's sight went dark. He wanted to shout at Penny. Drowning was preferable to suffocation. Let me breathe. I don't care what happens. Let me breathe.

Suddenly, as if Penny heard him, her metal hand released its grip. His mouth opened and someone clamped his jaw down on an object and his lungs took in a hurricane-force suck of cool air.

Buckle gasped so hard he wondered if his organs might burst with the effort. If this was drowning he welcomed it. But it was not. It was a curved, soft object in his mouth that tasted of rubber, leather and the tang of another human's saliva. As the oxygen blasted though his body and reanimated his brain he realized that he was being towed again, hauled along by a strong hand on his collar — the hand of Horatus — and Penny clung alongside him, keeping the breather pressed into his mouth.

Horatus had come back for him.

That was surprising.

XLIV

THE UNDERNEATH

"You insufferable fogsucking harlot!" Cicero snarled.

Gasping on the passageway deck, Buckle saw Cicero wipe a trickle of blood from a superficial cut over his jugular vein and peer at the little red smudge on his fingertip. "I'd like to have you know, Captain—this scarlet Lieutenant of yours—she had a knife to my throat!"

"You wouldn't have gone back for my Captain otherwise," Sabrina said.

Buckle sat up and spat the breather out of his mouth. His chest hurt and he was gagging up seawater but he was alive. Penny knelt beside him, holding his hand. They were in another narrow passageway but this one wasn't flooded.

Horatus, his armor dripping, leaned against a square hatch as he worked the hippocampus-shaped buttons on a combination cylinder. The Praetorians stood behind him, swords drawn. Sabrina and Welly stood off to the right, Sabrina sheathing her knife and smiling.

"It gave you no right to make a hostage out of me," Cicero grumbled. "Like it or not, my survival is the only priority. You slowed our escape. You made Horatus go back."

"You may well owe the Captain your life before this day is over," Sabrina replied, moving to help Buckle stand.

"Losses are to be expected," Horatus said.

Buckle got up on his feet with the assistance of Sabrina and Penny Dreadful; he blinked, unsteady, somewhat dizzy.

"Can you fight, Captain?" Sabrina asked.

"Send a dozen steampipers my way," Buckle replied, coughing up salty seawater. "Piece of cake, Lieutenant."

Horatus finished entering the code and spun the cylindrical lock mechanism. Buckle heard tumblers rattle. The hatch popped open with a slash of bright light and a burst of stale, warm air rich with the smells of burning wood and all manner of sour, boiled and braised seafood.

"We are entering the Underneath," Horatus said. "Move quickly along the catwalk to the far hatchway." And with that he swung outside with Cicero and the two Praetorians at his heels.

Buckle stepped through the hatchway and was immediately struck by a sense of vertigo; his boots rested on the grating of a catwalk suspended in an artificial sky. He stood five stories above a Roman-style metropolis which appeared to occupy the entire base of the Atlantean dome. Thousands of tightly packed terra-cotta rooftops lined a narrow, geometrically precise street grid and larger columned buildings dominated the squares, the walls of the stupendous chamber soaring in ribbed girders of copper and brass. Lines of white and gray smoke from cooking fires threaded upward and collected in vent holes drilled in the massive, shallow dome above him, its surface painted to look like a wide blue sky with towering white clouds, depthless and almost three-dimensional in its skilled application. At the apex of the sky dome rested a brilliant sun constructed from spiraling luminiferous aether tubes, providing a glowing, almost natural light for the residents.

And the residents were out in force, the streets and squares overflowing with crowds of men and women in white togas, clutching their children, all looking up in a multicolored sea of faces fifty feet below. Buckle could sense their apprehension, feel the movement of the atmosphere as they breathed in and out as one frightened mass.

The two Praetorians quickly resealed the hatch.

"Let's move!" Horatus hissed as he strode along the catwalk. Buckle followed with the group, their boots clanking on the metal grating and echoing ominously across the huge, silent space.

"Look!" Someone shouted from the street below, "It is Horatus, Commander of the Praetorians!"

The weight of so many focused eyes made Buckle's skin crawl. The people looked haggard but clean. They were the workers, the underclass of Atlantis, the sea-farmers, fishermen, carpenters, ironworkers, potters, and nursemaids who provided the nobility with the power to wrest a kingdom from the sea. Though their clothes were different, they surely resembled, in their simple clothes and worn faces, the citizens of the Crankshaft territory.

"Ho, Praetorians!" A white-bearded man with a gray toga shouted from below. "What has happened? We have felt disturbances! And our sea-farmers report Founders submarines on the attack!"

Horatus stopped and leaned over the rail. "Fear not, Galba!" he shouted with confidence. "Yes, a battle has been engaged with the Founders but they are being roundly repulsed, I assure you!"

"Then why have the watertight doors been closed?" Galba yelled back, angry. "There are rumors that the dome is flooding and yet our escape hatches have been sealed!"

"You are safe!" Horatus shouted.

"Then why do you run, drenched and dripping?" Galba pressed. "And why do you have one of the monster machines in your company? And a scarlet!"

"We are looking after the safety of the Keeper of the Aether!" Horatus responded. "And now I must see to that. You and your families are safe! I give you my word!"

Horatus turned and hurried after the group. Buckle had no idea whether the people below were safe or not, whether Horatus was lying to them or not. A low grumble of voices rose in the air to join the hollow clanking of their boots as they rushed along the catwalk.

"You abandon us!" Galba howled from below. "You lie, Horatus! You abandon us!"

The crowd's apprehensive mumbling morphed to a roar, thousands of angry voices, indignant, terrified, rising up in rage. A piece of rock, perhaps a chunk of brick, clanged off the bottom of the catwalk.

"Hurry!" Horatus said, sprinting through the group to take the lead.

Buckle ran alongside Sabrina and Welly as more objects—mostly small rocks and bricks—sailed up around them, a few ricocheting off the catwalk, but none had much momentum due to the height.

Horatus and the Praetorians arrived at the far hatchway and quickly set to applying the combination code to the cylinder.

"You lie to us!" Galba bellowed. "You abandon us! Where is the First Consul? Where is Marius?"

The hatch opened with a puff of pressurized air.

The two Praetorians yanked Cicero through it before it was even halfway open.

The thunder of the angry mob followed Buckle as he, Sabrina, Penny, and Welly swung through the hatchway. Horatus jumped into the passageway and the Praetorians hauled the heavy hatch shut behind him, cutting off the roar of the mob with the sharp clang of heavy metal.

"Your city is lost," Buckle said to Horatus as he spun the door wheel. "How could you lie to them in such a fashion?"

"The truth shall do them no good now," Horatus replied as he slapped the hatch-locking lever into place. "They shall not drown unless the Founders wish it. Their fate is already sealed, as is ours. The First Consul betrayed us all. Nothing matters now but the safety of the Keeper."

XLV

OCTAVIAN'S ESCAPE POD

Buckle became disoriented in the mad rush through a series of winding Atlantean passageways but it didn't matter. Horatus and his Praetorians knew where they were going; they led the group through the humid veins of the underwater city, clattering along one corridor after another under thousands of aether tubes and metal pipes glittering with a million pearls of condensation.

It was startling when Horatus finally halted at a hatchway, so accustomed had Buckle become to the relentless movement through the labyrinth.

"This hatch opens into the corridor leading to the First Consul's escape pod," Horatus said as he manipulated the combination cylinder. "The pilot will be in the pod unless she is captured or killed. Turn left and be ready to cross swords. Nothing matters except the Keeper, do you hear me? He must escape with us or die in the attempt."

"Aye," Buckle said, drawing his sword.

The locks slid aside and Horatus kicked the

414

hatch open, lunging out, gladius at the ready, followed by the two Praetorians with Cicero between. Exiting the hatchway, Buckle found himself in an ornate corridor with a crimson carpet and arched bulkheads plated with brass. To his left he saw a docking platform with a large circular hatch flung wide open flanked on each side by marble statues of Neptune and oblong windows providing wide views of the sea.

An Atlantean guard in white and gold armor stood at the ready on the platform, harpoon gripped against his chest. "Hurry, Commander!" he shouted.

An Atlantean officer, his white and gold armor coated with blood, raced into view from the opposite end of the curving passageway. "Commander Horatus! The guards are overwhelmed. They're coming! Dozens of them!"

"Atlanteans!" Horatus boomed. "With me! We make our stand here!" The two Praetorians and the two Atlantean soldiers jumped to form a line across the passageway with Horatus in the center.

Horatus grabbed Buckle by the collar and hauled him around. "I cannot ask you to die here, Captain—but the Keeper must not fall into the hands of the enemy. The power of the aether in the wrong hands would be the end of everything. If he is to be captured you must run him through. You must destroy him."

"He knows!" Cicero wailed.

"Get him into the pod!" Horatus snapped. "Get

him into the pod!"

Sabrina and Welly grabbed Cicero by the scruff of his toga and pushed him across the platform, Penny Dreadful bringing up the rear.

"You are a hero, commander Horatus," Cicero shouted back over his shoulder. "Your sacrifice shall not be forgotten!"

"Do you understand what I ask of you, Captain?" Horatus asked.

"I understand," Buckle replied.

"The survival of Atlantis depends upon him," Horatus pressed, gripping Buckle's collar tighter. "Promise me."

"I give you my word," Buckle said.

Horatus looked relieved, the tightness of the skin around his eyes easing. "Good. Get him to Seneca on Insulae Five. Nowhere else. Insulae Five. The Keeper shall show you the way."

A mass of blue-coated men and women appeared around the bend of the hallway, coming on the run, led by their flashing swords and pikes.

"We shall hold them off as along as we can," Horatus said, turning to join his soldiers. "Go!"

"Get in or you'll not be coming!" A female shouted from inside the pod.

Buckle swung through the hatchway and into a narrow cylindrical cabin lined with luminiferous aether tubes and portholes, offering barely enough room for six small seats. At the front a female pilot with pinned-back brown hair and a white uniform glanced back in apprehension as she threw switches and flipped toggles.

"Seal the hatch," the pilot shouted.

Cicero swung the hatch closed behind Buckle. "Hatch shut," he shouted back, winding the door wheel. "Seal engaged. Get us out of here, Valeria!" Cicero squeezed his bulbous form between Buckle and Welly and hurried forward to take the seat alongside the pilot.

The front of the pod had a big window through which Buckle glimpsed the towering, brilliantly lit curve of the Aventine dome glass alongside their pod, and beyond that the endless depths of the sunlit sea where the shadowy Founders submarines still circled like sharks. Through the metal of the hatch he heard muffled shouts, clashing steel and the cries of dying men—Horatus and his doomed Atlanteans being overrun.

Buckle saw Cicero force his fingers into his mouth as if his very life depended upon it. Cicero spat a glass ampule into the palm of his hand.

"Don't lose that, Keeper," Valeria said. "We're by no means out of danger yet."

Cicero took a deep breath and returned the ampule to its compartment in his golden dolphin ring.

A powerful vibration shook the pod, followed

by a hammer-blow concussion that canted the deck and nearly threw Buckle and everyone else into a pile. The lights sputtered and died, sending the submarine interior into a wavering, ocean-lit darkness. As he regained solid footing Buckle noticed that the Atlantean dome had also gone dark, its high glass walls now only reflecting sunlight from the ocean surface.

"My engineers have destroyed the city's luminiferous aether engines, as is their duty," Cicero announced grimly. Buckle took a seat in silence, as did Sabrina and Welly. Penny Dreadful stood against the bulkhead beside the hatch.

Valeria activated the cabin's boil agitators. Buckle heard the pitter-patter of the tiny machine arms spinning inside their glass housings as every instrument in the boat—which covered nearly every inch of hull not a window—rapidly lit up with green bioluminescence.

"Disengaging from docking bay," Valeria said, flipping a set of brass switches.

Buckle heard a loud metallic clank followed by a grinding rattle that shook the pod. Buckle tensed. It did not sound healthy.

Valeria flipped a set of wooden-handled switches back and forth. "Automatic disengage has failed," she said. "Keeper—perform emergency manual disengage."

"With all good speed," Cicero answered, leaping

up from his seat and squeezing along the tight aisle until he reached a hand wheel located in the upper right quadrant above the hatch. He pointed to an identical wheel in the upper left quadrant. "Clockwise, if you please?"

Buckle jumped up, grabbing the wheel and rotating it in a clockwise direction as Cicero did the same. Both cranks turned with very little resistance.

"The pod's docking pins are fully retracted," Cicero announced.

"Curse the luck!" Valeria shouted. "An airlock clamp must be stuck. I'll wager that shaking we took warped it. Step back from the hatchway! Firing emergency bolts!"

Buckle stepped back from the hatch along with Cicero, though that distance wasn't much inside the pod.

Valeria lifted a panel cover and flipped a red-painted lever. Two loud bangs hammered against the rear bulkhead. The pod bounced but did not swing free of the airlock.

"No good!" Cicero howled. "No good!"

Valeria spun around in her seat. "A docking bay clamp has malfunctioned. We cannot disengage. Our only hope is to eject the clamp itself from the docking bay."

"And how do we do that?" Buckle asked.

"It can only be done from inside the airlock,"

Valeria said grimly. "Two switches inside the emergency instrument compartment on the left side of the outer docking bay hatch."

"Then open the hatch!" Buckle said, drawing his sword in the cramped space. Sabrina hedged alongside him, saber already out of its sheath. Welly also drew his blade. "We shall form a defensive perimeter on the platform. We can hold the enemy at bay for the few seconds necessary to perform the task."

"You cannot," Valeria said.

Buckle glared at Valeria. "What now?"

"The one who goes out will be left behind," Valeria said, drawing her pistol, a polished white, elegant weapon, and laying it on the instrument panel beside her. "The airlock must be sealed before the clamp disengage will activate. Whichever of you goes out there will be left behind."

"Damn it!" Buckle snapped.

"I shall go," Penny Dreadful said, stepping forward.

"No, you won't," Buckle answered.

"The automaton isn't tall enough to reach the switches," Valeria said.

"It's me," Welly offered, his voice strong but shaking. "Just like who gets the breathers. It must be me."

"No, it's me," Sabrina announced.

"It's on me," Buckle said. "I appreciate the

overabundance of self-sacrifice here but it will be me. No arguments."

"No!" Penny Dreadful mewled softly. "No, no, no, no."

"But I must go with you," Welly began. "Someone has to defend your back or you won't have time to throw the switches!"

"The young man is right," Valeria said.

"Very well," Buckle said quietly. He knew when it was necessary to send zeppelineers to their deaths, including himself. "You're with me, Wellington. You take the fogsuckers while I throw the switches. That will only take a few seconds and then I shall be at your side."

"No," Sabrina whispered. "It should be me."

"Here, Captain," Valeria said as she tossed her pistol to Buckle.

"Thank you," Buckle replied and turned to Sabrina. "You and Penny see to it that the Keeper gets to Insulae Five and sees a man named Seneca. See to it."

"Damn it all to hell," Sabrina groaned.

"Piece of cake," Buckle said with a smile.

Sabrina looked at him, her green eyes glowing in the boil-lit cabin. "I'll find Elizabeth. I shall."

Buckle smiled. He felt good about that.

"Before I go," Welly said, moving with purpose in the tight space, taking Sabrina's right hand and kissing it. "Farewell, beloved Lieutenant."

"Not nearly good enough," Sabrina whispered quickly. She lifted Welly's chin and kissed him on the lips.

Welly glowed. "Now I am ready to die," he said.

"And for you, Romulus," Sabrina said. She leaned in and kissed him, her lips soft and warm, and her touch gave him resolve, strength, and sadness. She leaned back and gazed at him, her eyes brimming with tears. "Piece of cake."

"Piece of cake," Buckle replied.

"Hurry, damn it!" Valeria said.

Buckle leaned against the hatch, trying to listen over the pounding of his heart. All he heard was the gurgle of the sea and the creak of what was probably the damaged docking bay clamp scraping in its housing as it moved with the ebb of the currents. The sounds of fighting inside the passageway were gone.

"Open the hatch!" Buckle ordered. So this was it, he thought, his head lowered, his right hand clamped around the grip of his saber, his left hand clenching the pistol. He couldn't imagine surviving this one. But it was a good way to go. "And close it behind us as fast as you possibly can."

"Your sacrifice shall be remembered, Captain," Cicero said.

Buckle nodded. He wanted to punch Cicero in the mouth.

Cicero wound the wheel and flipped the locking lever.

The hatch swung open into darkness. The mist of a dozen jetting leaks filled the airlock, obscuring what Buckle knew was waiting a few yards beyond. Advancing with his sword and pistol, Buckle leaned into the hatchway and coiled for a charge. Still, he could see next to nothing. Weak sunlight obliquely filtered in from the undulating surface above and imparted a shivering blue-green light to the passageway. With the swirl of the mist it all had a haunting, otherworldly feel, an endless depth, like a place that existed both in the reality and in the other. Aether light occasionally spluttered from the cracked overhead tubes, the liquid spilling down here and there in sparkling cascades.

Then Buckle saw them, a dark irregular mass in the throat of the passageway, stepping over the bodies of Horatus and his men as they advanced, weapons glinting in the wobbling sea-light. The aether flashes revealed shadowed faces, silver buttons and blades.

"Now!" Buckle ordered, but as Welly plunged out past him he found himself anchored to the deck of the pod. Penny Dreadful had locked onto his thigh with her small, powerful arms, pinning his leg as effectively as if it were nailed down.

"You cannot go!" Penny Dreadful shrieked, her voice indistinguishable from that of an anguished human child.

"Penny!" Buckle howled, seeing Welly charging by himself. "Release my leg, now!"

"No!" Penny wailed.

Sabrina jumped through the hatch, snatching Valeria's pistol out of Buckle's hand as she passed.

"Sabrina!" Buckle screamed. "Get back!"

"Close the hatch!" Sabrina shouted. The roar of the pistol slammed Buckle's ears, its blinding flash biting his eyes, and Sabrina vanished through its billowing black cloud.

"Your bravery will be remembered, Lieutenant!" Cicero yelled, throwing his weight against the hatch.

"No!" Buckle yelled, kicking at Penny, clawing at Cicero's sleeve.

"Captain!" Cicero roared, fighting to free his arm from Buckle's grasp. "Please!"

"Close the hatch or we all drown!" Valeria shouted. "When the switch is thrown the airlock floods! Close the hatch!"

"Sabrina!" Buckle screamed. He hauled Penny off of his leg but it was too late. He released Cicero and staggered against a seat as the Keeper closed the hatch and spun the locking wheel.

"Hatch sealed," Cicero announced, already on his way back to the bow.

Buckle heard a loud bump of metal on metal from the stern and the pod slid forward, buoyant, loose, free, into the ocean.

"We have disengaged," Valeria said.

Buckle clutched the seats beside him; he felt weightless, dizzy, as the pod ascended and spun around.

"Engaging aether engines," Valeria said as Cicero slipped into the seat beside her. The pod interior hummed to life with a quiet, purring vibration. Electricity. Valeria's instrument panel tubes lit up with the soft glow of the luminiferous aether. "Hang on."

The deck tilted as Valeria accelerated and banked hard to starboard. Buckle scrambled to a starboard porthole and peered down. There, looking up through one of the oblong window ports in the docking bay, her face pale as a ghost behind the glass, was Sabrina. She pressed her hand against the inside of the window and disappeared, turning away to meet her fate.

"Sabrina!" Buckle shouted, clutching the back of the seat. The escape pod veered again, descending down and away from the Atlantean dome, leaving behind its towering mountain of dark, dead glass. The electric boat would have amazed Buckle had he not been shocked numb. It was as if his heart had been ripped from his body for a second time. He had lost another sister to the Founders.

And his soul was unsure if it could stand it.

XLVI

SHUBA

Her hand pressed against the cold glass, the clang of the docking bay clamp disengaging still ringing in her ears, Sabrina stared up through the rippling surface of the sea window. The Atlantean escape pod, gold and white and beautiful, rose away. She was glad they had escaped. But it hurt when she glimpsed Buckle looking down at her, his face terribly stricken, and she felt guilty at having caused him so much pain.

Sabrina did not regret acting without thinking, acting in Buckle's defense, but she hated the idea of dying before exacting her revenge, the old revenge which had lived with her for so many years. It would be an itch she could never scratch. It would itch in her dead bones for eternity.

She turned to face the passageway, balancing the weight of her saber in her hand. It would have been good to have her knife in her free hand but that had been left behind in the Vicar's skull. So, take as much blood as one can now, for now is all that is left.

She lowered her head, listening to the breathing

from the wall of enemies inching towards her in the dark, closing panther-like, their black and navy blue Founders uniforms lit up by sputtering bursts of the aether cascading from the tubes overhead, the crackling illumination shimmering across their forest of poised blades.

She raised her head and saw them lift their boots as they advanced, stepping over the lifeless body of Ensign Wellington Bratt.

Sabrina raised her sword. Welly had fought and died well. His charge and her pistol blast had put the enemy on their heels, if only for a moment, but long enough for her to throw the emergency release switches for the escape pod. It surprised her how calm she was, how at ease she was. She did have great affection for Welly but she hadn't the time to miss him — and she would be seeing him again very soon, for wherever he was she was sure to follow. She would, however, inflict as much damage as possible before the deal was sealed. She took a deep breath and smelled seawater and ambergris.

Sabrina had born a Founder and now she would die under Founders blows. There was some vein of irony in there if she had cared to mine it.

The enemy loomed closer now, not wary but rather enjoying the pause before the kill, safe in their numbers and the glacis of sword and pike blades in front of them.

"The First Consul's escape pod is away, sir!" one of the Founders reported.

"They won't get far," an officer's voice barked. "Senior Sergeants! End it!"

Two sailors, more shadows than light, leapt at Sabrina, both swinging cutlasses. She deflected their blows in sprays of sparks and sharp rings of metal. The sailors weren't attacking in perfect tandem and their alternate swipes gave her a chance to address each blade in turn. These were regular sailors, not steampipers, and the quality of their swordsmanship proved it.

It was time to kill somebody. Sabrina ducked the cutlass swipe from the figure on her left, the bulk of his shape silhouetted against the sea window, hearing the whip of his blade passing over her head.

Bringing her blade up and across, Sabrina slashed the man's neck. Hot blood sprayed her left cheek on the thin skin just under the eye. She heard the man gurgle, heard the thump of his body against the window glass. "That's for Wellington Bratt, you pigs!" she said.

The second attacker, a short, husky woman, lunged at Sabrina's now exposed right side. The spilling flash of a luminiferous aether tube lit up her cutlass as she raised it above her head and brought it down in a diagonal chop. Sabrina parried the blade and with a snap of her wrist sliced the woman's bicep. The woman gasped, her cutlass hitting the deck with a thump, and fell away.

Sabrina backed up. She felt the bristling heat of the mob, their hands gripping their swords so tightly the atmosphere hummed, now hedging toward her as the overhead aether tubes kicked out more bursts of jittering white sparks.

"The fools! Kill her!" the officer howled. "Just finish it!"

"What is this?" a new voice boomed, approaching from the rear of the Founders group. It was an odd voice, male, young, with a strange, throaty vibration. "Where is the First Consul?"

The group in front of Sabrina halted, quivering, their eyes locked on her.

"We have cornered the last defender, Shuba — but the First Consul's pod has escaped."

Sabrina's gut tightened up. She knew who Shuba was — one of the mysterious Founders Martians, a young male of the elite whom she had seen only a few times as a child.

"Escaped?" Shuba roared. "Fools! You shall be called before Parliament and Fawkes himself to answer for this failure, Commander."

"As you will, Shuba," the officer replied, his tone fearful, defeated.

"What is this?" Shuba asked. "Step aside."

The wall of Founders sailors parted for Shuba as

he strode through them, stopping to regard Sabrina from ten feet away. In the dying shudders of the aether light Sabrina could see him peering at her, tall and slender and wearing a long black cloak with red lining, his white face displaying a darting pattern of black stripes. Shuba was no half-breed like Max. His eyes, like a shark's eyes, glowing inside a large pair of goggles, faint, depthless violet-black in the dark, struck an unsettlingly primitive cord in her human soul, as if she remembered those eyes peering down at her in her cradle.

Sabrina considered attacking the Martian but he didn't come within her measure — and there were many Founders blades between them.

"The scarlet," Shuba announced. "This one is the scarlet; a Fawkes. The one the Vicar spoke of. Isambard's niece. Odessa's long lost sister. Do I need remind you that it is an offense punishable by death to kill a scarlet, Commander?"

"My apologies," the officer replied quickly. "We had no idea who she was, Master Shuba. I swear it."

"Redeem yourselves by capturing her alive," Shuba snarled. "Each and every scarlet is of interest to Isambard Fawkes!" He whirled on his heel and vanished into the passageway.

"Yes, sir," the commander replied. "It shall be done."

Now Shuba had given an order, an order which

would save Sabrina's life, if only long enough to be interrogated and torn to pieces as a traitor by her uncle, Isambard Fawkes. Sabrina gripped her sword tighter. She would die here, simply, cleanly. She would force the Founders to kill her. It would be easy for one of them to inflict a mortal blow while fighting for their life in the dark.

Even in death she could defy Isambard Fawkes.

Sabrina lunged to the attack, crashing into a body and driving her sword thrust into flesh as the skewered man cried out.

Hands clawed at Sabrina from every angle, strong hands dragging her down.

"Take it easy!" the Commander screamed. "If any one of you as much as scratches her I'll kill you myself, I will! Don't bleed her! Don't bleed her!"

Sabrina elbowed and punched as the shouting, grasping sailors compressed around her, preventing the swing of her blade. Fists struck from the shadows. Curses filled the air, flung at her in bursts of hot breath laden with the stink of bad teeth and stale grog. They had her arms. Her wrist was twisted terribly and her sword wrenched away. A hand clamped down on her face. She bit a finger, feeling the skin break between her teeth, the slick roll of a knuckle, the gush of hot blood on her tongue. A man howled and yanked the hand back, nearly breaking her jaw as he tore free of her gnashing.

"Put her down!" a deep voice hissed.

A big, meaty fist, gloved in leather, catapulted out of the shadows and slammed into the side of Sabrina's head.

Sparks exploded inside her eyes. The world fractured, flipped sideways.

The roar of the sea came to Sabrina, implacable and endless and ancient as the echo inside the nautilus, the sound not of waves but of unimaginable mass, of the immense pull of its gravity, of the spin of the earth and the pull of the tides. She fell into the sea and descended, slowly, gently, along the rippling green towers of a seaweed forest to the cold dark bottom where thousands of black mussels opened and nipped her skin and where she, ignoring the pinches, settled on the stony bottom to curl up with an octopus.

XLVII

ROCKETS IN THE MIST

Romulus Buckle sat in the last seat, the one closest to the hatch, listening to the weird sputter of the Atlantean escape pod's dying luminiferous aether engines. For one of the few times in his life he could remember, he was uncertain as to where he was. They had been traveling for hours, traveling for hours in a silence housing the weird hum of the aether engines, the hiss of the air fans, and the stream of the sea against the hull.

Valeria and Cicero sat with their backs to Buckle, occasionally clicking switches or peering into scopes, working the cockpit instruments under the wide sea window which was black with night.

Elizabeth was gone. Sabrina was gone. Welly was gone. Buckle had nothing to do. He was a mere passenger. He did not have the role of captain to save him with action, to force him to rise above his personal tragedies and appear strong for his crew. He had nothing to do to keep himself busy except plan rescues, plan to recover his shipmates through audacity, suicidal risk-taking and brute force.

Elizabeth was most certainly still alive — he had seen her. But why had the Founders brought Elizabeth to Atlantis with them, and how could she penetrate his dreams so vividly and lead him to her location inside the submersible? He thought he could still feel Elizabeth's presence, a trace of it, but that sensation was quickly ebbing away, dissolving in the unseen distance outside of him.

Sabrina might be dead but he was hoping that she wasn't. To him, she'd simply vanished into the Founders shadow world like Elizabeth. Her scarlet hair would save her life, he believed, if only for a little while. Of Welly's fate, the poor young fellow, Buckle had no idea.

Buckle rejected desperation, despair, motionlessness. He could not allow it. Such things were luxuries a captain could not afford, even when he was in limbo under the sea. He turned his mind to the next steps. When he reached the *Pneumatic Zeppelin* what was he to do? What would be his immediate course of action? His first mission would be to return the Keeper of the Aether to the Atlanteans, to escort him to the mysterious Insulae Five the doomed Horatus had mentioned. The Atlanteans apparently oversaw a sprawling sea empire much bigger and deeper than Buckle and his eastern contemporaries had ever estimated them capable of. But the Atlanteans had been overrun by the Founders, at least at the Aventine dome, while also embroiled in a civil war of their own. Buckle wasn't sure of what use they might be to the Grand Alliance now.

After that, it would be necessary to sail the *Pneumatic Zeppelin* back to Crankshaft territory and join the fleet. The Alliance would need every gun it could get. But if Buckle truly did believe Lady Andromeda's prophecy, that Elizabeth was the key to winning the war, should not every other concern be secondary to Elizabeth's recovery?

Including Sabrina and Welly?

Penny Dreadful, the little girl machine, slid into the seat next to Buckle and looked up at him with her inhuman gold eyes as she clasped her cold metal fingers around his. Buckle heard something odd, a mechanical wheezing, and he realized the sound was coming from Penny. Buckle felt a new pang of worry. The gunshot delivered by the Vicar must have damaged her internal system; now the ancient, compromised machinery sounded like it was struggling, pushing too hard, overtaxed. And in such a condition the decrepit living machine might go haywire — as had all of her brothers and sisters before her — and become dangerous.

It was in his concern for Penny Dreadful that Buckle found himself again. He'd lost important people in his life, yes, but many more needed his protection.

He still had a robot-child to worry about, a crew to worry about, a clan to worry about, a world to worry about. And they all needed him, at least, they all needed what little bit he could do to defend them.

Buckle decided he'd ask Ivan, the *Pneumatic Zeppelin*'s chief engineer and inventor, to look at Penny once they returned to the airship. He gathered himself. He must find his words again.

"I wish I could weep," Penny whispered. "I am so very sad."

Buckle patted Penny's iron shoulder as he would to comfort to a real child, even though she was much older than he was.

"Can't we save them?" Penny asked. "All the others, my brothers and sisters, I have never been able to save anyone."

"They must fight their own battles for now," Buckle said. "We must return to the *Pneumatic Zeppelin* before we can do anything for them."

"Aye, Captain," Penny said bravely. She placed her hands in her lap and sighed, again with that low, awful wheezing.

The little automaton was all that he had left of his Atlantis expedition team, Buckle realized.

"We are about to surface at your given coordinates, Captain Buckle," Valeria announced. "We've used the last of our aether fuel so I hope your airship is on the mark."

Feeling the escape pod ascend, Buckle stood up, stiff from hours of inaction, and steadied himself by taking hold of an overhead pipe. "She'll be here," he said. "She shall be here. Well done, pilot." Assuming that the Founders had laid siege to all of the Atlantean domes and their associated island ports, Valeria and Cicero had agreed to make a run for the rendezvous with the *Pneumatic Zeppelin*. The airship, with Valkyrie Smelt and Ivan Gorky in command, would be waiting in the sea mists to pick them up. The plan had been for the airship to be on station one mile due north of Santa Cruz and to move another mile due north if Founders activity conspired to make the first position unsustainable. With Vera Cruz captured, Buckle was certain that his cautious bridge officers would have relocated to the more distant position.

Of course, events had conspired to prevent Buckle from making the rendezvous. The Atlantean escape pod was designed as a short-range emergency lifeboat, its limited aether fuel further taxed by running deep. But they had made it through a combination of luck and Valeria's skill, slipping through the Founders blockade net.

The escape pod surfaced into uneven patches of sea mist, the moonlit, blue-gray clouds visible now and again through gaps in the fog banks. The sensation of the ocean changed, from the smooth flow of the underwater currents to the rolling push and pull of the surface waves.

"Shutting down propulsion," Valeria said as she depressed a brass lever. The stuttering propellers wound down into silence. "Drop sea anchor."

Cicero manipulated levers at his station. "Dropping sea anchor."

"Let us go see if your air machine is here, shall we?" Valeria said as she pulled two heavy oilskin coats out of a cubby, tossing one to Buckle before pulling hers on. She wound the crank of an overhead hatch. "Keeper, bring the flare gun."

Donning another oilskin coat—one which did not fit him around the middle—Cicero opened a compartment door and tucked a flare gun into his toga, along with a leather case containing five cartridges. "I would like to say with all sincerity, Captain," Cicero offered, "that I understand what sacrifices were made this day for my protection. I shall to see it that the memory of your officers is both exalted and immortalized."

"I am sure you shall build them fine statues," Buckle replied sourly.

"Please, Captain," Cicero responded, with considerably more softness than Buckle had witnessed in him before. "It is very little but it is all that I can do for a debt I can never repay."

Buckle nodded.

"Hole in the boat!" Valeria announced, lifting

the ceiling hatch. A small flood of cold seawater splashed down on the deck grating.

A rush of fresh sea air hit Buckle in the face. The slap of it was good for him. It helped clear his mind, settle his emotions. He climbed the ladder after Valeria and found himself standing on the small, open bridge, exposed to the weather and the spray, and he much preferred it to being inside the submarine. His face felt damp and cool but not uncomfortably so. It was an unnaturally warm mist.

Valeria snapped out a night glass and peered into it. "No sign of an air machine. Mind you, it could be right on top of us and we couldn't see it. Damned fog."

Buckle placed his hands on the rail and stared into the mountainous ebbs and flows of the moonlit fog. Icebergs floated by, white and blue giants lurking in the gray distance. Seagulls squawked from the icebergs, grounded by the near-constant mists and probably starving. The fog deadened sound but brought its own silent hum with it. Again Buckle was struck by the strange weight of the mist, moisture-laden and far too temperate for the icy wind which pushed it.

"By Salacia's seaweed crown, I hate the surface!" Cicero groaned, struggling to clear the hatch as the roll of the vessel cast him about. Buckle pulled him up by the hood of his coat.

"Ready flare," Valeria ordered, snapping her night glass shut and jamming it into her coat pocket. "Completely useless in this soup," she muttered.

"Aye," Buckle agreed. The fog bank, constantly shifting from translucent sheets to dense, opaque curtains, made telescopes useless, even misleading. The naked eye, far more sensitive than the glass, was a better tool under the circumstances.

"What are we going to do if this zeppelin can't find us?" Cicero asked.

"A lot of paddling and dining on raw seagull, most likely," Valeria answered.

"They'll find us," Buckle stated flatly. He simply chose to believe it. He'd had enough bad luck for one day. At some point Lady Fortune had to balance her scales.

"Very well, Captain," Valeria said with a smile.

Cicero clicked a cartridge into the firing chamber of the flare pistol. "Ready here."

"Loose the flare when ready," Valeria said.

"I suggest you aim north, more or less," Buckle offered.

"I have no idea what direction north might be from this tilting bucket," Cicero grumbled.

Pulling a compass from her pocket, Valeria pointed towards the forward port quarter. "North, Keeper."

"Thank you," Cicero replied. He aimed the flare

gun upward and fired. The glowing cartridge vaulted high into the mists before it popped, bursting into a bright red haze that arced away slowly on its parachute, burning smaller but brighter as the magnesium burned down to its wire.

Buckle scanned the wreathing, flare-lit mists. He couldn't see a damned thing. There was a very good chance the *Pneumatic Zeppelin*, even if it was only a few hundred yards away with a full complement of lookouts on station, would never see their flares.

A flash of green, soft but casting a wide, undulating glow, rose and fell in the fog to the northwest. It didn't appear close but it had to be close to be seen at all.

"There we go," Buckle said, his relief immense, his sense of what the *Pneumatic Zeppelin* would be like without Sabrina and Welly also brutally sharp and bitter.

"Bravo, Captain," Valeria said with a small smile. "I'm certainly glad we won't be sharing any uncooked seagull giblets in the near future. Fire another flare, Keeper."

"As you wish, Valeria," Cicero answered. He flipped a smoking cartridge out of the pistol chamber and replaced it with a new one.

"Do we board by a lowering of ropes, Captain?" Valeria asked.

"Yes," Buckle replied. He suddenly felt very

tired.

"You take the Keeper up with you first," Valeria said, watching Cicero fire the second flare. "I shall scuttle the pod and come up after you."

"We can probably salvage your vessel," Buckle offered.

"No," Valeria replied. "This pod carries a luminiferous aether generator; its secrets must be obliterated and go to the bottom with it."

"As you wish," Buckle said.

"I wanted to tell you, Captain," Valeria said. She was a skinny, hard-faced woman with a high, aquiline nose. "What your officers did, they saved us all, just as much as Horatus and the Praetorians. You should be proud of them."

"I am," Buckle replied, but he could bring himself to say no more.

A huge elliptical shadow, growing darker and darker in the fog overhead, announced the arrival of the *Pneumatic Zeppelin*. Buckle caught his breath as her great mass descended into view forty feet above, her copper and bronze gondola pods laced with spars and ratlines and her port windows glowing faintly of yellow buglights and green boil. With her propellers still and engines cut she came to him slowly, like a ghost ship, silent except for the wooden creaks of her decking and the light brush of the breeze across her skin.

"Captain below!" a lookout shouted. It sounded like Lansa Laslo, one of the riggers.

The *Pneumatic Zeppelin* suddenly took on life. Black forms sprang out into the rigging, buglights in their hands; the big maneuvering propellers whirred, steadying her against the drift of the ocean breeze. The massive airship slowed to a stop with her gunnery gondola suspended a mere fifteen feet above Buckle's head. The gondola's loading bay doors swung open and a long rope ladder rolled out, unfolding neatly as it flopped its way down to the bridge of the escape pod.

Buckle could feel her, his beloved airship, her titanic mass displacing the moonlit fog in the sky, the sweet sea air buried under the stink of her coal fires and damp canvas.

Buckle was home.

But Sabrina and Elizabeth and Welly were not home.

Not yet.

THE END

ACKNOWLEDGEMENTS

This is the third book in a long series and a lot of good people have helped me along the way. First, as always, I must thank my parents, Richard and Janet, and my wife, Shelley for their endless love and support. I thank my daughters, Sabrina and Amelia, for providing motivations and rewards of the most endearing kind. And Kellie the dog is always somewhere nearby.

My work is shepherded by my brilliant and patient agent, Mark Gottlieb, at Trident Media Group. I gratefully acknowledge the support of Adrienne Lombardo and Alex Carr who originally championed the series (and still do). I also wish to thank authors Jeff and Ann VanderMeer, whose continued encouragement and support for this series have helped me keep my chin up even in troubled waters. I would also be remiss if I did not thank my fellow authors at Westmarch Publishing, who know what it is to live the writing life.

A special thanks to artist Eamon O'Donoghue, whose fantastic cover illustrations surely have sold more books than the scribbles inside, and to Roberto Calas, whose wonderful Snow World map has been much anticipated by readers. I offer a heartfelt thanks to Robert Kroese for his superb copy edit and assistance in formatting, plus another heartfelt thanks to Cynthia L. Moyer for her crackerjack proofread and formatting aid. There are so many others to thank for their help along the way, including Julia Kenner, Jeremy Zerfoss and Jeremy L. C. Jones.

If you enjoyed the book, please consider joining my Newsletter list at richardellisprestonjr.com and posting an honest review at Amazon.com, which helps the novel obtain PR within the machine. Thank you!

Author Richard Ellis Preston, Jr. is fascinated by the steampunk genre, which he sees as a unique storytelling landscape. *Romulus Buckle and the Luminiferous Aether* is the third installment in his steampunk series, *The Chronicles of*

the Pneumatic Zeppelin. He has also published the first novel in his young adult adventure series, *The League of the Sphinx: the Purple Scarab*. Richard has also written for film and television. He lives in California and haunts Twitter @RichardEPreston. You can also find him on Facebook at Richard Ellis Preston, Jr. and on the web at richardellisprestonjr.com.

Made in the USA
San Bernardino, CA
16 December 2016